SINFUL MAGIC

A Wing Slayer Hunter Novel

JENNIFER LYON

SINFUL MAGIC: A WING SLAYER HUNTER NOVEL

Published by JenniferLyonBooks
www.jenniferlyonbooks.com

ISBN: 978-0-9967169-2-5

Cover Design: Jaycee DeLorenzo of Sweet 'N Spicy Designs
Copy Editor: http://www.kimberlycannoneditor.com
Formatted by: Author E.M.S.
Wing Slayer Hunter Logo Design: Jaycee DeLorenzo of Sweet 'N Spicy Designs

Originally published by Ballantine Books 2011

Published in the United States of America.

The Wing Slayer Hunter Series

Blood Magic

Soul Magic

Night Magic

Sinful Magic

Forbidden Magic (novella)

Caged Magic

1

SHE WAS THE IMAGE OF sex.

Pure sex.

No, she was more than sex. She invoked wild feelings, untamed ardor mixed with protective...

Shit, he didn't know! Kieran DeMicca kept drawing, desperate to reveal her.

Each line he stroked on the wall of his hotel room made his cock ache and harden. He was drawing beauty. Passion. Sensuality.

Normally he drew vigilante justice in bold charcoal splashed with red. That was his medium, his art, what he was famous for: Dyfyr, Dragon of Vengeance, exploding from the charcoal lines to spew his blood fury. Dyfyr had no restraint or moral boundaries; he only dealt in vengeance on behalf of those who couldn't fight back for themselves. He had a personal grudge against his sire, the demon dragon that had created him. That was what Key lived and what he drew.

Not this. Sweeping lines of sex and woman. Not a girl, not a lady, but a *woman.*

Still couldn't see her! Sweat ran down his back into the waistband of his jeans. He could see only the parts:

1

JENNIFER LYON

the sweep of her shoulder, the curve of her waist, the sweet contour of her thigh, the heart-shaped face.

He had no choice, no ability to control what he drew. It came from his soul; he drew because he had to. Her breasts were full and spilling over her arm. She wouldn't let him see her nipples and that infuriated him. But then he captured the enticing curve of her hip, with the one thigh turned and shielding her mound.

"Show me, damn it!" he snarled, needing to see all of her.

She refused, but his attention was on her stomach now. She wasn't anything like the other women he drew. Her stomach wasn't cut to rigid muscles, but rather, she had a slope that made him want to press his face into the softness of her belly.

More sweat slid down his chest. The air was cranked up high, but the heat came from within.

From the woman. But it was more than lust. He drew to drain off the fiery heat of violence writhing within him, leaving him cold and empty. But every line of this woman created a reverse flow that made him burn with lust and made him *feel*. Wild feelings, possessive feelings, tender feelings.

Who is she?

Key picked up another pencil and unveiled her face.

Stroke by stroke.

And when he was done, his breath caught. He'd never seen her before. The dragon tat on his chest shifted in his skin. His entire body went tight with red-hot, fierce, ball-exploding lust. She appealed to the man in him on a visceral level. He wanted to protect her, screw her and soothe her all at the same time.

Her tilted green eyes stared back at him and told the story.

Witch.

2

A shiver raced down his spine. Oh fuck! The witch appealed to something much darker within him, and a hell of a lot more dangerous. He was a witch hunter, cursed to crave the power in witch blood. If he killed a witch, his soul would be gone. He'd go rogue, turning into the murdering jackals his father, uncle, and half brother had been. He'd refused to let the curse turn him, fought it every day since puberty.

Was he losing the fight? Was that what made him draw her? A witch he'd never seen before? Just looking at her fractured him, part of him desperate to stroke, pleasure and protect her; another part wanting to destroy her by cutting her and letting the warm spill of her potent blood cool the burn of the curse on his skin.

His arm twitched, and when he looked down, he saw that he had picked up another pencil. *Red. For blood.*

Liam! he thought. Shit! His half brother was dead. It had been eleven years since Key had plunged his knife into Liam's chest and sliced out a chunk of his heart, then walked away. He had to be dead. Yet...the name *Liam* burned deep into his brain, as if he had an art-psychic connection with his half brother.

Had he survived? Or was the insanity of bloodlust claiming Key?

He fought the need to keep drawing, resisting the urge to destroy this beauty with his bloodred pencil. He struggled, hurling the pencil against an adjacent wall. No. He wouldn't draw the brutalization of this witch! Every time he'd slipped into his frenzied drawing mode, he'd been drained, dispassionate, pissed off on an intellectual level. Not this! Not feeling the agony of emotions, of caring. Goddamnit!

He was in a maelstrom that he could only vent by drawing. His hand shook with the need, the compulsion to draw and destroy. His muscles popped and burned, his veins swelled with bloodlust. From the first time he'd held a thick crayon in his hand at three years old, art had been his refuge, his solace. His sanity. Drawing drained off the core of violence inside him. Left him calm, reasonable, able to live.

But if he picked up that pencil and desecrated this sensual creature that embodied everything female, he would feel it. Feel too much: hatred, rage, anger, grief, disgust, horror—and it would drive him closer to the edge. Closer to losing control of the bloodlust, and going rogue.

Clenching his fists, he fought, struggled, and sweat coated him, pouring down his naked chest, soaking his skin. Shakes began from his bones and rattled outward.

Rage and violence exploded inside his chest. His dragon tat roared in his head. And Key lost.

He picked up the pencil.

Bloodred.

And he began to destroy her.

※

Roxanne Banfield moved through the crowded room, feeling the energy buzzing in her. The excitement of the fans, the creativity of the talent, practically took on a life of its own. The meet and greet was the opening event for the Comic Expression Conference.

Her stomach fluttered in excitement. She was confident that she was going to find exactly the right project for her dad's company, Spectral Productions. She had a comic book series and a graphic novel in mind, but she really wanted to see the authors mixing with their fans.

If she was going to work with them to develop their project into a movie or TV series, she needed to see how they interacted. Temperamental artists could make her life a special kind of hell. She moved through the milling folks, some in costume, some looking starstruck, many young women dressed for sex and obviously on the prowl.

Spotting the siblings Perry and Nina, creators of The Eternal Assassins, she headed toward them. They had an intriguing graphic novel series going of a shadow world empress who offered murder victims a chance to kill their murderer. The souls didn't know the cost of that deal until after they agreed and found themselves in a new body. If they made the kill, they became Eternal Assassins.

"Roxy."

That voice! She narrowed her eyes and spun around. Standing there, an expensive digital camera hanging off his neck, was Mack Daemon. What the hell was he doing here? Humiliation and fury burned up her fair skin. "Look what the scuzz pool burped up." She was proud of her restraint. What she wanted to do was shove his camera into a place that would take intimate photos of his colon.

He spread his hands out in a see-I'm-harmless gesture. "Look, I'm sorry, all right? I was just intrigued, and I couldn't help myself. My camera is like an extension of my hand."

She stepped toward the five foot eight, gym-bulked man. "Not during foreplay," she said in a low voice. Her birthmark on her inner thigh, the one that fascinated him enough to grab his camera and take a picture, felt cold and dead as ever. She hated that mark, wanted it gone.

Mack's voice hardened. "This isn't the place. Meet me for a drink later and we'll talk."

She had trusted him. He was a freelance photographer; they'd met at another conference and dated for a few weeks. When she was sure he wasn't her Awakening, the man who would unlock her fertility magic, she'd agreed to have sex with him. Roxy didn't want to be a witch, not the kind of witch her mother was, using sex only to feed her magic. Sex was a super big deal for her, and this guy broke her trust with his fetish. "Nope, I don't drink with perverts." She lifted her chin and turned to go find Perry and Nina.

"I know what the birthmark means."

She whipped back around and stared at him. His dark eyes looked calculating. Mack was smart, talented with a camera, and he had a kinetic energy she'd interpreted as a drive for success. She had liked that in him, liked that he had his own life and wasn't clingy or demanding of a long-term relationship.

He didn't flinch beneath her gaze and added, "Meet me at nine in the bar."

What was this? Blackmail? Or did he think she was some kind of genie he could get three wishes out of? What could he do to her? So what if he told the world she was a witch? No one would believe him; mortals rarely believed. Her powers were latent anyway, locked in her dying chakras.

But if rogues found out...that would be bad. "This is the only way you can get a date? Blackmail?" She aimed her best pity-the-pig look on him, but she knew she had to show up and see if he really was trying blackmail or something else.

"Just be there." He turned and walked off.

The energy of the room suddenly escalated. Dragging her gaze from Mack-the-worm, Roxy turned toward the door. A man walked in. He wore jeans, a black T-shirt, and so much attitude it prickled her skin. As he passed, people stopped what they were doing and stared. Even her hot-meter gonged. Hard. Beneath that shirt, his muscles rippled as if nothing could contain his strength. The guy gave off vibes of sex and danger.

The silence broke with hushed whispers.

He moved through people with panther grace, heading toward the end of the bar, zeroing in on a group of women.

She knew who he was: Kieran DeMicca, creator of the comic book series she was interested in possibly developing; Dyfyr, Dragon of Vengeance. She kept watching and evaluating, while ignoring the attraction that quivered through her.

Her interest was strictly professional.

And right now, her professional opinion was that Kieran DeMicca was a chick magnet. What she needed to know was if he had his priorities straight. If she optioned his series and he retained any creative control, Roxy wasn't going to play mommy and pull him out of a tangle of naked females to work.

She tracked his progress as he chatted up the growing group surrounding him, when he suddenly shifted his gaze and looked right at her.

Her stomach clenched and a strange tingling ran from her pelvis to her throat. The inside of her left thigh began to burn as if every cell in her body sparked to life. Her heart started to race, and her head spun for a second.

Reaching out, she grabbed the back of a nearby chair. His eyes narrowed on her as if he'd made an earth-shattering discovery. Then he took a step.

Toward her.

Her inner thigh still burned. Right where her birthmark was. It should feel dead, not—

Oh shit!

The closer Kieran DeMicca got, the more her thigh reacted. Her heart hammered, and she had to escape. Now! Roxy fast-walked out of the large conference room, down the hallway, and hit the door to the women's restroom.

Her heart was slamming against her ribs, blood pounding in her ears. Her hands shook and her palms were wet with sweat. Going into a stall, she yanked down her slim black pants, and looked at her inner thigh.

"Oh hell, no," she whispered, staring in disbelief.

The two-inch schema was coming to life. Fertility witches were born with a round reddish birthmark somewhere on their body. At puberty, it took shape. For most witches, it turned into half of a fertility goddess: a woman with her arms raised over her head in a circle, her breasts full, her hips rounded, then tapering down into a point. For some reason, Roxy had the full mark, not just half like the others did. But for all fertility witches, their magic was latent, waiting to find their Awakening, usually between the ages of nineteen and twenty-six. When that happened, the mark began to change, taking on color, and once the witch and her Awakening had sex, her magic was released. But if she didn't find her Awakening, the mark faded, and the witch's chakras died off. Roxy's mark had been rapidly fading.

Now she saw faint blue as if someone had brushed barely tinted watercolor over it.

"No," she whispered again, unable to believe it.

She was going to turn into her mother, choosing magic over those she loved.

"I won't," she said, determination firming her spine. Pulling up her pants, she thought quickly: Only one thing brought out a fertility witch's magic—her Awakening.

A man.

It wasn't Mack, she knew that. They hadn't actually had sex, since she'd thrown his ass out when he'd taken the picture, but her mark hadn't reacted to him at all. She'd been in a room full of men, but no one had affected her until...

Kieran DeMicca. She'd felt the reaction when he'd walked into the room, and it had grown stronger the closer he came to her.

Was it possible Kieran was her Awakening? She was so close to reaching her goal of her chakras dying and becoming mortal. All these years she'd waited and now it was all threatened.

If it was Kieran, then she had to keep her distance from him.

⤳ 2 ⤳

KEY WALKED INTO ILLUSIONS, THE largest bar at the Mystique hotel. The multilevel space was about the size of a large hotel suite. Every table was made of glass with colored lights that sat on a black floor for dramatic contrast. There was a long glass wall encasing dancing waterspouts. At each end of the wall, a long bar snaked out, the surface changing colors as the lights on the dancing water shifted.

He scanned the bar, looking for the woman from his wall. The one he hadn't been able to bring himself to paint over yet. He'd been shocked when he'd seen her in the meet and greet. *Alive. Real.* He wasn't crazy.

But why had he drawn her? Was Liam alive? Why would his brother surface now? Over the last eleven years, Key had occasional bursts of drawing Liam butchering witches. His best friend, Phoenix, thought it was guilt and bloodlust manifesting in him.

When he wasn't caught up in the power of the frenzied drawing, Key thought Phoenix might be right. Guilt and violence were his constant companions.

But now—how the hell did he draw a woman he'd never seen? And Christ, when he'd seen her in the flesh, his entire being twanged like a pitch pipe. As if his deepest cells were affected by her. He had to find out more, like why she'd run when Key had made his way toward her. Who was she?

Where is she? He'd already searched the restaurants and was running out of ideas. He scanned the people sitting at the tables when his gaze caught on a woman walking into the bar.

It's her!

Excitement tensed his muscles, but he checked the intense urge to approach her. When he'd tried that in the meet and greet, she'd run. He found a table and sat down to watch her.

She walked with purpose to the end of the bar farthest from him. Her red hair was pulled back in a sleek, low ponytail that showed her heart-shaped face and green eyes. Her spaghetti-strap top barely contained her full breasts, her slim black pants hugged the sweet curve of her hips and ended just above her shoes. Even dressed, she was softly sexy and romantic, not his usual type. Key gravitated to a harder type of woman, the kind he couldn't destroy easily. Women who just wanted the thrill of screwing him because he was famous. Women who didn't look too deeply past his surface.

He couldn't look away from her, and continued to watch as she approached a man, slid onto a bar stool next to him and accepted a glass of wine.

Narrowing his eyes, he repressed another urge to leap to his feet. He didn't like her with another man. It made his thoughts swirl in red violence and his chest burn.

What was happening to him? Was it because she was a witch? But he couldn't smell her witch blood or feel her power. Even across the room, a witch hunter could sniff out the power in witch blood. He inhaled to see if he could catch any scent and got a lungful of copper stink.

There was a rogue somewhere close: Adrenaline surged through him, causing all his enhanced hunter senses to sharpen even more. He didn't see any men with the over-bulked muscles and too-soft features that rogues had. Yet the hair on the back of his neck bristled an alarm. A rogue was there, but shielding himself to appear invisible. Key couldn't see him, but he sure as hell smelled him.

Then the scent began to fade.

Key jacked up out of his chair, and followed the odor out to the atrium that was in the center of several restaurants and shops. The stink of copper kept moving farther away from the bar.

A bad feeling stirred in his chest the farther he got from the woman in the bar. If she was a witch, had this rogue homed in on her, waiting to get her alone to kill her and harvest her blood? Key followed the smell to one of the long hallways, then hesitated, his instincts screaming not to leave the woman.

At the other end of the hallway, the rogue materialized.

Shock punched Key so hard, he froze to the spot. Time hung still as he took in the man standing at six foot five inches, about two hundred and sixty pounds with copper-colored hair surrounding a face that had a masculine jawline but feminine, hairless skin and delicate eyebrows. His arms were hairless, too, but packed with bulging muscles.

Liam. Alive. His half brother who had cut and tortured Vivian, the girl Key had loved, trying to make her tell him where the Dragon Tear was. Like a kaleidoscope, the memories kept changing—Key saw himself holding her in his arms as she died. She'd been innocent, carrying their child, and had had no idea the Tear even existed. His brother had tortured her. Liam cared nothing for anyone or anything but himself and that Dragon Tear.

12

The memories broke apart until all Key saw was Liam as they stared at each other. Then Liam spun and ran through a door at an astonishing speed even for a rogue witch hunter.

Key's shock shattered, and he snapped into action, racing after his brother, determined to finish the job of killing him. But he was too late—Liam got into a black SUV and peeled off into the night.

Why after all these years had his brother shown up now? How had he survived Key's knife to his heart? And why here, in Las Vegas, instead of where Key lived in Glassbreakers, California? He knew one answer; Liam was after the Dragon Tear. He'd do anything to get it. But how did the woman Key had drawn on the wall fit in?

The woman! Had Liam lured him away from her purposely?

He turned and hauled ass back to the bar.

⋙⋘

Roxy slid onto the bar stool, and keeping her face bland, she said, "What do you want, Mack?"

He pushed a glass toward her. "I ordered you a Chardonnay." Then he pulled his dark eyebrows together. "Look, Roxy, I'm worried about you."

"Why?" She accepted the glass of wine and took a sip. What did he know, and what did he want from her?

Mack sipped his Scotch then said, "That mark means you're in danger. I travel extensively with my work and come into contact with a lot of people. I've heard stories about women with that mark, and the group of fanatics who try to find and kill the women who have it. I couldn't believe it when I saw it on you."

A shiver trickled down her spine. Was he telling the truth? Witch hunts throughout history had proven how deeply mortals feared the idea of witches. But... "You took a picture."

He nodded. "I wanted to compare it to the images I'd seen. I had to be careful. I didn't want to reveal who you are or endanger you. The image matches. You're a"—he looked around then whispered—"witch."

She wasn't sure if he believed his story, but there were some nuts out there. How else would Mack know what that mark meant? "It's just a birthmark," she said to fill the silence while thinking.

"A birthmark in the shape of a fertility goddess?"

She jerked her gaze to him as alarm traveled through her. He knew too much, was too specific. Too intense. "You didn't say anything then," she pointed out while studying him.

He reached over to touch her arm. "You got so upset, too upset to listen. And I was worried. I wanted to check it out. Roxy..." he leaned toward her, "...let me take you to dinner. I've made reservations at a nice place. We'll talk and figure out how to keep you safe."

She pulled her arm free and took another drink of her wine. Like hell she'd go anywhere with him. He might be telling the truth, but taking a picture in such an intimate moment was just creepy. She needed more information. "Tell me how to find out more about this group."

He shook his head. "Too dangerous. What if they have other ways of discovering what you are? Better if you stay close to me for a while as I check into this more."

She shifted into full disbelief. He was maneuvering, withholding information to stay in control. Her instincts might have failed her once with him, but now they were pinging. "I haven't heard from you in two months and suddenly..." A buzz slid along her spine. She suddenly felt...exposed.

"I was being careful!" Mack sucked down more Scotch, then calmed his voice. "I will tell you everything at dinner. It'll be quieter there, and we can talk. I have my car." He stood up and took her elbow.

The buzz kept tingling from her pelvis to her heart. Her chakras! Mack cupping her elbow irritated her, his touch repellent. Jerking her arm from him, she stood. "I'm not going anywhere with you." If her chakras were reacting, her Awakening must be in the bar. She turned and searched. The dim and colored lighting made it harder.

"Roxy, I'm trying to help you. Just come to dinner with me. Don't make me—"

His words cut through her distraction. Sensing a threat, she whipped around to stare at his darkly determined eyes. His jaw was tight and his shoulders high. "Make you *what*?"

He visibly relaxed and softened his tone. "Worry about you. I want to clear this up between us."

That wasn't what he was going to say, she was sure of it. The skin of her inner thigh prickled insistently and distracted her again. Turning from Mack, she did another search. Would she recognize her Awakening once she saw him? Was it Kieran? She looked past the people lining both bars and moved on to the tables. She saw groups, and couples...

She spotted Kieran standing at the back of the room, his eyes focused on her. Her chakras shivered in reaction, and her schema prickled. Everyone else in the bar became background noise, meaningless to her. In that second, she knew he was her Awakening from the almost magnetic pull she felt, the urge to move closer to him. She couldn't look away and noticed that he stood alone, not even a drink in his hand. Blue and black lights spotlighted him, showing his hard edges. He had a long face, deep-set eyes, harsh mouth, and a chin that would crack knuckles. His shoulders strained his T-shirt.

His gaze was locked on her as if she were his prey. She actually felt dizzy, her limbs almost heavy. The intensity of his attention shivered over her skin and swirled inside her. The throb in her schema grew. Desire began to warm her body, tightening her nipples.

No! Dear Ancestors, her body was trying to call to him.

"Roxy..." Mack put his hand on her shoulder.

It felt like sandpaper on her skin. She didn't want his touch, not Mack. She jerked away, and, unwillingly, she turned back to Kieran. When their eyes met, she started to move, lifting a foot to walk toward him.

He started toward her, weaving through the crowd with a feral grace. Coming for her. He'd touch her, and she'd lose control.

No!

She turned, slapped the wineglass on the bar. Suddenly the room was too hot and the walls were closing in. She felt sluggish, almost ill. A headache was taking root behind her eyes. Something was wrong...but she had to leave, get away from her Awakening, from Kieran. She took a step, then another, focusing on the door.

The atrium. Get out there, then go to her room. Away from Kieran, away from Mack. She kept walking, faster and faster.

"Roxy, wait!"

Risking a look back, she saw Mack following her. She frowned at him. "Leave me alone!"

Then she looked over to Kieran.

He was following her, too.

She stumbled, caught the back of a chair. The flashing lights made her dizzier, her vision was getting fuzzy. Panic dumped adrenaline into her system and she shoved off the chair. She was half running and made it out into the atrium, then she looked around to get her bearings.

She couldn't focus, the room began to spin, her stomach heaved. Tried to make it to a bench along the wall. Couldn't, and suddenly, she was falling.

Two arms slid beneath her. Strong, warm, safe. Roxy struggled to focus. Kieran's face appeared. He lifted her off her feet and held her easily. "Feel sick. Something's wrong." Her words were slurred. Did he understand? She couldn't hold on.

"I've got you. You're safe."

She slipped into blackness.

⟶✷⟵

Key caught her just as she passed out. With so much happening, he couldn't sort it all out, but he knew the woman in his arms must be connected to Liam. His brother was really alive—

"Who the hell are you? Give her to me. She's my wife. Drunk. Can't hold her liquor. I'll take her."

Key shifted his gaze. It was the man from the bar. He stood at five eight, dark hair and eyes, wore a blazer over a T-shirt in the Hollywood-poser fashion. He'd distinctly heard the woman tell this guy to leave her alone. Fierce protective anger surged in Key, but he maintained his control. "Beat it."

"Hey! I said—"

The jackass looked right at him with a challenging stare. That gave Key the opportunity to use his hunter ability to shift memories by traveling through optic nerves to the other man's short-term memory. After two seconds, Key felt the sponginess in the nerves and knew he wasn't the first witch hunter to memory-shift this guy. It had been more than a coincidence that

Liam had picked tonight to show himself to Key. This guy was his brother's mortal flunky. They were working together.

Christ, things just kept getting weirder. The woman's scent of honey-almond curled around him, but he could also smell sour sickness taking hold. She wasn't drunk, he didn't smell enough alcohol on her to make her sick.

He felt pinpricks of witch power, but it was faint. What the hell was going on?

"What's the problem here?"

Key glanced at the man in the suit fitted with a lapel mike and he had an earpiece. *Hotel security.* He thought fast, worried about the clammy feel of the woman in his arms. Staring into the man's eyes, Key said, "Diabetic. I have her medicine in my room."

"Need a doctor?" he asked.

The man who'd been insisting the woman was his wife began edging away. His eyes dilated in fear and his hands twitched. Key had to make a choice, follow him and hope that trail led to Liam, or help the woman. He could hand her over and...

He couldn't. His muscles wouldn't do it. He knew that if the security guard called a doctor and they gave her synthetic medications, it could kill her. Resigning himself to tracking the mortal man later, he said, "I'll let you know. Usually she's fine a few minutes after a shot of insulin." He had no idea if that was true of diabetics, but it got the security guy off his back. He strode to the elevators, got on an empty one, shot up to his floor and hurried to his room. Once inside, he hustled toward the bed and gently laid her down.

As soon as he let go and stepped back, flickers of bloodlust licked at his veins. This close, he could tell she was a witch, but her power was almost flat. Sort of like when he found a dead witch drained of blood by rogues.

As if her power was dying or dead.

But she was alive, breathing fine but lying very still. Given the way that asshole with her acted, Key had a feeling he'd slipped something into her drink. Witches were highly evolved creatures, and synthetic drugs made them sick. On the upside, it looked as if she'd drunk less than half her wine, so she'd live.

As long as Liam didn't get ahold of her. That thought jolted him with a hot reminder of what it had felt like to desecrate her picture with cuts and blood. He looked at the picture still on the wall where he'd drawn it, seeing the dozen gruesome wounds gushing blood.

His brother would do it if he got her.

Key yanked out his phone, scrolled for the name, and hit call.

"Talk to me, comic boy," Phoenix Torq answered.

"Liam is alive."

"You're doing that frenzied drawing shit again?" the other hunter demanded.

"I saw him. Here in the hotel."

"It's been eleven years, Key. He's dead. You just saw a rogue—"

Key snarled, "For once in your life, shut up and listen." Then he explained exactly what happened. "He's alive, and if he's alive he wants the Dragon Tear." It's all any of his family ever wanted.

Phoenix swore, then asked, "Where's he been all this time? Why now?"

He felt dread wrap around his spine. "I cut out part of his heart, he should be dead. But I know it was him, and he was luring me away from this witch." He took a breath. "Maybe it takes that long to rise from the dead." He didn't know if he was serious or not.

"This isn't one of your freakazoid comic books. The dead don't rise."

He hoped not. "He didn't come after the Tear or me in all those years, so he must have been unable to. Nothing else would stop him. Nothing." Key knew it like he knew his own name. "You don't want to believe me, fine. But that Dragon Tear cannot be discovered. Ever. You are the only other person who knows about it." Key had told Phoenix so he would understand—if Key went rogue, Phoenix had to kill him before Key got to the Dragon Tear.

"Ailish and I will be there in a couple hours. Hang tight." He disconnected.

Stowing his phone, he dropped his gaze to the woman on his bed. He was pretty sure the slumber was so her weak magic could clear out the toxins of whatever shit was in her drink. Even semiconscious, she was incredibly alluring with lush, female curves. The way she'd felt in his arms, somehow instinctively trusting him, made him even more protective.

What did his brother want with her? How had this witch with the flat power caught Liam's attention? Where the hell had Liam been all this time? There was no time to waste; he had to find out how she'd crossed paths with Liam so he could protect her.

Then he had to kill his brother and make sure he stayed dead this time.

He needed her awake. Now.

He went into the bathroom and turned on the faucets in the tub. Returning to the room, he took off the witch's shoes, then scooped her into his arms. "Time to wake up, Sleeping Beauty."

—✳—

Roxy jerked awake when she landed in ice-cold water. Her heart slammed against her chest, adrenaline rushed and her head pounded. Bile rose up the back of her throat. Thrashing around, trying to escape the freezing wetness, she realized she was in a bathtub.

A large one made of marble.

Still wearing her clothes.

Her stomach churned as she shoved up to her feet and clambered out of the tub. What the hell had happened? Sleepwalking? But this wasn't her room in the hotel, none of her lotions or cosmetics or her curling iron sat on the counter.

She looked for a towel, caught sight of the huge man and went still. Her heart knocked hard enough to crack a rib. There, leaning against the closed bathroom door was Kieran DeMicca.

The one man in the entire world she wanted to avoid.

Her skin was ice-cold everywhere except on her mark. Needle-sharp heat prickled there. Throbbed. Hurt. "What the hell are you doing?" she tried to yell, but her teeth were chattering too much, and movement hurt her head. Tentatively, she reached for a towel off the stack and used it to dry her hair. Even that hurt her poor head. "What am I doing here?"

"You passed out in my arms. I'm pretty sure your drinking buddy in the bar put something in your wine."

She jerked her head up and then had to drop the towel and grab the counter to keep from falling. The bathroom spun. Bending over at the waist she concentrated on breathing and not vomiting all over the pretty veined marble on the floor. She imagined cooked skunk pelt tasted better than her mouth. *Think!* It was coming back to her that she'd met Mack in the bar. He drugged her? Why? Finally, she stood up, dripping cold water and fury. "I'll kill him."

He dragged his gaze from her wet hair, down her dripping top, second-skin pants all the way to her waterlogged toes. His expression was tight. "You might want to dry off first."

Still holding on to the edge of the counter for support, shivering violently, she remembered Mack in the bar and feeling sick. Then Kieran had caught her in his strong arms. And she'd felt safe. That was crazy! It had to be the schema unleashing hormones to get her to have sex with him. She had to get out of this bathroom and away from him. "What is your game, Mr. DeMicca? Why the hell did you bring me to your room and dump me in ice water? Are you as twisted as your art?"

His eyes widened. "You know who I am?"

She snorted. "I'm not one of your fangirls with a hankering to bang famous, so don't flex your ego."

He tilted his head, amusement bringing out the dimple on his left cheek. "Bang famous?"

"Okay, we're done here." Time to take control and leave. She forced herself to stand up to her full five foot six inches. The mark on her thigh was almost as irritating as he was.

He dropped his crossed arms, pushed off the door and stepped toward her. "No, we're not. What's your name?"

He was too close! His woodsy and darkly spiced Chianti scent swirled around her, filling her nostrils. She realized she was leaning toward him, a little part of her mind noting how big and solid he was, with bronze colored skin that contrasted with his short blond hair and light eyes. Pulling back, gripping the counter, real fear took root deep in her stomach and bubbled in her chest. She had to snap out of it; she could be in danger. "My father knows I'm here, and that I'm looking at Dyfyr to develop as a series for TV."

He took another step, crowding her against the counter. "Who are you?"

She tilted her head back to see his face. "Roxy

Banfield, executive producer for Spectral Productions."
She could feel his male warmth contrasting sharply
with the chill, making her shiver.

Kieran frowned. "Quit standing there freezing; use
your power to dry off."

Shocked, she said, "My...you know?"

"That you're a witch, yes."

How the hell could he know that? "Mack! That
blackmailing asshole." He'd told her about the fanatic
group looking for witches with her mark. Was Kieran a
part of them? Did he pay Mack to drug her and turn
her over to him? Forgetting her aching misery of cold
and sickness, she said, "How much did you pay him?
What do you want?"

He tilted his head, drifting his gaze over her. "This
second, I want you to stop suffering, use your power to
dry off and get warm."

She felt a tingle of heat everywhere he looked. He
was only one brief step away from her, and she had to
fight the urge to move toward him. Feeling his
heat...she clamped her jaw against the hormone-
induced urges. Roxy couldn't assess how much danger
she was in. Was he some crazy-ass mortal who killed
witches who had the schema mark? Or something
else? Should she deny she's a witch even though she'd
already tipped her hand? She tried another tactic.
Maybe she could convince him she'd reformed. "Can't,
I'm latent." She lifted her chin and added, "I refuse to
be a witch." That was true. Soon, her chakras would be
dead and she'd be gloriously, one-hundred-percent
mortal. If she didn't catch her death standing here in
icy wet clothes.

His face hardened, his bones jutting against his
tanned skin, but a light shifted in his eyes. "Ah. That
explains why I can barely smell your power."

"Smell my—" Alarm bells banged in her head,
brutally intensifying her headache. She wasn't dealing

with a wild-eyed fanatic, but something much more deadly. "Witch hunter," she whispered, trembling harder.

"Yes." He had his arms crossed over his chest, the muscles popping and shifting. Finally he held out one hand, palm up. He caught hold of her wrist, tugging it up. "Touch my lifelines, they're real." He settled her fingers on his palm.

She swept the pads of her fingers over the curving lines, the dips and ridges arcing over his callused hand and creating a sensual heat deep in her belly. He wasn't rogue; she could feel and see the evidence of that. When rogues killed an earth witch, they lost their souls and therefore, their lifelines. They also usually smelled like copper, not a rich, red wine like this man.

"Keep touching me like that..."

She jerked her gaze up to his face at the groan in his voice.

His gray eyes had flecks of blue as he finished his sentence, "...and I'll take those wet clothes off for you."

Her heart hammered in her chest, her body coiled tight, and she wanted to feel the texture of his palms brushing all over her skin. Shame had her jerk her hand away, breaking all contact.

She was allowing her baser hormones to control her!

He turned and reached for a thick white robe hanging on the back of the door and tossed it on the counter beside her. "Get out of those wet clothes and put this on." He pulled open the door, slipped out and closed it.

What had she almost done? Humiliation bent her over, and she forced herself to take deep breaths. He'd just been showing her his lifelines and she'd wanted to jump him. With Kieran gone, her headache and queasiness returned. She felt weak and shaky. Standing up, she debated her options. She could see from the black and gold logo on the robe that she was still in the Mystique hotel. Every room she'd seen in this hotel had the bathroom off the foyer of the room by the door to the hallway. Maybe she could go out the door, turn right, and make it to the hallway door before Muscle Man out there stopped her.

Witch hunter! They were supernaturally fast and strong; this was really bad news. What did he want? She couldn't figure it out. If the bloodlust from the curse was driving him to kill her, he wouldn't worry about her drying off and getting warm. Or showing her his lifelines.

Trembling with cold, and wincing from the rapid pounding in her head, she knew the smart thing would be to get dry, put on the robe, go out into the foyer, and then figure out how to get away. Even if Kieran meant no harm, he was still dangerous to her.

After stripping and drying off, she tossed down the towel and slipped into the warm robe. The mirror showed her pale face, huge eyes and a scraggly, half-gone ponytail. She tugged out the band and finger-combed the worst of the tangles, then gave up. Given her circumstances, it was better to go with the unattractive drowned-rat look.

Steeling herself to find a way to get out of this mess, she opened the door and stepped out into the foyer.

A scream locked in her throat.

Staring back from the wall across the hallway was a life-sized nude drawing of herself with hideous, bleeding cuts all over her.

Oh sweet crone! He was a lunatic! Terror burned through her, pounding her heart, roaring in her ears. *Run!* She whirled to her right and ran for the door five feet away.

Inches away from freedom, she was body-slammed into the door. It took her a full second to realize that the man had caught her face with his palm and had his arm around her waist preventing her from actually hitting the door. She was pinned so tightly, she couldn't even move her legs.

But she sure as hell could feel his thick, heavy erection pressing against her back.

Had she screamed? Would help come?

Or was she going to die here, right beneath her bloody, hideous picture drawn on the wall?

≫ 3 ≪

KEY HAD SEEN THE PANIC hit Roxy as soon as she saw the drawing. He caught her before she escaped. Standing there with her trapped between him and the door, his blood ran hot with every desperate breath she took. Her scent warmed to melted caramel with almonds. It was wickedly sensual, filling his lungs and his cock. But he could feel her heart pounding too fast like a small bird, and the sharp acrid scent of fear was burning through her natural scent. That picture had scared her senseless.

It was a sharp reminder of just how far gone he was. It hadn't even occurred to him what would happen when she saw it. He was so used to the violence in his head, in his world. This woman wasn't. He took his hands from her and slapped his palms on the door. "Turn around."

She did, and something inside him twisted at the sight of her flushed face and wild eyes. She was a good seven inches shorter than he. Looking down her length to her bare feet, he estimated she was a hundred and thirty pounds lighter. At one time in his life, he'd known what it felt like to be small and vulnerable. His father and brother regularly used him as a punching bag. Key had been born small by witch hunter standards, and worse, by the time he was three years old, he began drawing dragons and girls. That had been enough to make his dad feel the need to beat the pussy out of him. But his father had another motive as well. The Dragon Tear protected his mother, Beth, so Hogan would use their son Key, breaking his arm or leg, cracking ribs...all in an effort to force Beth to give him the Dragon Tear. She wouldn't risk letting Key wear the Tear, knowing he'd have given it to his father to save her. Key hadn't known how to fight back so he just let them hurt him.

Looking at Roxy now, he remembered that helpless, sick fear, then the blinding pain, and the only thing that had kept him focused was not giving the bastard what he wanted, to hear him scream or cry. Once Beth could get to Key and put her arms around him, the magic that protected her would protect him and help him heal. So his father had to do things like lock her in a room...

He jerked his mind back to the present and the woman standing between his outstretched arms, staring at him as if he were a nightmare come to life. She wasn't all that far off the mark. "I'm not going to hurt you." His voice came out thick. He pulled his hands off the door and fisted them at his sides to keep from touching her. She enticed him, and he wanted to touch her. She was too delicate, too breakable.

She sucked in a breath, lifted her chin and demanded, "What kind of freak are you?" She compressed her full lips, as if biting back a scream.

He hated that she saw the truth and ugliness that writhed inside him. Like his father had when he'd scream, *You're a freak! A spawn of magic so vile you make me puke. Should have drowned you!* Most women saw only his looks and reacted to his pheromones or his fame. "I'm trying to keep you alive.

It's not me that's going to kill you." The scent of her witch blood was so faint that it barely tripped his bloodlust. So why was Liam after her? How had she crossed his path? He had to find out.

"So you're stalking me to draw pictures like that." She tilted her head toward the drawing.

"No. I drew the picture first, then saw you in the meet and greet and recognized you." He narrowed his gaze. "You recognized me, too, and ran away. Why?" She had known who he was; okay, that made sense, she was a producer scouting for talent. But why would she rush away when she saw him?

"Because I didn't want to talk to you."

Might be true, but he thought there was more to it. "What's your connection to Liam? Do you know where he is?"

"Who?"

Her pupils were contracting into pinpoints, probably from a headache. She was leaning heavily against the door, breathing too fast, and the scent of sour sickness was very real. He'd thought her magic would heal her, and felt a sliver of regret for waking her up. "Liam is my half brother, and he's a rogue. That picture I drew? It means he's after you. That's what he'll do to you if he gets you." All these years he'd been having his episodes of drawing Liam—he hadn't been crazy or sinking into bloodlust. Liam was alive and Key's art knew it. This was real.

"But I don't know any Liam!" She winced, her shoulders rising in the white terry cloth robe.

Key fought sympathy. He knew witches felt pain intensely, but her misery from the aftereffects of the drug was nothing compared to what Liam would do to her. He had to find the connection between them both to keep her safe, and to track Liam. "He apparently knows you." Key watched her, wondering if she would lie.

She pulled herself together. "My magic is latent, so how would he even..." she trailed off, her eyes dropping. "Mack. He was up to something."

"The guy in the bar?" When he'd gone through the optic nerve to shift his memory, he'd found the man's short-term memories were mushy from another witch hunter's previous shifting. It had to be from Liam. "When I caught you in the atrium, he insisted you were his wife and tried to take you from me."

She grimaced. "Mack Daemon, he's an old boyfriend. We broke up. I never told him I'm a witch, but he knew and...damn, I can't think with this headache."

He felt a stab of regret and lifted his hand to her shoulder. "Let's go sit down." She was looking worse by the second.

"No, I want to leave—" The color drained from her face. Then Roxy ducked under his arm, ran into the bathroom, and dropped to her knees in front of the toilet.

Key winced at her violent vomiting. *Shit.* He went in and got her a wet washcloth. Lifting her hair, he held it against the back of her neck.

"Go a—" She couldn't finish as the next wave of sickness hit her.

Key waited, memories of another time, another woman throwing up, and him feeling helpless. He'd eventually learned the few things he could do. Cool cloth on the back of her neck, ginger ale or tea, and patience.

The spasms finally stopped. Key flushed the toilet, went to the sink, and wet another cloth. He handed that to her.

Roxy shifted on the floor, leaning back against the side of the tub by her damp clothes. She leaned her head back, appearing so drained she could barely move.

He couldn't stand her thick misery. Key hunkered down, slipped his arms beneath her and lifted her up.

"Kieran..."

He looked down at her too-pale face, her freckles vivid. "You're too sick to go anywhere." He walked out of the bathroom into the fresher air of the bedroom and headed to the bed. He held her in one arm and stripped the covers back, layered some pillows, then put her down.

"Resting for a minute, then leaving."

He didn't argue with her but went to the minibar and got out a small bottle of ginger ale, opened it and held it out. "You won't get far in your condition."

"Far enough to kill Mack," she muttered, took the bottle and sipped.

He sat down on the side of the bed, facing her with his hip brushing hers. That small contact reminded him of when she'd touched his palm. Lust had exploded in him. He had a supersized sex drive, but this woman did things to him unlike anyone else. She squinted against the light, dragging him back to the present. He reached over and turned off the bedside lamp. That left only the light from the bathroom around the corner. "What can I get you to help? Tea? Or I have a friend who is a witch, she won't be here for a couple hours, but she—"

"No witches."

Odd. "She could use magic to clear the toxins from whatever shit Mack put in your wine."

"No." She scooted away from him, putting a few inches between their hips. Taking another sip, she added, "I can't stay here with you." She turned her head toward the wall and added, "Or with *that*."

The picture. Key was furious with himself for not painting over it. These episodes didn't happen very often, but when they did, he either found paint or called the witches and they would magically erase it.

To her, he said, "You can't go back to your room. Mack drugged you. And I think he did it to take you to my brother. If Liam wants you, he can get you. He can walk right up to a security guard and, using his ability to shift memories, get the guard to hand over your room number and his passkey card."

The ginger ale slipped from her grip.

Key caught the bottle, his hand brushing a part of her thigh. A flare of warmth seared his hand and shot straight to his groin.

She tried to pull the robe tighter, but her hands were clumsy. "Something in the drink?" Her words were thick.

Key looked up at her struggling to keep her eyes open, her head listing to the side. He hated that she thought he drugged her. "No," he reached up, pushed her hair back. "I forced you awake when your body was trying to break down the drugs." It had been cruel of him, but he'd thought she could use her magic to dry and heal herself. "Sleep," he said gently. Then added, "You're safe."

Her eyes were sliding closed. "Not safe."

Leaning closer, he slipped one arm around her to pull her to his chest and then froze. Her scent slid down his throat and stirred deep inside him. More sensual than sexual, it made him want to hold her against him forever. He almost heard his dragon purr. *Damned strange reaction.* Moving two pillows so only one remained, he laid her back. She was nearly limp.

"Can't stay here." Her protest was real but she was too weak to follow through and her eyes closed.

Shit, his chest ached. He had to focus on his priorities: Find and kill Liam. Leaning over her once more, he asked, "Roxy, how did Mack know you're a witch?"

"Took a picture."

"Of your eyes?" She had classic witch eyes, they were exotically tilted up at the outside corners. The wall woman resembled her, but it wasn't quite right. His fingers curled, he wanted to either touch her, or get out his pencils and capture her on paper.

"No," she said slowly.

Focus! "Then what?"

"Schema. Have to..." Her lips moved then she sighed and fell into a healing sleep.

Schema? Like a diagram of something? He looked at the witch sleeping, and his chest expanded with protectiveness, but only because he knew what his brother would do to her if he got to her. Had to be. It was up to Key to make her safe.

He'd start with tracking Mack Daemon.

Key pulled out the passkey he'd gotten from the maid with a little memory-shifting. Sutton West, another Wing Slayer Hunter who was their computer expert, had located Mack Daemon staying in the hotel. Slipping the card into the lock, Key went into the room.

It was dark and quiet, just the air conditioner humming. Silently, he checked the bathroom on his left and found it empty. With his hunter vision, he could see the room perfectly well. There was a sitting area and desk on the right, a bed in the middle of the room against the bathroom wall, a small table and chairs, and a dresser and TV to the left.

But no Mack. Key took out his BlackBerry and checked on Roxy. He'd left her asleep in his room, with his laptop camera on her. She should be safe, but if something happened, he'd get to her. Satisfied that she was still asleep, he began searching the room and quickly went through the drawers; he found cameras and a laptop, but so far, nothing to link him to Liam or find where he was.

He took out the laptop, set it on the bed and booted

it up. Into his headset, he said, "Sutton, I'm disabling the firewall, can you hack in?"

"Can you draw?" Sutton replied, and then gave him directions to type into his browser.

"I'm in. What's your witch's name?"

She wasn't his witch. "Roxy. Roxanne Banfield."

The cursor on the laptop was moving by itself; pages were opening and closing. It was strange to watch. "Also look for Liam DeMicca."

"Your brother?" Sutton asked. "Thought he was dead."

"He looked alive when I saw him earlier."

"Unexpected family reunion," Sutton muttered, then went on, "He's added to the search. Carla is looking for information about latent witches."

"Good, thanks." Key did a second search of the room. He found a file of papers, airline tickets, hotel receipts, paperwork on the conference, nothing on Roxy or Liam.

"Got something."

He shot across the room. "Liam?"

"No, a file for *Roxanne Banfield,* in the folder *Witch Mark.*"

Key checked his BlackBerry again and Roxy was fine. He shifted his gaze to the computer screen as the pixels formed into a picture. It was a strange marking on delicate creamy skin, with a curve that would fit his palm. He could almost feel the softness, wanted to feel— "Shit, that's her thigh!" The inside of her thigh. Did Roxy know someone had taken that picture? He didn't like the idea of someone else that close to her inner thigh...

Forget it! Focus on the marking, not her thigh. "It's almost the color of clay bleached out by the sun...very light tan pink." Now that he was concentrating, he could see that it was in the shape of a goddess symbol, about two inches high, with her arms stretched up and her body clearly female. Like a fading sketch. "Schema." That's what she had called the picture Mack took. "Sutton, ask Carla what a schema is to witches."

"On it."

When he'd been drawing the wall-woman, he hadn't been able to see the marking. She'd turned her thigh, covering her mound, and that had pissed him off. He had wanted to see her, wanted to know every inch of her. But the way she'd stood, shielding herself not just from modesty, but hiding that marking...it twisted inside him. As if that mark connected them.

The skin beneath his dragon tat stretched and pulled.

"Key?" The voice of Sutton's mate, Dr. Carla Fisk, came over his headset. Sutton must have patched her through.

"Yeah, what do you have?"

"Schema is a representation of the true self." Carla's voice was fascinated. "It only happens with one kind of power that I know of—fertility witches."

Fertility witches! They were the single type of witch he distrusted. They screwed with nature and created monsters.

Like him.

Revulsion tried to shudder through him, but he repressed it. "So Roxy's a fertility witch. What does that mean? Her power is flat."

"I don't know much more. Fertility witches have always been shrouded in secrecy. I do know why you're not feeling her power; their magic is latent until they come into their power. Since their gift is sex magic, that's a good thing. I think that happens around their twenties, but that's about all I know."

Sutton broke in. "There's a picture and description of Roxy in that file. But there are files of other witches with partial marks in the folder."

He looked at the laptop and saw five witches, each

with a schema on different parts of their bodies, and in different stages. Two were brightly colored like a tattoo. All of those were just half of the goddess mark, not the fully formed one like Roxy's was. "What does it mean that Roxy has the full mark?"

"I'm not sure," Carla said. "I'll try to find out, but right now I'm checking on these five witches to see— Oh Ancestors! All five of them have been killed." She took a loud breath. "Someone is targeting fertility witches."

"The last file," Sutton said slowly, "is full of directions on how to disable the witch's power by cutting her, using a stun gun, etcetera. There's a number to call for sightings, directions, capture and delivery."

Key scanned the file, his stomach churning with a potent combination of disgust, outrage, and just enough of the darker craving to have those witches. *You have a witch in your room...*that seductively cool internal voice taunted while his veins swelled for the feel of witch blood. Hating that part of himself, he said, "I'll call the number."

"Wait, I want to trace it," Sutton said. "Okay, go." Key switched lines on his BlackBerry and dialed. Waited through the rings and forced himself to breathe. Finally it went to voice mail, three words: "Leave a message."

At the sound of Liam's voice, adrenaline dumped into his bloodstream, and his head pounded with renewed fury that he'd failed to kill Liam. He locked his jaw and disconnected. Switching lines, he said, "Voice mail." He heard his jaw crack with stress. "It's my brother, Liam." Thinking fast, he added, "Mack's a mortal, and I saw that his memory has been shifted by a witch hunter before. Liam must be recruiting mortal men to find these marks on women."

"I'm sure you're reeling that your brother is alive,

but do you know what he wants with fertility witches specifically?"

"No, but I'm going to find out. He's after more than these witches, that much I do know." Remembering Roxy in his room, he shifted screens on his BlackBerry as he finished his thought, "Liam is after— Oh shit!" The bed was empty. Roxy was gone.

—————

Key was furious with himself for getting so distracted by the schemas and learning that Roxy was a fertility witch that he hadn't seen her leave. He'd had to replay it to see when she woke, got out of bed, grabbed her clothes and left.

He could not believe how his night kept going from bad to worse. Phoenix and Ailish arrived—Phoenix must have broken the land speed records in his Mustang to get to Vegas so quickly and now they both stared at the wall where he'd drawn Roxy.

Phoenix wore his customary leathers, and his dark eyes were troubled. "You left her in here with this?"

"She was practically unconscious." Key went to the minibar, pulled out a too-damned-small bottle of Scotch and drained it.

Ailish, Phoenix's soul-mirror mate, stood next to him. Her hair was getting longer, now past her shoulders. Dressed in a black camisole, skinny jeans and boots, she wasn't looking at the drawing; she wasn't looking at anything. She said, "Damn, Key, that picture gives me the creeps and I'm blind. Mind if I get rid of it?"

The soul-mirror bond that ended the curse for them also allowed Ailish to see through Phoenix's eyes. It'd been too much to hope that Phoenix wouldn't show her. He didn't like them seeing Roxy naked or cut, but he was the asshole who had left it on the wall. More guilt. "Go ahead."

He felt Ailish's magic rise in the room, then as he watched, the drawing faded from the wall until it was just a memory.

Phoenix strode over to Key. "You can't find Roxy anywhere?"

"She's not in her room." Frustration burned in his gut. The dragon tat on his chest shifted, too. "If Liam has her..." He couldn't stand still. He hated feeling helpless.

From his laptop, Sutton's voice came out, "I found her with the cameras in the hotel hallways. She's safe. I'll show you the feed."

Key turned to the laptop and watched as the images began. Roxy, still wearing the robe and carrying her clothes and shoes, knocked on the door of a room. A woman opened it, stood back as Roxy walked in, then closed the door.

"I know her, that's Meryl Chambers, she's a bookseller." Relief eased his knotted muscles.

Sutton said, "The door has stayed closed. We'll watch the camera and make sure no one goes in or out. Even better, I think I can code the computer in the door lock to alert me if anyone goes in or out. Even if a rogue is invisible, the door will still alert me."

Thankful for Sutton's incredible computer wizardry, he said, "Okay, good." He leaned against the dresser while Ailish and Phoenix walked over to the couch and sat down.

"Key," the voice of Axel Locke, the leader of the Wing Slayer Hunters, came over the laptop. "Sutton has filled me in so far, but we need more information. Start at the beginning."

He turned his head, seeing the green eyes and hard face of his leader on the screen. Key, Phoenix, Sutton and Axel and another hunter named Ram had decided to commit themselves to their god, Wing Slayer. To show their allegiance, they each had a tattoo of a winged creature. Key did the tattoos, but when he'd inked the raven Axel asked for, it had magically changed into a hawk—the sign that Wing Slayer had chosen him as the leader.

Key felt the weight of the dragon inked on his chest. "I don't know what Liam's doing with fertility witches, but I know one thing he wants—the Dragon Tear. It's supposed to be the last in existence, and it's full of powerful dragon magic. My mother was an archaeologist and found it. After that, she wore it to keep my father, Liam, or anyone from getting it. She said it had the power to strip immortality from other dragons and make them mortal. It can also strip a god of immortality."

"A god-killer," Sutton said. "I've heard rumors, but I didn't believe it."

"Believe it," Key said. "It killed my mother. She wore the Tear and died of old age at thirty-nine." Bitterness roiled in him. "It was completely irrational—she could see she was getting older at an accelerated pace, but she wouldn't take it off. And that was only wearing the Tear as a necklace. Imagine if it was broken open, what the essence of it could do?" That was half the reason he'd kept his father, uncle and Liam from getting it. The other half was pure spite. They wanted it, had tortured him to get it. He'd never let that happen.

"The Tear is dangerous. If Asmodeus got ahold of it, he could strip Wing Slayer's immortality and then kill him," Axel said. "Wing Slayer is just regaining his god-power to fight the demon since the curse."

Key nodded. Wing Slayer was half god and half demon. He'd created the Wing Slayer Hunters and needed their complete faith in order to invoke his god-power. That was, and always had been, the one ironclad rule of the witch hunters: Never deny or renounce their god. Everything had been fine for centuries until three decades ago one hunter, Quinn Young, rejected Wing Slayer. That had been the loophole that Asmodeus and his demon witches needed to cast the curse and break the bond between the god and his witch hunters. "I have, the Tear hidden, Axel. It's in Glassbreakers, not here. So what drew Liam here?"

"You think it's the witch, Roxy?"

Key nodded. "But I can't figure out why. Her power barely registers with me."

"Okay, the Tear is safe for now," Axel said. "You need to protect the witch and find and kill Liam."

Key shoved off the dresser. "Going out now. He's got to be in Vegas somewhere."

Phoenix stood. "We're going with you."

Key stiffened. "No. You need to stay here and protect Roxy."

Visible tension radiated through Phoenix, lifting his shoulders as he leaned forward. "I swore I'd always have your back. That doesn't change because I'm mated." He ground his jaw and repeated. "That doesn't change—ever."

Ailish stood up and put her hand on Phoenix's shoulder and added, "Except now, you get a two-for-one deal."

Phoenix added, "I saw that drawing." He lifted his hand toward the wall. "That's your frenzied shit. What if it happens while you're out hunting? I'm not letting Liam or anyone get the drop on you."

Phoenix knew Key better than anyone alive. After his mother died when he was thirteen, Key had taken the Tear and run away. Shortly after that he'd met Phoenix; they survived the streets together and that made them brothers in every way but DNA. He knew Phoenix's stubbornness well, but he had one weakness—women in trouble. "Roxy's defenseless. She doesn't even have her magic. And if Liam does go after her, I need you there to stop him. Dead."

Phoenix crossed his arms over his chest, clearly frustrated. "You'd better not get killed, dragon boy."

Key grinned. "Can't. You still haven't let Ailish see my dragon tattoo."

Ailish laughed. "Oh! Maybe you should show me now, before you go out."

"Damn it," Phoenix said and a second later, purple and blue wings sprang from his back. One wing hit the wall, and the other curled around Ailish, stroking her possessively.

"That shit never gets old." Key laughed. The soul-mirror bond gave the witch hunters real wings to protect their witch. Phoenix's bird was insanely jealous of Key's dragon. He never cared that Ailish saw the other hunters' tats or wings, but the dragon made the bird crazy. So far, Phoenix hadn't let Ailish see the dragon, and since she had to use his vision to do it, he was winning the battle.

Ailish smiled and stroked the wings.

"Leave before I cut out your liver and feed it to the bird," Phoenix growled.

Key's humor faded and he strode out to track his resurrected brother.

≫ 4 ≪

ROXY LET THE SECURITY GUY open her hotel room door. Heeding Kieran's warning about rogues being able to get into her room, she was being careful. When she left his hotel room, she'd gone to her friend Meryl's room and stayed there. No one would know she was there. All she wanted to do now was throw her things into the suitcase and move them to Meryl's room. She was booked on a flight out tomorrow.

She could just go home now.

She should.

But she'd done months of research, and she'd believed that either Dyfyr or The Eternal Assassins were the project that she and her cousin, Shayla Banfield, had been looking for to work together on. Shayla needed work as a screenwriter, but even more, she needed something to be passionate about. Plus if Roxy went home now, her father would know something was up. She could tell him, but he'd be upset. Her father was adamant that she let her chakras die and become mortal. If he knew she'd found her Awakening, he'd watch her like a hawk. Question her, refuse to send her on assignments.

Roxy could do this. Mack she could handle; she

wouldn't give him the opportunity to drug her again.

But Key...she had to keep her distance from him. The picture on his wall had scared her, but what truly terrified her was the reaction of her schema. When she'd showered this morning, she saw more color invading her schema, obviously from being with Kieran. It was a shock to see it after watching it fade. The whole area was sensitive, the brush of her fingers tingled in a way that made her really uneasy. Something edgy and unfamiliar was happening in her.

Sexual heat.

No. She refused to turn into a passionately destructive witch. Ever. The schema would stop as long as she stayed away from Kieran. It had to. She hadn't even told Shayla that she'd found her Awakening.

The security guard walked up to her. "Ma'am, I checked and your room is empty." He handed the key card over to her.

Relieved, she stepped into the hallway next to the bathroom and closet, thanked him, then closed and locked the door. Taking a deep breath, she turned and choked when Kieran suddenly appeared in front of her. "Argh!" She strangled on the sound, as she stared. Where'd he come from? He towered over her by at least a half-dozen inches, and his body filled the foyer. The scent of Chianti came off him in waves. His eyes were a mix of blue water and smoky anger. He took a step toward her. "No more running. We're going to talk."

Adrenaline surged through her, and she almost turned to run, but she was a quick learner. Last time she'd done that, he'd pinned her against the door. Instead, she lifted her head and said, "How did the security guy not see you? Were you invisible or do you have some power to just pop in wherever you want?"

"I appeared invisible to the security guard. I broke into your room when I found you missing. I also broke into Mack Daemon's room and found an interesting picture."

His voice was low, but the black muscle shirt stretched over his chest shifted strangely. She stared, but all she saw was the shirt straining to contain the rise and fall of a massive chest as Key reached for something in his pocket. She noticed his arms were thickly muscled. The man had been lifting more than pencils. He looked like he could bench-press her. And given how easily he'd lifted her last night...

"Look."

The sharp word made her jump and she jerked her gaze to the BlackBerry he held out. Her heart slammed against her breastbone. Blood surged through her as embarrassment and humiliation burned her fiery blush. "My schema." The mark that symbolized everything she hated. All her life, she'd been torn between her parents—her mother insisting she give her life over to magic, her father demanding she become mortal. And both made her feel that their love was conditional on how that mark ended up—dead and gone or alive in full color.

It had been magic that tore her parents apart, turning her father's love into something ugly. It made Roxy's stomach churn. Would her father come to hate her if her powers Awakened?

And what if she fell in love with a man? Her limited experience with sex had already shown her that she made men uneasy; they complained that she was too demanding, wanting too much from them. And that was without her magic; once her magic surfaced, she would need sex to feed her power. Would one man be enough? Or would he resent feeling like a stud service for her magic?

All this circled in her mind as she saw the picture on his phone. "How did you get that?" She made a grab for his phone, desperate to delete it.

He snatched the phone back. "Better question is how he got the shot, since this appears to be the inside of your thigh."

The tone of his voice took her aback. *You're like your mother, aren't you? I can feel it. Since she's not here, you'll do.* Sweaty hands shoving up her nightgown... Roxy shook off the old memory. That man had been jacked up by her mother's sex magic. He broke into their house and when her mom hadn't been there, he'd come to Roxy's room. She'd only been eleven, just a little girl. But the guy hadn't cared; her mother's sex magic had him insane with lust. Fortunately her mom arrived home at that moment and all kinds of hell had broken loose. And now there stood Key, using that tone, like she somehow deserved this. "How do you think?" she snapped, then turned to the closet, yanked out her suitcase, and stormed into the room.

Key turned aside so she could pass.

She walked back to the closet and wrenched clothing off the hangers and hurried back to dump them into her suitcase. Next she got her shoes, and threw those in.

She went to the dresser and reached in, pulling out her underwear.

"Pretty."

His voice was so close she could feel it on her neck. Roxy looked down. Siren red and robin's egg blue silk spilled over her fingers. The cool satin contrasted sharply with his warm damp breath.

The schema on her inner thigh tingled. And spread...her skin began to feel tight, and—

No! Oh sweet crone, this was everything she had feared. Her Awakening invoked intense desire and feelings, and she barely knew him. He could be a crazy killer! Okay, she knew he wasn't; if he'd wanted to hurt her, he could have last night. He'd helped her when she'd thrown up. But he was a witch hunter, which made this even more impossible. As her Awakening, sex with him would release her magic. And she believed, destroy her dreams of finding real love and having a family. As a mortal she could have that. As a fertility witch? She didn't think so, not from what she'd seen between her parents and her own experiences.

He was also physically dangerous to her. That sudden, intense surge of magic in her blood could incite the bloodlust in Key and he'd kill her. Cut her over and over, smearing her blood over his skin to absorb the power.

The feel of his breath on her suddenly felt accusing instead of sensual. *Better question is how he got the shot, since this appears to be the inside of your thigh.* She didn't care what he thought of her. Dropping the panties and bras, she whipped around and said, "That picture is why I broke up with him." She closed her eyes, trying to get control. "I didn't know he had his camera in the bedroom."

"He took it while you were asleep?"

She opened her eyes and corrected him. "Sex." It had been so long, and Mack had seemed like a good enough guy. She'd known he wasn't her Awakening, and she just craved...touch, intimacy. And secretly, she was hoping that since her schema had begun to fade, no magic would surface during sex. It was the only time she showed any power, and it was just a trickle, but it opened up a pit of want in her that no one could seem to touch. The only two other men she'd slept with had reacted like there was something wrong with her. Something...unnatural.

"He used sex to get close enough to take that picture?"

She remembered how Mack had told her he wanted to see all of her. Then telling her to close her eyes, let him. "As soon as I saw the flash, I realized he was a sick creep and I threw him out. I should have destroyed the camera." She'd been so upset, embarrassed. Ashamed. Stupid.

"He tricked you." Lifting a hand off the dresser, he touched her face. "What did he do? Tell you to close your eyes and then acted like he was going to go down on you, bring you pleasure, then when you're lying there, spread out for him..." His eyes burned molten gray with flecks of blue.

She had a whole different image in her head. Key, kneeling between her legs, his fingers skimming that mark, and then rising higher, toward her desperate heat. The mark flamed hot, little tendrils of warmth spreading outward. She squeezed her thighs. "Don't." Curls of shame made her turn her face away from his touch, from his eyes. "Back off."

He dropped his hand and stepped back.

Growing edgier, she demanded, "What do you want? Why can't you leave me alone?" She scooped up the bras and panties and threw them into the suitcase.

He perched on the edge of the dresser. "We found—"

"We?" Her paranoia reared up.

Without a pause he said, "Wing Slayer Hunters. We're witch hunters who have recommitted to our Wing Slayer god. We've vowed to protect witches like you."

She nodded. "Axel Locke and his crew." Her mother had told her about them. She bitched about Darcy and Carla trying to take over the Circle Witches online group that she had started. Did Key know who her mother was?

"Yes. Axel is our leader chosen by Wing Slayer. But the hunter helping me with Mack's computer was Sutton West. He's a computer expert, and mated to a witch named Carla."

"Soul mirrors," Roxy said, surprised how much information she'd absorbed from her mother. Gwen Banfield was bitter that these witches had found a solution to the curse that had stripped witches of their familiars and high magic, while she hadn't. It all stemmed from the curse cast three decades ago by demon witches trying to bind witch hunters as their familiars. The spell twisted into a blood and sex curse, causing all the witches' and hunters' souls to be pulled out, joined and then halved. The result was their souls were damaged. The hunters' bond with their god was broken, causing them to lose their immortality and saddling them with a ferocious craving for sex and the power in witch blood. Witches lost their bond with their familiars and their high magic. The hunters that had once guarded earth witches now slaughtered them for the power in their blood. Then Axel and Darcy discovered they were two halves of the same soul, and once they were joined, the curse broke for them. She pulled out of her thoughts when she realized Kieran was talking.

"Mack is working for Liam, my brother. It was all there on his computer, including pictures of five other fertility witches that are known to have been killed by rogues."

Roxy sank down on the edge of the bed. "But I'm latent! How did they know I'm a fertility witch? How did Mack know? I never told him, I don't tell anyone I'm a witch. Or was it just an accident that we dated and he found the schema?"

Kieran's mouth pulled tight. "I don't think it was an accident." He pushed off the dresser, took out his phone, scrolled, then walked over to hold it out to her. "I had Sutton email the file to my phone. Look for yourself."

Her palms were slick with sweat, but she took the BlackBerry. The throb spread to her entire head as she went through five pages of different witches with the schema, although none of them had the complete schema as she did. "This was on Mack's computer?"

"Same place I got the picture of your schema."

Handing his phone back, she felt the betrayal burn in her chest. "You're sure about this? That Mack was drugging me to take me to your brother?"

Key shoved his phone into his pocket. "I called the phone number we got off Mack's computer—it was my brother's voicemail. Sutton will try to track the phone, but it'll be a prepaid. I went out searching for any sign of him last night, but didn't find anything." He stared down at her, frustration tightening his face. "You said you're latent. When do fertility witches come into their power?"

Roxy was so rattled, she answered without thinking. "When they find their Awakening."

He sat next to her. "Which is?"

She hesitated, her hand digging into the bedspread between them.

"Roxy, we're trying to help." He covered her hand. "Witches are being killed."

The warmth of his fingers covering hers raced up her arm, inflaming her schema while settling her churning stomach. "A man. The fertility witch has to find the man that causes the chemical reaction in her to release the magic in her chakras. If the witch doesn't find him, her chakras die off, and she becomes mortal."

"The schemas with color..."

"Means the witch found her Awakening," she explained. "The full color means they had sex."

"Sex magic," he said softly. "Your power is based in sex."

She looked over at the hunter next to her. Images filled her mind—Kieran pushing her back, covering her with his huge body, and then kissing her. Heat pulsed in her schema, sending out those tendrils of desire to flicker enticingly. What was wrong with her? She never fantasized! Just being near him for a few minutes weakened her. She needed distance. She was so close to her chakras dying. Ignoring the desire forming a throb between her legs, she pulled her hand free and stood up. "I'll be careful. I'm moving to a friend's room and—"

"Not good enough," he practically roared at her

Pinned between his huge body and the bed, she couldn't step back. "What is wrong with you? You warned me, your job here is done."

He ground his jaw, his hands flexing at his sides. "My job is to protect you. We'll move you into my room and—"

"No, and I'm not your job." Even if he hadn't been her Awakening, she wasn't moving into a man's room, a man who was practically a stranger. A man who drew a naked picture of her cut and bleeding on his wall. She could hire a bodyguard, if needed.

He put his hands on her shoulders. "Do fertility witches have needs?"

His warm hands made her catch her breath. "Needs?"

He caressed soft circles. "I can feel you, I know you respond to me." He lowered his head, and said in a thick tone, "I can smell your caramel desire."

Too much! Roxy froze beneath the onslaught. The feel of his warm hands sliding down her arms, and then back up and over her shoulders. He brushed his full mouth, so solid and hot, against hers. Tremors ran down her spine, her nipples tightened, and a pulse began to beat deep in her pelvis. It was more than she could handle. "What are you doing?" She meant to yell, to push him away, but it came out a soft whisper.

He raised his hand to capture her face. His eyes were igniting to a fierce blue. Pulling his head back a fraction, he said, "You feel it, too, there's a pull between us." He pressed his swollen cock against her belly, "I want to give you pleasure, give you everything you need."

Frustrated fury nearly choked her. She had to get away from him. The pinpricks in her schema intensified to a near burning, crying out for the touch of her Awakening. He was turning her into exactly what she didn't want to be—a witch controlled by her hormones. She'd lose everything she was working for—a chance to be loved without fear of her magic destroying it. A chance for a family. Her thoughts gave her strength and she caught his arms, jerked his hands off her face. "No!" Her heart hammered, her blood thundered, and adrenaline blew her anger into an inferno. "Last time I tried to have sex, that creep took a picture of my schema. That's what happens when I let passion and hormones control me. So I don't have sex."

"I won't hurt you." He ground his jaw in anger. "I sure as hell wouldn't take a picture of you and put it on the Internet."

"No, you just draw naked, mutilated pictures on the wall of your hotel room. That's so much better." Remembering that, she said, "Is it still there?" What if housekeeping saw it or—

"It's gone." He snapped the words. "And that was different. If you don't want sex, fine, but you need protection."

From him. She ripped her gaze away and stormed into the bathroom, gathered up her stuff and dropped it all into her travel bags. Then she went out and shoved those into her suitcase. She zipped it up, yanked it off the bed and dumped it on the floor. Her hands were shaking, the mark on her thigh burned, and her life was spiraling out of control. So she told him the blunt truth. "My schema is trying to make me have sex to find my Awakening."

Kieran's face softened. "Roxy—"

"No. I'm not going to Awaken. Not now or ever. I want my chakras to die off, and I will become fully, completely mortal."

His mouth dropped.

Finally she was getting through. "Kieran, I appreciate the warning about Mack and Liam. I'll be careful. You've done your job, now leave me alone." She pulled out the handle, rolled the suitcase toward the door and left.

❋

The multi-author signing was scheduled for two hours.

He'd made it an hour and twenty minutes so far. The noise in the large room was thunderous. The scent of sweat, perfume, latex and marker was cloying. Many of the fans were dressed in costumes; Star Trek and Star Wars were always popular. So were X-Men and Transformers, a few even dressed as Dyfyr. Some stayed true to the comic books, keeping the dragon charcoal or black with only bloodred accents. A few added their own color.

Key's line for autographs still snaked around the room. Impatience pounded in his head and tightened the muscles of his neck. His hand cramped and his bloodlust was starting to burn and swell his veins. He needed sex.

Automatically, he searched the room, his gaze passing over the authors and fans until he saw Roxy. She stood with a large man sporting a cop haircut and wearing a lightweight jacket over his gun.

Bodyguard.

But a mortal one, and that wasn't good enough. Liam or any witch hunter could shift his memory and get him to do whatever they wanted. Hell, they didn't even need to do that; Key could pick up Roxy and run, and he'd be out the hotel and partway down the street before the bodyguard reacted.

A darker emotion slithered through him. What if she let that man touch her? Ease her? He clamped down on that thought. But damn, she looked hot. She wore a black skirt, a blue green, sleeveless, button-down top, and had her red hair pulled back into a clip. Fresh, yet so curvaceous and enticing.

He was attracted to a fertility witch. That gave him pause. He wasn't dumb enough to assume all fertility witches were willing to pervert their magic as the one who helped his mother had done. Still, he wasn't a fan. But Roxy was latent, she didn't have her magic, so what did he care?

She must have felt his gaze, turned and looked at him. Her fair skin darkened. They were hyperaware of each other. She turned away, resuming her conversation.

He felt the loss, a return to the emptiness. Weird shit. He drew to pour out his rage and violence to be empty and clearheaded. But Roxy, when he drew her, saw her, or touched her, reversed the flow and made him feel as if a vital part of him had been drained and asleep, and was now waking.

Soul mirror.

The thought stunned him, and he rejected it. In the soul-mirror couples so far, the tattoos on the witch hunter came to life, giving the hunter real wings and acting as a familiar for the witch and helping her control her high magic. The way to find out if they were soul mirrors was usually for the hunter to touch the witch's blood, and the wing tattoo recognized his soul mirror.

But Roxy was latent. She wasn't his soul mirror. Hell, Kieran was a product of magic. When his mother had been pregnant with him, she'd taken the Tear to a fertility witch and had her do a spell to call the soul of a dragon into him. When he'd started drawing dragons as soon as he could hold a crayon, his mother said it worked. Key had always known the dragon was there, even knew his name: Dyfyr. It was like his hand or his foot, just there.

But he soon came to understand that he was a freak of magic, produced by a powerful Dragon Tear, a mother obsessed with immortality, and an unscrupulous fertility witch. A monster. Not the stuff of soul mirrors. No way in hell was he unleashing this dragon on any woman. The creature, when he surfaced, was furious.

Besides, soul mirrors exchanged sex and blood, and formed a bond. A relationship. Key didn't do relationships—he had destroyed people he loved or who loved him. While dying, his mother blamed him for not saving her, though he never knew how he was supposed to when she wouldn't take the Tear off. Then there was Vivian and their baby...

He shut it down before the old guilt suffocated him. No, he didn't sign up for that kind of grief. He could endure any physical pain. He'd had enough practice thanks to his father and Liam, so he knew how to survive that. But he wouldn't allow himself to destroy another woman.

His mind was in a turmoil trying to sort it all out. And yet his gaze returned to Roxy, sliding down her back, over that full ass and the length of her legs. His groin tightened, and the need to touch her ached in his chest. Sex he could do, but she didn't want it. At the very least, he had to make sure she was safe. Finish this signing while Phoenix and Ailish were out sniffing around town seeing if they could get any information on Liam.

Vivian flashed in his mind again, her skin so pale, her lips gray as he held her. He'd been desperate to save her, but it had been hopeless. His hatred of Liam burst like a firework finale in his head. Being an artist, his mind redrew the scene so it was Roxy's face...

Low complaints cut into his thoughts.

"Hey!" said a woman dressed as Princess Leia.

"Wait your turn!" demanded a storm trooper.

"You can't cut in line!" a slave girl shouted from farther back in the line.

Key spotted the two troublemakers. They were in their early twenties; one had on a black hoodie and a bulge in his front waistband. *Gun.* The second man was hauling a duffel bag.

"Beat it, kid." Hoodie shoved the approximately thirteen-year-old boy from the front of the line.

"But I was in line!" The kid was about five foot two and had on a Dyfyr hat over his shaggy brown hair, along with a too-big, black T-shirt, baggy camo pants tucked in sad looking boots.

"Get lost." The other man dropped a stack of comic books on the table. "Do your thing, dude."

His tat went hot. The rage wanted to boil up and out of him. It was the kid... Key only had to look at him to see he'd had a life of being pushed around.

On top of that, he knew what the thugs were doing, getting the comics and graphic books signed to sell online. They were bullying and intimidating all the authors into doing it.

"The boy was next," Key said, threading steel into his voice.

Hoodie lifted his sweatshirt to reveal the gun. "Sign them, asshole."

Key dropped his Sharpie on the table. "Can't. Got a cramp in my hand." He scanned the line of fans, saw they sensed trouble and moved back a few feet.

The bigger man with the duffel bag grabbed Key's wrist and tried to slam his hand onto the desk.

Key froze his hand in midair, using his hunter strength.

The man's dark eyes widened.

Hoodie pulled out his gun.

The other guy let go and turned to guard his gunman's back.

Key leaped over the table and jerked the gun out of Hoodie's hand.

"Knife!" It was the kid's panicked voice.

Key slammed his fist into Hoodie's jaw. His head snapped back, his legs buckled and he went down hard. Key spun, and went still. The second man had yanked the kid in front of him, the knife at his throat. Key looked into the boy's brown eyes shimmering with tears and helpless fear.

"Hey!"

It was Roxy's voice. She must have run across the room toward the commotion. Key kept his eyes on the knife at the kid's throat.

"Let me go!" Roxy yelled.

"Shut up, bitch!" Then a slap.

He knew that was Hoodie. He must have gotten up and grabbed Roxy.

"Umph! Damn!"

From the sound of it, she was clearly fighting him.

The man with the knife looked away from Key to see his partner scuffling with Roxy. Key seized the opportunity and lunged, grabbed the forearm holding the knife, and yanked it back. A sickening crack echoed in the room.

Key put his hand on the boy's shoulder and moved him out of reach. Then he turned, taking in the entire room in a sweep. Roxy's bodyguard was in a tussle with two security guys. He'd pulled his gun and they'd assumed he was the problem. Hoodie had hold of Roxy's ponytail, a small pocketknife at her throat. The man had blood running from his mouth and nose from Key's earlier punch.

"You move and I'll cut her!" Hoodie said, his dark eyes wild with pain and panic.

Key still held the first thug's gun in his hand. In a show of cooperation, he ejected the magazine to the ground, then reached over and set the gun on the table.

The guy watched his movements, his grip on the knife easing as he thought he'd gotten control.

Key snapped into action, drawing his knife from the holster at the small of his back and throwing it with dead-perfect aim.

The blade buried in the man's arm, just above the elbow. His nerveless fingers dropped the little pocket knife. He bellowed in pain and fear, shoved Roxy with his good arm and tried to pull the knife out.

Key leaped over where Roxy had fallen to her knees, pulled out his knife and yanked the bellowing asshole to his feet. After wiping off his blade on the thug's pants, Key threw him down next to his buddy.

Security swarmed around them. Key ignored them, his gaze zeroing in on Roxy. She got to her feet and stood there, shivering, a bruise forming on the left side of her face. He jerked off the light jacket he wore to cover his knife holster. Putting it around her shoulders, he yanked her up to his face. "What the hell were you doing getting close to that scumbag?"

She glared right back at him. "I had to get that man with the knife to look away from you. He would have cut that kid!"

A buzz filled his head. He could hear all the chatter going on around them, but his entire focus was on this little witch in front of him. "You did it *on purpose*?"

"To give you an opening to save the boy." She lifted her hand to her cheek.

A maelstrom of feelings erupted inside him. Pride

in her, fear for her, rage that she'd been hit, satisfaction that she believed he'd save the boy, respect that she cared enough about a boy she didn't know to put herself in danger...

"I'm sorry."

Both he and Roxy turned at the same time to see the boy standing to his right. The kid's hat had come off, he still clutched his rolled up comic book, and his face was a picture of shame and misery. "For what?" He was so wrapped up in Roxy, he couldn't get his head around why the kid was apologizing.

The boy stared down at the book in his hands. "For starting this. I should have moved when the guy told me to, but I wanted to meet you...sorry." He turned and started to walk away.

Key let go of Roxy and turned. "Hey kid, what's your name?"

The boy stopped and looked back. "Tyler."

He walked to the young man, put his hand on his shoulder and felt the sharp bones beneath the kid's shirt. "This isn't your fault, Tyler. You tried to stop the guy with the knife, didn't you?"

Finally the kid looked up, his face flushing. "I tried to grab his arm, but he's stronger." He looked down at his comic book. "I don't know how to fight or anything."

Oh Christ. Key was looking at himself about sixteen years ago. Twelve or thirteen-ish, thin, gangly, and clueless on how to defend himself. No wonder the kid liked Dyfyr, the Dragon of Vengeance. If Dyfyr were here, he'd defend this boy. "Do you still want me to sign your book?"

"Really?" He looked down again. "It's kind of messed up. I read it a lot."

This kid was the reason he did signings. "That's why I create them, dude. Not for plastic sleeves and display cases, but to be read." He took the book from him, hiding his grin at the tattered condition, turned to his table, and grabbed the pen. He wrote, "To Tyler, a man with the bravery of a dragon," before signing his name. He handed it back when a page slid out.

Tyler didn't notice the falling paper as he read the inscription. "Oh. Awesome! Thanks Mr. DeMicca!"

Key bent down and picked up the page. It was a drawing, a pencil sketch of him at the table, bent over to sign a comic book. Behind his right shoulder, Dyfyr was crouched; his eyes watchful, his spiked tail partway up and he looked ready to explode into action. It was damned good. He looked up. "You drew this?"

Tyler looked up and flushed a deep red. "Uh, I was, you know, just standing in line, and sketching. Just fooling around."

Key said, "Can I keep it?"

The boy's mouth dropped open. "Uh, yeah. If you want."

Hell, yeah, he wanted it. He'd put this up over his drafting table at the club, another reminder of who his real fans were. He held out the drawing and the pen. "Sign it."

Tyler's eyes grew bigger. "Like an autograph?"

"Exactly."

The boy took the pen and paper, leaned over the table, and wrote across the bottom, *Tyler Yandell*. Then he turned and held it out.

Key took the drawing. "Thanks. You interested in learning some self-defense?"

Tyler stood up straight, his shoulders back. "From you?"

Key could teach the boy, but he had another idea. "I could show you a few things, but I know someone even better. She used to be a professional kickboxer. Her name is Ailish, and she's here in town with me and a friend of mine."

He grimaced. "A girl?"

"Ever hear of the Blind Kickboxer?"

Recognition rearranged his face into awe. "Oh man, really? You know her?"

He smiled. "Yep." He turned to Roxy.

Gone.

Looking up, he saw her heading toward the door. Glancing to the kid, he said, "Stay here." Then he ran over, winding between people, and caught up with her at the door. "Roxy."

She turned back to him. "Oh, your jacket." She slid it off her shoulders and handed it to him.

Ignoring her outstretched hand, he saw the delicate skin beneath her eye getting dark and puffy. "Damn. Your eye is bruising."

"I'll put ice on it later." She shoved his jacket into his hand; then both of them turned as police swarmed into the room. They insisted on talking to everyone.

"Stay here with your bodyguard," Key said, then walked over with the police to where security had the two thugs contained, giving his statement as he did so.

He glanced back over to see a cop taking Roxy's statement. Tyler was sticking close to him, so Key took out his phone and made the call he'd promised the kid.

"Yeah," she answered.

That got a smile from him. "Ailish, it's me."

"No info on Liam, but I won two hundred bucks! On slots!"

He smiled. "Good, you're buying dinner. Hey, I have a favor. A friend of mine wants to learn to fight." He slid behind his table and sat down. "Could you meet us in the signing room?"

"The fertility witch?"

He checked on Roxy again, saw her still talking to a cop, her bodyguard next to her. He answered Ailish, "Nope. Name's Tyler, just met him today."

"So mysterious, dragon boy. Okay, we'll be there in a few."

"Later." He hung up and looked at Tyler standing by him. "She's on her way."

"Thanks, Mr. DeMicca."

"Call me Key." Then he sobered and gave the boy fair warning. "You might not be thanking me after you go one round with her. She won't go easy on you, but if you really want to learn, Ailish will teach you."

His own memory of learning to fight came back to him. Phoenix had found Key on the ground getting the shit kicked out of him and then beaten the hell out of the group of boys and sent them packing. Furious, he'd brutally yanked Key off the dirt and asked him if he was too dumb or too scared to fight.

Don't know how. All he knew how to do was not show pain.

I'll teach you.

And he hadn't been nice about it. But Key learned. No one knew that, not a single soul. Phoenix had his faults, hotheaded, hardheaded, always spoke his mind, but he never told anyone about that scene. Ever. He'd call Key pansy-ass artist, comic boy, dragon lover, all day long, but he'd never humiliate him with that story.

Tyler looked him directly in the eye. "I want to learn."

"Good man," Key said. They'd find out more about this boy, what his situation was. If he needed real help, they'd get it for him.

He stowed his phone and walked toward Roxy.

But she was gone. Again. Damn it, losing her was getting to be a bad habit.

⇒ 5 ⇐

ROXY WAS EXHAUSTED, AND THE herb tea she'd sipped hadn't done anything for the throb in her left cheek and eye. She'd just concluded her last meeting and had a little time to herself. She'd sent her bodyguard, Joel, on a break so he could get something to eat and walk around a bit. She would call him to meet her before she left the cafe. Her stomach rumbled and she thought about ordering dinner.

She opened her jaw, winced and decided to wait. The place was full, but she had the booth, and had paid for several rounds of drinks and food for the people she met with. First she'd had discussions with some key merchandising people about current projects, and she'd just concluded a meeting with Perry and Nina Jenkins, who assured her the dramatic rights were available. She really liked them and loved their series of Eternal Assassins. She could visualize it as a movie, beginning with the murder of the first assassin and Aya, Empress of Shadowland, offering the shocked soul a deal for revenge. The soul would have no idea of the true cost.

The over-arcing story question would be *Is there a way out of the eternal contract?* Fighting against a trick of nature, or supernatural beings, appealed to her on so many levels. She loved themes like that, where each choice mattered, where the characters played an important role in the universe.

She picked up her pen, jotting down all the information she'd need for a profit and loss statement to include in her pitch to her dad. Then they'd come up with an offer and contact the agent...

Someone sat down across from her.

Looking up, Roxy fought back a groan. It was the man in the Bart Simpson costume. He'd been following her around the signing, repeatedly pitching his "Groundbreaking animated series about a family..."

She'd told him politely that she wasn't interested the first two times, then more sternly the third time, and after that her bodyguard had chased him off. She thought he'd gotten the message.

Apparently not. That plastic head with the frozen cartoon expression was disturbing. His voice came through a hole in the mouth. "Since you're not busy now, I'll finish what I was telling you about my project. It's X-Men meets the Munsters."

She'd had enough of this. "I've told you no. You need to leave or I'm calling my bodyguard." She reached for her phone.

His shoulders snapped back and the head wobbled. "You won't even give me a chance! You're all the same, a bunch of stick-up-your-ass cretins who refuse to recognize my talent!" He got up, snatched a full glass of water from the next table and dumped it on her.

Roxy gasped in shock as the water and ice tumbled over her.

Everyone in the cafe went silent, except for the sound of a cellphone ringing somewhere. Bart Simpson stomped out.

"Hell," she muttered, feeling hot tears of

humiliation, tiredness, frustration and loneliness fill her throat. She never cried, never gave in to her emotions.

"You have a lemon slice in your hair."

She looked up to see Kieran looming over her, his wide shoulders blocking out the world. His mouth was half-cocked, one side turned up in a smirk, the other side flat. It felt strangely as if it was just the two of them. "It's my citrus look. You like?" What else was she going to say?

She could feel his gaze slide over her face, travel along her neck like a warm caress, and catch on the soaked silk shirt molded to her breasts. Her nipples tingled and hardened in response.

He lifted his gaze. Putting one hand on the table, he leaned in. "You have a habit of getting wet."

In spite of the cold water, heat bloomed in her belly and in her schema. She was losing her mind, or maybe it drowned in the water. "First you and now Bart Simpson."

His grin slid into high voltage as he pulled the slice of lemon from her hair. "The cartoon character? He gets you wet? Kinky."

"No!" She picked up a cloth napkin and wiped her face. "I mean—" She was flustered. That voice, his grin, just the solid feel of him leaning into her made her forget her own name. "Bart Simpson's been stalking me!"

His dimples appeared. "Where's your bodyguard? Off at Moe's Bar?"

Her mouth twitched. "I gave Joel a break. I didn't know I'd be accosted by Bart. He had a cutting-edge animated series idea. X-Men meets the Munsters."

Key dropped his head and laughed.

It was too much. Roxy was drenched, humiliated, tired, sore, but she started to laugh, too. Until finally the hot pain in her face got her attention. She cupped her left cheek in her hand. "Could have used the ice in that glass for my face."

Key sobered instantly. He reached over, pulled her hand off, and took her chin in his palm. "Hell, woman, why didn't you put some ice on this?"

The sudden touch stunned her. "Uh...I had work." Business first. She was responsible, not flighty and reckless.

"The bruising is worse." He ran one long finger over the tender skin.

She shivered, a little tremor sliding down her body, touching her nipples and...

He stood up, slid off his jacket and placed it around her shoulders. "Come on." Using the edges, he pulled her to her feet.

Chunks of ice clunked on the polished marble floor. She hardly noticed with the feel of his jacket, warm from his body and full of his spicy scent, and Key standing right in front of her. "Thanks."

He smiled down at her. "Let's get you in dry clothes and do something about your face." He let go of the edges and pressed his hand into the small of her back.

Waitstaff rushed in behind her to clean up the mess. Diners watched as they walked out into the atrium with the colored water feature in the center. Every step she took with his hand on her back pulsed in her schema. "You don't need to come with me." She held up the phone still clutched in her hand. "I'll call Joel." She should have done that earlier, but Kieran had a way of distracting her.

He kept his hand on her, guiding her into the elevator, then gestured to the buttons for her to push her floor and said, "Can't take a chance with Bart Simpson on the loose. Call your bodyguard from the room."

She put her phone away and pushed the button, then she leaned against the elevator wall and pulled his jacket tighter around her. She'd been watching Kieran in the signing, she couldn't help it. The man was her Awakening, and she was curious. Then she'd seen the kid shoved aside, the man show his gun, and Kieran explode into action. He'd leaped over that table like he could fly. He'd moved so fast, she could barely track him. He'd looked every bit as fierce and frightening as the dragon he drew.

She'd reacted when that man put the knife to the boy's throat, rushing over there, planning to distract the man. She hadn't anticipated the thug on the floor getting up and grabbing her, but her plan had worked.

Even when he'd pressed that knife to her throat, she'd been scared for only an instant. Then Kieran turned around, she'd seen his eyes drain to gray menace, and she'd known he'd free her. She hadn't expected him to throw a knife that landed two or three inches from her arm. Was his aim that good or had it been luck?

She looked up to see him staring at her from two feet away. Wearing a black shirt and jeans, he filled the elevator, dominated the space with his powerful male presence. He was so...capable. "How did you know you wouldn't hit me? With your knife, I mean."

"I don't miss." The doors opened; he stepped out and then held the door.

"Ever?" She went into the hallway. For any other man, she'd say he was bragging. But she'd seen Kieran in action today.

He fell into step beside her as they walked down the hall. "Not in a long time. You weren't in any danger from me."

But she was. And she was playing with fire by prolonging her contact with him. Questions bubbled up, her desire to know more about him, learn everything she could. Where he came from, how he learned to fight like that, what his skin felt like, what it would feel like to let herself go in a hot, deep, wet kiss with him.

Stop it! She had to control her thoughts. She grabbed her key card from the side pocket of her purse and fumbled to get it into the slot.

Then he moved up behind her, one of his hands taking the card from her fingers, the other reaching for the door handle. The heat of him sank into her from all sides.

"Nervous?" he said against her ear.

She shivered and watched as he lined the card up and slid it in. Slowly. His long fingers pushed the card down a fraction at a time. Holy vibrators, she was in trouble if she thought a key card was sensual. "Hurry up!"

"Impatient to get inside with me?" He rammed the card home and pushed the door open.

Roxy took a step to get some distance, then turned, took off his jacket and held it out for him. "Thanks, I'm safely to my room now."

⁕

He ignored the jacket, reached for her arm and pulled her behind him where she was safe. Then he walked into the room.

"Damn it, you can't..."

He paid no attention to her protest. First he checked the bathroom, then the closet, and finally the room. This one had two queen beds. He walked around them both to make sure no one was crouched and waiting for her. Then he turned back and saw her standing there holding the door open.

She arched one delicate eyebrow and said, "Done playing superhero?"

He walked up to her. The closer he got, the more her natural honey-almond scent deepened. He knew desire when he scented it. It'd been growing since they got into the elevator. It was tantalizing, seductive, and beginning to get an edge that suggested she was going to be in pain if she didn't follow her urges.

He wouldn't leave her in pain. Not when she obviously desired him and he wanted her with a desperation that was growing by the second. He dropped his gaze to her breasts, so lush and full, beneath the flirty little silk shirt. His body began to hum. Then he saw her shiver. Lifting his gaze, he reached out and caressed her wrist. "Close the door, Roxy."

Her eyes widened. "After you leave."

He drew his finger up the inside of her elbow. "Now," he said gently. He wasn't leaving her hurt, cold and alone. He sure as hell didn't want to leave her unsatisfied, although that was ultimately up to her. But he could be persuasive.

She shook her head and then winced. Raising her shoulders, she rolled her head, obviously trying to loosen tight muscles. Then she abruptly let go of the door, dropped his jacket and grabbed her left shoulder, her face tightening.

Judging by the suddenness of her movement, he assumed it was a muscle spasm. Key reached behind her shoulder and felt the knotted muscle twitch beneath her cold, soggy shirt. Her scent was getting sharper from the pain. Quickly he began undoing the little row of buttons. "Get this off."

She dropped her arms, and he slid the shirt off.

Letting the garment fall to the ground, he caught her shoulders and turned her. Moving her damp hair aside, he pressed his fingers against the muscles where her neck curved into her shoulder.

"There," she said, her voice tight.

He began massaging, working in circles, warming the muscles and tendons so they'd relax. With his other hand, he slid the strap of her gold-colored bra over her arm, working the entire area. She'd probably wrenched the muscle when the guy in the signing had grabbed her or slapped her, and then the cold water and stress finally set off a spasm. Hot anger sizzled inside him. He knew it wasn't logical to think he could have prevented what had happened, but her pain pushed his buttons.

The woman made him feel too much.

She was turning him inside out. He'd had a quick glimpse of her abundant breasts spilling over the cups of her bra. And now even as he was trying to ease her pain, he was thinking about how her skin felt satiny-soft beneath his fingers. She was the color of a seashell, creamy with a hint of pink. He even noticed the way her damp hair was curling.

Heat flared in his body, a protective and deeply erotic sensation rising and grabbing hold.

He sucked in a breath to get control and realized the sharp scent of her pain was fading. "Better?"

"Yes." It came out a groan. "Keep going."

As if he'd stop. The slope of her neck enticed him just like every other part of her. He wanted to press his mouth to that spot. He looked down her back at the curve of her waist and the flare of her hips beneath her skirt. Christ, she was built for sex, for a man to lose himself in her.

For him to lose himself in her.

"Ahh." She dropped her head forward, relaxing.

Her voice vibrated, almost a deep purr that sent red-hot shivers down his spine and thrummed in his groin. Her scent was caramelizing, so potent he leaned forward and brushed his mouth over the curve of her shoulder.

She shivered.

More! The command came from the most primitive part of his brain.

"Kieran…"

Her voice in sex mode, he wanted *that*. Lifting his mouth from her shoulder, he turned her and pressed her to the wall. Careful of the bruise, he leaned in, cupped her face and brushed his mouth over her lips. Feathering and gentle, learning the lines and curves of her lips. Those brushes tempted the shit out of him. Her lips were soft and full, with a hint of what lay inside.

She made a soft sound.

A primal groan tried to surge in him, but he ruthlessly controlled it, refusing to hurt her. He kissed and licked, while using his thumbs to stroke her face, her jaw, feeling the kick in her pulse. Oh yeah, he was giving her pleasure.

She opened beneath him, responded to his touch in a way that shuddered right down his spine. He dipped his tongue into her mouth, tasting the warm depths as hunger exploded. A growl rumbled in his chest, while he skimmed his hands over her shoulders, over her waist, filling his palms with the curve of her hips.

Roxy moaned and grabbed his arms, her fingers digging into his muscles. She rose up on her toes and kissed him back.

Hard.

Her tongue rubbed against his. Full breasts pressed to his chest, making his dragon shift restlessly. Her scent was thickening with her need.

Ease her! The words thumped through his brain in time with the lust pounding in his cock. Key reached lower, cupped her ass and lifted her. Aggressive, needy, hot, he had to have her. He shoved the skirt up and pressed his hips between her thighs. Seeking her heat, her most intimate ache…

She cried out, tearing her mouth from his. "Hurts. No!"

He froze. He was *hurting* her? Her jaw? "Where?"

he demanded while fighting down the crazed primal urge throbbing in his cock, tightening his balls and pounding in his blood.

She was panting, her nails ripping into the skin on his biceps. "My schema."

Something really was wrong. Holding her, he strode to the bed, set her down and shoved up her skirt. She had smooth full thighs that made him swallow. He ignored that and zeroed his gaze in on the upper left leg.

His blood pounded in his ears, and he crouched down to eye level. Her scent was hotter, richer, and made his mouth water. But his gaze caught and held on the mark. Nestled up close to the copper silk panties was a two inch figure of the fertility goddess outlined in the thinnest line of emerald green and filled in with the barest tinge of sea blue and green. It was stunning. He wanted to touch the symbol, stroke it, pet it...

Roxy caught his hand sliding up her thigh. "No!"

He forced his gaze up to hers. "I can stop the pain." How the hell did he know that? It was some elemental instinct. It wound deep within him, creating erotic images that hardened his cock unbearably. And when he inhaled, he caught more than her desire, he smelled a whiff of magic. *Danger!* his mind screamed. He was so hot, so on edge, if he stopped touching her, the curse would burst out and he'd want her blood. Crave it. "What the hell is going on?"

Her eyes were the color of spring grass, fragile and layered with emotions. "It's starting...you have to stop touching me."

He fought the urge to look again, to see her creamy thighs with the mark of the fertility goddess and her panties that hid the part of her he was desperate to see, touch and so much more. Ripping his hands away, he rose and took two steps back. His veins began to pulse and twitch, but he was still in control. Barely.

She got up and shoved her skirt down.

He couldn't look away. Standing there, shimmying her skirt over her hips, her mouth kiss-swollen, her breasts jiggling in the cups of her bra and her scent enticing him. He forced his gaze up to her face. "Tell me."

She looked at him like he'd kicked her puppy. Like he was the enemy. Her shoulders dropped and her eyes closed. "It's starting." Then she opened her eyes and they shimmered with unshed tears. "You're my Awakening. You're destroying me."

Her last words ripped through him, getting too damned close to places better left alone. "What the hell does that mean? If I'm your Awakening...shit!" It hit him what she must mean. If her magic released suddenly, it would inflame his curse, and he could lose control. Kill her. Frustration brutally clamped his neck muscles. "I won't hurt you." He'd plunge his knife into his own chest before he let himself hurt another woman.

The tears turned to glittering anger. "You are hurting me! I don't want to be a fertility witch, but when I'm near you, my schema hurts, my body aches...I don't want it!"

He was hurting her just standing there? His gut burned, but he couldn't just leave her. Yet a kernel of low-grade panic formed in his chest. Everything was happening too fast, going too deep. "We have to talk about this, figure it out. There are things we need to—"

"No. I can't be near you. Not now, not ever." She sucked in a deep breath. "This attraction, it's not real. It's manufactured by my schema to release my magic."

Anger leaped up into the brew of frustration, worry and helplessness. "Bullshit." He fisted his hands to keep from reaching out, hauling her up to his mouth and silencing her. Untamed possessiveness dragged him a step closer to her. "What's between us is real." He would not let her make this attraction between them *ugly*. Since he'd drawn the picture, she'd touched his life with a singular beauty. He'd treasure that memory always.

She turned her face away. "Once we had sex, I'd come into my magic. The woman you know now, the one you see now, she'd be gone. And you'd grow to hate me." She added quietly, "I'd grow to hate me."

Key blinked at the whispered shame crawling through her words. It beat at him, made his skin itch. She really didn't want this. Their attraction really was ugly to her. He hated the fertility witch who had perverted him into a monster. Roxy was a fertility witch, but when he looked at her...he didn't see it. She'd put herself in danger to help him save that kid. He was sure she'd use her magic responsibly. So why did she think her sex magic would be so bad? He didn't dare touch her, didn't dare bring out any more of her power that could incite his curse. But he couldn't bear her suffering. "How do you know that?"

She turned back. "It's what happened with my parents. My mother needed more and more sex to feed her magic. My father got tired of being nothing but a power source to her. Now all she has is her power. I don't want that."

How had this gone so wrong? He'd been trying to keep her safe from Liam, but he was destroying her. Quietly, he asked, "What do you want?"

"To become fully mortal. Find a man who can love me, really love me. Have a family. Live my life in a real and meaningful way. I want sex to mean something, be an expression of caring, not just be used as a way to get power."

He stood perfectly still, yet a kernel of panic exploded inside him. This was exactly what he didn't want. Love was a fragile emotion, so easily broken, and when it broke, it destroyed the people involved. *Family?* He couldn't go there.

He'd destroy her. Somehow, someway, he always did.

"Please, Key, just leave."

His chest hurt. "I can't leave you alone and unprotected. Liam's out there, Roxy. He's going to find a way to get you." She was too vulnerable. He flashed on the picture he drew of her, cut up.

She lifted her head, the bruising on her cheekbone more vivid when her eyes were empty. "I can live with that risk, but I can't live with my magic."

$$\rightleftharpoons 6 \rightleftharpoons$$

ROXY ACHED DEEP IN HER pelvis where her first chakra resided, and in her lower abdomen where her second chakra, the one that held sexuality, cramped in protest. The schema tingled.

She got up, stripped off her skirt, found a pair of jeans and a T-shirt. Then she grabbed her cellphone and called the one person who would understand.

"Roxy, I've been waiting!" Shayla answered. "So did you meet them? Nina, Perry and Kieran?"

"He's my Awakening," she blurted out.

"Who? What happened? You found your Awakening? Oh God, I knew I should have gone!"

"Shayla, you can't." Her cousin was tainted. In the Banfield line of witches, one witch in every generation carried a mutation of infertility. They discovered it at puberty when their schema formed into a black barren tree instead of the goddess mark. Shayla had the barren tree mark. No one knew how the original mutation had happened or why it continued generation after generation. Just using their magic spread infertility, and over the centuries, if discovered, infertility witches were sometimes killed by mortals and even witches. Most tried very hard to avoid their

Awakening and become mortal. Shayla was grimly determined to let her chakras die, so they couldn't risk Shayla accidentally running into her Awakening. Her cousin spent most of her time at home or places she knew were safe, like Roxy's, or all-women gyms, etcetera. "My Awakening is Kieran DeMicca."

"Creator of Dyfyr? Unfreakingbelievable. Okay, that means DeMicca is now dead to us. Get the fuck away from him!"

"It gets better. He's a witch hunter. One of the Wing Slayer Hunters."

"No shit? Roxy, run. Now. Or I'm coming to get you."

That made her stomach tighten. "No, Shayla, I'm coming home. I'm going to call for an earlier flight and leave the hotel."

"Roxy, how's your schema?"

She hesitated, but lying wouldn't help. She hated herself for being weak. Even now, she ached for the touch of the man who would awaken her fertility magic. "There's color, it's started. And sweet crone, I want him." She straightened her back. "But I'll fight it, Shayla." She had to. Roxy wanted more in her life then a series of sex partners to feed her magic that could never be satisfied. "I'm going to be mortal, have a real family." A lover who wouldn't grow to hate her for what she was. She didn't want her father to hate her like he hated her mom and magic. Her father insisted she become mortal, while her mother pushed her to find her Awakening. *What do you want?* Kieran had asked her, the only one to ask her that. And the answer? *To be loved for who I am. To be safe to be myself.*

"I'll help you. We made a pact. You'll stay with me, and somehow we'll find a way to stop your schema."

Her cousin's words pulled her from her confused thoughts. "Okay. And, Shayla, I'm going to pitch buying the dramatic rights for Eternal Assassins to my dad."

"Just get home. We'll deal with all that later." She hung up.

Roxy hoped so.

Quickly, she repacked her suitcase and called the airline and booked a flight. Then she called her dad, but thankfully he was in a meeting, so she just left a message that she had what she needed and was coming home early.

Then she made her last call to her bodyguard, Joel, and asked him to arrange transportation to the airport. She wasn't taking any chances and would have her bodyguard with her until she was through security. With that done, she then sent a text to Meryl, letting her know she was leaving. Just as she hit SEND, the screen bloomed into a picture.

It was her mother. Gwen Banfield had red hair similar to Roxy's, but her mother's had several distinctive silver streaks. They shared the same green eyes. "Roxy, you've found your Awakening."

Old anger and longing mixed with everything else to give Roxy, a pounding headache. "How do you know?"

"Circle Witches. Apparently, the witch hunter told some witches who asked us if there was a way to repress the attraction."

Key had done that? He had heard her when she said she didn't want her magic, and was trying to find a way to help her. God, just thinking about him...

Don't.

Instead she focused on the question. "Is it possible?" Her mother had created the Circle Witches years ago as a way for witches to meet safely to share knowledge and power. If Kieran knew who her mother was, he and his crew wouldn't be so eager to help. Her mother hated the soul-mirror witches, hated how they were taking control away from her. She'd formed the loop because the curse had forced them into hiding from rogues, so witches rarely ever risked gathering in person. They were just too vulnerable. Witch karma kept them from doing any harm with their powers, even to protect themselves. Before the curse, witch hunters protected earth witches, hunting only demon witches who had traded their souls for dark magic, but now earth witches had no protection at all. The men who had once guarded them now hunted and killed them.

Gwen's mouth thinned. "Roxy, you can't fight this. Your father has poisoned you against your magic. He's made it into something dirty and disgusting. It's not, our gift is sex magic. It can be beautiful..."

She felt her throat tighten at the memories of the various men in the house when she'd lived with her mom. Their voices as they stormed out, *What are you, some kind of sex freak? It's never enough! You're draining me.* Or the opposite, the ones begging to stay, to have more of her. Then there were the whispers from her teachers or the parents about her mom, about all the men, so they looked at Roxy with a pitying expression. Or suspicion—would she grow up to be like her mother? It all came to a head on the night when she'd been eleven years old and woke up with a man in her room. Frightened, Roxy had called her dad. He'd been furious and demanded that Gwen choose—either change her life, or Roxy would live with him. Gwen chose sex magic over her daughter, and Roxy moved in with her father.

She wasn't going there with her mother, wasn't getting into the old stuff. Gwen had made her choices and now Roxy was making hers. "I don't want sex magic." She'd tried casual sex, tried to fill the growing emptiness inside her, but she'd felt worse.

"It'll be different with your Awakening," her mom said gently.

"That's not reassuring. My father was your Awakening, and you two hate each other."

"I met him before the curse, Roxy," her mom said heavily. "I had my high magic, the sex drive was manageable. But then I lost my familiar and couldn't reach my top three chakras. Everything got out of control." She drew her breath through her teeth. "Mortal men are weak. He said he loved me until it got tough. Until I had needs he couldn't handle." She looked away, somewhere offscreen.

She saw vivid pain in her mom's profile. Her parents had never married, but their love had been real once. Keeping her words soft, she said, "That's why I want to be mortal."

Her mom looked at her. "Roxy, it won't stop. The desire will keep growing until you go insane with it. You have to follow through and gain your magic."

No. She refused to believe it. "I'll find a way. Besides, he's a witch hunter. If my powers suddenly unlock, it could make him insane with bloodlust, and he'll kill me."

Her mom didn't even pause. "It's a sex and blood-curse; sex often tames the bloodlust." Her face darkened with bitterness. "Other witches are doing it, and they are gaining power. This hunter could be your soul mirror, Roxy. Then you'll be as powerful as the others: Darcy, Carla and Ailish."

Soul mirror? Kieran? Not just her Awakening, but the other half of her soul? Fear tingled along her spine and made her stomach cramp. Bubbling along with that was old hurt. "You're willing to risk my life to find out? What if he's not my soul mirror? What if he kills me?" Or she survived with a sex-based magic that she couldn't handle? Her dreams dead, her life consumed by the magic she didn't want? Or what if Kieran was her soul mirror, but he didn't want that relationship so he rejected her?

"You have the fully formed schema!" Her mom's voice rose a notch.

On one of her day visits to her mom—her father never allowed Roxy to stay overnight—Gwen offered to teach Roxy to shave her legs and she had seen the schema. Even now, she felt a chill at the memory of the almost wild look in her mother's eyes.

Gwen went on, "As far as we know, you're the only fertility witch born with one since the curse. We think that means you might be able to increase all our magic in our ceremonies, creating more fertility in witches, mortals and crops without the terrible drain on those of us with half a schema."

She tried to digest all that. Her mother was infuriatingly secretive about the magic and ceremonies of fertility witches. "You've never told me that before. Why would my full schema make a difference?"

After a pause, her mother said, "The schema is an important part of our history. Only Awakened fertility witches can read the spells and legends handed down from the very first fertility witch. Once you Awaken, you'll—"

"More evasions. Big surprise." Her mother had held out that carrot for years: Find your Awakening and join the secret club. There was a knock at the door and Roxy felt a wave of exhaustion. "I'm coming home. If you want to quit playing games, we can talk then." She got up, shoved the phone deep into her purse. Her mother would get the hint and cut the magic she was using to talk to Roxy.

Beyond tired, she took a last look around the room, picked up her purse, left her key card on the dresser, then pulled the handle out of the suitcase and opened the door.

"Ready?" Joel asked.

She stepped out into the hall and looked up at his

longish face with the slightly big nose and deep brown eyes. "Were you able to get a car?"

Joel took the suitcase handle from her, pulling it into the hallway so the door could close. "Yes, it should be out front by the time we get down there."

The sound of the door closing reverberated through her, as if she were slamming a door on an essential part of herself. The witch. She had the deep urge to find Kieran and...but no. She made her decision. "Okay, let's go." They headed down the hall, got into the elevator and were in the lobby in less than a minute. They passed by the occasional elf or wolverine as they headed for the glass exit doors.

Stepping outside into the bright sunlight and warm air was a shock. The sounds of traffic and voices flowed around her. She reached into her purse, pulled out her sunglasses and slipped them on. Able to see, she glanced around at the velvet-roped line for taxis and valet on her left. On the right, she felt the cool spray from the fountains. Cement seating surrounded the water feature, and she caught sight of a boy in a Dyfyr hat sitting on a bench, pencil in hand, sketching.

"Over here." Joel took her arm, leading her toward the curb where a few town cars, limos and SUVs idled.

Roxy pulled her arm away. "One minute." Then she walked over to the kid. "Hi there."

The boy lifted his head and squinted at her. "You're the lady that got smacked."

"That's me," she said. "My name is Roxy. You okay? That was pretty scary in there."

His eyes rounded. "Did you see him? He was fierce! And he signed my book, even though it's kind of messed up." The boy shifted his papers and turned his comic book over to show her.

Roxy looked at the message, and she felt something shift in her chest. She'd seen Kieran's face when he saw the knife at the kid's throat. The man protected a stray, gangly-looking kid, then wrote a message that any boy would love. She smiled, trying not to wince at the flash of pain in her left cheek and eye. "Cool. And yeah, I saw him. Fierce," she repeated the boy's word. "What's your name?"

"Tyler. Key's friend is going to teach me self-defense. It's a girl, but she's cool. Blind, too. Ever heard of the Blind Kickboxer? She said she'll work with me for a couple days, until she goes home. She and the big dude with her, they are going to talk to my mom and see if it's okay."

"Roxy, the car is waiting," Joel said, his voice sharp.

She glanced over her shoulder at him. "I have plenty of time to make my plane." Turning back to Tyler, she said, "They left you here to go talk to your mom?" Why wouldn't they take Tyler with them to his house?

"She's on the casino floor. I can't go there, I'm twelve and you gotta be twenty-one. My mom deals blackjack. She's real good."

Roxy began to see the pattern. "You hang out around the hotel while your mom works?"

"I like it here. A lot of the staff know me; they don't mind as long as I don't pester the guests." He looked up. "I probably wasn't supposed to bother Key, but I wanted to meet him. He's so awesome."

The boy had a case of hero worship. And why not? Kieran was tremendously talented, and he'd saved the boy's life. Maybe hers, too. "What are you drawing?"

He looked up again. "Dyfyr. Key took one of my drawings. He wanted my autograph on it."

"Roxy," Joel said, "sitting out here like this isn't smart."

He was right. She'd hired him to protect her, and ignoring his advice was stupid. She rose and said, "Nice to meet you, Tyler. Good luck with your self-defense."

His smiled shyly. "Thanks."

Joel took hold of her elbow, and they walked to one of the SUVs with blackout windows. He opened the back door, letting out a blast of cool air. Roxy put her hand on the doorframe, stepped up on the running board, and squinted as her eyes tried to adjust to the gloom inside.

A thread of uneasiness tightened her stomach, and she hesitated.

Two hands reached out, grabbed her forearms and yanked her into the car. "Hey!" She screamed as she was dragged across seats and the door slammed behind her.

She twisted and fought, kicking the door with her sandals. A hand grabbed the back of her neck, shoved her face into the leather seat. "Got you now, Roxy."

It was Mack! She could barely drag in any air with her nose and mouth smashed into the seat. Something cold was pressed against the side of her neck.

Oh God. Where was her bodyguard? Why wasn't he doing something? She was being kidnapped! She redoubled her efforts to twist and fight.

A sudden buzz, and the pain shot through her. Her body twitched and jerked and then...

Nothing.

⇒ 7 ⇐

KEY PACED IN HIS ROOM. The bloodlust was rising, filling his veins like the burn of acid. He had his laptop opened on his dresser. Darcy MacAlister said, "I'm still waiting to see if anyone in Circle Witches has a way to repress the attraction between a fertility witch and her Awakening. But didn't you say the schema had color?"

Turning, he met Darcy's brown gaze on the laptop screen. "Yes, a thin outline of emerald green and faint watery sweeps of blue and green." He'd wanted so desperately to touch that mark. It was the source of Roxy's pain and he'd intuitively known he could turn that pain to pleasure.

"It's starting. Her schema already recognizes you and is coming to life. The power is probably rising in her chakras, filling them. We'd be trying to repress a magic that's already begun working. Much harder."

Key's drawing hand began to twitch, but he ignored it and focused on Darcy. "We—" The ringing of his cell interrupted him. Pulling the BlackBerry out, he looked at the screen and saw it was Phoenix. "What?"

"Got Tyler here with me. The kid saw Roxy get yanked into a black SUV, her suitcase left behind."

Fury quieted Phoenix's voice to soft death. "I'm on my way to get my car. Meet me out front." He hung up.

Key's anger went hot, and the dragon shifted on his chest, the spiked tail scraping his skin. Liam was behind this, he was sure of it. Key had drawn it.

His head filled with images of all those years ago when he'd come home to find Vivian cut and screaming at the hands of his brother. Now Roxy. His chest burned with rage. She was his! He'd drawn her, he'd touched her, kissed her.

He looked at Darcy on the screen. "Tell Axel—"

"He's on the phone with Phoenix. Go, find her!"

Key shut the laptop and ran to the door. Urgency pounded through him as he bypassed the elevator, ran for the stairs and raced down the eight floors. Going at the inhuman hunter speed, he hit the ground floor and made it out the door in seconds. Phoenix's powerful Mustang GT rumbled at the curb. Ailish stood next to the car, holding the door open. Tyler was next to her and turned to look at Key with big eyes and a pale face. Holding out a sheet of paper, he said, "Sketched this and I saw the three-one-seven and the letter J from the license plate."

He grabbed it and saw the side and back of a Cadillac Escalade, black with chrome wheels, and the partial license plate. As desperate as he was to get moving, he put his hand on Tyler's shoulder. "Thanks."

Tyler said, "You'll save her, I know you will."

The boy's earnestness redoubled his determination. He nodded once and slid into the backseat, and Ailish got into the front and closed the door. Phoenix floored it and shot the car out onto Las Vegas Boulevard, heading north.

Phoenix drove like he did everything else, hard and fast. His profile was rigid, his dark eyes hidden behind his shades. "Sutton's hacking into the news cameras on light poles or on traffic signals to see if he can spot the SUV and partial license." He wove around traffic and pedestrians. It was early afternoon; people milled around in slow motion in the glaring sunlight. The strip came alive after dark.

Sutton's voice came through the speakers. "Found them heading left on Bedazzled."

Phoenix raced past Desert Inn, then past Sahara, swung a left on the street named for the old hotel.

"Anything more?" Key asked Sutton.

"They passed one camera but I don't see them at the next." They could hear his fingers flying over the keys. "The SUV didn't turn at the next intersection. They must have stopped between these two cameras." He put the coordinates on the GPS screen.

"What's there?" Phoenix asked.

More clicking, then he said, "Some strip joints, a nightclub, and the old Bedazzled hotel and casino. It's scheduled for destruction in just over a week."

"There's the hotel." Key pointed to the blocky, sprawling five-story building that had several steeples. In the heyday of the hotel, each steeple was covered in colored lights representing sapphires, diamonds and rubies. It was surrounded by a seven-foot fence, and posted with plenty of No Trespassing signs. "Let me out. You go check out the other places while Sutton watches the cameras."

Phoenix swerved to a stop. Ailish let Key out and got back in, and the car peeled off. Key shielded his presence so no security cameras could see him, and then he rushed up to the fence, grabbed the top and leaped over. He landed on the other side and took stock.

The building's huge marquee was covered in graffiti, and the large sign, Bedazzled, that once blinked different jewel colors, had some letters missing; others were cracked or broken. There were boards over the front doors and windows, and the asphalt had deep fissures.

Moving silently toward the building, he heard the traffic whizzing by behind him. Was Roxy here? Was Liam?

Then he heard noise coming from the underground garage—a pain-filled cry that stabbed at his memories and tore at his old guilt. He shoved it aside and homed in on his target.

⚜

Roxy fought to breathe, terror pounding in her veins as the monster looming over her cut off her clothes, leaving her in her bra and panties.

Then he cut *her*.

Pain, it was a blazing agony that rang in her ears. "No, stop!" Why? Oh Ancestors, why? The gloom was cut by the headlights from the SUV, revealing her tormentor. Stripped to the waist, he knelt over her, smelling like oily copper. He was huge, ripped with muscles and hairless.

He looked wrong, too-delicate eyebrows, no beard shadow.

There was no help; her bodyguard lay dead in a pool of blood. Her wrists and ankles were handcuffed to something in the cement. She was helpless to escape.

"Stop? But I've only started." He wiped the blood coating the knife on his chest.

Her blood. Bile burned her throat and she twisted, fighting the restraints.

He laughed. "I've been looking for you. You have the mark that can wake the dragon."

She stared up at him. "What dragon?" He was crazy. And she was going to die. Sweaty fear twisted through her, making her hot and sick as tears ran down her face. "I don't know what you're talking about!"

His eyes gleamed. "It's taken me a decade to learn all about fertility witches and the dragon." He leaned closer. "To learn about you. You have the fertility mark." He grabbed her thigh, wrenching her legs apart. "Color is starting to appear. Whore magic. You're all born to be whores. Answer my two questions, and the pain will stop. Where is the Tear, and did you wake the dragon?"

Panic clawed at her stomach. "I don't know what—" He moved in a blur, then agony slashed across her stomach. Roxy screamed, jerking against the chains, her entire world narrowing to the pain. She sucked in a breath and begged, "Don't! Please!"

"One more time...where is the Tear, and did you wake the dragon?" he asked in a soft voice, and then he shoved his hand against the cut on her stomach.

It felt like he was reaching into her and tearing out her organs. She heard hoarse cries and realized they were coming from her. He took his hand away, and she looked at him, desperate for some sign of humanity in him.

He rubbed her blood over his chest. "Where is the Tear? Did you wake the dragon?"

The pain eased enough to breathe, and she choked on the fumes from the idling SUV. With the lights behind her tormentor, she couldn't see who was in that truck. Looking back to him, she saw her blood staining his chest, and she gagged. If she vomited, she'd choke. *Think!* But she couldn't grab on to her thoughts; this whole nightmare was too much like that drawing Kieran had done. Kieran said his brother would do this to her. "You're Liam." A thread of wild hope gave her strength. "He'll find you. Kill you."

Liam laughed. "He tried, but I rose from the dead."

Cold shudders snapped her mind back to reality—

she'd told Kieran to go away. Leave her alone. He wouldn't even know, and she was at the mercy of this monster. "What are you?" The words scraped her raw throat.

"Blood-born. You have the mark, you know about the dragon. Did you wake him?"

Frantic, she scrambled for any answer. "Dyfyr! In Kieran's comic books! That dragon?"

She saw his eyes narrow.

"No!" She squeezed her eyes shut, shaking her head back and forth, but the pain came anyway. A slice or her thigh. She screamed, then choked on a sob. It consumed her, ate her, until she was drowning in agony. And her mind swam free...escaped from her body *Tear? Dragon?* Her thoughts locked in on Dyfyr. She could see him in her mind! Oh Ancestors, she wanted him, missed him. Her dragon. Real, full of color, his ruby eyes furious. He would save her. He always saved her.

✦

Key ruthlessly stayed invisible and in control as he took in the scene in the underground garage. He saw Roxy framed in the car lights on the oil-stained cement, clad in only her bra and panties, a dozen cuts on her stomach, thighs and arms. Her hands and feet were cuffed to eye hooks in the ground. A truck idled to the right of her, and her bodyguard lay dead to the left.

Liam knelt over her, Roxy's blood on his hands and chest.

Key's rage exploded; he materialized and launched himself. He hit Liam, throwing them both several feet beyond Roxy's head. He whipped out his knife and, with his brother flat on his back beneath him, aimed for the heart. He would shred it into a pulp this time.

Liam grabbed his wrist, stopping his strike. "Still a weak runt."

Surprised, Key looked at his brother's face and saw his blue eyes bright with the high of witch blood. He stunk of copper, but he was stronger than Key had anticipated. Icy rage fueled his muscles. He'd been weak and helpless once, but no more. "You're going shade." The words were nearly drowned out by the gunning of an engine.

A second later, the front grille of the SUV hit Key and knocked him off Liam. Slamming onto the ground, he ignored the hot flash of pain in his shoulder and rolled up to his feet. The SUV had backed up and Liam was yanking open the door to escape.

Oh hell, no! Key flipped his knife to the blade end and threw with deadly aim to the center of his brother's back.

Liam spun and caught the handle of the knife. Standing on the running board of the SUV, he looked at Key. "Dragon's not awake, is he? He's never going to wake now." He turned and threw the knife.

Not at Key.

But at Roxy. A perfect curving arc that would bury the deadly tip in her heart.

A ferocious energy took hold of Key's muscles and he sprang. He threw every bit of strength and will into his body, determined to fly if he had to. Stretching, he sailed parallel to the ground, his arm reached, his fingers extended, his gaze locked on the silver blade as it descended.

Liam's taunt rang in his head—what the hell was he talking about, waking the dragon? Didn't matter, Key couldn't let her die!

The blade was inches from her chest. One inch from his fingers. He heard his brother laughing as the SUV peeled out. His brain screamed, *Reach! One more inch!*

Pain tore through the end of his middle finger. Then there was a thunk as the knife bounced off something and changed direction. Key didn't have time to figure it out; he was going to land right on Roxy. Using every muscle he possessed, he flipped himself to the right and hit the ground on his bad shoulder, and stars burst behind his eyes. He grunted, rolling up to his hands and knees.

He heard a crash as the SUV drove through the gate and out onto the road.

He'd missed his chance to kill Liam. He'd screwed up. How the hell had his brother caught that knife? The rogue was almost as fast and strong as Axel. Hunters who found and bonded with their soul mirrors acquired more strength and speed.

With the headlights of the SUV gone, the garage was dark, gloomy, only a sliver of light slipping in from the entrance. His eyes adjusted quickly, and he reached for his knife lying between him and Roxy. That's when he saw it.

The fingernail of his middle finger was an inch and a half long. Curved. His cuticle was crusted in blood. "What the fuck?" Then it hit him, that's how he stopped the knife from killing Roxy.

He'd grown a fingernail. Like a dragon claw.

Freaking weird.

He scooped up his knife, sliced off the nail and holstered his blade.

"Dyfyr?" Roxy said in a whisper.

The dragon tat on his chest moved, as if stretching to reach her.

"Kieran?" Her voice was raspy and trembled.

He sucked in a breath and smelled the faint power in her blood. His veins pulsed in reaction. Her face was damp with sweat and tears, her eyes haunted by pain and fear, her lips cracked and bloody. He looked down her body; saw the cuts on the ripe swells over her breasts, her belly and her thighs. His skin pulled tight, air locked in his chest, the bloodlust buzzed in his ears. If Roxy wasn't latent, the bloodlust would be like live wires shoved through his veins and the juice turned up to torture. "It's me," he said softly.

Yanking his phone from his pocket, he texted *9-1-1, Bedazzled underground garage* to Phoenix. He should have done it once he heard them in the garage. But the need to get to Roxy had pushed out every other thought. Sliding the phone into his pocket, he crouched next to her.

"How did you know?" she asked in a hoarse voice.

"Tyler saw them take you." Her wrists were cuffed over her head, and the chain between the bracelets threaded through the eye hook of a bolt drilled into the cement. He leaned over, grabbed both sides of the chain, and yanked. The chain held for a few seconds, but Key put his strength into it despite the scream in his shoulder and snapped it.

"And you came."

He took hold of her wrists and lowered them to her sides. "I never should have left you alone." Then he moved to her feet and worked on breaking the chain between those cuffs.

Her eyes filled with more tears. "I wanted you to go. I don't want this...I don't want..." Tremors wracked her body.

Her broken words scraped his guts. How the hell could she ever trust him after he'd let this happen to her? Key heard the Mustang coming, the growl of the engine matching his own helpless fury. He hadn't been quick enough! He'd walked out of that room and left her vulnerable. He moved back to her side. He would not allow her to lie there bleeding on the dirty floor.

The sharp smell of her pain burned his nose and made the tattoo hiss. The dragon wanted her. Key knew it and yanked his shirt off. Then he slipped his arms beneath her body, lifted her up, and cradled her against his chest.

Her blood touched his skin. Touched the tattoo.

Her blood touched the dragon.

The beast shuddered as if trying to waken from a long nap. Bloodlust thickened in his veins, while protectiveness tightened his arms around her. A throb in his groin swelled his cock. He could feel the agony rolling off her.

The Mustang roared into the garage.

Roxy stiffened.

"Easy, green eyes. It's a friend coming to get us out of here." He looked up as Phoenix spun the car so it skidded to a stop three feet from where Key stood.

Ailish jumped out, shoved the seat up and held it for them. Key eased inside, holding Roxy as close to the dragon as he could. Ailish crawled into the back with them. Using her magic, she shut the door.

Phoenix peeled out.

Ailish said, "You have to be my eyes, Key. Show me where she's hurt. The worst cuts first."

He laid her across his thighs. "Roxy, this is Ailish. She's a witch." Taking Ailish's hand, he laid it on the worst wound on her stomach.

Roxy sucked in air and stiffened, but didn't say anything.

He pulled her face closer to his chest and felt the bloom of Ailish's magic. A pure white light radiated from her hand, and the wound stopped bleeding. Then Key moved Ailish's hand to a deep wound on Roxy's thigh. He was careful not to touch her schema, not wanting to cause her any more discomfort. That wound closed.

"How's the witch?" Axel's voice boomed over the speakers.

Key directed Ailish's hand to the next wound, while answering, "We have her; Ailish is healing her cuts.

Liam and his mortal flunky, Mack, got away." Just saying the words pissed him off. "Liam is different, faster. I threw my knife at his back when he was trying to get into the SUV to escape. He turned and caught it."

Phoenix looked into the mirror over the rims of his shades. "You throw like a rocket."

He moved Ailish's hand to the last cut on Roxy's breast over the cup of her bra. "The power in witch blood makes rogues stronger and faster, but this seems like more." Key looked down at Roxy. Her closed eyes looked bruised, and he pushed back her sweaty tangled hair, sickened by what she'd suffered. "I heard him tell Roxy he'd risen from the dead. Called himself blood-born." He barely noticed Ailish putting her hand on his right shoulder and healing whatever he'd torn in there when the SUV hit him. He had no idea how she knew he'd been hurt.

"Liam wanted Roxy specifically and went to a lot of trouble to get her. Do you know why?" Axel asked.

"Said she could wake the dragon. She has the fertility mark." He wasn't sure what it meant.

Sutton broke in, "Her schema? Is that why she has the full mark, not the half marks we saw on the other fertility witches? And if it's the dragon in you, how would Liam know this and not you?"

Frustration roiled in him. "When I find my brother, I'll be sure to ask him right before I rip his heart out of his chest and burn it."

Axel said, "Get the witch back here to Glassbreakers where we can set up better protection. We'll go from there."

He took Ailish's hand to show her the handcuffs on Roxy's wrists and ankles. Once she was free, he looked down at her pale, strained face. Her scattered freckles stood out like blood specks. His gut burned with the memory of her chained and cut. He realized that she was still wearing only the bra and panties, dried blood staining her skin. "She needs a chance to clean up and get some clothes."

Her eyes widened. "I'm not dressed."

Shock. She wasn't quite tracking what was happening around her. He wrapped her in his arms. "It's dark, no one can see you." Not exactly true since he and Phoenix had enhanced hunter vision, but they didn't make a habit of leering at women they rescued from rogues. "When we go into the hotel, I'll hold you. I can make both of us appear invisible."

Sutton broke in, "Linc has a house not far from where you are. It's safer. Roxy can clean up, and we'll conference there." He gave the directions.

"Here," Ailish said, handing over his shirt. "I stepped on it when I got out of the car and picked it up."

He stared at it as Phoenix made a series of turns and took them on a long, private road with few homes. In the parking garage, when he'd seen and smelled Roxy's suffering, he'd needed to take off his shirt so he could hold her close to the dragon. Was she waking the dragon in him? As screwed up as Key was, how stupid was it to wake an ancient beast forced into Key by fertility magic? Shit. "Thanks."

Phoenix turned into a gated driveway, stopped and rolled down the window. "Sutton, we're at the house, what's the code for the gates?"

"There's a palm scanner. I've already inputted you, Key and Ailish."

"Got it." Phoenix leaned out and pressed his palm against the mechanism, and the gates slid open with a soft whirring. They pulled up to the house. "Holy mansions," Phoenix said. "Linc must be as rich as you, comic boy."

Key ignored him as he helped Roxy put the shirt on. When the car stopped, Phoenix said, "Stay there until I come around." He got out of the car, opened the passenger side, and helped Ailish out.

Then Phoenix leaned in and reached for Roxy.

Key caught his wrist before he touched her. Looking up into Phoenix's dark shades hiding his eyes, he almost growled, "I've got her. Back off."

The other hunter tilted his head down and looked over the rim of his glasses. His gaze slid to Key's chest, then he held up both hands in a sign of surrender and stepped back.

"Wait, I can do it, just...dizzy," Roxy said, her eyes closing.

"Just rest," he told her, then slipped his arm beneath her legs and stepped out of the car. Phoenix shut the door, and they headed up to the massive front doors. The house was a two-story villa that had to be five thousand square feet.

Phoenix located the scanner and put his hand against it, and they heard a soft click. He opened the front door, and they walked into the cool interior.

Key headed for the stairs, moving through the dark gloom of the house with no problem. Ailish had done a good job, but they both had blood on them. He wanted to get Roxy cleaned up and into a bed where she could recover from shock and blood loss.

"Dude," Phoenix said.

Key stopped halfway to the staircase. Turning back he saw Phoenix with his arm around Ailish. "You'd better look at your tat. Your dragon's not a female."

When Key had inked the dragon, Phoenix had started calling it "she," and Key had gone along. He'd always known Dyfyr was male, but what had it really mattered? He shifted Roxy a bit and looked down. His mouth went dry and a buzzing filled his head at what he saw. The dragon had a lock of Roxy's hair wrapped around his front claw and held it against his face. He claimed her. And where there used to be cluster of amethyst scales on his head, now two very male horns stood proudly.

"You touched her blood," Phoenix said.

He felt it right through to his heart. Dyfyr was waking, and he'd claimed his soul mirror. He'd known on some level from the first strokes of his pencil on the wall when he'd drawn her. But now he'd touched her blood, and the dragon recognized her. That's why he'd taken his shirt off in the garage, to let the dragon touch her.

It was like being hit with a ton of bricks and fractured into several pieces. A deep part of him craved his soul mirror. She would free him from the curse, and he would help her with her magic. But another part of him knew he wasn't cut out for this. He destroyed people he loved. And it didn't matter anyway.

She didn't want her magic.

She didn't want him.

⁕

Roxy wasn't used to being weak and helpless. She'd built her life so carefully, each choice a step farther into the mortal world. She'd been so sure of her decision.

Now her world was shattered, and she was too damned weak to do anything but let Kieran carry her like a child as he walked through the huge house. Finally he stopped moving, and she heard a door close. She had to pull herself together. Opening her eyes, she said, "I can stand."

He set her on her feet. She grabbed the doorframe to get the dizziness under control. Moving her head carefully, she realized she was holding on to the doorway between a large bedroom and an attached bath. "Where are we?"

"Another hunter's house, Linc Dillinger. He uses palm-scanner security, which is good protection. Rogues like Liam don't have lifelines, and that will set off alarms." He walked past her into the bathroom, leaned into the shower and turned it on.

"Okay." She followed him with her gaze, trying to get her bearings.

He turned around, and she saw his naked chest. It'd been too dark in the garage and the car to really see, and she'd been slipping in and out of full consciousness. She was awake now, and her breath caught at the sheer beauty of the dragon inked there. Kieran's shoulders and chest were a wide, muscular canvas, and the dragon sat slightly turned, his massive chest thrust out, snout angled down, and gleaming ruby eyes watching her. His scales were vibrant colors of emerald green and sapphire blue, while his chest, wings, horns and underside of his tail were amethyst. His wings were bent behind him, and the tail curled around his back feet. And wrapped around one of his front claws was a lock of hair exactly the same color as hers. Unable to resist, she walked across the chilled marble. "That looks like my hair."

Kieran glanced down, then back at her. "It is."

How? It was a tattoo, wasn't it? There was something ancient and powerful about the beast. The amethyst horns were incredibly sensual in the way they jutted out, then curved at the tips. *Did you wake the dragon?* Shivering at the memory of Liam asking that, feeling lost and unsure, she lifted her hand and laid it flat over the dragon's chest. A second later, she felt twin hearts beat against her palm. They pulsed with a deep and brutal longing so profound that she gasped in response to the force of it, the absolute purity. It wasn't bloodlust or sexual lust, but something more emotional and *real*. Then it was gone, and all she felt was warm skin and a single heartbeat of the lethal artist.

"Is this the dragon I'm supposed to wake? I thought I saw him, he came to me and I knew he'd save me. Then you were there, and for a second I thought you were him." She kept touching him.

"You called his name. Dyfyr."

"I knew him. Know him." She lifted her gaze up to Kieran's face. "What's happening? Nothing makes sense."

Steam began trailing around them as they stood in front of the open door of the shower. Kieran's massive shoulders tensed. "Evidently, I touched your blood, and he recognizes you." He paused, laying his hand over hers pressed against the dragon. "We're soul mirrors."

She heard a clang in her head, like cymbals clashing, and pulled her hand away. "But I'm latent. I'm..." Her stomach twisted with bitter fear as she remembered the hot burn of that knife slicing her skin, her own screams ringing in her ears. "Whore magic. That's what he called it. I don't want that, I don't want to—"

Key took hold of her arms. "Stop it. Don't you dare let him define you, Roxy. Don't you fucking dare."

The hot fury pulsing in his words cut through her cold panic. "I hate your brother and want him dead."

"We're on the same page there, green eyes." His face eased and he let go of her. "Not just dead, but his soul trapped in the between worlds, existing as a cold, pain-wracked shade for all of eternity." He reached to her knees where his shirt hung on her, grasped the hem and pulled it off.

The warm steam pouring from the shower surrounded them, making it feel like a secret room far away from reality. He reached for the front clasp of her bra and unhooked it. She finally realized he was undressing her and grabbed his wrists.

He allowed her to hold him. "You're too weak to do

this yourself. I'm going to help you shower, find you something to wear, and get you into bed. Then figure out what to do next to keep you safe."

She tried to explain. "It's like I've been thrown into a fast-moving river and I can't get out, can't even catch my breath." Her breasts were exposed, she was exposed, but Kieran looked into her eyes, listening. "I know what soul mirror means; we bond our souls and the curse breaks and frees you from bloodlust. But you're my Awakening. Once my magic rises, I'll need more and more sex. I don't want that life. Sex magic twists and taints everything."

"How can you be so sure?" His voice was soft.

"Because my mom chose sex and magic over my father, and then over me. She didn't want me anymore." Oh Ancestors, she sounded like a child. But she was scared, tired, unsure...nothing made sense. She'd worked so hard to become mortal, to fit somewhere. Belong. She could find a man to love, and sex would be normal. Not about magic and power.

"You're mother sounds like a bitch, not a witch."

His hard words jerked her gaze to his face. "My father grew to hate her. He was her Awakening, just like you're mine. He loved her in the beginning, but now he hates her. Hates her magic. I can remember their fights when I was young and they thought I was asleep. *We don't make love, I just screw you until your magic is full! And if we do go out, then I have to deal with all the men swarming around wanting a taste of your sex magic!*" She shook her head and dizziness made the room sway.

"Idiots. Letting a child hear that." He flicked his wrists, breaking her grip, then took hold of her arms to steady her. "Easy, Roxy. You lost a lot of blood."

She held perfectly still and the room righted. The warm steam helped fight off her deep chill. She couldn't believe she'd told him so much of her past when they needed to focus on now. "What do we do?"

He reached up and slid her bra straps down her arms and let it fall to the floor. "We'll figure it out in time. Right now, I'm going to protect you, not hurt you. I won't try to seduce you or in any way bring out your magic."

"But the schema, and your bloodlust and—" It was so overwhelming.

He crouched and tugged her panties down. "Your power scent is so light, I can deal with it. And touching you ices it."

She looked down at the powerful hunter gently easing off her underwear. "And the attraction?"

"Hold on to my shoulders for balance," he said, wrapping one large hand around her ankle.

Roxy put her hands on him and her schema woke up with hot tingles. They started in the center of the little goddess mark. Kieran got the panties off, then his shoulders tensed. He jerked his head up until he was eye level with the schema. She felt his skin grow hot beneath her hands. "Kieran?"

"Caramel with a hint of pain. Getting worse."

The feel of his shoulders, the sight of him crouched down before her, the touch of his hand on her ankle sent pleasure winging through her. She had the unbearable feeling that being with Kieran would be more intense and intoxicating than anything she'd ever experienced.

Desperate heat blazed in the goddess mark and spread outward, making her body throb even as her mind shied away. Fear mixed in, and the mark pierced her skin with hunger. "It's the schema! It's not real!" *Whore magic.* Those two words bounced in her head. This wasn't going to work. "We can't be near each other."

He released her ankle, reached behind him to pull out his knife.

The sight of the sharp blade made her gasp with memories and terror. The bloodlust! He was going to cut her, hurt her. She turned to run, but dizziness spun the walls and she felt herself falling...

Kieran caught her around the waist, instantly steadying her. He pulled her back to his chest. "Not going to cut you. Never. I won't hurt you." She could feel his heart pounding, sweat and steam coating their skin. "You're safe with me."

Something more than Kieran touched her back, she felt gentling strokes so light she might have been imagining it. But it calmed her. She sucked in a breath. "I panicked." She was naked and felt so damned vulnerable. "What are you going to do?"

"Lean back, just lean on me. I've got you."

She sagged against him, against his strength. His arm around her waist held her up. "I'm stronger than this, usually."

"You survived. It's the blood loss and shock making you feel weak, but you're damned strong. Now I'm going to help you. We're going to have to be together until my brother is dead and you're safe. We have to tame the schema."

She put her hands on his forearm, borrowing some of his strength. "How?"

"We're soul mirrors, and some of your blood got on me, opening a connection between us. I think that's inflaming your schema even more because the soul-mirror bond requires a blood exchange. I have your blood, you need mine. I'm going to try a drop or two of my blood on the mark. I think it'll soothe it for a while."

"What if it makes it worse?"

"Then I'll take care of you." His voice thickened and she felt the ridge of his erection pressing against her spine. "I'll ease your lust without sealing our bond. As long as I don't enter you, the bond won't complete.

We'll keep trying until we find what works together." She felt him swallow, then he added, "Okay? Trust me?"

Her schema burned and hurt. And she began to have real sympathy for her mother. Was this what she endured, over and over? "Yes."

He pressed his face next to hers. "Trusting me after what my brother did to you...that's bravery." He released her waist, switched the knife to his right hand and pressed the tip against his left palm.

A bubble of blood welled up.

"Show me the mark. Hurry," it came out a growl.

Fighting embarrassment, she turned her left leg and exposed the goddess marking on the high inside of her thigh. The emerald green outline was darker, clearer, and the blue coloring filled more area than before.

He lowered his hand.

She arched toward him, desperate for his touch. "Kieran..." Shame fought with desire, with aching need.

He caught her hip with his other hand, his fingers firm as he held her. Then he curved his hand over her thigh, his thumb brushing her pubic hair. That touch shuddered through her center.

But the hungry pain began to ease. The pounding, mindless need notched down as a languid feeling softened her muscles. A fluttering along her spine where her chakras were surprised her. It was a sweet sensation. A hum soothed her mind, almost forming into words, but she couldn't quite hear them. Yet the gentle rhythm of the hummed words comforted her. "It's working." She felt a bit stronger, less dizzy.

"Good." He pulled his hand away. "Get in the shower."

She turned and stepped in, grateful for the warm spray of water. She reached to pull the door closed, thankful for a minute to herself when Kieran stepped in.

Naked.

Oh-my-stars-naked. Holy-hot-naked. Roxy pressed herself against the marble wall as he filled the oversized stall. Water sprayed on his head, running over those shoulders, finding the ridges and valleys of his muscles, over his dragon-inked chest, the ridges of his abdomen, and down into the dark blond pubic hair and...

She jerked her eyes up. "You're hard. Huge!"

He snorted. "Thanks," he said as he reached for a bottle of shampoo and poured some into his palm. "It's not going away anytime soon with you standing there looking like a sex goddess." He stepped toward her.

She pressed herself back. "But the schema! It's calm now! Why are you aroused?"

Key sank his fingers into her hair and started lathering. "This attraction is real, my green-eyed witch." He took hold of her arms and moved her to the stream of water. "Close your eyes."

He really desired her, it wasn't just the schema forcing it? *Real.* With the steamy water cascading over her hair and body, Kieran's hands on her, helping her, she wondered if it would be so bad to make love with him.

But what would happen to his attraction to her after her magic took hold? When sex became a burden?

He'd leave. Even if they were soul mirrors, he'd walk out, just like her father had.

And she'd be left with nothing but her magic.

≫ 8 ≪

SWEAT POURED DOWN KEY'S BACK, his hand and fingers ached, his shoulder burned, but he kept drawing with a fierce urgency. He shoved a dresser out of his way to give himself more room and kept going. The only thing in that room he was aware of was Roxy, each breath she took. Each time she moved in the big king-sized bed where she slept, he and the dragon knew it.

He was in a frenzy, the violence writhing in him, fury rising. He had to draw, kill, or have sex. Touching her blood and her schema had inflamed him. He wanted sex. Wanted Roxy. Craved her. Her scent was imprinted on him.

Stripping off her panties, seeing her revealed to him, her scent...he shuddered, his cock rigid in the sweatpants he'd found on the bed after they'd come out of the shower. For Roxy, there'd been a pair of black yoga pants and tank top she slept in now.

My witch, he thought, yet she didn't want to bond with him. She didn't want her magic, feared its power, and he was the one bringing it out in her. How the hell was he going to keep her safe without destroying her? His brother had already hurt her, and that made Key insane with rage.

The dragon shifted restlessly, tapping a claw against his skin. *Our treasure.* Key blinked. He'd just written the words beneath the first panel he'd drawn; the scene of the dragon carrying a woman.

Dragons were notorious for guarding their treasure. His dragon considered Roxy his treasure.

The thought slipped away as he dropped a piece of sidewalk chalk Ailish had conjured for him, got out another color, and went back to work on the last panel.

Revealing.

Something hit his shoulder. "Key—"

He turned, grabbed the man and threw him into the wall, then crouched between the bed where Roxy was and the intruder. He'd kill—

"Key, goddammit, it's me." The voice was whisper-soft and furious.

Snapping up to his full height, Key blinked. *Phoenix.* He stood close to where Key had shoved the dresser out of the way, his dark eyes angry, and his arms bulging in his leather vest. As the seconds ticked by, his awareness radiated out from where Roxy lay sleeping. Turning his head, he saw Axel standing just inside the door. He had his arms crossed over his bare chest, a sign that he'd used his wings to get to Vegas. It was impossible to get a shirt over wings.

It took him another few seconds to bank the violence, to fully understand that they weren't going to harm Roxy. He'd always been protective, but the intensity of this rocked him.

"Kieran?" Roxy said behind him. "What's going on?"

Her voice, the sheer confusion and slight edge ripped through him. He turned to her and felt the dragon sigh. Her eyes were sleepy, her hair a mass of soft waves, and she looked so damned sensual tucked in the bed. His hand twitched around the chalk, he wanted to draw her, capture this look that was uniquely hers. "Axel is here. You go back to sleep, I'll just be downstairs."

"You're leaving?" She sat up, threw back the cream colored covers, and stood up. "I—" her mouth hung open as she caught sight of the walls. Starting from the left, she tracked the images to the last one he'd been working on. "You did this? All this? How long have I been asleep?"

"Three hours."

She walked around the bed, past him, her sleep-warmed scent hitting him in his gut. No magic, just honey-almond mixed with shampoo and soap. His blood heated, his cock tested the seam of his sweats. Ignoring his erection, he watched Roxy glance at the two other hunters, then back to the first panel. She stopped in front of it, her red hair spilling over her shoulders, her face absorbed with the drawing. A few seconds later, her skin took on a soft glow.

"It's Dyfyr. Just like your tattoo."

Key felt the dragon's chest swell with pride. He had drawn four panels reaching from the floor to seven feet high in places, the first two on the wall where Roxy stood, and two more on the adjacent wall. Roxy was studying the first panel where Dyfyr flew across the skies, his wings majestic, his ruby eyes gleaming as he carefully cradled a woman in his arms. Key had drawn variations of this as long as he could remember, but he didn't know why.

She moved to the second panel and her shoulders hunched. "He's crying. Where's his lover?"

Chills went down his back, while his chest was warm. He caught a whiff of dark chocolate. Her magic! Did she realize? She was using magic. A shimmer rose to her skin. Only witch hunters could see the shimmer on a witch; mortals couldn't. "How do you know the woman is the dragon's lover?"

She looked over her shoulder at him. "Because his heart beats, and he holds her like a treasure."

Key couldn't stop himself and walked closer until he stood by her left shoulder. He looked into her eyes. "How do you know his heart beats?"

She closed her eyes for a second.

Her scent swirled around him, the chocolate sliding into his veins, firing his bloodlust.

Then she opened them and said, "I feel him."

Stunned, he realized that she was magically connecting with the dragon in him, with Dyfyr, through the drawings.

She turned back to the wall. "But now he's crying, curling up in this remote, barren place, his tears crystallizing with his grief. Oh," she lifted her hand, placing it on the chalk dragon's head, "I hear him. Earlier it was just a hum...but now I can hear him."

The need for her blood ate through his veins, cramped his gut. But he couldn't look away, captivated by the way she stood there, her gaze on the dragon, drawing in her lower lip, her body loosening and filling with magic. "What's he saying?"

Her eyes slid closed and she said:

> *The dragon soars across the skies*
> *And sees below all those lives*
> *He wonders anew why they go on*
> *Lives so fragile and time so short*
>
> *They cannot see him*
> *In his fiery glory*
> *Not his eyes of gleaming rubies*
> *Or his scales of timeless beauty*
>
> *A strange sensation, what is this?*
> *Looking down, he is captivated*
> *Gold of hair and fair of skin*

With eyes that truly see him.

His silent heart begins to beat
To know a want he can't resist
He swoops down low to claim his love
They soar along in tremendous passion

Time is cruel and takes his woman
But his heart beats on
Each strike more brutal
And wishes that he, too, was mortal

He falls to the land and cries the tears
His heart stops beating and to stone he turns
Leaving his tears as a gift
Of mortality to the wounded souls

Stone he will stay
No life beating in his chest
Until the woman bearing the fertile mark
Wakes his heart with her touch

Key had to touch her before he burst into flames from dual cravings for her blood and sex. The growing need to finish their bond created a pressure on his soul. He settled his hands on her bare shoulders and felt the gentle stirring of her magic. All his life, he'd been suspicious of fertility magic, but this felt like a sweet and sensual kiss over his skin. And he wanted more.

She leaned back against him. "He stopped his heart and turned to stone, rather than feel the loss. He loved her, truly loved her."

The contact, the feel of her body against his, calmed the burn swelling his veins. He knew she was so caught up in the dragon she didn't realize she was leaning against him. He focused on her story. "So that's where the Dragon Tear came from."

Roxy looked at him. "The same Tear Liam was going on about?"

He clenched his jaw at the memory of what Liam had done to her. "Yes. My mother gave it to me when she died. She said it was the only remaining Tear—"

"The other dragons must have used all the other tears to become mortal, leaving only the one," Roxy filled in.

He rubbed his thumbs over the skin of her shoulders. "Guess so. And I became the guardian of the last Tear. My mother wore it until it killed her. Drained the life out of her."

She frowned. "Why didn't she tell you more? Liam says I can wake the dragon. Did she tell you that? Did she know?"

"No." Blood-deep anger simmered and threatened. He took a breath and felt Roxy's skin beneath his hands. What would she think if she knew what he was? A real live Frankenstein, a magic monster. He added, "I was only thirteen, and she refused to believe she was going to die until the very end." And then she was mad at him for it. He shook his head. "It was a powerful delusion, maybe from wearing the Tear."

Phoenix broke in, "Now we know why it strips immortality. Dragons are extinct...the tears destroyed an entire species."

"Except for one," Key said. "Dyfyr is alive and sleeping in me."

"Apparently, that Tear has quite a history," Axel said. "Phoenix, come look at this."

Key turned with Roxy to see the two remaining panels. The first panel had a large man, large by mortal standards, climbing treacherous cliffs over a churning sea. His gold-colored hair blew in a harsh wind, and from his closed fist, a rainbow of colors arced outward.

Key's chest tightened. He knew what was in the

mortal's fist—the Dragon Tear. It was the size of the end of Key's little finger, shaped in a perfect teardrop. The extremely hard, almost unbreakable outer shell changed colors as the liquid sealed inside moved and shifted, catching the light and reflecting stunning rainbow shades. The Dragon Tear was the ultimate prism.

The next frame showed the man burying the Tear in the side of the cliff, and as he placed it in the hole and let go, massive gold wings sprang out on his back, and he grew larger, stronger, more powerful. And not human, or mortal. His gold eyes burned red, and his face was stamped with fury.

Phoenix strode to the wall and said, "That's Wing Slayer. The first panel has to be when he disguised himself as mortal when he lived on earth centuries ago." Axel asked, "That's the Tear in his hand, isn't it?"

"Yes." Key was stunned as he grasped the scenes. "Wing Slayer had it? Why?"

Axel turned to look at the drawing of Wing Slayer, then back to Key. "Wing Slayer is half demon from his mother's side, and half god from his father's. He lived in the Underworld with his mother, and when he began resembling his father, both in some powers and in looks, his mother cast him out. Neither the gods nor the demons wanted him, and he was essentially alone. He chose to live on Earth, but if he'd been discovered by a witch, he'd have been banished for being half demon. This drawing depicts how Wing Slayer disguised his immortal god and demon sides with that Tear. Just carrying it unbroken allowed Wing Slayer to appear mortal."

Key processed that information. "I guess as long as he carried it unbroken, it just drained his immortality temporarily. The problem is that if the Tear had broken on Wing Slayer, it would have turned him into a mortal permanently. It still could—"

"And then Asmodeus can kill him easily," Axel said. "It is a true god-killer." The man turned his commanding gaze on Key. "Where is the Tear now?"

Before this, Key had told only Phoenix, but Axel was his leader. "It's at the club in the archway between the club and the warehouse. In the gargoyle."

Surprise blanked Axel's face. "How long have you hidden it there?"

Key understood his shock since Axel of Evil was his club. "When your mom and I designed the archways with the gargoyles and dragons, I had one specially made. I hide the Tear there off and on. When I'm out of town, I always put it there."

Finally he nodded. "That works."

"Asmodeus has to be behind Liam trying to get that Tear. The demon and Wing Slayer have been at war over Earth ever since they both realized their power was tied to it. Killing off Wing Slayer would remove the biggest obstacle in Asmodeus's way. With that Tear, the demon could finally kill his rival."

Axel narrowed his eyes as he glanced back at the drawings. "Wing Slayer was hiding the Tear. I'm betting Asmodeus was trying to get it even then, and Wing Slayer must have used his god-power to shield the hiding place so the demon couldn't get it." Turning, he added, "Wing Slayer was banished from Earth by a witch who found out he was half demon. Since he was carrying that Tear, there's only one way the witch could have known—Asmodeus somehow revealed it to her."

"Demons suck," Phoenix said. "But it looks like the god was one step ahead of the demon and made sure he couldn't get the Tear." Facing Key, he asked, "But if Wing Slayer shielded it, how did your mother find it?"

Key related the story she'd told him. "She was descended from a dragon. The story of this Tear was passed down in her family, and it became her obsession. That's probably why the Tear took longer to kill her than it would have a mortal without dragon blood. It also allowed her to see through the magic Wing Slayer used to shield the Tear."

Axel grimaced. "Once your mother moved it from its hiding place, the Tear became visible to Asmodeus."

It made sense. "And that's how my dad came into my mom's life. He was already rogue and sent by Asmodeus to get the Tear. My mother didn't know about witch hunters. He convinced her that he loved her, trying to seduce her into giving up the Tear. But she loved the Tear more than him. The Tear wouldn't allow him to take it from her by force." He left off the part about how his father used him, breaking his bones and burning him with cigarettes.

Phoenix's voice pulled him back. "How did you draw this if you didn't know any of it?"

Key shrugged, more comfortable with his art than his memories. "Before Roxy, my frenzied drawing has always been linked to witch murders and Liam. Since I thought he was dead, I figured it was some kind of guilt or manifestation of my bloodlust. But he's alive, so I must have been drawing his witch kills. No idea why. But this..." Key looked around. "I've always drawn Dyfyr, that's not new, but Wing Slayer is. Liam said Roxy can wake the dragon, maybe it's the dragon beginning to wake, and he's revealing information."

Axel and Phoenix both stared at him, while Roxy lifted her head. "He sensed me in the hotel? Knew Liam was after me?"

Her eyes were filled with wonder. He could see that she was enthralled with the romance of that idea. "It's the only explanation I can think of."

"Phoenix?"

They all turned to where Ailish stood in the

doorway. Phoenix strode to her, taking her arm and guiding her into the room. "Did you talk to the Ancestors?" he asked her.

"Yes." Her gaze drifted. "I asked about the Dragon Tear."

Surprised, Key asked, "What about it?"

Ailish turned toward his voice. "Phoenix wanted to know if there's any way to destroy it."

Her mate added, "Liam's back, the Tear is a god-killer, and I was telling Ailish everything we learned from your drawings through our link. She consulted the Ancestors." Phoenix looked down at her. "Tell us."

"The Ancestors said the Tear was formed in ancient dragon magic, very powerful. The only one who can destroy it is a dragon. They said to wake the dragon. It's our only hope of getting that Tear out of Asmodeus's reach."

Key felt Roxy stiffen as the silence settled around them. She didn't want that, didn't want her magic. She'd told him he was destroying her. And that was the one thing he couldn't live with.

Phoenix broke the silence. "Roxy's your soul mirror. When we seal our bonds with our soul mirrors, the winged creature in us wakes. Your dragon will wake when you do that."

"There must be another way," Key said. "I felt Roxy's magic when she saw the dragon panels. She's already connecting with Dyfyr—"

"You felt my magic?" Roxy said, her voice tight. She turned to look at the drawings. "It's already happening. Just like...it's happening."

The bewildered distress in her voice cut him. He was so damned sorry. Hadn't she suffered enough? Yet when her magic surfaced, her skin had lit with sunset colors and she'd been stunning. How could she not want that gift?

"Liam said I had the mark—" Roxy stepped away,

and spun to face them; her face bloomed with angry color and her eyes grew wide. "She knew."

Totally thrown off by that, Key said, "Who knew?" And how the hell had Liam known all this when Key didn't?

Roxy narrowed her eyes. "My mother. Before...I was on the phone with her in the hotel and she said that I had the only fully formed schema since the curse, and that it was really important, but she wouldn't tell me why." She looked up at him. "She didn't tell me, never warned me."

Key could see the raw pain in her expression. This is the kind of shit families did to one another. "You're safe now." Realizing how inadequate and useless that sounded, he asked, "You think she knew you could wake the dragon? Or about the Tear?"

She straightened. "I'll find out. She's not going to play her games now. I will get the full truth from her."

Axel cleared his throat. "We'll leave for Glassbreakers tonight. Then we'll get some sleep and reconvene tomorrow. Phoenix, you drive the four of you and I'll fly over, keeping watch from the sky."

Once she and Kieran were alone in the room, Roxy's mind kept spinning, filling with both wonder and betrayal. She looked up at the picture of Dyfyr holding his beloved. The more she stared, the more she felt the connection. Because she and Key were soul mirrors?

Or something else?

What secrets had her mother hidden from her? She knew her mother was manipulative and magic-hungry, but how deep did it go? How deep were her mother's secrets? Her stomach turned. What would the soul-mirror witches think of Roxy when they found out who her mother was?

Returning her attention to Dyfyr on the wall, she concentrated and felt a soft pop deep in her pelvis.

Her first chakra. It was happening. She felt trapped, scared and turned around. Kieran stood there, his legs spread, arms down, and the dragon on his chest holding her lock of hair like a priceless treasure. Looking at them, she didn't feel trapped any longer. Lifting her gaze to his eyes, she said, "It's not going to stop."

"What?"

"My magic. It's rising, and it won't stop." She was trying to come to terms with the decision she had to make.

Key's face softened. "I can stop it. My blood worked earlier."

Roxy did a full turn, looking at all his work, then back at him. "And it drove you to do all this. You didn't drain off the pain, you took it." He'd done that for her. First he'd saved her life, then suffered for her.

"I knew what I was doing. Drawing eases it. Don't worry."

She walked to him and took his chalk-stained hand in hers. "What's it like?"

"What?"

"To have such an amazing talent."

His eyes shone. "Being able to draw is like breathing to me. I've always done it, and I have to do it. It's survival. It's the one thing I can count on."

Roxy felt the truth in his words. "I envy your gift and passion. Since I don't have any talent of my own, I love searching out projects to develop for TV or movies." She shut up before she added that it helped to feed the emptiness inside her, the one that nothing else ever touched. She looked down, seeing her smaller hand stroking his bigger one. And she realized that his touch made that emptiness feel a little less frightening.

Kieran took hold of her chin. "You have the gift of

magic. The only problem I see is, you don't trust yourself or your magic."

She shivered, wanting desperately to sink into this man. "It's sex magic. It's not creating beauty or worlds like you do."

Rubbing his thumb along her cheek, he said in a low voice, "There's beauty in sex, green eyes. If you haven't experienced it, you haven't been doing it right."

He made it sound so simple. "But sex magic is just about harnessing the energy to fill our chakras, not sharing intimacy. People get hurt, get angry."

"People like your father?"

"Yes. But it's more than that. One night when I was eleven, it was a full moon, and my mom had to leave to do a fertility ceremony."

His fingers tensed on her face. "She left you alone?"

She nodded. "I finally fell asleep, watching the moon though my window and sort of hating it. The moon always took her away from me to do these ceremonies to bring children to the world." Pausing, she got herself back on track. "Anyway, I fell asleep and woke when a man's hand covered my mouth."

Key's eyes drained of any blue to icy gray. He slid his hand from her face to put it around her shoulder, pulling her against him, as if he could protect her from her own memories. "What happened?"

Fourteen years ago and it was still vivid. "I tried to scream, but I couldn't breathe. He was shoving up my nightgown and said, 'You're like your mother, aren't you? I can feel it. Since she's not here, you'll do.'"

"Shit, Roxy, did he—"

"No. My mother came home and chased him off. He was one of the men she'd slept with, and he came back for more. He was obsessed with her, with her sex magic. Some men fear the power, others are mesmerized by it. I guess he thought if I was her daughter—" She cut herself off. "My father came over, and they had a fight. In the end, my father took me home with him. And from then on, he told me I had to let my chakras die and become mortal in order to have any happiness. And when I did see my mother, she pushed me to find my Awakening and release my magic. It's always been one or the other. Choose, pick a side. And the mortal side seemed like a better bet." Because deep down, Roxy forced herself to admit silently that she didn't trust her mother, or her motives in pushing so hard for Roxy to Awaken her magic.

He brushed her hair back from her eyes. "Sounds like your parents played a game of tug-of-war with you. And maybe shaded the truth to their own liking. Your father made you believe that man in your room had something to do with your magic, didn't he?"

She frowned at him. "The man said—"

"You were eleven years old! Your magic didn't attract him, he was a pervert and a rapist. Your father should have found him and killed him. Not blamed you! Not made you feel shame in your gift. And your mother should never have left you alone and vulnerable to a predator."

Roxy was so startled she couldn't think of anything to say. His entire body was heating with his anger *on her behalf*. He made her feel she mattered.

He dragged in a breath and added, "No one is going to pressure you, not while I'm around. I'm here to keep you safe."

She leaned back, looking up into his eyes. "According to my mother, there's no stopping my Awakening now. I didn't want to believe her, but you saw it in the shower, the schema is filling with more and more color. The pain, well, you felt it, and it's only going to get worse. It's time I faced the reality. I will never be mortal." Hearing herself say the words stopped her for a second. But then she pressed on. "And it's not just about me anymore. You need me to help you wake Dyfyr and find out how to get rid of the Tear. Even I know how important Wing Slayer is in the fight with Asmodeus. I can't let him be killed by the Tear if I have the power to stop it." It was time to let go of her impossible dreams, grow up, and deal in reality. Kieran had saved her life. How could she not help him in return? "Can you teach me to, I don't know, trust my magic?"

His gaze heated, but his voice was gentle. "Hell, yes. I can show you beauty in sex and pleasure." He took a breath. "That's the easy part."

"What's the hard part?"

His stare grew remote. "We're soul mirrors, and if we finish this bond, you're going to need me. We'll have to be a part of each other's lives." Running a hand through his hair, his voice tensed. "Your dream is some romantic love story that I don't know if I can do. I'm not good at relationships. Look at Dyfyr. He loved a woman, and it caused him so much grief, he cried dangerous tears, then put himself in a sleep. Where you see romance in that, I see misery."

Her chest grew heavy. She hadn't even realized she'd had a secret hope that as soul mirrors, she and Key would have a love story, or maybe it was from the drawings of Dyfyr. As soon as she saw them, her magic had bubbled in recognition, and she'd wanted desperately to wake the dragon. Like part of her was missing and... *"Romantic Roxy,* that's what my cousin Shayla calls me. But you don't believe in romance, or love?"

He pulled his mouth tight, then said, "I believe in actions, and taking care of responsibilities. Dyfyr will be your familiar. He'll help you reach your top chakras, and that should help you with your sex magic. I won't take Dyfyr away from you, Roxy. You're giving me freedom from the curse and the Tear. I won't reject you. Anytime you need me for magic, or sex, I'll be there for you."

"I see. So you'll be my on-call stud service?"

A primitive blue flickered in his eyes. "No, damn it." He fisted his hand at his side. "I put my passion, my faith into my art. Not people."

Her heart squeezed. What had happened to him to make him feel that way? "Why?"

He looked down at her, his eyes turbulent. "People destroy each other. I don't want to destroy you."

This man who had taken her pain had been trying to save her, not destroy her. He was bringing out her magic, but that wasn't something he'd set out to do. He'd left that decision to her. And she'd made her choice—there was no going back. "We'll concentrate on waking the dragon and finding out how to safeguard the Tear."

9

KEY JOLTED AWAKE, LEAPED TO his feet with his knife in his hand. Witch blood. He could smell it...

Want it.

As he came fully awake, he realized it wasn't real, but images in his head. His fingers tightened around the silver hilt of his knife. The burn slithered and grew. He looked down at his arm and saw the veins swelling beneath his skin.

Craving witch blood.

Want it. He wanted to feel the warm power pouring over his skin and cooling the burn in his veins. Filling the emptiness. The hollowness that gnawed at him.

Witch blood in your room, sleeping in your bed.

"No," he said, his voice dry with need. He looked across the length of his loft, toward his bedroom. Roxy was in there, the sound of her soft breathing telling him she was still asleep.

Sex. He could bring out her power with sex, then harvest it with his knife. His mind splattered with images: sex, blood, the patterns her blood would make on his chest when he cut her. The feel...

The rancid smell of burning skin jolted him. Then he felt a searing line on the right side of his chest. He

121

looked down and saw a row of burn blisters from the dragon's snout up to his right shoulder.

Dyfyr was pissed. Showing more signs of life to protect Roxy. His ruby eyes glowed with anger. The pain didn't do much, but the smell of his flesh burning was enough to mask the lingering scent of witch blood.

But he still felt the urgency, the rage building into cold emptiness that sucked at him, pulled at him, trying to draw his mind into the endless vortex.

Recognizing the signs, Key knew he needed to vent the cold rage. Sex, violence, or drawing...that was how he did it.

Draw. He grabbed the jeans he'd thrown on the floor when he'd gone to sleep on the couch, yanked them on, then strapped on the holster he used for his knife. Securing the weapon, he looked at his bedroom again.

Don't. Even the faint scent of her dark chocolate power might set him off.

It wasn't her scent that had woken him. It hadn't been her scent he'd smelled, so strong, so jacked up with adrenaline...

Liam. He'd struck again. Furious, Key began to twitch with the need to draw, to spill out his venomous hatred of his brother. It was just after ten, giving him about five hours' sleep. He turned his back on the loft and headed for the wide metal stairs going down to a studio on the first level.

The walls were brick and the floor cement. He had a large U-shaped work space. His computer faced out, equipped with a graphics tablet and stylus when he wanted to do digital drawings, a scanner for when he wanted to scan in freehand work. He also had a drafting table. And on one large wall he had sheets of paper to allow him to draw at will.

Like now.

He opened a drawer in his desk and got out a fresh

supply of pencils. Going to the largest page, he selected a pencil and began to track his brother. He worked fast, not trying to remember the dream or control his art. He didn't judge, didn't even look.

He just drew.

And then finally he could inhale without the cold violence searing his lungs. Key wiped his arm over his forehead and was surprised by a knock at his door. Adrenaline seared his veins, and he pulled his knife from the holster. Common sense told him that Liam wasn't going to knock on his door, but Roxy was upstairs, and he wasn't taking any chances. Going to the door, he looked out the peephole.

A tank-sized man with a bald head and an eagle earring stood there—Sutton West. Key's surprise kept mounting. He pulled open the door. "Why are you here?"

Sutton strode in, turned and said, "Axel filled me in." He looked around and paused on the drawing. Then turned back to Key. "Where's Roxy?"

Adrenaline had primed Key's body for a fight; his muscles twitched, and his blood raced. "She's asleep."

Sutton stilled, turned his body slightly, so immobile it looked like he had silenced his heart. Seconds stretched out, then his shoulders eased slightly, and he hit Key with his gaze. "I hear her breathing. That's good."

"I'm not going to kill her."

The other hunter wore a black T-shirt, black fatigues and hiking boots. "Axel says that you have an ancient dragon named Dyfyr sleeping in you"—he lowered his eyes to the tat—"and now he's waking up."

Key wasn't sure where this was going, so he said nothing.

"I've been with you when you fight. You start off fine, like any hunter, but when you get pissed, something happens. You go into a cold, killing frenzy, ignoring pain like it's not even there. And I think it's something to do with that dragon."

Key shrugged. Sutton was very close to the truth. Dyfyr had always been inside him, and Key had felt the dragon reach out and pull him to the cold gray place where he existed. Key didn't feel pain as much there, and Dyfyr and Key often merged, working together to destroy what had pissed them off. Usually rogues. But it had started long before Key began killing rogues. It's what Key was, the creature that his mom and the fertility witch had created.

"So what I'm wondering is, what if Dyfyr doesn't want to wake up? And Roxy forces him and really pisses him off?"

Key frowned. "I don't hurt women, or innocents." That wasn't entirely true, he had once. But never again. "You've hunted with me countless times, and I've never noticed you being afraid I'd lose it and hurt you. Getting soft since you mated, old man?" Sutton was four years older than Key.

A corner of his mouth lifted. Dropping his arms, he flexed his massive hands. "Anytime your dragon wants to come after me, I'm willing. Always good to have a sparring partner."

He wasn't kidding. Sutton was always looking for a stronger, faster, more brutal sparring partner.

Lowering his hands to his side, Sutton glanced at the latest drawing and said, "What is this, Key?"

He turned and got a good look at the scene he'd drawn. "That's Liam." His half brother was on his knees bent over a woman, cutting and smearing her blood over his bare, hairless chest. Key could see the fading places on his body where the blood was being absorbed through, feeding the sick craving for the witch's power in her blood. Liam had been rogue as long as Key could remember, and he'd always had the strange contrast of hard, bulging muscles and soft, hairless, almost feminine skin. They believed the stark contrast was from absorbing all the power in witch blood—the power gave rogues more strength, but the female hormones also gave them some feminine traits. In the garage, part of Key's mind had realized that Liam was bigger and yet more feminine than he remembered. He had to be getting a lot of witch blood.

He shifted his gaze to study the woman, trying to determine more about her. She'd been stripped to her underwear, but she was so drained of blood, her skin was caving in around the wounds. Walking closer, he pointed, "This mark above her right breast, it's a schema."

Sutton stepped up beside him. "The top half of the fertility goddess. It's outlined in black and filled in with brown and green. So she was a fertility witch who had her power."

"And now she's dead. I woke up with the scent of blood and the pounding urge to draw this scene." He didn't mention the bloodlust.

"Weird shit. You draw your brother's kills through some psychic connection." He fell silent, then said in a flat voice, "Look at the setting."

He examined the landscape around Liam and the dead witch. He saw the dirt lot, the cars parked nearby, the small building off to the side, and the old antennas overhead. Recognition hit him—it was the old radio station out past the cemetery. "Rogue Cadre headquarters." His adrenaline spiked again. "Liam is here in Glassbreakers." He pulled out his phone and called Axel, told him what he had.

"I'll send out some recruits to look for the witch," Axel said. "We'll meet later today."

Key hung up.

Sutton said, "Watch that dragon, Key. Later." He left.

Key locked the door, then he went upstairs.

Roxy walked around Kieran's loft, trying to get her bearings. He'd told her last night he owned the building and used the bottom floor as a studio. The living area upstairs was a huge space with exposed brick walls, ductwork overhead and wood floors. The best feature was the long wall of floor-to-ceiling windows across the room that opened to a balcony.

The kitchen was in the center on the opposite side of the windows. The long granite countertop divided the space and had bar stools.

The living area had a red rug on the hardwood floor with a metallic gray curved couch topped with red throw pillows. It faced a big-screen TV mounted in the corner so it could be seen from almost any place in the living area.

The other end of the loft was split into a large master bedroom and bathroom. Roxy had slept in there at Key's insistence, and he'd slept on the couch. She sank onto the soft cushions, looking out the windows to the landscape of the beach city.

Kieran walked out of the bedroom wearing jeans, boots and a blue T-shirt that made his eyes look more blue than gray. His face appeared tanned, but Roxy had seen him naked and knew that was his natural color. It really stood out with his blond hair. He barely looked at her and went into the kitchen.

His scent swirled around her, dark and spicy mixed with soap. It made her stomach tighten and her schema start to throb. She ignored it.

"Do you want coffee?" He filled the coffeemaker with water, then scooped in grounds. "Or tea?"

"Tea." She felt displaced. She didn't have even the most basic of items. He'd given her a toothbrush, and she'd used his comb to work through her hair. She'd had to put on her same clothes. "I need to use a phone. I have to call my mom, my dad, and make some business calls." She wasn't going to give up everything. She'd still be a producer for her dad, find a way to get him to keep trusting her. She wanted the Eternal Assassins books. Maybe it would help Shayla forgive Roxy for her decision.

He set the kettle on the stove, turned on the flame, then walked around the island toward her. Taking his phone out of his pocket, he handed it to her. "Call whoever you want. We'll get you a phone, clothes and other stuff later today."

He turned and went back to the kitchen.

"I'll have my dad send over a laptop, a phone and maybe I can have Shayla pack some things from my apartment," she said as she dialed her mom.

"No," Key turned with two mugs in his hand. "I'll get you whatever you need. I don't want to risk people knowing where you are and possibly compromising your safety or theirs."

She frowned as she thought about that, but then a voice answered, "Yes?" in her ear.

"Mom..." For a second her throat tightened and her eyes burned. And then the anger and betrayal took hold. "I need information, no more secrets."

Key set a cup of tea on the table in front of her, along with a plate of chocolate and powdered donuts. He picked up a chocolate one, bit into it and vanished again.

"What happened to you?" her mom asked. "The soul-mirror witches are asking all kinds of questions. Roxy, how do they know about waking the dragon? That is sacred!"

Key came back with his coffee and a sketch pad. He sat in the chair with his back to the window, crossed his ankle over his knee, flipped open the pad and looked up at her. Realizing she was staring, she quickly answered her mother's question, "I was kidnapped and taken to a rogue. He knew about my full goddess schema. He demanded to know if I'd woken the dragon and where the Tear was."

"Oh Roxy! No!" Her mom's voice rose. "Did he hurt you? You got away?"

She sucked in a breath, hearing the real panic. "I'm okay. Key and his friends rescued me. Mom, the rogue had been looking for me, or more specifically, my schema. How could you not tell me?"

"I didn't know! Roxy, you can't think I knew the rogue was looking for you. I only knew how important you are to the fertility witches! We need you to Awaken your magic, but I didn't know..." She took a deep breath and asked, "How could he know about your schema and that you can wake the dragon? It's a sacred secret, told only to Awakened fertility witches."

"Trust me, getting cut a few times will make you reveal anything." She squeezed her eyes shut, trying to suppress those memories.

"Blessed Ancestors, Roxy! Do you need me? Where are you? Still in Vegas? Wherever you are, I'll get there and heal you. Or I can find a witch closer to—" Her mom's voice cracked.

"I'm healed, Mom. What I need from you is the truth. Your secrets and lies damn near got me killed."

"Roxanne! You cannot blame me for that! How—"

"Stop it." She stared out at the rooftops of city buildings. It felt like her mind was leaping from roof to roof, but unable to find any answers. "I am not playing your games, Mom. I want to know about my schema and how it can wake the dragon. And anything you know about a Dragon Tear."

Her mom sighed. "You will need to Awaken your magic, and then we'll do a ritual trying to wake the dragon. We'll need a man to represent the dragon in his human form, and you'll perform sex magic."

She cringed and kept her gaze trained on the windows. She knew Key could hear the conversation. This was what she didn't want. Maybe to someone like Kieran it seemed stupid, maybe it was just sex. But to her... "No. I'm not having sex with some random guy." She could hear the smooth strokes of Key's pencils on the page and wondered if that wasn't exactly what she'd agreed to with him.

Was she losing herself, trading her values, her beliefs, for magic? Would sex eventually be just a power source to her? Not about a connection, a way of sharing herself with a man?

"Roxy, you don't understand. This is why I didn't tell you, why we don't tell anyone who is not an Awakened fertility witch." Passion enriched her mother's voice. "It's a beautiful ceremony reenacting the creation of fertility witches in the story 'The Dragon's Lover.'"

Roxy's chakras tightened in some kind of visceral response. She glanced over to see Key's hand still as he heard what her mother said. She remembered Key's drawing of the dragon and his lover. Was she the first fertility witch? "How was she...created? What does it have to do with a dragon?"

There was a pause, then, "I've already told you more—"

She would not be put off. "A rogue knows, and he seems to be one step ahead of us. If you want me alive to Awaken my powers, then start talking."

Her mom took a breath and said, "This is the story passed down from the lover."

> *She gazed at the skies*
> *Day and night*
> *More than sun, moon and stars*
> *She saw soaring dragons*

Earthbound and lonely
Believing she, too, was magic
She dreamed of flying
Wrapped in dragon wings.

And then one majestic creature
Plucked her from the earth
Taking her to the heavens
Teaching her of love

Passion heated their blood
Shifting him to his man-form
Laid her on the sweet grass
And gave her true magic

Her dragon loved her so
He bestowed his magic kiss
A gift of fertility magic
In the mark of a goddess

Her magic and love bloomed
Growing eternally stronger
Until death ripped her away
Vowing to return one day

Her magic swelled until her heart ached. "The mark, that's the fertility goddess?" That's what Liam had said when he had her.

"Yes. But the curse broke our power. We've done countless ceremonies trying to wake the dragon in the hopes that he would help us strengthen our power back to the pre-curse levels. Eventually we realized it wasn't going to work that way. We couldn't wake him. But then your schema began to take shape as the fully formed goddess, and we realized you had the full mark just like the one the dragon gave his lover."

It swirled in her head. "Mom, do you know the name of the dragon?"

"No, we only know the lover's story. Why?"

Her stomach bubbled with excitement. "Key has a tattoo of a dragon. His name is Dyfyr, and I think he might be the dragon that bestowed fertility on his lover." The pieces all fit. The goddess mark connected the stories of Dyfyr and the lover. Even now, just remembering the drawings Key had done of Dyfyr and his lover had the power to make her heart swell and her throat tighten with powerful emotion. She added in a soft voice, "He's my soul mirror."

"Roxy, don't you see? You have to do this! You're our hope! You'll be able to wake the dragon, he'll become your familiar, and then in the ceremonies, he will increase all our magic through you." Her mom took a deep breath. "It won't break the curse for all of us, but it will at least help control the sex drive and give us more power."

But no pressure or anything. She was confused on one point. "How will it help you control your sex drives?" She was not going to have sex in front of a bunch of old crones, no matter what the reason. *Don't look at Key,* she told herself.

"Our magic is sexual in nature. When we Awaken, that drive is powerful to help us reach our high magic in our top three chakras. The curse trapped us at the fourth chakra and leaves us in a loop of needing sex to get more power to reach those chakras but being unable to do it. It's an unending cycle. But when we circle our magic with you in the ceremonies, we'll reach our chakras through yours. It will satisfy that need in our magic, at least temporarily."

Tension built in her. "Do all these ceremonies require sex?" She weakened and glanced at Kieran.

He raised his eyebrows and grinned.

Jerking her gaze back to the view, she waited.

Gwen finally said, "No. Well, you may need to gather energy in your chakras from sex before the ceremonies, but no. That kind of sex magic is very powerful and used sparingly." She added, "Your father had no right to turn you against magic, against your heritage."

"I don't want to hear it, Mom. He wanted to keep me safe. If my chakras died, my schema would have vanished. The rogues would have no interest in me." A throb started behind her eyes. She added, "Dad wanted me, he loves me." But would he still?

"I love you, Roxy. I shouldn't have left you alone that night. Your father was supposed to come over but canceled. I made a mistake." She bit off the word, then said, "Your father's the one who walked out on us. In the beginning I had my high magic and he was fine. But when the curse took away my familiar and things got rough, he walked." She sighed and added, "All that matters is that you don't suffer this way. Roxy, stop fighting and Awaken your magic. Wake the dragon."

Why argue? It's what she was going to do anyway. "I'm not doing this in a ceremony with other witches around. Tell me how to wake the dragon with just the two of us."

Gwen hesitated again, then said, "It's sex magic. You need your magic, then you call the dragon, he Awakens and fertilizes you."

Roxy blinked, keeping her eyes focused on the windows. "Lovely."

"It is!" Gwen snapped. "It was the dragon's gift to his lover. He made love to her in human form, gifting her with fertility. He shared his own magic with her."

It did sound romantic and lovely put like that. She looked at Key. His hand moved over the page, sure and steady, his face angled down and backlit by the windows. Even sitting he appeared big and strong, with an edge of ancient power in the lines of his muscles. She had to remind herself that it wasn't going to be anything more than sex between them. "Thank you for the information, Mom." Another thought occurred to her. "Please be careful. If the rogues find out you're my mother, they might go after you to get to me." The very idea made her queasy.

"I know how to protect myself. Roxy, you can do this, you'll be one of the most powerful witches. And things will be...better."

Roxy felt a weird vibration at her mother's pause. More secrets? Or because she thought Roxy waking Dyfyr would help all the fertility witches? "Mom, what are you not telling me? I swear if you hold out—"

"Nothing. Roxy, I know you had a bad experience, but I'm not the enemy here. I'm trying to help."

She thought it through. "What about the Dragon Tear? Do you know anything about it?"

A beat passed. "You're being paranoid. These emotional swings are natural when you begin your Awakening. But you need to fully Awaken so that—"

Her evasion infuriated Roxy. "Mom, answer the question!"

"No. I mean I've heard rumors, but that's all."

Roxy opened her mouth, then shut it. Was her mom lying? Gwen had told her about the ceremony, so why lie about this? "I have to go. Bye." She hung up. With her mind spinning, she reached for her mug and took a drink of tea. Holding the cup, she set the phone beside her. "You heard."

He lifted his gaze and grinned. "I am to fertilize you. Will we need manure?"

She flushed to her roots. "Shut up."

"Maybe I should water you, too?"

She leaned forward, grabbed a powdered-sugar donut, and threw it at him.

Key caught it and took a bite. "Fertilize, fertilize, it has such a romantic ring to it."

"No less romantic than having sex in public," she snapped.

"That's not happening, not like your mom described. Now hot sex outside where no one can see us, oh yeah, that'll happen. But it'll be just us. You and me."

Warmth moved through her at his throaty description.

He added, "Because it seems like I really should fertilize you outside." Then he broke into laughter.

"Jackass." But his laughter was infectious and she laughed, too. Finally, she said, "Did you hear anything else besides that?"

He finished the donut and went back to shading something on the drawing. "Yes. Dyfyr created fertility witches." His eyebrows drew together and he looked up. "That makes sense. Dyfyr's connection to fertility witches and Liam—that's why I'm drawing it when Liam kills them. The dragon is furious."

Roxy felt that resonate in her chakras. "Dyfyr is their creator, like Wing Slayer is yours."

Key shifted in the chair. "Wing Slayer had a little help in my case."

Roxy turned to study him. "What do you mean?"

"My mom got pregnant with me. She had the Tear, but she needed to bring Dyfyr back to life to get what she really wanted—immortality."

Roxy said, "That doesn't make sense. The Tear left other dragons mortal."

"Yes, but I think as this story about being descended from dragons and finding the Tear was passed down in her family, it was embellished and changed."

Roxy got it. "Like whoever found the Tear and woke the dragon would get immortality."

He nodded. "She believed it. So much so that she became an archaeologist in preparation to find the

Tear. Then when she did unearth it, she took that achievement as a sign that she would be the one to achieve immortality. But she needed the dragon, Dyfyr, for that."

"What did she do?" Roxy wanted to know.

"When she was a few weeks pregnant with me, she went to a fertility witch. While she wore the Tear, they did some spell or ceremony that called the soul of Dyfyr into me."

Roxy stared at him. "A fertility witch did that? Is that even possible?" Even as she said it, a memory stirred, but she couldn't quite bring it up.

His face filled with shadows as anger rippled within him. "I'm here. They created a monster."

No! "You're not a monster!"

He stared at her with cold eyes. "I'm a freak of magic, Roxy. The fertility witch who did this abused her power and twisted nature by joining a fetus with the soul of Dyfyr. What would you call it?"

Her breath caught as the memory surfaced. Roxy and her mother were fighting when Roxy said she didn't want to Awaken, she wanted to be mortal and have a real family. Gwen snapped back that fertility witches helped mortals create those families. *But they do so much more,* Gwen said, explaining that she had done a spell so incredible, it was bigger than the miracle of birth. That memory ignited a flush of suspicion. Her mother had been evasive when Roxy asked about the Dragon Tear. Oh God, could her mother have been the fertility witch who did this to Kieran? Merging a dragon soul into an unborn child could be considered bigger than the miracle of birth. The risk to the child... But Gwen had brushed off the risk when Roxy told her that her Awakening was a witch hunter and dangerous to her. If she'd risk her own daughter's life, was it such a stretch to think she'd risk an unborn baby? Panic rolled through her as she stared out at the cityscape, trying to think. To Kieran, she said, "You hate fertility magic, but you said my magic was a gift."

The coldness in his gaze melted. "You put yourself in danger to save a kid. Hell, you didn't even want your magic. You won't do that, Roxy. You won't try to alter nature."

He believed in her. And if she told him what she suspected about her mother, what would he do? Her stomach twisted in knots. She just had too much coming at her. Roxy cradled the cup of tea. Fear froze her, but she focused on Key. It was easier to think about him. "Is that why you don't think you know how to love, to have a relationship? Have you ever been in love?"

His hand stilled, and he looked up. "Once. She died." Then he resumed sketching, his cold dismissal a clear signal that the subject was closed.

"I'm sorry, Kieran." He'd endured so much. He made her want to take care of him, to reach past his emotional walls and ease the pain in him. Did he still love that woman who died? She hated that he'd suffered that way. "I shouldn't have asked, I'll just call my father." She'd been avoiding calling him even though he'd be worried, but now she picked up the BlackBerry and dialed. "Heath Viking."

His voice wrapped around her chest and squeezed. "Dad, it's me," she said, struggling to get control of her wildly fluctuating emotions.

"Roxy! I have people in Vegas looking for you! You checked out of your room and vanished. You didn't get on your flight, what happened?"

She launched into the story, quickly telling him what happened and explaining that Kieran was protecting her.

"You're choosing magic."

The flat betrayal in his voice almost undid her. She

could try to explain, but she didn't think he'd listen, so she simply said, "Yes." Then she added, "I'm going to work from here. I want to buy the dramatic rights to the Eternal Assassins." She rushed on to reassure him. "As soon as I can, as soon as it's safe, I'll be back in the office. Nothing is going to change."

"Roxy, don't do this. Stop before it's too late! We'll find a way. Don't do this. You'll become...you won't be my daughter. Your mother said the same thing all those years ago. But she changed, until I was just a means to feed her magic. And it was never enough. She...goddammit."

His anger and disappointment made her head throb. Her chest seized, and her eyes burned. She couldn't do this right now, so she said, "I've already had a preliminary meeting with the two authors, Nina and Perry, and I feel good about them. I can work up a profit and loss as soon as I get a laptop, and then I can pitch it at the meeting by video conference. This project will be perfect for Shayla to write the screenplay. It can be huge, like *Twilight* or *X-Men*."

"You won't even try to fight this? You're going to let magic ruin you?" His voice dropped to angry despair.

"I don't have a choice. Please, Dad, I swear—"

"You swore you wouldn't choose magic. When I hired you, Roxy, you promised. You broke the promise. You're fired." He hung up.

She held the phone in shock, seconds ticking by. He fired her. As his employee or his daughter? Both. She knew it was both. Finally she made herself press the end button and stared out the window. It was sunny and warm. Everything she had feared would happen was happening. Her father had fired her, hated her. Hated what she was becoming. He'd only loved her until she screwed up.

Her schema began to ache.

Key caught her attention as he got up and walked

over to her. Sitting on the arm of the couch, he slid his hand to her neck and rubbed the tight muscles. "I'm going to get you your life back, Roxy. I swear it. I'm your soul mirror; you're going to get your high magic. The sex drive is supposed to calm then. You'll be in control, and there's no reason you can't keep working."

He was right. Hope sprang up in her. Lifting her gaze, she said, "Working where? My father fired me."

Key stared at her. "Form your own production company and kick his ass."

The image surprised a laugh out of her. "I could, couldn't I?" Her father's reaction hurt down to her soul, but maybe he'd cool off, forgive her.

He nodded. "Damn right. If you need financial backing, I'm here, sweetheart. Over time, your dad will see how special you are and realize he's an ass who should have supported you when you needed him most."

He got it. The man who claimed not to know much about relationships understood what love was supposed to be.

"Once Liam is dead, you can work with your dad or do whatever you want. You'll have to be careful, though. We should develop enough of a bond, a sort of psychic link that will enable you to let me know if you're in danger from rogues or demon witches." He slid his arm around her. "I'll protect you. I'll be there for you."

She believed him. "I know you will." She took a breath and said, "There's no going back, so we move forward."

His gaze burned into her. "I'm going to show you the beauty in your magic, Roxy. Show you that it's a gift." He rubbed his palm down her arm, then cupped his hand around her side and let his thumb slide over her rib cage.

Her nipples tightened from the feel of his thumbs caressing her through the tank. "How?" Fear twisted with her desire, confusing her. It was all happening too fast. Her world spun, her goals changed, and she couldn't get a handle on anything.

"You were doing magic last night when you woke up and saw the dragon on the wall. Before you had a chance to think, or worry about consequences. What did that feel like?" He slid one hand up, gliding over the swell of her breast, barely skimming her nipple.

She shivered, goose bumps springing up her arms. The way he was touching her was sensual and soft, without being too invasive. Thinking back, she remembered being confused; waking up to find those men in the room. Then she saw the dragon Key had drawn. "It was like deja vu, and then I felt a soft...pop is the only word I can think of...in my pelvis, and a sort of energy rising to my rib cage."

His gaze stayed locked on to her face. "Your chakras. Your witch-shimmer came to the surface, the fiery glow of sunset. It was faint but there."

He handed her his sketch pad and said, "Here's how you look this morning. The light spilling in, catching the colors of your hair."

Roxy looked down. He'd caught her sitting at an angle, facing him, and a wistful expression glazed her green eyes with her mouth soft and slightly parted, as if she were going back in time in her head. She had her head slightly tilted, exposing the lines of her neck. It was so vivid, she recognized that was the moment she was thinking about the romance of Dyfyr and his lover. Her hair was blond over a light brown base, but he'd shaded it with red, somehow capturing the true color. Her breasts rose against the small tank top as if she were sucking a breath for a sigh. "It's lovely. I look better here than I did in the mirror." Though she appeared a little remote and melancholy.

He tossed the tablet on the table. "That's how I see you. But I want to see that witch-shimmer again, and your sensuality. When you're not holding back, not consciously repressing your magic and your desire." He throttled his voice down. "I want to bring out that sexy shimmer of yours and then capture it on paper. Show you there's nothing to fear in your power or beauty." He brushed his fingers up over her clavicle, along her jaw, and cupped her cheek.

She tilted her head back, caught up in his gaze. "You don't have to do this. What about your bloodlust?" He was going slowly with her, giving her some time, but she knew that they had to have sex. "We can just do it."

His fingers tensed. "Touching you eases my bloodlust. I want to learn you and teach you to trust my touch. To feel safe with me."

"I am safe with you." He'd rescued her, taken care of her, taken her pain away and stayed with her while she slept. "I know that."

His hand on her face relaxed, wisps of blue heat flared in his eyes. "Safe enough to let me take off your shirt? Allow me to touch and kiss you until your magic rises and fires your shimmer?" His voice thickened. "Can you sit on the couch, with the sunlight pouring over your breasts, and let me draw you?"

A knot in her stomach eased, her heart picked up speed and excitement skipped through her. Anticipation. She glanced at the long wall of glass. "But the windows..."

"Specially treated glass. No one can see you, except me." He ran his thumb over her lips. "Only me."

"Only you," she said as he kept brushing her mouth, then dipped inside. She touched her tongue to his thumb and his jaw clenched.

He drew his thumb out and lowered his mouth to

hers, while his hand on her waist crept up to brush the underside of her breast. He stroked her with his tongue and nipped her lower lip. Then licked it.

She shivered, feeling overpowered by just a kiss. Her body was softening, while her schema heated and thin threads of desire began spreading. It was never like this with anyone else. He kept brushing the tender skin under her breast until her nipple ached, while stroking her mouth with his tongue.

Pressure built low in her belly.

He cupped her breast, brushing her nipple through the shirt. Tremors of pleasure shot through her, arrowing down, and she felt a pop, then the energy flowing out, spreading, filling.

Key lifted his head. "Your magic. Feel it?" He drew his fingers around her breasts.

Her magic streamed toward it, turning her skin sensitive to his touch. "Yes," she breathed, wondering at the new, full feeling of it. The way it followed Key's fingers.

He switched direction and trailed his fingers down to the hem of her shirt. Grasped the edge and pulled it up.

Expectation heated her skin as her breasts spilled out.

Then he guided the top over her head and tossed it down. He got up, stepped between her legs and knelt down. His hands settled on her thighs, his heat penetrating the soft cotton of the yoga pants.

Roxy sat on the couch, unsure what to do. Her nerves pulled tight, her emotions flinging between excitement and uncertainty. Key had seen her completely naked, yet this felt more revealing, more personal.

He lowered his gaze, his eyes growing hotter, taking on more blue. "Breathtaking." He leaned up to her mouth and kissed her. Hot, open mouthed, demanding tongue. He ran his hands up over her hips to the bare skin of her waist.

Then higher.

Skimming, his palms created friction that her magic chased. She wrapped her arms around his neck, needing to taste him, wanting to know and savor the depths of Kieran's mouth.

A hint of dark spice that fired hunger in her.

He drew his hands up to cup her breasts, feathered his thumbs over her nipples. She felt another chakra open, more magic, more pleasure.

Key moved from her mouth, kissing down her throat, until he captured one distended nipple between his lips, then grazed it with his teeth, followed by gentle swipes of his tongue. Then he switched to the other side, making love to her breasts with his mouth.

She was drowning in the sensations, her body heating, and her schema began to ache, burn, demand. She arched her body, thrusting her breasts high in an offering, to concentrate on that pleasure, not the pain in her...

Key dropped his hands and caught her hips, pulling her tight to his erection. His hip was pressed to her schema, the firm contact easing the pain. Lifting his head from her, he raked his gaze down her body. "So damned beautiful." He sucked in a breath, his nostrils flaring, color riding his cheekbones.

His long, thick erection pressed exactly where she needed it, a hot pressure between her thighs.

He leaned up, kissed her mouth, then slid to her ear. "Going to draw you now. Right now when you're so fucking hot, I can't think straight."

She shivered.

"And then, little witch, I'm going to take these pants off of you. I want you to think about that. Lie back and think about what it's going to be like when I touch you. You'll be wet and slippery..." He groaned in her ear. "And I'll have to taste you. Find out if you are as delicious as I'm imagining. Think about that, Roxy, what it's going feel like when I spread your thighs and kiss you until you come for me."

~ *10* ~

KEY SAT ON THE COFFEE table, thrumming with the need to capture her on the page. Roxy glowed with the fiery colors of sunset, desire softening her lines and swelling her lips and breasts. He looked down to her cleft in those yoga pants.

Damn. She was swollen there, too, her caramel scent so tempting he gripped the pencil tighter. He began sketching.

Fast.

Needing to record this. Not for him, it was imprinted on his brain, on his soul forever. But for her. To show her, before he took her completely, before he stripped off her pants, spread her open and filled her, he wanted her to know how incredibly beautiful and special she was.

Drawing at hyperspeed, so fast a mortal would see only a blur, he saw her forming on the page. It inflamed his lust. He wanted her with ferocious desire that beat at his spine and swelled his cock so big, he was surprised the buttons of his jeans didn't fly off.

Beneath his shirt, he felt the dragon moving, trying to wake. For her.

He glanced up at her, wearing just her pants, still

flushed with desire and magic. It hit him how much she trusted him. She was giving herself over to his care, to their care, him and the dragon. It made his chest go so tight, he was nearly dizzy with it. This witch who'd fought her sexual magic for years trusted them to bring out her power. He changed pencils, desperate to capture the color of her witch-shimmer. He had his knees touching hers to keep the bloodlust under control.

As he looked up again, his gut tightened. Did she know how much he loved doing this? To him, drawing was sensual. Creating her lines on the page was foreplay. And she let him, gave it to him, didn't fill the space with chatter.

She was special. Too special. He didn't want to think about that.

The dragon shifted and moved, restless, desperate to come fully awake. To claim her. A small part of his brain noted it, wondered why this woman was so important to the dragon.

For Roxy. *Our treasure.*

It played over his mind briefly that the dragon thought that Roxy was his treasure. That was significant...his pencil slowed. A grain of anxiety he couldn't name slipped into the heat blazing through him. He shifted his position so that he was no longer touching her.

His BlackBerry dinged a text message. His veins began swelling from bloodlust, his cock ached for relief, and Roxy watched him with suspiciously soft eyes. He grabbed the phone from where it was next to her on the couch and opened the text.

A picture filled his screen. "Damn!" It was Tyler and another woman, tied up. Both were pale and terrified. The accompanying message read: "I have the kid and his mother. I'll give them to you for Roxy. I'll call with instructions. Screw with me and I'll kill them."

He wasn't going to screw with him, he was going to kill the weasel bastard. But was it Liam? Or his dumb shit flunky? Wouldn't Liam demand the Tear? Key flipped the sketchbook closed and slammed it down on the coffee table.

"What?" Roxy bent over and looked at the picture on his BlackBerry. "Oh no, it's Tyler!"

Her desire faded under the heavy scent of worry and fear. "They saw me talking to him. Right before Joel led me to their car, I was talking to Tyler."

He was furious at himself. They'd left Vegas and forgot about the kid. Mack could have been in costume and hanging around the signing, seen Roxy and him work together to save the kid. "Get dressed." He forwarded the message to the other hunters, quickly explaining who the kid was.

Phoenix called and Key answered with, "We screwed up."

"Roger that. Listen, the woman is the kid's mom. Ailish and I both recognize her, her name is Paige. I'm going to get Sutton on tracking this. Meet us at the warehouse."

He looked at Roxy, his loyalties torn. "I can't bring Roxy."

"She'll be okay, she's not releasing enough power to make the others lose control."

"Her power's getting stronger. I don't want the unbonded hunters near her." Once a hunter found his soul mirror and sealed the bond, the curse broke for them. But Roxy was caught in the middle, her powers releasing now, but not yet bonded.

To him. *She belongs to me!* The words rang in his head and worried him. Shit, he had to focus on Tyler. He added to Phoenix, "I can't leave her alone."

"Bring her to my house. Ailish is here, they'll be safe. I'll wait while Sutton's tracing the message."

"Done. And Phoenix, we're going to save that kid."

"Fucking A." He hung up.

Key went into his bedroom and armed himself. He strapped on his knife harness, slid another into his boot. He unlocked his weapons safe and took out a Glock 10mm semiautomatic pistol. He carried that in his hand and walked back out to the living area.

Roxy was dressed and standing there waiting. Her gaze took in the gun in his hand, and her mouth tightened, but she didn't say anything. Her muscles were tense, she had her arms crossed over her middle, and her witch-shimmer flickered on her skin. He smelled flares of her power.

A slow burn in his veins developed barbs, irritating the shit out of him. He knew the curse was rising to a dangerous level. Maybe it'd be better to leave Roxy in his loft. There was an excellent alarm system and he could close the bulletproof shutters over the windows.

But her flickering power changed his mind; she needed to control her magic, and Ailish could help her with that. He would stay in control. The drive to Phoenix's house was only ten minutes. "Let's go." He strode to the stairs and started down.

"Where?" She followed, the sound of her flip-flops ringing loudly on the metal stairs.

"Phoenix and Ailish's house. You'll be safe there, and Ailish can help you control the magic you've released so far." He stayed a few feet in front of her, trying to avoid her scent as much as possible. He went to the door behind the staircase that led to his garage. Waiting for Roxy to pass, he closed and locked it. Then he strode to his truck and opened the passenger door. The interior light showed him Roxy picking her way across the cement.

He could see in the dark and hadn't thought to turn on the light. It was cool and gloomy in here, and he saw her shiver as she got in. Her tank top, while sexy, was barely legal the way it hugged her breasts and had only spaghetti straps over her shoulders. It was no defense against the chill of the garage. She didn't have any other clothes, not even decent shoes.

He needed to take better care of her. Moving around the truck, he opened his door, got in, and slid the gun beneath his thigh. Then he reached behind the seats and grabbed a Windbreaker and tossed it across her legs. "Put this on."

"Thanks." She slipped into the blue Windbreaker and wrapped it around her.

Key opened the garage, started the truck, and backed out. He waited until the door was completely closed before he gunned the engine and took off.

His phone rang. Key pulled it out and looked.

Tyler's phone.

He pushed the button and answered it through the Bluetooth installed in his truck. He said one short word: "Where?"

"Inland Storage in one hour. If you're one minute late, I'll kill the woman in front of the kid. We have people watching, don't try anything, DeMicca."

Key looked over at Roxy and mouthed, "Mack?" He was almost positive but she'd know his voice better.

She nodded, her face pale and tight.

Was Liam there? A flash fire of old rage and anger threatened to erupt, but he ruthlessly suppressed the emotions. "Why do you think I give a rat's ass what you do?"

"Because you saved the kid. I was there, DeMicca, I saw it. And this is just the beginning. Bring me Roxy or I'll kill both of them and move on to your friends."

Those words released more memories of being beaten and tortured. But this wasn't about him, it was about saving the kid. "I'll be there in an hour with Roxy. You can have her as long as Tyler and his mom are alive." He cut the call before he told the dickhead the gory details of how he was going to die.

"I can't believe I almost had sex with him. I trusted him. After a year of no dating, no sex, I..." she trailed off, running her hand over her face.

Key tightened his fingers on the steering wheel. Another reason to kill the man. Bile-tasting acid made his chest burn. He didn't like the thought of Mack touching Roxy.

Or any other man.

Getting control of himself, he asked, "You what?"

"I was lonely, empty, and I guess I thought sex would help. I should have known better. And now, it's my fault. I got Joel killed; you told me a mortal bodyguard was a bad idea, but I didn't listen. They must have done that memory-shifting thing on him." She dropped her hands. "After they kidnapped me, Joel was really confused. At the underground garage, he got out of the SUV, looked around, and said, 'This isn't the airport.' Liam laughed and said, 'It's your last stop' and cut his throat. All that blood, poor Joel's shocked face." She folded her arms across her stomach and leaned forward. Guilt hunched her shoulders. Her scent soured with self-recrimination and queasiness.

He reached out and put his hand on Roxy's hunched shoulder. "Are you going to be sick?"

She lifted her head and looked at him. "No. Just stop him, Kieran. Please. Don't let him hurt Tyler or his mom to get me." Her green eyes were fierce, yet damp with unshed tears. "I'll go with you. That way Mack can see me, you can even give me to him to get Tyler out. Then come back for me."

Her utter sincerity echoed through his head. His blood boiled at the thought, and he smelled singed skin, followed a second later by a searing on his chest where the dragon's mouth was. The creature was as outraged as he was. "No." He realized he'd roared that out when she cringed back. He rubbed her shoulder, feeling the icy tension in her muscles. "I won't risk you. But believe me, we're going to get the kid and his mom out."

Nodding, she leaned back.

Moving his fingers from her shoulder, he took hold of her hand. The skin-to-skin contact eased back his bloodlust and helped him stay in control. It settled the dragon down as well. In control again, he called Phoenix and filled in the other hunter about the phone call from Mack.

Roxy worried that she should have insisted on going along with Kieran to help divert Mack's attention.

"They'll be fine, Roxy," Ailish said. "Phoenix is immortal, and he has wings. He's going to fly over and scope it out first. They have other hunters meeting them there."

She was still trying to get used to Ailish's eyes. They were a strangely compelling silvery blue and bracketed by a fine webbing of scars. The rest of her face was lean and strong, just like her body. Being blind, she didn't meet Roxy's gaze, and it was slightly disconcerting. "I can't help but worry. It's me Mack wants."

Ailish moved around the big kitchen, pouring out glasses of iced tea with ease. "We'll get to work, and you won't have time to worry." She slid a glass across the granite counter to where Roxy sat on a tall bar stool.

Out of nowhere a voice said, "Ailish, it's Darcy. I'm at the front door."

"Do you have an intercom?" Roxy asked.

"She's using magic." Ailish headed around the counter and out toward the living room. Over her shoulder, she added, "I can't see the camera views on the house, so she's letting me know she's here."

Roxy heard the door open, followed by the two witches talking. Her nerves pulled tighter. *Darcy MacAlister.* She was the soul mirror of Axel Locke and very powerful. She and Axel were the first two to bond their souls, discover that it broke the curse for them, and gain immortality. She turned, feeling self-conscious in her borrowed clothes. She thought about her mother, how much Gwen resented the soul-mirror witches because they'd found a way to reach their high magic, and Gwen hadn't. What did they think of Gwen, whom they knew only as Silver? As soon as Tyler was safe, she would tell them all who her mother was. She didn't even want to think about the possibility of Gwen being involved in Key's creation. She'd ask her when she got a phone and a little privacy.

Both witches walked back in, Ailish first, her dark hair a contrast to the sleek mahogany with red highlights of Darcy's hair. Both witches glowed with their witch-shimmer, making them appear unearthly.

She wished she'd seen the picture Kieran drew of her—had he caught her witch-shimmer? She glanced down at her hands, but her skin looked just milky white to her.

"Hi, Roxy, I'm Darcy."

She jerked her head up and planted a smile on her face. Roxy knew how to deal with people; it was her job. She needed to stop doubting herself. Sliding off the bar stool, she stood up straight, shoulders back, and held out her hand. "Nice to meet you, Darcy. I met your..." She couldn't think of what to call him. Mate? Soul mirror? "...uh, Axel last night."

Darcy's face lit up as she took Roxy's hand. "Mate is fine." She let go and held up a large bag with handles.

"I brought some clothes. Axel said we're close to the same size. I'm a little taller, and you're definitely bigger in the bust." She grinned again, then said, "There is some new underwear and a bra. Axel showed me his memory of you and I guessed thirty-six C."

She took the bag, feeling the weight. "Thank you. I don't have my purse or—"

Darcy shook her head, reached out and touched her arm. "Key took care of it, don't worry. You've been through a terrible ordeal, and we want to help you. Make you feel safe."

"And," Ailish added, "you may be able to save Key. He's been getting closer and closer to the edge, doing what Phoenix calls his frenzied drawing. Phoenix is worried that Key's going to encounter witch blood and not be able to control himself. If he went rogue, that would tear Phoenix apart."

"I won't let that happen." If he hadn't stopped to draw her, they'd already have sealed their bond before he got the text message showing Tyler and his mom kidnapped. Sealing their bond was imperative to saving his soul. He'd done so much for her, she was going to do this for him. Just the memory of the way Kieran made her feel, so strong and sexy, warmed her.

"Good," Darcy said. "Let's get started on seeing how much of your power and control you have, unless you'd like to change first?"

She did feel a bit grubby in her clothes, but she said, "Work first, then I'll change."

Both witches nodded approvingly. Using her magic, Darcy waved her hand and pushed the tables and chairs back, clearing an area. Then she reached into her purse and pulled out four candles. "These are to help you focus on your chakras."

She set them at the four cardinal points. "Red is for earth, symbolizing the first chakra at the base of your spine."

Roxy felt a tug above her tailbone.

"Orange for water in your pelvis. Yellow for fire, your third chakra in the area of your solar plexus."

She felt two more tugs, each one getting weaker as they moved up.

"And green for air, the fourth chakra behind your heart." Darcy stood and said, "Come sit in the center, Roxy."

She took off Key's jacket, set it down, walked to the middle, and sank down on the cool tile floor. Immediately, a bubble of energy fizzed around the base of her spine. "I feel my first chakra."

Darcy crouched in front of her, on the other side of the red candle. "That's because you're close to the earth. Focus on this red candle and try to direct the energy you feel to light it."

Roxy stared, seeing the long, tapered shape, the white wick standing proud. The first eleven years of her life, she'd seen her mother and her friends do magic. She'd felt it moving around her, the magical energy as natural as breathing.

"Funnel the magic up, directing it through your hands."

Darcy's voice was becoming more distant as she concentrated, mentally calling the energy swirling at the base of her spine up and through her hand. She lifted her right hand to aim at the candle. A buzzing sensation rose through her. It seemed to stall and sputter. She pushed harder, willing her magic to work.

Roxy didn't want to fail in front of these witches.

She redoubled her efforts. Harder, deeper, she concentrated until she heard a pop, then a sizzle, and the next thing she knew a flame flew out of her hand, missed the candle and—

Darcy dove to her right, leaping out of the way as the flame turned into a missile.

"Shit!" Roxy exclaimed, throwing up both hands. "Come back!"

The flame slammed into one of the dining room chairs and exploded into a raging fire.

Roxy leaped to her feet. "Oh God! I'm sorry!"

The piercing shriek of multiple smoke alarms blared through the house.

Ailish ran past her, held out her hands and doused the fire with water. The thick smell of smoke made it hard to breathe, soot burned her eyes, and the shrieking of the alarm threatened to make her brain bleed.

Darcy rose to her feet, waved her hands and the shrieking stopped.

Roxy moved to stand by Darcy and Ailish. She turned to the blind witch standing next to her. "I set your chair on fire."

Darcy looked over. "And scorched the wall and floor."

She was so horribly embarrassed she couldn't think what to say. She just kept seeing the streak of flames hit the chair before it exploded into bright oranges and yellows. "Kieran said my witch-shimmer has the fiery glow of sunset. Maybe a little too fiery?"

Darcy snorted and then started to laugh. "Did you see the flame erupt from her?"

Ailish said, "Hello, blind here? But I felt the energy and heard the chair explode!" She started to laugh, too.

Roxy stared at the two of them laughing. "But the chair is ruined. And your wall..." There was a huge plume of black staining the paint. "I really wanted to impress you both. I've heard so much about you. Instead, I practically set your house on fire."

Darcy grabbed on to the back of another chair, laughing so hard she couldn't catch her breath.

The whole absurdity of the situation hit Roxy and

she broke into laughter. She sank to the floor, tears running down her face, unable to stop laughing. "It's not that funny," she wheezed.

"It is!" Darcy said. "I couldn't believe it when I saw the flames erupt from your hand."

"I almost hit you!" Then she remembered the shock on Darcy's face, and the way she leaped to the right. "You jumped like a frog." The fits of giggles started again.

"Damn, wish I'd seen that," Ailish said.

They sat together and laughed until finally, Roxy pulled herself together. "I'm sorry, seriously. Darcy, you could have been hurt. And Ailish, I'll pay to fix everything."

"I got it," Darcy said, sitting up and focusing on the chair.

Roxy watched as the gold lights floated in Darcy's brown gaze, her golden shimmer brightened on her skin, and she held out her hands. She could feel magic rise, the energy creating an answering swirl in her first four chakras. As she watched, the chair repaired itself, the blackened wall returned to the light brown, and the acrid smell of smoke damage vanished. The swirling energy rushing along her spine calmed as Darcy lowered her arms. "Amazing."

Darcy turned to her and put an arm around Roxy's shoulders as if they'd been friends for years. "I was never in any danger, Roxy. I chose to jump out of the way, but I could have doused that flame in water. I didn't because I wanted to see what you could do. You have power. You just need a little more control."

There was such easy acceptance with these two witches. "I'll practice."

"We'll practice together," Ailish said. "Darcy and I aren't going to let you get hurt by a magic accident. No need to hold back, Roxy. We're here; we can counter anything you do by mistake." Ailish was sitting facing them. "Including trying to burn my house down."

It was such a relief. She felt better after laughing like an idiot. It had released the horrible knot sitting below her rib cage ever since being kidnapped and taken to Liam. "Thank you."

"You're welcome." Darcy dropped her arm, but stayed next to her. "Let's try again. This time, I want you to consciously open as many chakras as you can, then control the energy to light the orange candle."

She closed her eyes and concentrated, picturing the red sphere of energy, and felt her first chakra pop. "One."

"Keep going," Ailish encouraged.

She mentally moved up her spine and pictured orange. She had to work harden but that one finally burst open. She kept going, finding it a struggle to open three chakras, and by then her schema was growing hungry, the pain piercing.

She couldn't force her fourth chakra open, so she began working on control.

≥ 11 ≤

KEY DROVE, WHILE PHOENIX FLEW on ahead with Axel. The location of the storage yard was just up the street from the Rogue Cadre stronghold.

"What do you see?" Key asked into his Bluetooth, tense with leftover sexual arousal, bloodlust, and the need to kill Liam.

This might be his chance.

Except, why would Liam demand Roxy and not the Dragon Tear? That kept nagging at the edge of his brain, but he needed to stay focused on what he was doing. Liam was dangerous. Too fast even for a rogue.

Phoenix answered, "Three rows of storage garages—the middle one is double-sided—and an office trailer with a chain-link fence surrounding it all. The gate is open, and there are two black SUVs parked at the trailer. Don't see anyone inside, but hard to be sure."

"I'm circling," Axel said. "Don't see anyone on the roofs, but rogues could be hiding beneath the overhangs of the roof in the shadows, under or in the cars, and that trailer is big enough to hold fifteen men."

"No sign of the kid or his mother?" They needed to know where they were to protect them.

"Not so far," Axel said.

Another voice broke in. "I've enlarged the picture text and enhanced the quality," Sutton said, working from the warehouse. "Both of them are lying on a cement floor. If they haven't moved them, they must be in one of the storage units."

Key pulled up two blocks from the strip mall where all the Wing Slayer Hunters were gathering to plan their strategy. The storage unit was two blocks away. He switched to his headset, then quietly slid out of the truck and strode around to the back alley that boasted broken asphalt, trash and a rusted Dumpster that did little to shield the three big witch hunters. The first was Ram Virtos, one of the original five Wing Slayer Hunters. He was ex-military, had a thunderbird tattoo, and lived by the code of duty and discipline. Linc Dillinger stood next to him and was the newest full Wing Slayer Hunter. He often wore designer clothes to match his excessive charm, but beneath that was a feral fighter. And the third was Eli Stone; he had the outline of a griffin tattoo on his back and was just waiting for his test. Once he passed, the hunters would have an Induction Ceremony, and if their god finished the tattoo, Eli would be a full member of the Wing Slayer Hunters. Sutton was doing their technical backup at the warehouse, while Axel and Phoenix were doing recon from the air.

Key strode up to the three waiting hunters. "Since Roxy's not here, the direct approach won't work. As soon as Mack and the rest see me without her, they'll know it's an attack."

Ram looked at his watch. "Fourteen minutes to his deadline." Lifting his steel blue gaze, he said, "If Sutton's right, we have enough time to spread out and locate the victims."

"Everyone goes invisible," Key added. "We can't tip our hand."

Ram said, "They'll be safer if we leave them in the unit, with one hunter protecting it until we neutralize the threat."

"Unless they have someone in the unit with them," Linc pointed out in his velvet-smooth voice. "It's what I would do."

"Shit," Key muttered. Linc was a high-stakes gambler and obviously damned successful at it judging by his house in Vegas. Not to mention that he drove a cherry Viper and had a Rolex for each day of the week. All the highlights in his casually tousled hair weren't from the hand of nature either. Glancing at Linc again, he noticed that he'd dressed down, black fatigue pants and T-shirt.

"Good point." Ram began ticking off a new plan. "Simultaneous attacks. Locate the victims. Assess the target, how many and where, then we launch attack and rescue at the same time. Two hunters on the vics, rest on the target." He looked at the three hunters standing around him. "We have to assume rogues are here, maybe even Quinn Young and his Immortal Death Dagger."

The only antidote for that dagger burned into the leader of the rogues' arm was the blood of a bonded soul mirror. "The Rogue Cadre is just down the road. It's also possible the mini-Death Daggers might be around," Key pointed out. So far, they knew only about the mini-Death Daggers that protected the headquarters. Young grew them on his body; they had a very limited range and had to be recharged somehow. Sinister as hell.

"We've been looking from the air," Phoenix said through their headsets. "Haven't seen any yet."

Eli said, "I'll take the vics." His light green eyes blazed against the darker skin.

Since Eli hadn't yet passed his test to become a full Wing Slayer Hunter, Key was uneasy leaving the lives of Tyler and his mom in his hands. "Who else?"

"I'll back him up from the air," Axel said as he landed in the middle of the alley.

Key looked over. Axel's brown and gold eagle wings were spread wide, a span of at least twelve feet, before he folded them behind him.

Phoenix touched down next, his bright blue and purple phoenix wings a startling contrast to the man himself.

"Thirteen minutes," Ram said. "Find the vics, then assess the targets. We'll divide the units into four rows. Linc, you take the first row, Eli the second, Axel the third, I'll take the fourth. Key, you work with Phoenix to assess the trailer and the perimeter. Any questions?"

Everyone deferred to Ram's military experience. When no one had questions, Key said to Phoenix, "I'll take the trailer and SUVs, you check the perimeter."

Phoenix nodded, and they all used their ability to bend light and shield themselves to appear invisible.

"Just over twelve minutes until the stated deadline, go."

Key turned and ran, covering the two blocks in less than a minute. He would approach from the ground and Phoenix from the air. They'd worked together for so long, they both knew their roles. Getting to the storage unit, Key slowed and moved as lightly as he could. The road was asphalt, making it easier to cover his tracks, but rogues also had enhanced hearing. He passed the two SUVs. Both had blackout windows. He edged along the front of the vehicles and didn't see anyone inside. He dropped to the ground and looked beneath the vehicle; nothing. He didn't hear any sound either, so he cleared the SUVs and moved on to the trailer. It was a standard office trailer, approximately thirty-two by ten feet, and set with the back close to the chain-link fence and the front looking toward the parking lot and the storage units.

Key heard several voices and movement inside. He prowled around the back, sliding between the fence and the trailer to look through the first window. Two big men were sitting on folding chairs, their soft faces and hairless arms contrasting sharply with their super-bulked muscles. They were rogue, and they each held knives. A middle-aged, frightened woman sat on another chair. Key assumed she was the employee or owner. He slid up to the other window.

Mack stood across from him by the first door, watching the parking lot through a window in the upper half of the door with a gun hanging from his right hand. There was another rogue in there with him.

Key moved out and went to the rows of garages. Standing in a shadow he took out his phone and texted that there were two rogues and a civilian in the back, Mack and a rogue in the front of the trailer.

Phoenix texted back that he'd found an SUV with at least four more rogues a half mile up the street under a tree, undetectable from the air.

"Noise in unit twenty-three," Eli texted. "Muffled breathing and moans."

Adrenaline spike in Key at Eli's report—that must be Tyler and his mom.

"My row is clear, moving to twenty-three," Axel responded.

"Clear," Linc messaged.

"Clear," Ram added.

"I'm behind the row of units closest to the trailer," Key texted.

"Linc, meet me there," Ram instructed.

"I'm here," Phoenix sent his message.

Key felt the presence as the other three hunters joined him.

"Six minutes," Ram spoke aloud, so quiet Key had to strain to hear. "Key, you go in the front. Linc you're in the back. Phoenix, go cut off that truck, and I'll back you up. Axel, can you get in the air, stick close to Eli until one of us calls for backup?"

"Yes."

"Go," Ram said.

Key slipped his knife from his holster and took off running. When he got to the steps, he leaped over them, landed and jerked the door open.

In his peripheral vision he saw the door on his left slam open and knew that was Linc. He focused on his job. Mack stumbled, then lifted the gun.

Key seized his wrist and squeezed. The bones crunched and Mack screamed, dropping to his knees, and the gun fell to the floor. Hearing movement, Key shoved Mack aside just as the other rogue jumped up and lunged.

Key pivoted into a full roundhouse and slammed his boot into the rogue's ear, throwing him five feet into the wall.

The crash rocked the trailer. Key heard and felt the fight from the other end. He ran after the rogue and shoved his knife into his heart. Then he twisted, making damned sure to shred it and send the bastard to his eternity as a shade.

"Where's Roxy?" Mack said in a thin, panting voice behind him.

Key pulled his knife free, then swung around and saw Mack had picked up the gun. This man had tricked Roxy to get a picture of her schema, then abducted her and handed her over to Liam. Icy hot rage gathered in his chest. "Where are Tyler and his mom?"

Mack was on his knees; his face was sweaty pale,

his right hand hung useless. But he managed to level the gun with his left. "Give me Roxy."

"Not a fucking chance."

He pointed the muzzle at Key's knee and fired.

Key sprang up, over the path of the bullet, crashed into Mack and landed on top of him. Before Mack could breathe, he caught his shattered right wrist and squeezed. "Where are they, dickhead?" He increased the pressure more and more.

"Twenty-three!" he screamed.

Key buried his knife in his chest, stopping his heart before he'd finished his scream.

Mack's eyes widened, then the life drained out. Key usually didn't kill humans. Too easy. Too much like his father beating on him. But Mack had signed his own death warrant by taking Roxy to Liam.

Getting up, he yanked out his phone and texted, "Targets dead, vics in twenty-three. Status?" Then he went to the connecting door to the back office. It was quiet but for a woman's sobbing. He opened the door.

Two rogues lay dead on the floor, and Linc had his arm around the woman. "I'll text it in," he said, and typed out "Linc's targets dead, civilian safe."

Ram texted, "Four rogues in SUV dead."

Key looked down. Nothing from Eli. Shit. He turned, burst out the door, leaped down the steps and hauled ass to unit twenty-three. In a second, Key took in the scene. The lock on the door was in pieces on the ground; the door was up. Three dead rogues littered the front. In the dark interior, more folding chairs were scattered, one more dead rogue and Tyler and his mom tied up, tape on their mouths, both of them staring at Axel leaning over Eli. There was a knife in the unconscious hunter's back.

"Think it nicked the heart," Axel said. "He's losing too much blood!"

Key ripped off his shirt, dropped to his knee, and

pressed it around the knife. "Want me to get my truck?"

Axel shook his head. "Sutton's bringing Carla here. We just have to keep him alive." He lifted his gaze to Key. "Eli forced the door. The rogues inside rushed him and the fourth went for the woman with his knife. Eli threw himself between them, saved her."

Key knew Axel had killed the ones out front. He eyed the man he hadn't been sure of. Axel had ripped his shirt away from the wound, revealing the outline of the griffin Key had inked on Eli's back. There was a long cut from the blade sliding across his skin, before the rogue had pushed it in. Returning his gaze to his hawk, he knew. "His test?"

"Yes. Saving a woman and a kid."

Key put his hand on the man's shoulder, "Hold on, Eli. Carla will be here." That's why Sutton had stayed back in the warehouse and kept Carla with him, so he could fly her here faster to help with life-threatening wounds.

The unit filled up as Ram and Phoenix came in. "Ah fuck," Phoenix snarled when he saw Eli.

Ram crouched next to Key, his silence heavy.

"Sutton's here," Axel said. "Move."

Key went to Tyler, while Phoenix went to Paige. Key ripped the tape off the boy's mouth. "You're safe now, kid."

Tyler stared up at Key. "He was going to kill my mom."

"I know. Phoenix has your mom, see? She's safe."

The boy turned as Phoenix remove the tape from Paige's mouth, then cut the ropes with his knife.

"I'm going to cut your ropes, and then you can go to her. Hold still." He slid his knife in and sliced the rope on his arms; then he freed the boy's legs.

Sutton ran in, still carrying Carla. His wings were out, but folded to allow him to get into the unit.

Tyler's eyes widened.

Sutton set Carla on her feet, and she dropped down next to Eli, across from Axel. "Sutton, I need your blood. Axel, your knife."

Without question, he handed her his knife. Carla sliced her palm and gave it back. "Ram, hold him down. Axel, on three, pull out the blade."

Axel sheathed his knife, then grabbed the hilt of the blade in Eli's back.

Sutton knelt behind Carla, sliced his palm, and waited.

Carla said, "One, two, three."

Axel pulled the knife free with a wet pop. Carla pressed her hand down on the wound. Sutton put his next to hers. Then she began to chant, her witch-shimmer brightening.

"What are they doing?"

He looked at Tyler's too-white face. "Healing him. Carla's a doctor." Of psychology, and she was using witchcraft, not medicine, to heal Eli, but Tyler was in shock and terrified. The simplest answer was best.

Paige put her arms around Tyler. "Thank you. That man there, he saved my life. Probably Tyler's—" She choked and started to cry.

Phoenix wrapped his arm around her shoulder. "Paige, I'm sorry, but I swear this won't happen again. We'll keep you safe."

"Mom, don't cry. Key and Phoenix are superheroes. Like Dyfyr." Tyler pressed himself into his mom's side.

Key was so furious that he'd let this happen, he opened his mouth to tell the kid that wasn't true.

Phoenix cut him off by saying, "You got it, dude." He eyed Key over their heads.

Key got the message; the boy needed a superhero.

"He's awake," Axel said. "Carla, thank you."

Eli sat up. "I felt that knife go deep, I can't believe

I'm alive." He reached over and grasped Carla's hand. "Thank you. I felt your magic pulling me back."

She smiled, looking a little wan, but relieved.

Sutton sat back, and pulled her onto his lap. "Sit here until the pain is gone, Carly."

Key watched the way Sutton cradled her, the look of pride in her on his face, the way he kept touching her, drawing off the pain of healing Eli. Carla's witch-shimmer was losing the ragged edge of red pain, and she relaxed against him. What was it like to be soul-deep partners like that? For a second, he thought of Roxy...

Then he remembered holding Vivian's body as she died, and cold dread spread in him. Love like that was too fragile, too unreliable, or maybe it just wasn't real at all. *You want to go to the hockey game with me, son?* The voice was so real in his memory.

Key had been six, and playing in front of the house. He should have known better, but there'd been something in him that craved his father's love. Approval. Attention. Maybe even being hurt was better than being ignored. He'd said yes. Followed his dad out, gotten into his truck, and then his dad got in and locked the doors. He brought out a pair of pliers and broke every bone in his hand. One by one. Key had vomited all over his dad, but he hadn't screamed, hadn't cried. Even that young, he knew his father was hurting him to try to force his mother to turn over the Dragon Tear. In frustration, his dad had laid on the horn to get his mother's attention.

Beth had run out, seen what had happened. Even now, Key remembered her tortured face. She'd gotten the jack out of the car and had broken the window. She'd taken Key away from his dad and the magic in the Tear helped heal his hand. She'd cried, "You're destroying me, Key! Don't you know to run from your father? If you could just figure out how to wake the dragon."

He hadn't been able to grasp how he was destroying her. But now, yeah, he got that she had wanted Dyfyr to wake up and grant her immortality for returning his Tear. Then the Tear would be gone and his father wouldn't have any reason to stay around. His mother obviously hadn't known what would wake Dyfyr; she was operating on flawed information and a lot of delusion. Much like a compulsive gambler has just enough small wins to believe in the big jackpot, his mother had seen enough small wins, like finding the Tear and seeing the magic in it, that she absolutely believed she'd achieve the big win of immortality. She couldn't give up or that would mean that she had put her son in a position to be hurt, over and over, for no reason. *You're destroying me, Key*. It echoed in his head, those words defining him... He jerked himself out of his memories and met Sutton's icy gaze. Watching him. Key forced himself to relax.

Sutton broke eye contact and took out his BlackBerry, pushing Carla's long blond hair out of his way so he could see over her shoulder. "Going to clear the phones. I blocked all but our internal transmission...oh hell."

"Now what?" Axel said.

Sutton turned his blue eyes on Key. "Your loft alarm was tripped about fifteen minutes ago."

"Liam." He was sure of it. Shit! This whole thing was a diversion. "He's going after the Tear." And Key wasn't there to kill his brother.

Axel leaped to his feet. "Is the Tear there?"

"No." Key rose, too. "I'm going, see if I can catch him." He took a few steps and turned back. "Roxy is—"

Sutton shifted Carla and rose. "At Phoenix's house. Carly and I will go there now. Your witch will be safe."

Phoenix said, "I'm going to fly ahead of you, Key, scope it out."

Key nodded and took off running for his truck, thankful that he'd done one thing right and hadn't left Roxy at his house.

⚜

The smell of the blood made his veins throb with fiery need. On the floor of his loft was the body of a slaughtered witch. Her blond hair was dark and sticky with blood, her clothes stripped off and her thighs spread open to reveal the schema. This witch had only the left half of a fertility goddess and it blazed with the gold and blue colors.

Next to her on the wood floor was written in blood, "Give me the Tear, or I'll kill everyone you care about."

Key shuddered, fighting the craving for witch blood. It was scraping his veins raw. He looked down at his arms and saw his veins bulging, darkening to almost black. As he watched, they expanded, thickened, throbbed with hunger. Need.

Witch blood. Not this dead shit lying on his floor, but living blood, warm and potent. He could plunge his knife into Roxy's arteries, letting the blood spray over him.

Then he could use it to draw—draw her death, draw—

Something slammed into him. Key flew back, the granite counter banging into his kidneys. He heard the stone crack. Or his back did. Furious, he got his feet under him and looked around.

Axel stood by the dead witch, his arms crossed, his eyes sober.

Phoenix stood directly between him and the witch, blocking his view. The hunter's hands were down at his side, but his naked arms and chest bulged. "Get out of here. You're losing control."

Key damn near pulled his knife and buried it in

Phoenix's chest when he caught himself. The bloodlust was short-circuiting his brain. He'd walked right into the witch's blood and had been staring down at her when Phoenix shoved him back. Liam knew this would make Key crazy. "Do you see what my brother did? He tore my loft apart looking for that Tear and murdered a witch right here!" The fury piled on his bloodlust and he stalked up to Phoenix, shoved him aside and went into his bedroom. He yanked the handmade quilt off his bed and stormed back into the living area. "That wasn't enough, though. He had to humiliate her. Spreading her legs open like a whore, just so we'd see the mark inside her thigh." He snapped the quilt out and covered her. His blood burned like a blowtorch. He was losing control. His hands shook with the need to draw or kill. He jerked his gaze around his apartment, the torn-apart furniture, the broken pottery, the—

His sketchbook. It had been thrown into a corner, still closed. Leaning down he picked it up and opened it. He saw the picture of Roxy sitting on the couch, her face wistful as she talked about the dragon legend.

His heart rate calmed. The dragon shifted as if trying to touch her.

He felt Phoenix standing over his shoulder, looking.

Key turned, took a step back, shielding the book, and flipped the page. There she was half-nude, leaning back against his couch, covered in her sunset witch-shimmer...

His. In those moments, she had given herself so completely, trusting him to show her the beauty of her sexuality and magic.

Phoenix moved to see.

He slapped the picture against his chest, lifted his head. "No." No one would ever see this but Roxy and him. Sliding the book up, he sniffed.

Very faint scent of copper. Liam hadn't looked; he'd just tossed it out of the way. Stupid fucker hadn't even seen the biggest treasure in the loft. This picture of Roxy.

"Hold it together, Key," Phoenix said.

"I am." He met his friend's gaze. "This is Roxy as only I will ever see her."

His dark eyes softened. "I hear that. Close the book. I won't look, and neither will Axel."

That was one thing Key could believe in. He eased the book back and closed it. "Liam is getting desperate and he wanted to leave me his little message." His gaze went to the witch again. He felt the dragon undulate in aggravation, while dread weighed down his gut. "There's more to this than just pissing me off or trying to get me to turn. Liam told Roxy he's blood-born. He'd suffered a fatal heart strike, yet he's not dead. What kept him alive? Where was he all these years?"

Axel walked up to him, both he and Phoenix cutting off his view of the dead witch beneath the quilt. "Something to do with the fertility witch blood?"

The dragon shifted again and the cold rage tried to pull Key in. He was so near the edge, he could barely think. "He's doing something with that witch blood. He had a group of mortals searching for and disabling witches, then bringing them to him. Blood-born..." The dread in him swelled. "Could enough fertility witch blood heal a heart? And now he's taken so much he thinks he can track the Tear? Dyfyr created fertility witches..."

Axel's face hardened. "You might want to think about moving the Tear from the club in case he is tracking it somehow."

Key agreed, but said, "You, Phoenix and Sutton are immortal; I don't want you touching the Tear. You're not a god like Wing Slayer, just immortal from his magic. Even unbroken, that Tear might do serious damage to you."

Axel nodded. "Key, gather up what you need here and get out. Stay somewhere else tonight. I'll take care of the witch and have the place cleaned up. We'll meet later at Phoenix's place." Axel took a breath and added, "Then you and Roxy need to wake the dragon. Find out how to get rid of this Tear."

His fingers tightened on the sketchbook as he thought of the picture he'd drawn of her and thought of the one time he'd tried to reach for love and happiness with a woman.

Then he'd destroyed her.

How the hell could he keep from destroying Roxy?

≫ *12* ≪

KEY AND PHOENIX WALKED INTO the house through the garage and found Dee, the housekeeper, driver for Ailish, and all-around friend bustling around the kitchen.

"Dee, hey, what's cooking? Smells good," Phoenix said.

"Barbecue beef sandwiches and potato salad," Dee answered. "There's beer in the fridge." She glanced at them. "Key, you look like you could use a keg."

"Hi, Dee," Key said, struggling to keep himself contained. With his overnight bag in his hand, he said to Phoenix, "Going down to shower in your gym." He had to wash off the scent of that witch blood. Wash off his brother. Clear his head before he saw Roxy.

Get control of himself before he smelled her blood.

Phoenix's house was a trilevel, and Key was currently on the main floor. He walked through the kitchen, past the dining room. There were two sets of stairs across from a sunken living room. He heard soft footsteps and looked up to see Roxy coming down from the media room.

She'd changed into jeans that hugged her thighs and ass, and then pooled around her slim ankles. Her shirt was grass green and cut low enough to show her generous cleavage. She had her hair twisted up on her head in a casual knot, long strands spilling out like rays of fiery sunshine. On her face, bare arms and upper chest, he could see the subtle glow of her sunset-colored witch-shimmer. She stopped on the last step. "Kieran, are you okay?"

His groin filled with liquid heat. Yet he could smell remnants of her magic clinging to her, and it fired his bloodlust to raging. The dual hungers broke him out in a sweat and buzzed in his ears. "Your magic, I can see it in your shimmer."

She flushed. "Three chakras. Darcy, Ailish and Carla have all helped me." She took a deep breath and added, "I heard about the fertility witch in your loft."

He saw that dead witch again in his head. Smelled her blood. His mind was fracturing with various images. That could have been Roxy. If he hadn't gotten there in time to save her from Liam in the parking garage, she'd be dead. Another part of his mind thought about her blood, how good it would feel, how the warm power in her blood would cool the burn of the curse.

"Kieran?" She reached for him.

"Don't touch me. Bloodlust. Don't." It was more than bloodlust; he was slipping into that empty, cold place that knew only violence and vengeance. A gray world where blood was the only color. Angry, hot, violent, spewing blood.

Sutton came down the stairs, squeezed Roxy's shoulder and said, "It's okay. Just give him a little time." Then he said to Key, "Let's go."

Key didn't look back, didn't dare. He knew Sutton had heard every word and recognized how close to the edge Key was. By the time Key got down into the gym, Sutton had stripped down to his pants. The man was six foot three, and at least two-twenty, maybe more since bonding to Carla. His bald head gleamed under the lights, the small eagle earring in his ear twinkled, and pure power rolled off the man himself.

Key dropped the bag, ripped off his boots and socks, jerked off his shirt, unsheathed his knife, and laid it next to the bag, then he went to the mat. He circled Sutton, taking in the eagle tat on his back, and the scars from when he'd forced out his wings to save his mate. Normally, wings were a flawless magic, the tattoo disappearing when the wings sprang out. Then when they vanished, the tattoo reappeared.

But Carla hadn't been Sutton's soul mirror, not then, not until his deep love for the witch turned them into soul mirrors.

Sutton whirled around and slammed his fist into Key's jaw, throwing him six feet back onto his ass.

It was on.

Key popped up, went low and caught Sutton with a knee strike that dropped him to the mat. Key spun into a kick for his head.

Sutton caught his leg and flipped him up so he landed on his back. Before Key blinked, the man straddled him.

Key swung his fist, aiming for under the jaw.

Sutton caught it and squeezed. "That dragon is fucking dangerous, Key. You and I both know it. Phoenix loves you like a brother, and he can't see it. But I can and so can you."

"So?"

Sutton squeezed and Key heard the first bone break in his hand. The swirling cold pulled him deeper inside himself. He didn't blink.

"You didn't feel that, did you?"

"Felt it, and don't give a shit. Break another bone, asshole."

Sutton squeezed.

Another bone shattered.

He was starting to see red at the edges of his vision. *Never cry, never scream, don't even groan. Ever.* "There are twenty-seven bones in my hand, my man. We could be here awhile, you have twenty-five more to go."

Sutton's expression was horrified. "Who tortured you, Key?"

How did he know? That was his last full thought before the rage blew the red spots all over the gray fog. He looked at the other hunter's face and all he saw was his father. Something in him broke loose. He caught Sutton's ankle between his knees, ancient strength filling him as he threw the man down. Leaping to his feet, he fought with brutal punches, vicious kicks until a pure, sweet voice, said, "Kieran, stop!"

He froze, panic turning his slow and killing heartbeat into a fast hammering. Whipping his head around he saw that, though everything else was grayed out except the blood, *she* was in perfect color. His treasure. Her face was so pale, the scattering of freckles stood out like blood.

"Your hands, Kieran," she said, walking toward him.

Through the fog, he saw that there were more people in the gym. He knew them all; Carla, Darcy, Ailish, Phoenix. And his goddess, his treasure. Their treasure.

"Roxy," Carla said in her calm, easygoing voice. "The dragon is partially awake, tell him to go back to sleep."

"But his hands!" Roxy said, her tone pitched to frantic worry.

He knew his hand was broken. So what? He'd heard the bones pop. He tried to look directly at Roxy, but it was hard. It hurt. Reminded him that she'd left him. Went away to a place he couldn't go. Hurt. God, it just hurt. So he looked at Sutton.

Lots of blood on him.

Didn't want to look at him either. So he looked down.

At his hands.

Claws? They were the color of fingernails, but at least two inches long, and curved. Was this what had everyone freaked? Of course a dragon had claws, didn't they know that? The gray swirled around him. He lifted the unbroken hand and looked. Yes, those were definitely claws. He extended his index finger, brought up his other arm and drew it across his forearm.

Watched blood well up. Very red. Red was good against the gray world.

"No!" Roxy yelled.

Her voice agitated him. Reminding him. Hurt. He turned to look at her. Hurt more. Sleep, sleep would be better but he couldn't stop looking at her. Looking past the red hair, green eyes, pretty skin to that soul he had missed for centuries.

Hurt. Sad.

She kept coming toward him. He wanted to hold her close, lift his wings and soar the skies with her in his arms. But his wings wouldn't lift or expand. He was trapped. She was part of his dreams, his memories. He hated the hurt, hated the hurt of Kieran, hated the hurt of all his witches, hated the hurt that assaulted him every time he partially woke.

His heart tried to beat for her, wanted to beat for her, but it was trapped in the magic of his grief.

"Dyfyr."

Her voice, it called him. Called the hurt. He looked at her from Kieran's chest, where he perched. Her witch-shimmer...it was exactly as he remembered. Then she touched him, her small hand pressed against his face. Her scent, her skin, her very essence made him sigh. Better.

"Go back to sleep, Dyfyr."

Yes, sleep. No more hurt when he slept. Just...dreams of flying with her in his arms. Dreams of taking his man form and making love to her. Dreams...

━━━※━━━

Roxy's first three chakras popped open, and the energy began funneling up. With her hand on Kieran's chest, against the face of the dragon, she said, "That's right, sleep, Dyfyr." There was a damp cold rising from both the man and the dragon.

Hurts.

She almost jumped as the word trembled in her head. Her chest began to ache, and shivering damp cold penetrated her fingers, swam up her arm, and searched out her bones, her muscles, right down to her cells. Gray filled her vision. And along with all that, Roxy felt a thread of old magic—a power that she recognized like her own mother, because it was Gwen's magic. She shivered but didn't let go. Instead, she soothed Dyfyr by saying, "It's okay."

"Carly, is she in danger?"

"I don't think so. Don't disturb her, just stand close."

Roxy heard them talking. Felt the men, Sutton and Phoenix, flank her shoulders. They were warm. But she was frozen with Dyfyr's pain and near certainty that her mother had done this, forced Dyfyr's soul into Kieran.

"Don't touch her," Carla warned. "The dragon won't like it."

The cold fog thickened and slowed. The brutal ache in the icy bones of her arm began to subside. "Sleep, Dyfyr. That's it," she said softly. She felt him sink back into his dreams. Her magic percolated, sending light-filled energy to the creature. As she felt the dragon relax and go back into his slumber, hot pain began seeping through the connection. She frowned, forgetting about her mother. Was she feeling Kieran's pain?

Key suddenly stepped back, severing the magical bond. It caused her powers to rush around, looking for him. She concentrated as the witches had shown her, calling her magic back to her first three chakras. Finally it calmed.

"Damn it, Roxy, I felt you trying to pull my pain away," Key snapped at her.

She looked up. Blue color warmed the churning gray in Kieran's eyes. "You're back."

"I wasn't gone." He tore his gaze from hers and lifted his hands. "Claws." Then he shifted his gaze to Sutton. "You shouldn't have broken my hand, it pissed off the dragon."

Roxy turned to the hunter on her left. He had four long, deep gouges down his chest. Carla hurried up to his side, settled her hand over the deepest one and began healing him. Her magic rippled in the air around them.

"You remember?" Sutton asked.

"Yes," he said, his voice tired. "The claws are new, though."

Roxy's nerves pulled tight. "Why did Dyfyr attack Sutton? It doesn't make sense. I thought you were friends?" She couldn't get a handle on what was happening. She'd connected so strongly with Dyfyr it rattled her. And then feeling the old thread of her mother's magic. She'd been around Gwen's magic all her life; it was as familiar as her mother's voice.

"Because Key didn't see me, did you?" Sutton said in a level voice. "Dyfyr wasn't attacking me."

Roxy jerked her thoughts back. "Then who? The dragon didn't want to be awake. He said it hurts to be awake. Was it the witch blood in your loft? According to the story of his lover, Dyfyr created fertility witches by gifting his lover with fertility. Did he wake when you smelled the blood?"

"That was part of it." Key went to the edge of the mat, picked up his knife. "But once Sutton pinned me and started breaking bones, all I saw was my father. And I wanted to kill him. Again."

"That's who tortured you, your father," Sutton said. "Okay, got it; the dragon's been protecting you. He rouses when he feels your old rage against your dad. But he's no threat to Roxy, which was all I cared about."

Key's shoulders tensed. "I won't let him hurt Roxy. I don't think he even wants to. I told you that."

Roxy was still caught up in the horror of Key's dad torturing him. He had experienced such violence that it was no wonder he didn't trust love. And yet he was so careful with her, so gentle. She stared at Kieran, his eyes cold and gray, remote. Shutting down. Protecting himself. Now she knew why, or at least part of it.

Key shifted, grabbed the overnight bag in his unbroken hand, and headed across the mat. Without looking back, he said, "I'm going to take a shower."

Roxy said, "Wait! Your hand! Maybe I can heal it." He didn't answer, just shut the door.

Shut her out.

That was so not happening. She started after him.

"Roxy." Phoenix put his hand on her shoulder.

She whipped around and stared at him.

"Key needs his space. You don't know him like—"

"You do? So what am I supposed to do, wait around until you say it's okay to go to him? Just leave him suffering and alone with a broken hand? Is that your plan? Because if so, it sucks!"

Phoenix's mouth fell open.

Roxy sucked in a breath. "Look, I know you're his friend, that you're like brothers, but right now, he

needs me. Maybe not forever, maybe that'll change—"
Tears burned her eyes, for herself and Kieran. Because
didn't it always change? She'd do something wrong, or
they'd find out what her mother had done, and they'd
all turn their backs on her. Like her father. Her
emotions were riding so close to the surface, she
couldn't sort them out. Kieran had seen something in
Roxy no one had ever seen before. He made her see
that it was okay to embrace her magic, that she was
strong enough to do it. He gave her permission to be
herself with no apologies. He gave so much to her but
wouldn't let her give to him. Wouldn't let her help
him. He closed himself off from others that way. "I
don't know if we'll be like you and Ailish, but right
now, he needs me. I can heal his hand, and I can save
his soul. So back off." She realized now that she had to
do that first. Seal their souls so he was free of the
bloodlust. She was shaking, and she was embarrassing
the hell out of herself. But she wasn't leaving Kieran
alone, she was going to help him just like he helped
her. She jerked her shoulder from Phoenix and walked
to the bathroom door, reached out and turned the
handle.

Locked.

"Damn it." She didn't dare look around. Were they
all staring at her? It'd be really dramatic if she kicked
in the door instead of standing there with her hand
wrapped around a locked knob. That'd give them all
something to talk about. Refusing to acknowledge
defeat, or let her frustrated tears fall, she gathered
herself and opened her chakras. The energy streamed
out.

She heard a click.

Roxy took a breath and turned the knob. She'd
done it! Going inside, she closed the door and turned
the lock.

The bathroom was fairly large and filled with steam

from the oversized glass shower on the right. Glancing left, she saw his knife lying on the double-sink vanity. Dropping her gaze, she spotted the trash can. He'd sliced off the claws and thrown them away. Turning to the shower, through the foggy glass, she saw him. He had his back to her, and water sluiced over his broad shoulders, ran in uneven trails down his muscular back, traveling lower to that sexy dip and then...

His butt. God, she wanted to squeeze his rounded, sculptured butt. Her skin grew hot, her clothes irritating her. She watched more water stream over his thighs to his calves.

Looking back up, she saw his left hand hung down, swollen and darkening with bruises. His drawing hand! What were the streaks of red? Looking up to the forearm, she saw the gash he'd sliced into his arm with the claw. It was still bleeding.

The memory of his pain got her moving. She yanked off her clothes. Pulling open the door, she stepped in.

Key had his right hand up, working shampoo into his hair. His shoulder and back moved with fluid muscles.

"I'm not going away," she said softly.

He kept scrubbing his hair with one hand. "I gathered that when you used your magic to unlock the door."

Roxy's heart thumped in her chest. "Give me your hand. I'm going to heal it. Or try anyway."

"It's fine. I'll heal in a few hours." He braced his good hand against the wall, bent over and stuck his head under the spray, washing off the suds.

She couldn't walk away from him. He'd been alone too long. Yes, he had friends, good friends. But he'd carried the burden of the Dragon Tear...she didn't even know how long. And his father, what had he done to Key? Her heart twisted in her chest. It had been bad enough that the dragon had found a way to help him. She scooted up close to him, pressed her body to his back, leaning over so that he held both their weight. Water bounced off him and spattered over her face.

"Roxy," he groaned the word.

The need in those words pulled out her magic. "I'm here, Kieran." She laid her hand over the bleeding gash.

Her magic burst from her chakras, flowing so fast, she wrapped her arm around his waist to keep from falling. With unerring accuracy, her magic raced to his blood, then back, then out again. Finally the wound closed up completely, but her magic felt fuller, stronger. Her schema pinged and throbbed, as if sparks of electricity danced there. "That was a rush."

"My blood. I only gave you one or two drops before on your schema. This was more, this fed your magic."

"Then I'll have enough to heal your hand." She skimmed her palm down over his thick wrist and gently cupped his hand. His skin was hot, and she focused her magic, sending in healing energy.

She began getting a backlash, first a trickle of pain that grew into a stream. She forced herself to keep breathing, to accept the pain without making a sound.

Key slipped his hand from hers, with the water still spraying over his head; he opened it and then made a fist. She had healed him. Moments ago, he'd been empty, hurting and feeling exhausted and like a damned freak. Now her magic was swimming through him, her breasts pressed against his back, her pelvis against his ass. Her touch, her voice, her scent, it was all breaking through the gray, damp coldness that usually kept him numb. She was making him feel.

"Don't move," she said softly as she pulled back.

"Why?" He had no defense against her. Hadn't she heard him out there? His life was a bad horror movie. Why was she here?

"Because it's my turn."

"To?" He heard her moving, heard the snap of a bottle cap opening, the soft thunk of setting it down.

"Wash you. Take care of you." Her soapy hands came down on his shoulders.

Key dropped his head, feeling the slickness of the soap beneath the warmth of her hands. His cock was already rock hard from her magic, now it jerked and danced. Turn. Take her. Lift her up, thrust inside her and make her yours.

Her hands worked over his shoulders, down his back, up his sides. "Arms up."

He couldn't fight this, didn't know how. He raised both arms, pressed them to the cool shower wall. Her soapy hands went up, then around, sliding over his nipples. He shuddered, but even more powerful than her touch was the realization that she was seducing him. Giving him what he desperately needed. "Roxy...not here. I'm not going to take you in the shower of Phoenix's gym." She deserved more than that, he needed to give her more than that. Take her to a special place with privacy to let herself go, to moan, to scream if she wanted to. Not here where other witches, and hunters with super hearing, would inhibit her.

She deserved more. He wanted to give her more. But he needed her. As long as she touched him, the bloodlust stayed quiet.

Her hands went down. He opened his eyes, seeing her ivory hands against his stomach. Healing hands. Hands that tamed the dragon. Strong hands. She slicked back and forth, then changed direction again, rubbing her hands over his ass. Her fingers sliding deep to touch his balls.

"Oh God." He spread his thighs apart and leaned

his forehead against the tile. It was the sweetest torment, the feel of her hands on him, her breath feathering over his back, her hard nipples teasing his skin.

She got more soap. Then crouched, running her hands over one thigh, down to his foot, then back up his other thigh until she edged up and circled his balls with her wicked fingers.

She stopped, rising behind him. He heard that lid of the soap bottle pop again. Was she going to touch him more? He wanted to ask. Okay, beg. But he didn't. He endured. He didn't move, didn't dare breathe, waiting...

Enduring.

Shit. This was wrong. He should be taking care of her. Giving her pleasure. Her schema had to be hurting her.

She leaned against him again, reached around him and brushed her soapy fingers over the head of his cock. His breath left him in a rush. She wrapped her fingers around his shaft and slid down all the way to his base.

Then up, all the fucking way up.

Her other hand cupped his balls. And then she opened her chakras. He knew because her magic streamed out through her fingers and hands, igniting a firestorm of pleasure. Her scent, honey-almond, caramel and dark chocolate, filled him as her hands slid and pumped. Her magic caressed, and she pressed her hot mouth to his back in wet kisses, all up his spine. He lost all control, all will to do anything but feel this. His hips pumped against her hands, and fiery hot pleasure raced down his spine and exploded.

When he finally settled, when enough blood returned to his brain to think, he turned and pulled her into his arms. Held her against his heart. He tilted her head back and kissed her. He reached down between them, parted her curls and found her clit. So slick and swollen. She'd gotten this excited touching him. He groaned into her mouth, wishing they were someplace private, where he could lay her down and learn her inch by inch. Denying himself the pleasure of sliding down her body, spreading her legs open and tasting her was torture, but he could at least ease her now. He wrapped his arm around her middle and lifted her higher. Then he slid two fingers into her sheath and felt her magic pulse.

His blood heated and he began to stroke her, in and out while feathering her clit with his thumb. She writhed on him and he soon figured out it was her schema. He pressed the outside edge of his hand against that mark, and she shuddered, began pumping, panting into his mouth.

Oh yeah. He liked this, he liked it a hell of a lot. Once he found her rhythm, he pushed her, touched her and stroked her until she came apart. He could feel her chest pounding as intense pleasure raced through her.

Lifting his mouth from hers, he looked at her flushed face, her knot a tangled mess of wet hair, her green eyes soft and unfocused. She had come to him, healed him, and given him pleasure.

She'd chased out the cold gray.

Key sucked in a breath. She was making him too vulnerable. Doing something to him. Bringing to life more than the dragon. She was making him *feel*. And that scared him. Maybe she didn't get it yet, didn't realize how twisted by violence and ugliness he was. Look what he and the dragon had done to Sutton.

The dragon wouldn't claw Roxy, Key was sure of that. She'd gentled him with her soft words and touches. But somehow, someway, they'd still destroy her.

They always did.

≫ *13* ≪

ROXY SHIFTED ON THE COUCH, uncomfortable. Connecting with Dyfyr and experiencing his thoughts and emotions had made him even more real to her. And then there was Kieran—sharing comfort and pleasure in the shower with him deepened her restlessness. She felt unfinished, fractured, like all her pieces weren't fitting together correctly. Her schema heated, pinched, settled, then did it again, like hot flashes. Her womb ached, her chakras twisted.

She needed Kieran's touch. But when anyone else touched her, it felt like sandpaper.

She, Darcy and Carla were going over what Roxy knew, trying to see if there was any merit to Key's theory about Liam and fertility blood.

"Dyfyr is angry about his witches. Kieran believes he's been drawing Dyfyr's fury when Liam kills a fertility witch."

"What do you mean, 'his witches'?" Carla asked from the chair on her left. "I saw the way Dyfyr responded to you, but what's his connection to all fertility witches?"

Roxy hesitated, remembering her mother's insistence that the story was sacred. But these witches were trying to help her, asking nothing in return, unlike her mother. She'd had to demand the information from Gwen, and it was very likely her mother had lied. If she'd been involved in that spell with Kieran, then she had to know about the Dragon Tear, since Kieran's mom had it.

God, if her mother really had done this, would Key blame Roxy? She wanted to tell him her suspicion, but now that she'd seen, really seen, what was happening to Key and how worried his friends were that he'd go rogue, she was afraid. Her first priority was to save his soul.

What if he refused to bond with her? Just...left her.

Like her father. Tears filled her throat. For the last thirteen years of her life, her dad had been her rock. He'd loved her, never walked out...

"Roxy?" Darcy put her hand on her arm. "What's wrong?"

She sucked in a breath. "Sorry, I, uh, I got fired. By my dad. Today. Because I chose magic." *Shut up!* They didn't want to know this.

Darcy gently squeezed her arm. "I'm sorry, Roxy. That's just cruel."

"Maybe he'll change his mind with a little time," Carla suggested.

"Thanks. My mom said emotional swings were normal as I Awaken."

"She's a fertility witch, too? It runs in families?"

Here. Now. She should at least tell them her that her mom, Gwen Banfield, was actually known as Silver in the Circle Witches. Her mother fought the soul-mirror witches for power. Gwen was bitterly jealous that the Ancestors had chosen Carla as the Moon Witch Advisor over her. She should tell them that much. "Yes," she said. Fear made her palms sweaty, and she just couldn't do it. Not right now, so she went on with, "Our creation as witches is different from yours," she said. "You all came from a process of evolution, exceptional mortal women who began reincarnating. But we came from Dyfyr bestowing magic on his lover." She recited the story as her mother had told it to her.

There was a moment of silence as everyone processed what it meant.

Then Carla repeated part of the tale:

Laid her on the sweet grass
And gave her true magic

Her dragon loved her so
He bestowed his magic kiss

"That's why fertility magic is based in sex magic," Carla said. "Dyfyr bestowed the power during sex, and became the creator of fertility witches."

Ailish spoke up from the other side of Darcy. "No wonder Dyfyr is pissed. Some asshole is killing his witches."

"Dyfyr has homed in on Liam, too," Darcy added. "I get that the dragon is connected to his fertility witches, but he also seems connected to Liam."

Axel came up the stairs and strode to the back of the couch. He put his hands on Darcy's shoulders.

The witch leaned back, and he kissed her.

Roxy looked away from the easy intimacy of the two soul mirrors and then felt the shift in the room.

Kieran.

Turning, she saw Key, Phoenix and Sutton walk up the steps and crowd into the media room. Four large men took up a lot of space. Phoenix moved to Ailish at the other end of the couch, and Sutton walked over to Carla.

Axel kept his hand on Darcy and said, "We are going out to do a little recon. And Sutton needs to look at Key's loft to redo that alarm system." He looked around at all of them. "Will you be all right?"

A knot formed in Roxy's stomach, and her schema itched violently at the idea of Kieran being too far away. Too far to Awaken her magic.

Darcy answered, "Yes."

"What's wrong, Roxy?" Key's voice came from her left shoulder.

She was so startled, she jumped up and turned to face his cool gray eyes. "You scared me! I didn't hear you move." He was three feet in front of her. Pulling herself together, she said, "Nothing's wrong. We're just going over information, trying to figure out the blood-born thing. I told them how Dyfyr's connected to fertility witches." She stopped babbling.

He narrowed his eyes. "You're tense, jumpy."

Hell, yeah, she was tense. She wanted to throw herself at him. Beg him to make it stop. Make the pounding, dark, writhing *need* stop. It felt like her chakras were too full; she was jumpy, irritable and horny. She hated feeling so out of control.

Carla said, "Key, you've drawn Liam for years, even when you thought he was dead, right?"

He pulled his gaze away from Roxy. "Yes."

"Why did you think he was dead?" Sutton asked.

"I killed him. Or thought I did."

"Explain," Axel said.

Key glanced at her, then sighed and said, "After I ran away, my father sent rogues after me. He thought if they beat me up enough, I'd go running to him. The bastard was delusional. Anyway, I learned to fight and eventually started killing the rogues."

"Then drawing their deaths and sending the pictures to his father," Phoenix said. "The stupid bastard didn't get the message. He sent Key's uncle to force Key to talk and reveal where he'd hidden the Tear. And when Key killed him, his father came after him."

Roxy stared at Key's cold, blank face. His own family. She knew how she felt at her father's rejection, but she was an adult. Key had been tormented all his life. How could they do that? Her magic swelled in an effort to get to him, to stop his pain.

"Liam?" Axel prodded.

"He was smarter. He figured out that physical pain wasn't going to get me to tell him where the Tear was. So he went after someone I cared about."

Her chest hurt. Oh dear Ancestors, he'd said he loved a woman once and that she'd died. "Kieran..." she said softly.

He ignored her. "I tracked him, we fought and I stabbed him in the heart, cutting out a piece of it when a swarm of rogues showed up. I fought my way through them and got the hell out of there." He ground his jaw. "I thought he was dead."

"Blood-born," Carla said. "It has to have something to do with fertility witch blood. Maybe healing the heart? Regrowing it? Is that possible?"

They all looked at Roxy as if she had the answers. She flushed, her emotions swirling. "I don't know. Sex magic is supposed to help create pregnancies." She thought back. "My mom did fertility ceremonies for mortal women wanting to get pregnant, and then for crops and plants...pretty much whatever needed to grow. Sometimes animal breeders used her, too. I never heard of the blood healing a heart."

"It's been eleven years," Key said. "Where would Liam have been all this time?"

"He said it took him a decade to learn about fertility witches and me." Roxy shivered and strived to stay in control. She had to help, not be weak.

Key put his arm around her shoulder and pulled her close to him. His warmth eased her tight muscles and chased out the deep fear. "We're just guessing right now."

190

"When Roxy wakes the dragon," Sutton suggested, "maybe she can ask him. That critter obviously likes her."

Carla said, "Actually I have a theory about that, especially after hearing you tell the story 'The Dragon's Lover.' Roxy, I think you have the soul of the dragon's lover. In that story, Dyfyr's lover said:

> *Until death ripped her away*
> *Vowing to return one day*

"You vowed to return to him. He waited, now you're here, and that's why you can wake Dyfyr," Carla said.

"But..." she trailed off. She'd felt the dragon, heard him. Knew him. And since seeing him down in the gym, she felt like a piece of her was missing. Was it possible? Witches reincarnated, but they rarely if ever knew who they were in past lives. All these years, she'd craved love: real, soul-deep love.

Suddenly, her throat grew tight and her chakras quivered with need. Then her power rushed out, spinning and making it hard to breathe. Like a memory, she could almost feel Dyfyr's wings wrap around her and the two of them soaring across the skies. Almost feel his love, see him as he shifted to man form. Her magic reached for Dyfyr in a desperate painful need.

"Your magic," Key said roughly.

She looked up, saw a flush riding his face. Felt the tension in his arm around her. She realized her magic was out, rushing around. "Oh, your bloodlust! Sorry."

He leaned down, brushing his mouth near her ear. "Not bloodlust, green eyes."

Her magic flared hotter.

"You're throwing enough sex magic to give a dead man a boner," Phoenix said in a croaky voice.

Axel and Sutton laughed.

Heat bloomed in her chest and climbed up her face. She desperately tried to concentrate and call her power back. Her schema prickled and began to ache, churning out more and more desire as her powers throbbed. Horrified at her raging powers and lust, she pulled away from Key and tried to focus.

"Jerks," Ailish snapped, rising from the couch, walking over and putting her hand on Roxy's arm.

In seconds she felt a bright, cool and calming energy flowing into her, searching out her power and slowing it.

"Roxy worked her ass off today to learn control. And you Neanderthals make fun of her, act like it's funny that she's hurting."

Roxy felt Ailish's fury riding on the surface of her magic. She looked up to the witch, grateful for her support and her help. Her magic was returning to her chakras and the lust dialing back. "It's okay, I'm going to have to get used to being—"

"The hell it is. I know what it feels like, Roxy. A demon tortured me with lust for years. And Phoenix making crude remarks, the other idiots laughing—"

"Shit, Roxy, I'm sorry," Phoenix broke in. He moved behind Ailish, laying his hand on her shoulder. "Ailish went through hell. Your magic surprised me, and I mouthed off. I didn't mean—"

"It was cruel," Ailish said. "She's a fertility witch. Sex magic is her gift, and you all make it a joke."

"Oh hell," Key said in a tight voice and reached toward her. "Roxy—"

She backed up. If he touched her, she'd lose control again. "I'll be right back." She hurried down the stairs and went into the kitchen. She opened the fridge and looked for something cold, like maybe a black hole. Since she couldn't find that, she settled on grabbing a bottle of water. Shutting the fridge, she turned and almost screamed. "Damn it!"

"I'm sorry," Key said, looking miserable with his hands hanging down at his side, his jaw tight.

She shook her head. "You didn't do anything. I'm the one that let my magic, and hormones, get out of control. It's just that learning I might be the reincarnation of Dyfyr's lover...it unlocked something in me and suddenly I could almost remember what it felt like to be *her*, the dragon's lover. I felt Dyfyr's pain in you down in the gym earlier. He loved her so much. Hurts so much. I hate that." She twisted the top off the bottle and drank some water. This was what she was, what she was becoming. A witch ruled by hormones and lust.

Give a dead man a boner. Yeah, there was some magic to be proud of.

She closed her eyes against the taunt in her head.

"Oh hell, Roxy, don't cry."

She realized hot tears were sliding down her face. She turned away, setting the bottle on the counter, and put her hands flat on the cool granite. "It's the hormones or something. I'll stop. Just give me a minute." She squeezed her eyes shut, clenching her teeth to get control.

"Screw this," he growled, taking her arm, turning her around and pulling her against his T-shirt-covered chest. He wrapped one arm around her back and pressed her face close to him with his hand.

She inhaled his scent, soap from the shower over the dark spice of him.

"You have no idea what you do to me. Your magic is more than sexy, it makes me *feel*. It touches me and fills up the empty places. And that's scaring the ever-lovin' shit out of me."

"Why?" She brought up a hand to wipe her eyes, done with that weak crying crap.

He tugged her head back and looked down to her face. "I don't want to feel, not like that. Not ever again."

His words were so raw, so honest. Her magic felt his pain and tried to stroke him. She asks softly, "Do you still love her? The woman who died?" How terrible that must have been for him.

He stared down at her, blue flecks darkening his gray eyes, and his hand wrapped around her hair tightened. "I carry the guilt every second of every day."

Her heart squeezed for him. "What happened?"

He let go of her, walked to the fridge and pulled out a beer. After opening it and taking a drink, he leaned against the counter across from her. "We were seventeen. Living on the streets, you grow up fast. But Viv, she was different. Not so hard, but smart. She loved food, and her dream was to have her own little restaurant someday. I'd be an artist, she'd be a chef...we were in love. Then she got pregnant."

"You have a child?" Boy or girl? How old? Where was he or she living?

He looked past her and went on as if she hadn't asked the question. "We were young and stupid enough to believe in dreams, to believe we could have a family. I thought love was enough, that I'd made a clean break from that shit I grew up in. I never told her about the Dragon Tear. I kept it hidden, sure that none of it would touch her. And I'd protect our child...so stupid."

Oh dear crone. This time, she stayed quiet and let him tell his story.

He looked up and said, "I was both working in construction with Phoenix and doing freelance art jobs, and Viv found a job as a cook. We had an apartment. I worked late one night on a mural. When I got home..." His face tightened and he took a long drink of his beer. Then he said, "I smelled the blood, then heard Viv's cries. My first thought was that something had gone

wrong with the baby. She was just over three

months pregnant. Then I smelled copper, and I knew. It was a little one-bedroom place. I got inside and found Liam cutting up Vivian, demanding to know where the Tear was." He jerked his gaze to Roxy. "She didn't know anything about the goddamned Tear."

"Oh, Kieran." It was all she said, all she could say.

"I pulled out my knife and attacked Liam, and both of us got cut up. Then he broke away from me, putting about ten feet between us. It was the perfect opportunity for me, I knew I could kill him then. I took aim with my knife."

She remembered Key saying he didn't miss when he threw his knife.

"It was all happening so fast. I heard Viv cry out my name. She'd gotten up and run toward me at the same time I threw my knife at Liam."

Roxy's heart pounded; bile burned up her throat. His gaze had drained to the color of hot mercury.

"He grabbed Vivian, jerking her in front of him. My knife hit her in the throat."

Her knees went weak. She grabbed the counter behind her and said, "Oh God."

Key stared at her, his gaze brutal. "She died in my arms, able to say only one last word, 'Why?' I was never sure if she was asking why Liam attacked her or why I killed her and our baby."

Horrified for him, she saw the haunted looked in his eyes, and it crashed in her chest, leaving her wordless.

"That's when I began to draw the truth of myself—the dark and violent world I know. It's what I am, and it follows me like a foul odor."

She pushed off the counter and took a step toward him. "It wasn't your fault!"

There was no mercy for himself in his eyes. "I killed her with my knife, her and our baby. She loved me and trusted me. I didn't warn her, didn't tell her about the

Dragon Tear, or that I came from a sadistic, screwed-up gene pool, or that I was a witch hunter. If she'd never met me, Liam would have left her alone and she'd be alive."

His voice was tight with guilt. Her heart broke for him. She crossed the kitchen and pressed into his arms. He stiffened. She wouldn't let him do this. "I'm not Vivian, Kieran. And I know about Liam, the Tear, I know it all."

He sighed, the tension easing in his muscles. He set his beer down and touched her face. "I want to show you something." He stepped back, took her hand, and said, "Come with me." He led her down the stairs into the gym. "One second." He dropped her hand, strode across the mat, picked up his overnight bag, and walked back. Then he grabbed her hand, and they headed to a weight bench. He sat, then tugged her to sit on his lap.

She hesitated, wanting to stay calm, in control, and sitting on his lap would make that difficult.

He rubbed his thumb over her hand. "It's easier if you let me hold you. It keeps the bloodlust down."

"That's a great line, hunter," she said, but she settled on his thighs. She would keep her magic contained and her chakras closed, she thought fiercely. Even with the feel of his hard thighs beneath her, his left arm around her back, his hand resting on her leg. She focused on watching his right hand dip into the bag and then pull out his sketchbook.

"I want you to see through my eyes." He opened it to the picture he'd already shown her. "I don't see your magic here, just you, and that's pretty damned fine. But once you let me bring out some of your magic..." He began to turn the page.

Her stomach fluttered with nerves. She could hear the sound of the page turning and wasn't sure she wanted to see this. And then he revealed the drawing.

She sucked in her breath. She was sitting in the corner of his couch, wearing only the black yoga pants. She had her right arm across her stomach and her breasts spilled over like they were too full, her nipples erect. Her skin glowed with a golden shimmer that seemed to take on all the colors of a sunset. She didn't know how he did it, how he captured those colors dancing over her skin.

Against the backdrop of her flushed skin and fiery golden shimmer, a crystal teardrop hung on a silver chain and was nestled between her breasts. It was silvery clear, yet she thought she caught colors simmering in it if she tilted her head. Then they vanished, and reappeared. "Is that Dyfyr's Tear?"

Kieran said, "I didn't intend to draw that there, but then I had to."

"Do you see colors in it?" she asked, staring at the drop.

"No." He turned to look at her. "Do you?"

"Almost, I don't know how to explain it. Flashes, glimpses, then I turn my head and it's gone."

"Must be your magic. The real Tear has colors, but even I can't draw that kind of magic."

"It's painfully exquisite. Hard to look at, yet hard not to." She reached out, touching the tip of her finger to it, almost feeling the hot dampness.

"I know it's too dangerous, but I would give anything to see that Tear on you." He seemed to shake himself and added softly, "Look at your face."

Her chin was up, her mouth full, relaxed and parted. Her green eyes were looking right at Kieran, full of confidence. So certain. So...rich with more than sex. That same feeling she'd had while he drew her washed over her now; hot rivers of desire, the longing to pull Kieran to her, and knowing...what? *That I can give him something no one else can.*

"Do you see it, Roxy?" His voice was throttled low.

"The beauty? The fire? The radiance in you when you let your magic surface? Roxy, this is *you*. It's more than sexual beauty, it's magic. And so goddamned enticing it makes my guts twist just looking." He turned his face to hers, his gaze magnetic. "It's you. And when I look at you, I know that if I fell for you, if I let myself care, my feelings for you would be a hundred times more powerful than what I felt for Vivian." He touched his finger to the Tear between her breasts in the picture. "And then, somehow, I'd destroy you. Just like Vivian."

He thought if he loved her he'd destroy her? That wasn't even logical, but fears like that usually weren't.

She touched his face. "Did you ever think that maybe together we'll be stronger? The curse will break, you'll be free of your bloodlust, I'll get my high magic, and we'll work together. We'll defeat your brother and safeguard that Tear." And maybe she could teach him to trust love, to trust himself.

Bits of blue flared in his gray eyes. "You make me want that, Roxy. Want to believe we can really have something together." He leaned in and kissed her.

"Key?" Axel called from the stairs.

Roxy scrambled off his lap. Key folded the sketchbook and put it away, then answered, "Yeah."

"We need to go. Darcy and Carla got a text that a witch is missing."

≋ 14 ≋

KEY WAS THE LAST ONE to get back to Phoenix's house. Roxy, Axel, Darcy, Phoenix, Ailish, Carla and Sutton were around the big table. As soon as he walked in, Roxy's scent surfed over the dinner aromas and hit him hard.

Dark chocolate; her magic was rising.

He went straight to the kitchen sink to wash his hands and saw his veins swelling, turning dark with the acid craving for her blood. Lust pounded down his spine. After drying his hands, he grabbed a beer from the fridge and went around the granite bar to the table. There was an empty chair next to Roxy.

She set a dish in front of him heaped with a BBQ beef sandwich, potato salad and fruit. "You must be starved. I fixed you a plate."

"Thanks." His throat tightened. It was a small gesture, something he saw the other bonded hunters and witches do all the time for one another.

"After I left you tonight, I went by your condo. I have a couple recruits wiring a new alarm system right now," Sutton said. "I'll go by and test it later tonight."

Key glanced up at the hunter across from him.

"Good. Liam's going to make another move soon. His desperation is rising. He really thought I'd leave both Roxy and the Tear in my loft." He took a drink of beer, washing down his rage.

Roxy set down her fork. "Where is he? What's he doing? Darcy said you rescued the missing witch and she's okay."

He looked at her. "We did. She sent a text that she thought she was being followed. Smart of her to send an emergency text like that."

"Emergency text?"

Carla set down her glass of water. "Sutton, Darcy and I have set up an emergency text system. If a witch is threatened or has been taken by a rogue and can alert us, the hunters try to find her. If she is able to keep her phone with her, we tap into the GPS and find her quicker."

"Impressive."

Key told her, "We arrived at the witch's house just as the rogue broke in. Before he died, the rogue told me Liam is at the Rogue Cadre headquarters. Said he and Quinn Young are tight. We dumped the rogue's body close to their headquarters, but we can't get too close." Frustration coiled in his stomach. He had to get to Liam. "It's protected by mini-Death Daggers."

Roxy's eyes were huge. "What is that?"

"Quinn Young is the leader of the rogues. He bargained with Asmodeus and got the Immortal Death Dagger. That thing can kill immortals. It's burned into Young's arm and is damned creepy. Now we've learned he's growing mini-death daggers that protect their headquarters."

"Kieran! You didn't get too close to those things, did you?"

He could feel her worry for him. "No. I'm not going to get killed and leave you without protection." Or someone to tame her schema and feed her magic. She needed him alive.

"He did use his knife to save me. I was hauling the rogue's body, planning to drop it at the rogue headquarters, then go from there head over to Key's condo and look at the alarm system. But I got too close, and the fun started. Kieran saw the dagger coming and threw his knife, knocking it off the path before it hit me," Sutton said. "Then we played a game of chicken because hot-shot rocket-arm just had to have his knife back."

Phoenix laughed. "Sutton and I flew overhead, drawing the daggers up while Key ran in and got the knife."

"I like that knife," Key said and took another bite of his sandwich.

"You could have been killed! All of you!" Roxy said. "Why would you do that?"

"Because they are idiots," Ailish announced. "And because they know that the only antidote to the Immortal Death Dagger is the blood of a soul mirror." She turned her face toward Roxy. "Phoenix and Sutton made sure the dagger didn't hit Key. They both have soul mirrors who could save them. But they are still idiots."

"Sounds like it," Roxy glared at Key.

Damn, she looked mad. "We were testing the range of the daggers, Roxy, looking for a pattern, a way to get by them. Wing Slayer and Asmodeus are in a war for control of Earth. The rogues are the demon's soldiers, and we are Wing Slayer's. We have to get to the rogues to kill them."

"And keep the Dragon Tear away from them," she added.

"Speaking of that, did you move the Tear?" Axel asked.

"Yes." That's why he was so much later getting to

the house than the rest of them. He was going to need to keep moving the Tear in case Liam really did have a way of tracking it with fertility witch blood.

"About the Tear," Roxy said. "I've been thinking. You know that drawing you did of me wearing the Tear?"

Her voice was tense, and he turned to her. He saw the flush rising up her throat. Did she think he could forget that drawing, or the real thing? He put his hand on her thigh. Before he opened his mouth to say anything, he felt streams of itching, discomfort... Shit! She was hurting! For sex. For him. His cock responded with enthusiasm, but his chest ached for her. He'd been out, and she'd been here suffering. "What about it?"

"I think that was you channeling Dyfyr again. He's telling us that I should wear the Tear tonight."

"No!" Realizing he snarled at her, he softened his tone. "I don't want you touching the Tear." He didn't want anything to hurt her.

"Key, you drew it," she emphasized. "Like when you drew on the wall in the bedroom in Vegas. It's Dyfyr, I know it is. I think once he's awake, he can get rid of the Tear."

He didn't know why he'd drawn it on her, and now he regretted it. "Roxy, that Tear is too dangerous. Wait until the dragon is awake. Until you have enough power to communicate with him. I'm not going to risk you. It could drain off some of your life. First we'll wake the dragon and go from there."

"But is that really a risk?" Phoenix said. "Wing Slayer will grant you both immortality. He's done it for all of us soul mirrors. That will counteract any small amount of life drained from her."

Immortality. With Roxy. She'd be his to protect, to make love to...and she'd be damn hard to kill. He would be able to relax a little bit if she had immortality. Maybe figure out how to be her lover and not destroy her.

Roxy put her hand on his arm. "What if I'm right and Dyfyr can use his magic to destroy the Tear as soon as he wakes?" She took a breath.

Kieran looked into her eyes and discovered something that shocked him—it was hard to deny her what she wanted. But she was his soul mirror, he couldn't risk her. "I don't think—"

"Key," Carla said, "Roxy had a real connection with the dragon in the gym. You know she did. I think she might have a point."

"Don't forget Linc's house," Axel added. "The way her magic rose and she connected to your drawings." He shifted his gaze to Roxy. "You were magical then, Roxy. Your witch-shimmer surfaced and there was almost an otherworldliness to you. Like you were with us, but also there with the dragon centuries ago at the same moment."

Ailish added, "The Ancestors said that only the dragon can destroy the Tear. Roxy's been right so far, hasn't she?"

Key was torn, realizing that Roxy was getting real support, making her face glow with their acceptance. But he was worried, damn it.

"Have you worn the Tear?" Sutton asked.

He looked at the man across from him. "Yeah. I wore it when I ran away and for a couple days until I started finding places to hide it. And various times when I was moving it."

Sutton lifted an eyebrow. "You don't look like an old man, so your life didn't drain away instantly."

He didn't want to do this.

Roxy said, "Please, Key. If you don't trust me, at least trust Dyfyr. He tried to tell you all those years that Liam wasn't dead, didn't he?"

He looked into her eyes again and knew he was

lost. "Fine. But just for a short time. When I say so." He was going to put it on her at the pivotal moment. Not before.

She gave him a tense smile. "Thanks."

Key took his hand away and tried to eat. But he was still uneasy. He heard the others talk but only half listened.

"Roxy," Carla said, "how could you hear the dragon's story? You don't have your fifth chakra that is your communication with other realms."

"When Liam kept demanding to know if I woke the dragon and about the Tear, I was desperate to answer him. I'd have told him anything. The only dragon I could think of was Dyfyr from Key's comic book. And then it felt like my mind splintered and Dyfyr was there. I remembered him, and I knew he was coming, that he'd save me. And then Kieran came."

"Amazing. Dyfyr reached out to you," Carla said. "That's one powerful dragon. He cares so much about you."

"Damn, you're doing it again," Phoenix said in a hoarse voice.

Key snapped out of his thoughts as a wave of hot sex magic rushed over him. Turning, he saw Roxy's witch-shimmer flickering between rich sunsets and a sickly pallid yellow. He could smell her pain. He moved his chair closer and put his arm around her. Her schema was going apeshit. The lust hit him right in his balls.

"What happened?" he asked gently, trying to get her to relax. She was too tense.

"My magic just...surged. Thinking about Dyfyr helping me, you rescuing me." Her voice was strained, and she bent forward slightly as another wave burst out.

Her magic was too wild, he could feel her clenching and fighting it, fighting *him,* as she tried to get control.

Phoenix fisted his hand on the table in reaction and said, "I figured you're just paying me back for being an asshole earlier today, Elf Witch."

She lifted her head, looking at the other hunter. "Elf Witch?"

While she was distracted, Key laid his other hand on her stomach, hoping to call her wild, sexual magic back to her chakras. Seconds later, he smelled more power in the room as the other witches managed to connect with Roxy's chakras and help.

"Red hair, green eyes, freckles—do the math and it adds up to elf. Then there's your magic, it's making me sweat. You want to punish a man, throw that at him when he can't do anything about it," Phoenix groused.

Key felt her power rush to his hand. It was calming down, aided by the other witches.

Roxy frowned at Phoenix. "I didn't mean to...wait I feel that. *Power.* Other witches," she looked around the table. "You're helping me."

"Yes," Carla said gently. "We just needed you distracted for a minute. You were too tense and blocking us."

Roxy looked incredulous. "Thank you." She turned to Phoenix. "Ailish told you to distract me, didn't she?" Phoenix grinned.

"She said I was a jackass earlier today. Really hurt my feelings."

Relaxing against Key, Roxy said to the other hunter, "You have feelings? Like real people?"

Key laughed, feeling the tension break. He let his hand fall from her stomach. Her shimmer was just a flicker now, very pretty. He could still feel the power of the others, they were all working to keep her schema under control. But once they stopped, it was going to rise fast and hurt her again. It was time for them to go, to take her to the place he'd chosen. He started to stand when his phone rang. Sinking back in his chair, he reached for the device on the table and saw it was Ram. He answered, "Ram, I put you on speaker."

"Good, I'm at Roxy's apartment."

"Why?" Roxy asked, surprised.

Key answered, "We put a camera on your apartment to see if Liam or any of the mortals he's got looking for fertility witches show up." He turned toward the phone on the table. "So did you get a hit?"

"No. The camera died and I went to check it out. I heard someone moving inside. I entered, went around a corner and got blasted in the face."

Key's gut went tight. "Shot? How bad?" Roxy's apartment was in Sherman Oaks. How fast could one of them fly a witch there to heal him?

"Ram?" Axel snapped when the hunter took too long to answer.

"Fire extinguisher. I couldn't see, couldn't smell...target got away. It wasn't a rogue. I think maybe a female; the blast came from someone smaller than a full-grown man."

"What the hell, a woman got the drop on you?" Sutton stared at the phone like it had morphed into a snake.

Roxy straightened. "A woman in my apartment? Maybe it was my cousin looking for me."

"Doubtful unless your cousin has a high-tech weapon," Ram said. "Something caused me to freeze, as if I'd been lit with a supersized stun gun."

Key growled, "Some kind of new weapon? Engineered for witch hunters?"

"Could be. Don't see a mark on me anywhere, but that could have healed. I have to wonder, though, why the fire extinguisher?" Ram said. "This isn't tracking. First-class strange is what it is. Even now, it feels like something is crawling on my skin."

Sutton stood up. "Hold your position, Ram. I'll be

there in fifteen minutes tops. We'll figure it out." He turned to Axel.

Their leader nodded, and Sutton kissed his mate. "Stay here, Carly, where you're safe. Please?"

"Sure, I want to talk to Tyler and his mom anyway. See if I can help them. They didn't want dinner, but Tyler's getting restless; he just docsn't want to leave his mom alone."

He smiled. "Do your magic, baby." Then he turned and went out the back.

"I'll stay but I think there's something I need to do," Ram mused. "Feels urgent. Important."

Christ, Key thought, something rattled Ram. He never thought he'd see the day. "What about Roxy's apartment?"

"I'll send you pics, but her laptop is open and running. Desk drawers are opened. If Roxy is normally neat—"

"I am," Roxy said, sounding almost as baffled as the hunter in her apartment.

Ram went on, "Then they've been searched. Kitchen looks orderly, just a mug on the counter. I think she only got as far as the desk before I got here."

Now that sounded calm and methodical like Ram normally was.

"Ram," Axel said. "I'm going to call you back on my phone in a couple minutes. Key needs to leave."

"I'll take the pictures," Ram said. "And try to remember what I'm supposed to do." He hung up.

Key lifted his gaze to Axel.

"Hell if I know," the man said, rubbing his hand over his face. "Go. We'll deal with Ram."

Key needed to take care of Roxy. He knew that once the witches pulled back their magic, she was going to hurt.

And he was going to ease her. Make love to her. Fill them both with pleasure.

By the time they got to Kieran's truck in front of the house, she was hot with rushes of desire, the need for his touch. She gritted her teeth, took her hand from his and hurried around to the passenger side.

But he was there already, pulling open the door and holding it while she slid into the seat. "You need to learn to stay behind me when we're out in the open," he told her. "I'm protecting you, remember? Think of my body as a shield."

He stood in the opened door, looming over her, his cent filling her lungs. "I can't." She closed her eyes and saw him in the shower. He was powerful enough to be a shield, but all she wanted to feel was him against her. She opened her eyes and told him the truth. "I think of you as my Awakening. The man who can make the pain stop."

He leaned in, touched her face, his eyes darkening to blue. "I'll make it stop, and then I'll bring you pleasure, all the pleasure you want." He slammed the door. And before she could turn her head, he was sliding in on the driver's side.

She needed him with a desperation that was deeper than sex. It was a connection so profound, she knew she wasn't going to be able to breathe again without it. It was like she was finally getting her soul back. "Do you feel it, too?" Was she alone?

"You. I feel you." Key pulled out onto the street and turned his gaze on her, radiating hot intensity. "Jesus, woman, your scent, your magic, everything about you is consuming me inside out."

Her nerves stretched and pulled until she couldn't sit still. They were going to have sex. She tried to think of something else. She wanted to know more about him. His own family had been cruel to him, hurting him to get the Tear. His father sending those rogues after Key, then his uncle...

She remembered what Phoenix said about Key drawing the pictures of their deaths and sending them to his father. "You sent your father the pictures to warn him, didn't you? You knew the dragon in you was going to kill him."

His jaw hardened. "I knew *I'd* kill him if he came after me. Back then, I was still trying not to be the animal they made me into. All of them, my mother playing with magic, my father...all of them. But I couldn't escape." His mouth pulled into a flat line. "He didn't believe it, I guess. Thought I was still the spineless boy who took the abuse without fighting back."

Her heart bled for him. He wasn't an animal, but man with the soul of a dragon. His father had deserve to die. "Is that how you learned to fight? From being attacked?"

He was quiet for a few seconds, skillfully driving through the dark city.

"If you don't want to talk about it, I shouldn't pry. Sorry." She had her own secrets. Like who her mother was and what Roxy believed she'd done, and Shayla being an infertility witch. Roxy was going to tell them as soon as she knew Key's soul was safe. But still, they were going to feel betrayed, and how could she blame them?

He looked over at her. "Phoenix taught me to fight. He found me getting my ass kicked by a group of boys. First, he bloodied them and sent them crying for the mothers. Then he yanked me up and asked me what the hell was wrong with me."

"You didn't know how to fight. All those times your father hurt you..." She couldn't bear it. "Your mother should have protected you—"

He cut her off. "It's pointless to go there. She was

209

addicted to the idea of immortality. Like a gambler. She couldn't stop and justified everything in her mind."

She didn't care. "I would have protected my child," she said fiercely. It was all so wrong. "I'm glad you killed him."

He looked over at her. "I'm good at killing, Roxy, and I learned from the best. Phoenix made damn sure I learned."

"Why?" She didn't know Phoenix well, didn't really understand him.

Key stared out at the road, then answered, "Those boys who were beating me up? They'd been tormenting Phoenix's mother and were going to rape her. I couldn't fight, but I gave them a new target, and Sheri, his mother, got away and found Phoenix."

She felt that down to her chakras. "You protected his mother, so he taught you to protect yourself." But it was more, much more. They became brothers that day. Because Phoenix respected strength—not bully strength, but true strength. She thought of Phoenix stopping her from going to Key in the shower, trying to tell her Key needed space. No wonder he was so protective.

"You okay?"

"Yes." Nervous as hell. Her stomach was flipping over. It had been different in the shower when all she'd wanted to do was take care of him. She hadn't been thinking about her own inadequacies. She took a breath and blurted out, "I haven't had much sexual experience, but I'm not...I think I do something wrong." She didn't dare look at him but stared out at the city, digging her fingers into her thighs. "I haven't really had real relationships. Mack wasn't serious. I knew he wasn't, you know, totally into me. I was just convenient or something. When a guy really liked me, I didn't sleep with him." She couldn't look at him. It was completely dark now, the moon was past half full, and she had no idea why she was spilling her guts.

"You had sex with men who didn't care about you?" The words sounded harsh, like they hurt.

"I didn't want to end up hurting them." She dug her fingers into the leather seat. "If my Awakening came along, and I wasn't strong enough to resist, and some man cared about me..." She closed her eyes, feeling the pull of Kieran.

Key snatched her hand up off the seat, his warm fingers wrapping around hers. "Got it."

"Didn't matter anyway. There were only two guys and afterward, they could never get away from me fast enough. No calls, no texts, no emails. Even the one that I thought was a friend. He said I was too intense, trying to get too much from him. That's my sex magic, I guess trying to draw energy from him. We weren't friends after that. He wouldn't look at me, like I was a dirty secret." She couldn't seem to shut up. "So I stopped trying to, I don't know, to fill something missing inside me, guess. Until Mack. I trusted him." She had no idea where Key was going. He drove like he did everything with utter confidence, winding into a part of town with older buildings.

"Mack signed his death warrant when he hurt you." He turned to look at her. "I told you I'm not good at relationships, but I can kill anything that threatens you." Looking back at the road, he said, "We're soul mirrors. We'll have eternity for me to figure this out. Tell me you birthday."

The sudden shift confused her. "May twenty-first. I'll be twenty-five. Why?"

He glanced over. "I won't forget. Ever. I'll figure out what you like and get you a present. See? I'll learn."

Roxy's heart forgot to beat. "Kieran—"

He squeezed her hand. "You won't ever want for anything. And sweetheart, after we have sex, we'll develop a mental link like the other soul mirrors. I'll know if you need anything. For sure, the dragon will know if you're in danger."

She dropped her gaze to his hand wrapped around hers. He was trying to give her affection, romance. She knew he didn't think he was capable of love, yet for her, he was going to try. It filled her with warmth and hope, and thick emotion. How could she not care about him? Yet, she had to ask, "What if I do that to you, too? Try to take too much of your energy or something?" The need for him was overwhelming her.

He turned to look at her, his gaze so hot, she should have gotten sunburned. "I'm going to take you into my arms and give you as much as you need to release your magic. And then I'm going to give you more, and more, until we're both exhausted. Even then, Roxy, I don't know if I'll be able to stop." He shifted his gaze back to the dark road. "I just don't fucking know."

Her chakras trembled in response, pressure growing along her spine. Her schema itched violently, and it felt like her pores were opening, seeking, making even her skin ache.

His hand tightened on her fingers. "Hang on, we're almost there."

She shifted in the seat, trying to focus. "Where?"

He turned down a city street where a huge walled compound took up a block. "Mural Maze." He pulled up to the gate and used his BlackBerry to code something in, and the massive, solid wood gate slid open.

"I've heard of this place. Like a museum of graffiti, owned by the city or the homeless shelter or something."

"I know the owner, he won't care." He pulled in and shut the gate, parking in a concrete lot off to the right.

She could only see what the lights from the truck illuminated. There were rows of concrete walls zigzagging, turning and doubling back. She couldn't see well enough to make out the art on the walls. "Only select people get in here. Are you sure this is okay?"

"Positive."

She wasn't completely stupid. "You own this, don't you? You bought up all this land..." The sheer magnitude of it dazzled her. "Why do you keep it secret?"

He turned off the truck and got out.

Roxy reached for her door handle but he was already there, pulling it open. "Because it would ruin it for the artists. I don't want my fame overshadowing their work. I have all the attention I want with Dyfyr."

Sitting up in the truck, she was eye level with him. She turned, her knees brushing against his stomach. "You really mean that." He cared about these young artists. It wrapped around her heart as it fully sank in who this man was. She reached out and laid her hand on his chest. Through the T-shirt, she felt the heat of him and the dragon.

A deep groan rumbled up his chest.

The contact rippled through her fingers, up her arm and hit her chakras. Her magic exploded out, racing through her. She gasped, bending forward at that sheer power with little control.

Key reached in and swept her up off the seat. "Put your legs around me." She heard the door slam and then he broke into a run, moving so fast that the walls covered in art blurred as he raced through the maze. With her arms around his neck, her body pressed to his chest, and her legs around his hips, she felt his muscles working effortlessly, churning up the ground.

It was strangely beautiful, the two of them alone in this concrete museum with the night sky opened above them and the only light from the moon.

He burst out of the maze and slowed, then stopped.

They were in a square space of land, covered in

lush grass surrounding a huge fountain in the center with multiple jets spraying up from different angles. A two-foot tiled bench surrounded the pond. She could smell the chlorine. "It's a park in the middle of a concrete jungle." So like Kieran; hard, with little spots of softness.

Like his art, and what he was doing for these kids. That he brought her here, to such a special place... She looked down into his face. "I can do this."

"We can. Together." He walked to the fountain while holding her, bent his knees, braced her with one hand and flipped a tile open with the other. He pulled out a black velvet bag.

She stared at it, feeling the brush of energy ripple over her skin, inflaming her with heat and magic. "The Tear?"

"Yes." He shoved it into his pocket, put the tile back, then slid his hands down until he cupped her ass. "I can feel the heat of you through your jeans." He pressed the hard ridge of his cock against her. "Unbutton your shirt for me. Take it off. I want to see the moonlight on you."

The heat grew in her schema and spread. She quickly undid the row of buttons, then slid the shirt off and let it fall.

"Bra," his voice was dry.

She released the front snap and her breasts, heavy with desire, sprang free. The cool night air dampened by the fountain rushed over her bare skin, and the white light of the moon filled her pores. Roxy tilted back, trusting him to hold her.

Kieran shifted, bracing one hand in the middle of her back. "More, Roxy. Feel it, your shimmer is rising." He leaned down, closing his mouth over her nipple.

Her whole body clenched at the hot, wet feel. "Kieran, it's too much. Too full."

He released her nipple and set her on her feet. Kneeling down, he stripped off her sandals, undid her pants, and pulled them down and off. Looking up, his eyes gleaming with pride. "This is your magic, your gift. Sex and magic. I can already see it rising on your skin, sunset fire." He reached his fingers into the elastic of her panties.

She dug her hands into his shoulders, frustrated at the feel of his T-shirt when she wanted skin. Wanted him. Kieran anchored her when everything else was spinning...his shirt vanished. Her magic! She'd willed his shirt gone and it vanished.

He shuddered. "Can't stop. Your scent, your magic, you." He drew her panties down. Then he lifted her leg.

She thought he was just slipping off her underwear.

"Hold on," he growled, then hooked her knee over his arm, raised her leg higher and spread her open.

Her schema throbbed, needed. Hungered.

His gaze locked on the goddess mark. "She's so damned hot. Almost full of color." A dark tint rode his cheekbones as he lifted his fingers and touched the mark.

Streaks of hot magic and lava desire raced out. "Key!"

"Oh hell, yeah. Felt that right to my cock." He leaned in and brushed his mouth over the mark. Then he drew his tongue over it, the wet heat bathing it, kissing away the pain and leaving trails of pleasure. Her sex swelled and dampened. Renewed, strengthened power raced up her spine and released a sizzle of energy in her chest.

"Fourth chakra opened." She was panting, holding on to him. "More magic." She wanted to bring out as much magic as she could to wake Dyfyr, but she couldn't get the words out.

He stroked the pad of his finger over her clit.

Rubbed. Circled. Petted. Then he slid deeper, separating her folds. Pressing inside her. Sliding back out. Circling her clit while holding her left leg up. "Roxy."

She looked down and her heart chakra filled, already pressing the chakra at her throat. "I can open it." *Just looking at you.* "Just need the Tear."

"You want the Tear?"

"Yes."

"Then give me this. For this moment, you are mine," he growled the last word deep in his chest. "Mine to taste." He leaned in, raising her leg so that her sex was completely exposed. He nuzzled, inhaling her and then he touched his tongue softly to her clit.

She cried out, her body going wicked hot, and held on to him. Trusted him.

He sucked and stroked her clit, and used the pad of his finger to circle the entrance to her body. Against her, he said, "Give me your magic." He slid his finger into her and closed his lips over her swollen nub.

Her body obeyed him, shattering in an orgasm. She cried out, leaning her head back, feeling the pleasure and power mix and grow. It rushed through her, revealing the soul of the witch inside her. As Roxy embraced it, the power shot up to press on her throat. It would be terrifying if not for Kieran. He anchored her with his hand on her hip, his kiss milking her pleasure, his *care* reassuring her.

Her fifth chakra whooshed open amid tremors of pleasure and self-discovery.

Kieran rose to his feet, his mouth wet, his pupils so big his eyes looked almost black and the dragon spread his wings in the tattoo as if reaching to gather her up so they could soar...

Her heart chakra filled with something more powerful and ancient than magic.

$$\rightleftharpoons 15 \Longleftarrow$$

KEY HAD TO STRUGGLE TO stay in control. The dark chocolate scent of her magic, the caramel scent of her desire, wrapped around his guts and engorged his cock to *take her now*. But, Jesus, the way she let herself go, and trusted his hands to hold her...and then the dragon stretching his wings to catch her magic. The creature was helping her, sweeping her power, giving her control. Roxy's magic streamed through him like water through a funnel. The intimacy of it shook him, he knew her now in a way no one else ever could. He'd felt the essence of her magic.

She was his. Hot, deep, protective feelings raced through him, and in that moment, he'd give her anything. He knew she wanted the Tear, so against his better judgment, he reached into his pocket and fished it out of the black velvet bag. Tiny sparks escaped the bag, from being near either the dragon or Roxy, a fertility witch, who might carry the soul of the dragon's lover.

She had to be. The dragon knew her, knew her power, and when he'd tasted her, ripples of energy began rising from inside him, quickening, burning off the damp coldness that had been there as long as he could remember. Oh yeah, the dragon was waking.

Careful of the Tear, he took off his boots, undid his pants and shoved them off. He felt her gaze on him, scented the spike in her desire, and shuddered. Quickly, he unwrapped the cloth, looped the fine silver chain over his finger and lifted out the Tear so that it dangled between them. As it gently spun, the impossibly clear crystal caught the moonlight, and the liquid inside sparkled with dazzling brightness, throwing off sharp beams of colored light.

He looked at Roxy, her shell pink skin flickering with the fiery colors of sunset. Her hair fell in waves around her shoulders and her eyes, gods and demons, her eyes swam with magic and so many emotions: pleasure, joy, excitement, and one emotion he didn't dare identify. He stepped to her and slid the chain over her head. Cupping the Tear, he hesitated.

What if it hurts her? He knew the dragon wouldn't intentionally hurt her, but the magic in that Tear was so powerful it could strip Wing Slayer's immortality and turn him into a mortal. The only way to contain it was for Dyfyr to wake and use his ancient magic. What if the Tear drained even a single moment of her life? He didn't want to chance it.

Roxy seemed to understand his hesitation and put her hands on his chest, sliding her palms over the dragon. "That drawing you did of me, remember you told me you were compelled to draw the Tear on me?"

Her magic poured from her palms to stream though him. Deep. Seeking and reaching with such *fertile,* life-giving magic that his balls tightened, his cock strained. "Yes," he could barely get the word out. But the memory of that drawing of her was imprinted on his brain.

She smiled. "Trust your art, Kieran. Let go of the Tear."

Another wave of her sexy, sinful magic rolled

through him, and he was caught in her spell. He released the Tear, watching as it fell to nestle against the curve of her left breast. The sparks and flashes of light grew more vibrant and powerful.

She closed her eyes. "I hear a hum." Her magic spiked and she said:

> *My dragon sleeps*
> *In stony slumber*
> *Wings unused for centuries*
> *Unfurl and stretch*
>
> *Power, ancient and mystic*
> *Rise and flex*
> *I cannot breathe again*
> *Without the beat of your heart*

Her magic lit up his insides, marked him, commanded him, waking the beast as old as the mountains. The creature roared through Key, truly melding man and dragon to become one, and redoubled the primitive need to protect, possess and take care of their treasure: Roxy.

Fierce, driving need exploded within him. He couldn't wait any longer, couldn't draw another breath until he claimed her, sealing her to him. Forever. He curved his arm around her waist, lifted Roxy, and slanted his mouth over hers. She tasted so damned good, so warm and rich that he couldn't stop. *More. Deeper.*

She melted against him and parted her lips, her tongue meeting his and her magic rushing through him. It hunted and pushed, one half of a soul searching for its mate, for completion. Key shifted her, cupping her ass, and raised her higher. "Now."

She wrapped her legs around him and rode the tip of his cock with a heat so silky and slick he growled into her mouth. He pulled back from the kiss and looked into her eyes.

And saw the soul of his lover. Laid bare for him to take and break. She loved him. *Loved.* She held nothing back, giving him everything right down to her heart and soul. "Roxy, oh God..." Her gift tore through him, profound and terrifying at the same time. He didn't know if he could be the man she needed, but he wanted to be. The love shimmering in her eyes was so powerful it reshaped him and caused the dragon's heart to break free of stone, surging through him with tremendous power.

She touched the dragon and looked into Key's eyes. "Take the beat of my heart. And make it yours." Then she unleashed her magic.

He couldn't deny her. Driven by selfish need and by timeless desire, he thrust into her, sliding into the silky source of her magic. It was an endless journey so hot and pure, he shuddered all the way down to his heels. He sank deeper and deeper, her magic pulsing around him, milking his cock, welcoming him, as he felt each beat of her heart moving through the Tear.

To him.

She was giving him her heart.

Hot pleasure raced over his skin, twined around his spine, forcing him deeper inside her. She took him, opened for him, and gave him complete access. Denied him nothing.

Her magic grew and twirled until finally he was completely buried inside her. Joined. He kissed her, tasting her magic as he pulled out to his very tip and thrust again. And again. Desperate to fill and feed her, willing to give her all his body, give her all his strength and passion.

Her body was tightening, squeezing him with her pleasure and magic.

The Tear shot out colors between them.

Words built in his throat. Not understanding where they came from, he instinctively fought them. Instead, he tried to give her everything else, rocking his cock into her, feeding her pleasure. But eventually her magic and love revealed the heart of the dragon inside him. The creature rose and, through Key, accepted her offering with the words that spilled from his mouth, "Your heart is mine." He slammed up in her, invading her to her soul, and he held her tight as the world splintered into the colors of fire pulsing with a new beat.

It matched the rhythm of the newly awakened dragon's heart. Each beat fed their pleasure until it felt like they were flying together, their souls finding each other, then twisting and binding until they were whole.

Joined.

Soul mirrors, bonded together.

Slowly, they settled back into themselves. Key held her tightly, feeling the gentle pulse of her sheath, the tightness of her thighs around his hips, the softness of her breasts against his chest. Even as he felt the dragon's heart now beating in his chest. She'd done it, Roxy had awakened the beast. He buried his hand in her thick, satiny hair, barely able to stand. But he did because he'd never allow Roxy to fall. Never allow harm to come to her.

She'd given her heart to wake the dragon. *She'd awakened him with love.* He could feel the emotion beating in the tattoo. He tugged her head back and looked into her eyes. Wide, green and completely guileless. "You did it, you woke Dyfyr. Roxy..." he trailed off, unsure what to say. She'd been so brave, so sure, and there wasn't an ounce of regret in her gaze. "You gave him your love. I didn't know that you were going to do that." Shit, that was lame. Cowardly.

"It's what he needed to wake. I realized it from Dyfyr's story. His heart began to beat when he first saw her, and her love kept it beating. He stopped his heartbeat when she died and left him." She stared up at him. "And you, Kieran. You need love, too."

He was lost in her. The beauty of Roxy was truly soul-deep. She gave and asked for nothing back. "It's not just the dragon you've awakened."

He felt the leap in her pulse, the heated swirl of her magic, and he saw in her eyes such a raw hope it made his chest ache. She gave him the power to hurt her. "You're making me want to believe in...us." Not good enough; he knew it, but he couldn't say the words.

She leaned into him, kissing him, causing blood to rush to his dick buried inside of her, when she suddenly pulled back.

"What?"

"The Tear. I feel it. It's still here." She leaned back and they both looked down.

The Tear rested in the valley of her breasts, the moonlight bouncing off it and casting beams of light. He was too consumed with her to worry about it too much. Lifting his gaze, he said, "We'll figure it out. Together." He tested that last word and found he liked it too damned much. Not alone anymore, but together. They would do it. "The dragon is awake; we'll help you with your magic until you're powerful enough to communicate with him." He lifted her off him and sank down so that he could cradle her on his thighs. He had to make sure that her schema was satisfied now. Not that they were done, he was going to make love to her again and again. He brushed his hand down her arm, over her hip, then slipped between her thighs to pull them apart.

On that swell of flesh high on the inside of her left thigh, the schema of the fertility goddess was solid with a fully blended turquoise color. The dragon fluttered in his chest as Key slid his hand up her thigh and caressed that spot with his thumb.

She moaned softly.

He shifted his gaze to her face. "Oh yeah. We're going to feed this little beauty, over and over." She was slick and hot, and his heart pounded with desire. More. He'd never get enough of her. His cock jumped, growing hard and ready for her. Key's chest tightened and he rolled them over, laying her beneath him and kissing her. With the sweet grass under them, cool moonlight pouring over them, and soul-deep passion raging between them, Key sank into her heat.

This, he thought, was what *home* felt like.

⇥✳⇤

Roxy was languid and sated. Her heart was full; Kieran hadn't rejected her love. She refused to wish that he loved her, that he'd say the words. He was opening himself, willing to try, and that was enough. She wanted to enjoy this new intimacy, both mind and body, that she had with him. She'd never had it before, and she didn't want to let go of it now.

Key rolled to his side and pulled her against him. She closed her eyes, letting her mind drift in the afterglow of pleasure while safe in her hunter's arms. Thoughts came and went lazily, like leaves on a stream when one image finally took hold. Visions of Dyfyr filled her mind and suddenly she wanted to know, "Will you get wings?"

"Probably. They seem to come out when our witches are in danger, though, so I'm not in any hurry." He traced his finger up her stomach, following the underside of her breast.

"Do you think I'd be too heavy for you to carry while you fly?" She would love the feel of that, soaring over the earth, just the two of them.

"Depends," he said, his finger trailing around her right breast.

Turning, she opened her eyes to look to him, and asked, "On?"

His eyes gleamed in the moonlight. "If you're wearing clothes or not."

She laughed at the idea. "I'm not flying naked! Where everyone can see me!"

"I'd shield you, Roxy." He shifted his gaze down her body. "You're mine. No one else will see you like this, soft and full from lovemaking." Looking up to her face, he said, "You're mine."

She felt *claimed* and smiled. "Hmm."

He dipped the pad of his finger between her breasts. "What?"

"If I'm naked then you have to fly naked, too. And I'd have to wrap my legs around you to hold on..."

He leaned close to her face, his eyes filling with blue heat. "And slide down on my cock?"

A ripple of excitement went through her. Amazing, she'd been so afraid of her sexuality, and yet with Key, she felt free and strong in her magic and lovemaking. Between them, there was no shame, just pleasure and sharing. "Yes."

"Hell, yeah." He leaned back on his elbow watching as he drew some pattern over her chest. "I think we'd better practice. Flying sex could be..." His eyebrows drew together and a line appeared between his eyes. He looked down to her breasts.

A faint tingle of alarm went through her. "What?" She angled her head down to see. Key ran his finger over the fine silver chain holding the Tear. She felt a twinge as the chain pressed against her skin.

"The Tear," Key said, his voice sharp, all signs of sexy playfulness gone. He shoved up to his knees and loomed over her. "Don't move!"

"Why?" Her heart started to race, her skin getting hot, but she stayed perfectly still. Panic clawed at her, but she held tight to the fact that Kieran was with her.

He'd protect her, she knew it, so she tried to draw on his innate strength.

"Hold still, Roxy," he whispered. "I have to get the Tear off you."

"What? Why?" She felt his entire body coil. Then he shot out his hand, aiming for the Tear.

A shaft of pain shocked a cry out of her. Key jerked his hand back before he touched her. Yet it felt almost like when Liam cut her. Sick fear exploded in her stomach. She looked at the spot where the Dragon Tear had been. A bubble of blood welled there, but she couldn't see the crystal Tear.

"Damn it, no!" Key lunged to his feet. "No!"

Roxy looked up at him. His face was a tight, vicious mask of rage. But he wasn't looking at her, he was looking at his hands.

Claws. Razor sharp claws, two or three inches long, protruded from the ends of his fingers.

But he hadn't touched her. He'd jerked his hand back, Roxy was sure of it. Yet she had felt a sharp pain on her chest. She looked down and saw a fine line of blood flowing from the inside swell of her left breast. She wiped it away and there, she saw a scab was forming. The spot hurt like a healing cut.

But the strangest of all were the muted beams of colored lights pulsing *beneath* her skin. Roxy reached up and touched the spot. She could feel a strange vibration.

"Fuck!" Key roared, low and vicious.

Roxy looked up and saw his jaw bulging and the cords on his neck standing out. "What's happening to me?"

His gray gaze slid to her, and she felt the chill of it. The warm, sexy lover she'd been with only moments ago was gone, and a steely-eyed hunter stood in his place. "The Dragon Tear. It's locked on to you somehow. When I tried to get it, it burrowed into you and," he lifted his hands, "these claws sprang out."

She looked down again, too stunned to comprehend it. She could see the fine silver chain pressed tight against her skin. She ran her finger over it; the chain was embedded so tightly she could feel it but not move it. The apex of the chain, where the Tear dangled, dipped *into* her skin. "I don't understand. The dragon is supposed to help us get rid of the Tear." She looked up. "You drew the picture of me wearing the Tear!"

Key stared at her with cold and dead, gray eyes. "He lied. The dragon tried to kill you." He stormed toward the maze.

"No!" She jumped to her feet.

Key stopped at the first block of concrete and smashed the claws against the wall over and over. Roxy was transfixed in horror when she saw the red stains of his blood spreading over the concrete in the silvery moonlight. She heard his bones cracking. "Kieran stop!" She ran to him, throwing herself at his back and locking her arms around his waist. "Oh God, stop!" Raging heat poured from his skin, his unyielding muscles, and the emotional pain ripping him apart. He pulled her off her feet as he kept slamming his hands against the wall. She hung on to him, her chakras flinging open, and her magic rushing to him. "Please!" Hot tears trailed down her face.

He went still. "Don't touch me. How can you touch me?" He pulled her arms off him and turned to face her. "That Tear is *inside* you, it'll kill you!"

The torment in his eyes was unbearable. "Kieran, we'll—"

"Don't you get it yet?" he roared at her. "I'm destroying you."

≫ 16 ≪

KEY GOT ROXY TO THE warehouse next to the nightclub, Axel of Evil, that served as the Wing Slayer Hunters' headquarters. For the entire drive, he couldn't even look at her. At what he'd done to her. What *they'd* done to her, he and that fucking dragon. Why had he trusted Dyfyr? All these years, he'd felt the cold rage of that creature. Seen what happened when he partially woke.

Blood happened.

God, he was every bit the freak of twisted, perverted magic that his father accused him of being. He wished the old man had done the job right and killed him.

Roxy had to live. She couldn't die. There had to be a way. He'd called ahead and told Axel the situation. He took Roxy through the garage door, past the pool table in the center. He was heading toward Axel, Sutton and Ram, but Roxy had stopped.

Key turned to see her standing by the pool table, her hair tousled, her eyes wide and haunted as she looked around. He dropped his gaze to her chest. She wore the green shirt with the row of buttons, and through the material, he could see the pulsing lights of the Tear lodged beneath her skin. The skin on his chest burned. The dragon had been burning his chest, raising blisters, off and on since it happened.

Did Dyfyr hate her that much? Key didn't understand; he'd thought the dragon loved her. But when Key tried to grab that Tear, his claws had sprung out—so lethal sharp, Key knew he would have sliced right through to her heart and killed her.

Roxy was staring at something to the right, then she walked around the pool table over to his drafting board and tattoo station. Key followed her, aware that Sutton, Axel and Ram were all by Sutton's high-tech computer area in the far corner. Moving up next to Roxy, he stopped.

Didn't touch her. He didn't dare trust the dragon not to make another attempt.

"That's Tyler's drawing of Dyfyr crouched on your shoulder. He showed me a similar one right before I was kidnapped." She turned to look at him. "You hung it."

It was just thumbtacked to the wall for now. "Kid's got talent. I'll have it framed when I have time." Why were they talking about this?

"Who did these other pictures?" She studied the various framed art; puppies that could fly, superheroes, one a sketch of Key himself.

"The puppy and a couple others are by Axel's little sister, Hannah. The others are kids I've met."

"Fans?"

He shrugged. "Just kids. This isn't important, Roxy. We need to see if Darcy—"

She settled her gaze on him. "They are important to you. So important you framed their art and hung it where you'd see it. These kids matter to you."

Key fought the sizzle of impatience. "We are here to get you help. That's all that matters!"

Her eyes filled with dry pain. "I thought the dragon

loved me, I thought it was real. I was so stupid. Maybe I'm not her, that woman he loved, and he's just mad. I had no right to wake him. I had no right," she said, her voice cracking like brittle twigs.

He lifted his arms to reach for her and caught himself. *Don't touch her!* What if his claws came out again? "Don't," he begged her, uncaring of who heard them. She was killing him. All Roxy had wanted was to be loved, to have a family.

She sucked in a breath. "I'm going to die, aren't I? I just need to know, because then it won't matter."

Why not just shove a hot poker through his heart? "I don't know, I just...I don't know." But he did know. What he'd done to Vivian had been more merciful than this. Viv had died in minutes. He couldn't stand looking at Roxy, seeing what he'd done. "Come on," he snapped, turned and strode toward the others.

Roxy followed and halted next to him.

Ram stepped forward. "Hi, Roxy, I'm Ram. Sutton and I grabbed some clothes and your laptop from your apartment for you. I put them in the condo."

"Uh, thanks, Ram. I appreciate it," she said tonelessly.

Sutton leaned back in his chair. "I checked the computer; it had been booted up but there was no activity. And I ran a scan on it just to be sure. It's clean." He leaned forward, picked up a BlackBerry and held it out. "Here's a phone. I hacked into your number and got all your contacts and added our numbers for you."

Roxy blinked, then took the phone without touching the other man. "Thanks."

Key was done with the niceties. "Where are the witches?"

Axel jerked his gaze from Roxy, anger simmering in his eyes. "Darcy's waiting upstairs in your condo, she's online with Carla and Ailish."

"Let's go." Key turned and led the way to the condos. He could hear the music and voices from the nightclub as they went up the stairs. "This is Axel and Darcy's condo here on the end." Turning right down a hallway, he added, "The second door on the left is the one Phoenix and I share. Ailish, too, now that they are mated." He reached out and opened the door.

He watched as she walked in, her gaze traveling over the spacious living room done in black leather and chrome on marble floors, taking in the wet bar across the room, then settling on Darcy. The witch sat on the leather couch with a laptop opened and her phone out.

Darcy set the laptop aside and stood. She had her hair clipped up and wore a pair of cropped pants and a T-shirt.

Key shut the door and asked, "Have you found out anything yet?"

"No." She walked over to Roxy. "I'm sorry, if I'd had any idea, I'd have warned you. It never occurred to me that the Tear would lock on to you." She paused, lowering her gaze. "I see the chain, and the soft lights flickering. Do you mind showing me where the Tear went into your skin?"

Roxy reached up and undid two buttons, pulling the left side of the shirt open.

Darcy grimaced. "I've never seen anything like that. It seems to be over your heart."

Key came up behind Roxy. "Can you get it out?"

Roxy pulled her shirt closed, her movements slow.

Darcy said, "I want to look with my third eye. Try to see what the Tear is doing." She reached out and took Roxy's arm.

Roxy looked down at her hand. "Is it safe to touch me?"

A renewed tremor of rage went through him. Key fisted his hands to keep from pulling her into his arms.

Kindness filled Darcy's gaze. "I'm sure it is." She led Roxy to the couch. "Carla and Ailish are on the computer. We're going to join our powers."

"Hi, Roxy," Carla's voice floated out.

"Hang in there, Roxy," Ailish said. "We'll figure this out."

Key stood a few feet back, and crossed his arms over his chest. He saw only the back of the laptop, but he was used to the way the witches often worked through the computer.

"We'll get started," Darcy said and her magic began blooming, her witch-shimmer coloring her skin with gold lights. Roxy's witch-shimmer rose and warmed her too-pale skin. A part of Key noticed the incredible beauty of the two witches, his artist's eye catching fingers of gold slipping through Roxy's sunset shimmer. Their magic was joining as Darcy used her third eye to see what the Tear was doing. He saw tiny flares of Carla's and Ailish's witch-shimmers, too, so they were circling their power or whatever they did.

Then he felt Roxy's magic as it streamed through him, the dragon flared to life, and the resulting thrum inside him was incredible. Hot arousal and life-giving light mixed and grew. He was acting as Roxy's familiar, he realized. They'd sealed their souls, and their intimate bond was coming to life.

For one second, fierce joy soared through him. The curse was truly broken, and he had a mate!

Then he looked at Roxy and saw the pulsing colored lights, muted from the layer of skin and clothing. The crystal Tear was in her and would kill her if they didn't get it out.

The magic began to recede. Key heard the door and turned to see Axel stride in, then walk over to stand at Darcy's shoulder. The two of them often communicated through their bond. Had the witch called him into the condo? Key had to know. "What did you find?"

Roxy laced her fingers together, turning her knuckles white. "It's bad, isn't it?"

Darcy's witch-shimmer faded to pale distress. She glanced at Key, then focused on Roxy. "I'm afraid it is. The pulses of light in the Tear are wrapping around your life force. If we pull it out, with magic or force, it'll kill you."

Key's hands fisted. "And if it stays in?"

Darcy bit her lip, then reached out to cover Roxy's joined hands. "It's draining your life."

The skin on Key's chest burned and blistered beneath his shirt. *What?* he thought darkly, now the dragon was pitching a fit that he'd failed to claw her to death? He wasn't satisfied with the Tear draining off her life?

—————※—————

Roxy was dying. Because she'd chosen magic. She didn't belong here with these powerful witches who had men who loved them. Darcy sat facing her on the couch, Axel standing at her shoulder. Carla and Ailish were on the laptop screen. She couldn't even look at Kieran. He blamed himself. But she'd been the one who bought into the stupid fairy tale, reciting a story about Dyfyr that she'd probably just imagined, convincing herself that the ancient dragon loved her. Or maybe her schema had fueled the fantasy to get her to Awaken her magic.

Hurts. Dyfyr had told her down in Phoenix's gym. Had that been real? If it had, he must have meant it as a warning, that it hurts to be awake, so leave him alone. Her eyes filled with tears, and she looked to the left, over the back of the couch at the wet bar. Dyfyr...he felt so real to her, like the part of her that had been missing for as long as she could remember. "Why does he hate me?" God, she was so pathetic. She didn't want them to see her like this. Didn't want Kieran to see her broken by a pain so profound that breathing hurt.

Hurts.

Her chakras shivered and swelled, her magic streaming out with a will of its own. Roxy didn't care. She had an inkling now of how much Dyfyr suffered in losing his lover.

Something brushed her arms. She jerked her gaze back, but Darcy touched only her linked hands in her lap. Key was still across the room. Yet she felt something, like buttery-soft leather stroking her bare arms.

Hurts.

That voice! It triggered a deja vu so powerful, Dyfyr's image filled her mind. Was it the dragon? Or was her sanity breaking?

"Roxy."

Carla's voice. She turned, looking at the witch on the laptop.

"I don't think that's it," Carla said.

"What?" Her head was filled with the dragon.

"I don't think Dyfyr hates you," the witch said patiently. "I saw the way he reacted to you when he partially woke in Phoenix's gym. That dragon did what you told him to and went back to sleep."

"Then why did he try to kill her?" Key demanded. "You weren't there, Carla. I tried to grab the Tear, and razor-sharp claws sprouted out. If I hadn't pulled back, I'd have pierced her heart."

"Something's going on, but I don't think Dyfyr is trying to kill her. I asked the Ancestors, and they believe Roxy is the reincarnation of the dragon's lover, too."

The brush of wings on her arms was still there.

Confused, she said, "I feel him," Roxy said, looking over to Key. "Dyfyr, I feel his soft, leathery wings."

Key stood unmoving in his shroud of anger and self-recrimination. "Don't trust him. It's a trick."

Roxy slid her hands from Darcy's and stood up. "Then what should I do, just give up and die?" Rage erupted inside her. "Come on, Kieran. Everyone is always telling me what to do, everyone knows what's best for me, so tell me what the hell am I supposed to do?"

His left eye twitched, then he exploded with, "I told you not to wear the goddamned Tear! But you wouldn't listen to me! You had to wear it! And now you're dying!"

That's right. He had told her what to do and she hadn't listened. So he'd leave. That's how it worked. People only wanted her when she did as they wished. The wings had left her and now she truly was alone. She lifted her chin. "So which is it? Are you drowning in all that dark, angsty guilt that you carry around, or is it all my fault? Why don't you go draw your pretty pictures until you figure it out." She turned toward the couch, then looked back over her shoulder. "Oh, and FYI, I'm going to fight to live, so deal with it." Kieran was right, it was her fault, but she was angry, hurt, scared, and so alone it felt as if she were going to fall into an endless hole of thick, choking darkness.

The silence made her want to run like a coward. Axel, Darcy, Carla and Ailish, they belonged to Kieran, not her. She just stood there, not knowing what to do. Leave? But where would she go? Would Liam still hunt her? She stared at the back of the leather couch. Then she remembered the phone Sutton had given her. She reached down and picked it up. "I'll call my mother and go stay—"

Key snatched the phone from her hand. "The hell

you are! Liam will have you within minutes. He'll cut that Tear out of you."

She shuddered.

"Roxy, damn it, I can't touch you." Blue mist flared in his eyes. "I don't dare touch you because I don't trust the dragon not to hurt you. But I want to. I know you're scared, upset, and I want to...I'm sorry."

Yeah, and she'd made him feel worse. "I shouldn't have snapped at you." She sank down on the couch. "Carla, if Dyfyr doesn't hate me, then what happened?" She hoped the witches would still help her after that special little outburst. Although Kieran made a good point, the Tear was in her, and they had to keep it out of Liam's hands. Exhaustion spread through her.

"I don't know. We're missing something, a piece somewhere." On the screen, Carla pushed her long blond hair back. "How many chakras did you open tonight?"

"Five."

"If you can open your third eye in your sixth chakra, you might be able to see Dyfyr and ask him. That's what the Ancestors suggested."

She thought about that. "I'd need more power than I have yet..."

Darcy leaned forward. "It builds as you and your soul mirror strengthen your connection."

She looked up to Key, knowing she'd need him. Her magic was based in sex and...

"I don't trust the dragon," he said.

So he wouldn't touch her, help her.

"Key." Ailish filled the screen. "You can try to touch Roxy and see what Dyfyr does. You have to try. Roxy's going to need more power. And her time is limited."

Time. Her life was draining. She hadn't thought to ask. Roxy turned to the witch. "How long?"

Ailish's silvery eyes darted around, revealing her distress. "From what we saw in our third eye, not long, maybe two months. I'd say you have to work fast, you have a week or two before you start losing strength."

Two months. Two months to live, two months to find the answer. Once Key calmed down, she'd get him to help her try to open her third eye and talk to Dyfyr. Then—

"Roxy," Carla flashed back on the screen. "You said your mother is a fertility witch, too. Talk to her, see if she has any ideas. I really feel like we're missing some vital part of the puzzle. Fertility witches are so secretive, she might know what we're missing."

My mother. Another wave of guilt snapped through her, causing her heart to hammer. "I should have told you this sooner." Her voice was as heavy as her heart. Each beat was painful.

Darcy laid her hand on Roxy's thigh. "What?"

Her mouth went dry. "My mother's name is Gwen Banfield, but on the Circle Witches, she goes by Silver."

The other witch jerked her hand back. "Silver. The witch who accused Carla of misusing her power?"

Roxy felt the bite of Darcy's anger in her voice. She reached up and rubbed her temple. "Yes. My mother started the Circle Witches and she's bitterly jealous of you three coming in and pushing her aside. Carla being chosen as Moon Witch Advisor by the Ancestors infuriated her. She's power hungry." She dropped her hand and added, "All my life, she refused to tell me the secrets of fertility witches until I had Awakened. She pushed me even when she found out my Awakening was a witch hunter, and my power releasing might inflame his bloodlust. All because she knew I had the full goddess mark, and I might be able to wake the dragon. But she never told me that, she just pushed and pushed." She stopped talking.

"Why didn't you say something when I asked about your mother?" Carla inquired.

"Or when you called your mother from my loft?" Key demanded. "Why didn't you tell us?"

What could she say? "I was afraid." Afraid Key would reject her, her new friends would reject her. Afraid she'd have to leave, afraid Liam would get her again. She wanted to save Key's soul by binding their souls. She just wanted to—

"What else are you hiding?" Key asked.

His voice rippled across her skin. She closed her eyes and knew she had to tell them all. "I think my mother was lying about the Tear. That she knows more." Whipping her head around, she opened her eyes and said, "I believe she was involved in the spell that created you. I felt her magic when I connected with Dyfyr in Phoenix's gym."

He stepped back like she'd hit him. His entire body tightened, and a tremor went through him. Then he turned and strode out.

And he was gone.

17

KEY STOOD ATOP THE HIGHEST building in Glassbreakers, Wave Runner Plaza. Years ago he'd painted a mural in the lobby and discovered the roof.

He stood at the three-foot-high wall, looking out. The night was dark and cool, lit by icy stars and the moon. The wind buffeted him, carrying the scents of the ocean and the city. If he leaped off the building, would his wings come out, allowing him to soar the skies? Or would he drop twenty stories, his body as heavy as his heart?

Even the sight of the city lights couldn't dim the memory of that Tear disappearing into Roxy or the claws coming out on his hands.

Or Roxy in the maze with the moonlight pouring over her, waking the dragon as he was buried inside her body. Or when he'd laid her back on the grass, sliding his body into her heat and watching her eyes shimmer with powerful emotion that echoed in his chest. She'd been his, and he'd felt a part of something special.

Then he'd nearly killed her. Was killing her. For his bellowing at her that she insisted on wearing the necklace, who was the freak of magic that drew the picture of her wearing it? Who took the necklace from its hiding place and settled it over her neck, letting the Tear fall against her breast?

Just like when he'd thrown his knife and hit Vivian in the throat. She'd been so young, pregnant with their child, and he'd killed her.

It never ended, no matter what he did, where he went, violence followed him.

His dry eyes ached.

Key turned from the city, facing the huge expanse of roof. He reached to the small of his back and pulled his knife from its sheath. He'd gladly cut the dragon from his chest if it would save Roxy, but he knew the creature was immortal.

Instead, Key dropped to his knees. Feeling the hard concrete bite into his kneecaps, he slid the blade across his palm. Then he laid the knife on the ground, bowed his head and called, "Wing Slayer." This had worked for Phoenix when he needed the god to help him save Ailish. Would Wing Slayer do the same for Roxy? Key had only one, single hope.

He could hear each drip of his blood splashing to the concrete as he stayed there, bowing down before his god, hoping for help. The wind rushed, in the distance the waves broke, and second by second, Key's desolation grew.

Each tick of time that he was away from Roxy was torture. He'd walked out on her. Abandoned her.

He'd had to. Because Dyfyr was enraged when she said she thought her mother had something to do with Key's creation. Both of them had been furious, but Key wasn't angry at Roxy. Not for that. She should have told him. God knows he had told her enough about himself. She should have trusted him.

But it was the Dyfyr's fury that had made Key leave. Fearing the creature would wait until Key was close enough to her and do something to hurt her.

The dripping of blood slowed and stopped. He healed fast, so Key snatched up his knife and cut again, a deeper, longer line. He returned the knife to the ground, the symbol showing his submission to the god.

Prayed and waited.

Seconds later, he felt the shift in the atmosphere as the air crackled with power. The hair on his arms stood up, his skin pebbled and a shadow fell over him. "Hunter."

Key lifted his head. His god hovered inches off the ground, the moonlight illuminating him in all his power. Even his calves were huge, massive thighs, arms wrapped in bronzed bands stamped with wings, a wall of chest and a face that was indescribably brutal and beautiful. He had gold eyes flecked with red. Spread out behind him were wings woven with gold feathers outlined in bronze. They must have spanned at least fourteen feet. He was too much to take in. "Wing Slayer. Can you save Roxy? Can you grant us immortality to stop the Tear from killing her?"

The god's wings darkened to a deep bronze, and his face lost the beauty to pure rage. "No. The Tear has bound to her life force. The Ancestors and I cannot do the required shift in her life force to make her immortal while the Tear is in her."

Hope crashed around him. He saw Roxy's strained face when she whispered, *Why does he hate me?* "What do I do to help her?"

"Only Dyfyr can save her now. I can't undo his magic, Kieran. But you and Dyfyr must save her."

He didn't know how. "The dragon was going to hurt her. I don't trust him."

"Find out why." The god's wings brightened, the air thickened with the scent of flowers, a scent much too feminine for the god. "Roxy must live, she's vital. Guard her at all costs; do not let Liam or any rogue get her."

His brother. "Liam claims to be blood-born. What does that mean?"

The building beneath him began to shake and sway. The stars in the sky dimmed. A sulfur smell burned Key's nose. "He is an abomination, a work of Asmodeus! After you stabbed him in the heart, he was dying as he should. The rogues took him to Young, who under Asmodeus's orders, did this."

The roof began to spin, and Key was caught up in a whirling funnel. He had no control over his body. Then suddenly, he was looking at a scene as it played out:

Liam lay on a bed, a ragged, fist-sized hole in his chest where Key had cut out a chunk of his heart. On a gurney next to him lay a woman. She was strapped down helpless, her eyes wide with fear as a big man with dark hair hovered over her. He was familiar; Key tried to place him when he saw the man's right forearm: the black, shiny, squirming burn mark that was the Immortal Death Dagger.

Quinn Young!

Key watched as he jammed a needle into her vein. Blood filled a small tube, traveling...

To Liam.

He looked back at the witch. She'd been stripped naked, and he saw beneath her breast the half-goddess mark. Fertility witch. As he watched time went by. Days with just his brother lying there in some kind of suspended state. Eventually there was another fertility witch. Then another.

The scene spun away.

Key opened his eyes, kneeling once more before his god. "Blood-born. They regrew his heart with witch blood."

Wing Slayer's eyes seared with vicious red. "I'd already taken Liam's soul and destroyed it. So Asmodeus was able to keep his body going, creating a weapon to find the Tear. It took almost eleven years and the blood of many fertility witches to do it. The demon thinks to make me mortal and kill me."

"Can Liam die?"

"Yes. The witch blood, as long as he keeps getting it makes him faster and, if it's fresh enough, gives him some advantages. Finish the job. Cut out his heart or burn him. He'll go shade and be gone."

"And Roxy?"

The smell of flowers swirled on the air, mixing with the strong, masculine, metal scent of the god. "Save her. Before all else, save her."

Key blinked, and the god vanished.

He reached down and picked up his knife. The smooth handle was engraved with the wings of a dragon. His god had marked his knife. The traditional sign that Wing Slayer had accepted his hunter.

⋙⋘

Roxy startled awake when she heard something move in the room. She held her breath and listened. She was in Kieran's bedroom in the condo—she knew it must be his bedroom because she had found her clothes and laptop in there. She guessed it was close to four A.M. Her heart pounded, but she knew Liam couldn't get into the condos.

Could he?

She lay frozen, panicked when she realized anyone could see the lights pulsing from the Tear embedded in her chest. She had a black tank top on, but light still leaked out. She pressed her hand over the spot.

"It's me, Roxy." Key pulled the covers back and slid into the bed. "Go back to sleep."

He was getting into bed with her? Dropping her hand, she scooted to the far right and lay there, not sure what to do. It was his condo, his bedroom. The gulf between them ached like a wound. "I'm sorry," she said softly, trying to reach across that chasm. "I should have told you about my mother."

He was silent, then said, "I told you...things about what my mother did to create me, about Viv. I thought that's what a relationship is...showing the other person who you really are and hoping that maybe they could care about you anyway."

She'd hurt him and that made her sick. "You're right. I had all these reasons, but at the very core of it, I was a coward. I suspected my mother when you told me how you were created because she'd once told me that she'd done a spell so incredible it was bigger than the miracle of birth. But I didn't want to believe it. I just...didn't. Then in the gym, the feel of my mother's magic was a faint thread, but so familiar. Why else would I feel that touch of her magic unless she did the spell? Or was part of the spell?" She fisted her hands at her side, her stomach burning with regret and so many other things. "I should have told you then."

He turned on his side, facing her. "I'm not your father, sweetheart. I'm not going to leave you."

"But you did." She looked up to the ceiling, wishing she could call those words back. She had no right—

"Roxy, look at me."

She shifted onto her left side. There was just enough light floating in to show her his face. "I left because I felt the rage of Dyfyr. When you said you believed your mom was involved, the dragon grew furious. I was so damned afraid I'd lose control of him and he'd hurt you that I left. But it's killing me, right this second I want to touch you. Need to touch you."

Her chakras slipped open, reaching for him. Her schema itched, wanting more of him. And her heart just ached. She wanted to comfort him, wanted to ease him. "What if I touch you?" She scooted closer, reaching her hand out and touching his face. The warm contact of his skin against her palm felt like a full breath of sweet air. She rubbed her thumb over the ridge of his cheekbone. His eyes had more blue in the faint light.

"I don't want to hurt you. I don't understand Dyfyr. Why he would try to hurt you."

"We have to ask him." She trailed her hand below his jaw and around the back of his neck. Feeling the tension, she rubbed the muscles.

"I know." His eyes gleamed. "I saw Wing Slayer."

As Roxy recovered from surprise, she listened while he described his encounter with his god.

"Blood-born. He was reborn with fertility blood." Her stomach turned over at the horror.

"Roxy, we're going to find a way to get the Tear out. I won't stop until we do. I don't know how when I'm afraid to touch you, but we'll do it. Wing Slayer said I must save you above all else."

"Me?" She dropped her hand to the sheet, close to where his hand rested.

"Yes. And he marked my knife."

She forgot about herself at the sheer wonder in Kieran's voice.

"He impressed dragon wings on the hilt, showing that he'd accepted me as his hunter. He believes in us, Roxy. He can't give us immortality until we get the Tear out, but he believes we can find the way to free you." He dropped his gaze to the bed between them and slid his hand until he touched hers. Then he wrapped his fingers around hers, holding her hand with such care. He lifted his gaze. "The dragon's not angry now. He's letting me touch you." He released her fingers and edged toward the curve of her left breast. "I need to touch you, starting here."

Roxy looked down as his finger skimmed the swell of her breast over the tank top. The Tear pulsed softly, pinks, reds, blues...all the colors sliding over her skin as the lights shifted in a slow easy rhythm. "It looks so strange. I can feel a vibration to it. But I feel the touch of your finger more." Her magic streamed out and curled around his touch. Tingles rippled through her center, and her schema began to throb.

He skated his finger up to where the V of the chain pierced her skin. "It's nestled over your heart, mirroring your heartbeat." He looked up, heat warming his eyes. "Do you trust me? I swear if the dragon tries to hurt you..."

"Yes," she breathed the word. She had trusted him from the moment he'd seen her schema and walked away when she'd asked him to. He'd respected her choice, her needs, her wants.

He reached down and caught the edge of her shirt, and Roxy lifted her arms as he pulled the shirt off.

Key rose, slid his right arm beneath her shoulders, and pulled her to the shelter of his chest. She quickly realized he was naked and aroused. His skin was hot, his scent filled her lungs. And then he kissed her, his warm mouth covering hers, his tongue easing in, tasting her while he cupped her breast and teased her nipple with his thumb.

Her magic began to race up and down, fluttering around their joined mouths, seeking the heat of his hand, even grazing where her side was pressed into him. Her thoughts broke apart and drifted away, replaced by the feel of Kieran. He kept up the sensual onslaught to her breasts, circling them, petting, soft tugs on her nipples, his kiss growing hotter, deeper. She couldn't lie still beneath him, shifting her hips, her schema demanding attention and flooding the folds between her thighs.

Key broke the kiss, rising up to push the covers back. He watched her face as he trailed a hand down her ribs, over her stomach to the edge of her panties.

Hooking his fingers in them, he lifted her up to drag them down her legs.

Roxy bent her knees and kicked them off.

Key slid his hand up her left leg, caught her knee and lifted it over his hip. She lay on her back, spread open, his arm cradling her. The room was semidark, but the shadowy light on his face revealed how much he needed her trust. "I need to know I can give you pleasure, not pain. I need to."

Her magic, her body, her very soul answered him, swelling until she was desperate for his touch. "Please."

He moved his hand up her thigh until he came to her schema. He caressed the mark. "Your magic, it's so damned sexy," he said, hot color rising over his cheeks.

Her magic surged like a tidal wave. She couldn't bear the torment and twisted her hips, trying to get more. The need was too big, too deep. Panic was starting to constrict her chest. *It will keep growing with no relief!*

Kieran tightened his powerful arm around her shoulders, and a second later she felt wings wrapping around her.

"We have you," his voice was deeper and fuller. He trailed his hand between her thighs, to her slick swollen folds, and he stroked her where she needed it most. His fingers caressed her clit, up and down, back and forth until she was nearly weeping as the pressure built and built. But Kieran and Dyfyr held her, giving her more and more.

Then he slid his fingers inside her, filling her, and Roxy shattered, arching as hot, deep pleasure vibrated within her, all hers. Just for her. She felt Kieran and Dyfyr giving it to her, stroking her higher, supporting her as she flew, then catching her as she fell.

Key rolled over her, his shoulders bulging and his

eyes darkened to a fierce, possessive blue. He spread her legs wider, pressed the thick tip of his arousal to her entrance. "Do that again, baby. This time, with me." Then he thrust deep, his body joining hers in another flight of soul-binding pleasure.

—✦—

"Roxy."

She startled awake and looked around to see she was in Kieran's bedroom. Looking to her left, the bed was empty next to her. What time was it? She glanced at the clock. Almost noon.

Had she dreamed someone called her name? She blinked, trying to push back the fog of sleep.

"Roxanne!"

She jumped, recognizing the voice this time. "Mom?" Her magic bubbled, her chakras feeling another witch trying to connect. What the hell was her mom doing here? "Where are you?"

"Your laptop. It's taken me hours to find you!"

In seconds her first four chakras opened. She looked to the dresser across the room where her laptop rested next to a couple of piles of folded clothes that Ram and Sutton had gotten from her apartment. Roxy swung her legs out of bed and realized she was naked. She grabbed her panties, dragged them up her legs, and stood. For a second, black spots danced on the edges of her vision, and she had to put her hand on the bed to hold the room steady.

Damn, she'd slept hard.

"One second, Mom," she called out, then she went to the dresser, grabbed a high-neck, dark-colored shirt, and put it on, then tugged on a pair of jeans. She looked down; the pulsing colored lights from the tear were dimmed beneath the shirt. Another sound caused her to look up.

Kieran walked in wearing jeans and no shirt. Dyfyr sat on his chest, holding the lock of her hair. Key carried a steaming mug and crossed to her.

Closing her magic for a second so Gwen wouldn't hear, she said, "It's my mother."

He handed her the mug. "Yeah, I heard. You look a little pale." He touched her face. "You okay?" He lowered his hand to where the Tear was beneath her shirt. "Any pain? Weakness?"

"No, just slept hard and felt a little dizzy when I stood from being jarred awake." She took a sip of the tea, and said, "This helps. Thanks." Taking a breath, she added, "I don't want my mom to know you're in here, okay?" He leaned closer and kissed her, then stepped back and propped a shoulder against the closet. He hooked his thumbs in his jeans and appeared relaxed.

She picked up the computer and set it on the bed. She raised the lid, keeping Kieran behind it. Gwen's head and shoulders appeared on the screen. Roxy was surprised to see that her hair had more silver streaks, and there were deeper lines around her eyes and mouth. Her mom looked tired and worried. Immediately, her mother said, "You've Awakened."

That caused her to pause. "How do you know?"

"You're my daughter, of course I know. And I can feel the spike in your power through the computer connection." For a second, her tiredness vanished. "You've done it, Roxy. You're a soul-mirror witch. Did the dragon wake?"

Debating what to tell her mom, she looked up at Kieran, then gasped. His chest! Around the dragon's mouth, red welts and blisters were forming! The dragon was burning him. Yet all Kieran did was shake his head, as if telling her to ignore it.

Why was the dragon angry? Was it from talking

about his being awake? That made her think of the Tear. She looked at her mom and said, "Yes, he's awake, and he's angry."

"Angry? But you're—"

"I'm what?" Just how much had her mother lied? Frustration steamed through her.

Her mom said, "We'll do The Lover Ceremony and appease him. Yes, that will work. We'll show him how we honor his lover, our first fertility witch. You'll represent her. You'll need your sixth chakra, your third eye, and maybe you'll be able to see the dragon. Talk to him. Explain that we need him."

Roxy watched her mother evade the question, and spin out plans. "I doubt it. He tried to kill me."

"What?" Her mouth dropped and eyes rounded, making her face look like a comic-book sketch.

Roxy felt her mother's magic sputter with her surprise. She pushed harder. "He was so furious"—she yanked the neck of her shirt down—"he embedded the Tear in me and then tried to kill me with his claws."

"That can't be!" her mom cried, leaning forward until her face filled the screen. "How could this happen? What did you do to him?"

Roxy heard a *clang* in her head, the door slamming on her tiny hope that her mom hadn't lied about the Tear and more to her. "You knew. And you lied." The words hurt her throat.

"No! I've only heard rumors! Why would you have the Tear? I don't—" She narrowed her eyes and said, "It's the other soul-mirror witches turning you against me. They hate me. Carla does dangerous, risky magic; she takes people to the astral plane! She lost a mortal on the astral plane once, yet the Ancestors chose her. She'll lie about me, say I did things—"

"What things?" Roxy demanded. Last night when she'd told the witches who her mother was, Carla had just asked why she hadn't told them. It had been

Darcy who lashed out about Silver. Roxy didn't know the soul-mirror witches well yet, but her sense of Carla was of a kind and deeply compassionate woman.

"Making you think I know about the Tear!"

Carla hadn't done that. Heavy fatigue blanketed her. "Stop lying. You had something to do with calling Dyfyr's soul into Kieran, didn't you?"

"I knew it!" her mother said, her face going red. "Carla's telling lies about me, trying to discredit me. But she's the one who lost that mortal on the astral plane!"

Roxy had a vague recollection of that, and as she remembered, Carla found the mortal and retrieved her. Roxy might not be a psychologist like Carla, but she recognized guilt, and trying to accuse someone else of a crime to cover your own. "We're not talking about Carla." She leaned over and set the cooling mug of tea on Key's dresser and returned her gaze to her mother. "We're talking about what you did to Kieran. How you risked a baby's life by calling the soul of an ancient dragon into him when he was in his mother's womb."

She shook her head. "You don't know what you're talking about. You refused your magic all these years! You wouldn't do what I told you, you wouldn't even read the comic books until last year!"

Roxy went so still she heard her own heartbeat. She looked up at Kieran and saw that he'd caught it, too. The dragon's ruby eyes were blazing with fury, and Key's eyes were a flat gray menace. She returned her gaze to her mom. "You sent me those comic books?" People sent her books, graphic novels, comic books...all sorts of material all the time. Oh God, it was hitting her just how deep this went. "I felt your magic in Dyfyr. You were part of that spell, you kept track of Kieran..." She looked up at him. "I'm sorry."

"Who's there? Roxy, who are you talking to?"

Key strode to her, slammed the laptop closed and shoved it to the floor. He stood above her, his chest rippled, veins standing out on his arms, his hands fisted. "That bitch." He looked down at her. "She's been manipulating you, got you interested in my comics so you'd seek me out, and now that goddamned Tear is locked inside you!" He ground his jaw, the cords on his neck swelling.

She could feel the heat of his anger, like a band tightening around her head. But she was finished being naive and weak. She stood up. "I'm going to tell the other witches. They need to know that we've confirmed she did the spell."

Key stepped back and held his hands out in front of him, opening and closing his fists. "My fingers burn like the claws want to come out." He looked up at her. "I can't touch you. I better leave to be safe."

Roxy dropped her gaze to Dyfyr. The dragon was so angry, his two curved horns looked sharper and his claws were out in the tattoo. The burn marks from earlier were healing, though. She couldn't begin to understand what her mother had been thinking, putting a powerful, ancient dragon in a child. "Where are you going?"

Key turned, went to his dresser and pulled out a shirt. "Phoenix and I are going to make a show of moving the Dragon Tear. We had Linc plant the rumor about it last night in a poker game, and Ram informed the recruits this morning to be on the lookout. Word will get around." He strapped on his holster for his knife, then put a backup blade in his boot.

"But...I have the Tear, how can you move it?"

"Sutton and Carla bought a diamond teardrop pendant this morning. The witches will infuse the stone with enough magic to give it the illusion of being as powerful a prism as the real Tear."

Worry gnawed at her. "You're trying to draw out Liam." A shudder of fear and revulsion rippled down her spine. The memory of her own blood and screams made her queasy. He should have been dead, but the demon and Young regrew his heart with the blood of fertility witches. How many died so that abomination could live?

Key's eyes blazed with hatred. "I'm going make sure he's dead this time."

"It's too dangerous, he's—"

Key strode to her, looking down. "He's a threat to you. He dies."

She blinked and felt the impact of his simple words. "Be careful, please."

"I'm still running hot. Can't touch you or kiss you, but know this, Roxy—I'll be back."

Running hot; he meant the dragon's anger. "Stay still." She rose up on her toes and brushed her mouth over his. Just a soft kiss and then she moved back.

Blue warmth flickered in his eyes. "Stay here, Roxy, where you're safe. I'll call you later."

After he left, Roxy bent over to pick up the laptop and felt another wave of dizziness. Was it the Tear? Sickening her? Maybe working faster than the witches thought? She dropped the computer on the dresser and went into the bathroom.

For a second she smiled. Leave it to Kieran to have red walls accenting white fixtures and black towels. She turned on the shower, stripped out of her clothes, and got under the spray. Curious, she looked at her schema. The mark was full of color, a mix of blue and green. If her life was draining so quickly, would the color in the schema fade?

Yet the goddess looked almost fat with color. That must be a sign that Kieran was feeding her magic. With her confidence rising, she was determined that she'd attain enough power to communicate with Dyfyr and find a way to remove the Tear. She had to—Roxy had more reason than ever to live now.

Kieran.

And she was going to fight with everything she had to stay with him.

$$\rightleftharpoons 18 \rightleftharpoons$$

ROXY FINISHED EXPLAINING WHAT SHE had learned for sure that morning about her mom to Darcy, Carla and Ailish. The blind witch was on the computer, Carla sat next to Roxy on the couch, and Darcy paced furiously around them.

Darcy whirled around. "She accused Carla of doing dangerous magic. Tried to get the Circle Witches to turn their backs on Carla when she needed help!"

Roxy had no defense for her mother. "I've been thinking about it. I'm pretty sure she thought that the Ancestors would tell Carla, the Moon Witch Advisor, what my mom did. That's why she wanted that position so badly. But she had to realize, on some level, she wasn't going to get it. Aside from doing something so dangerous and *wrong* with her magic, she hadn't found her soul mirror. She just wasn't powerful enough." That took her thoughts in another direction. "In fact, that's probably what scared her about each of you becoming soul-mirror witches; you might have enough power to find out what she did."

"With our third eye," Darcy said.

"And knowledge chakras," Ailish added.

"We would have needed to know what to look for,"

Carla said. "And we don't seem to have the connection to dragon magic that would have allowed us to see it anyway."

"I do," Roxy said. "But I'm not powerful enough yet." Nor was she sure she wanted to actually see what her mom had done. "I haven't opened my sixth chakra yet." She went on, needing to get this clear. "You're suspicious of me because I'm her daughter, I understand. But the Tear is in me, and we need Dyfyr to figure out how to get it out and destroy it. I need to know how to open my sixth chakra."

They were silent.

"If we don't find out why the dragon is so angry and I die, Kieran is trapped. I know the curse is broken for him, but what happens to the dragon if I die?"

Darcy sank down in the chair to Roxy's right. "The hunters only get their wings for their witch. Without her, the familiar dies off. Key will be free."

"Darcy," Carla rebuked her.

Roxy looked at Darcy. "But Dyfyr is immortal."

The other witch drew her eyebrows together. "Crap."

That made Roxy laugh, she couldn't help it. Darcy was loyal to her friends, and that was something Roxy respected and valued. "Yeah, crap." Then she sobered. "Look, maybe Dyfyr can't or won't save me." That hurt, but she had to focus on Kieran and the Tear. "But if I find out why he's so angry and fix that, then he and Kieran can exist together. And maybe he can tell us what to do about the Tear. Because once I'm dead, isn't someone going to have to take out the Tear to keep rogues from getting it?" Wasn't her day just brimming with pleasant thoughts?

"How do we know you're not manipulating us?" Darcy asked.

"Oh, give it a rest!" Ailish snapped. "Roxy is the victim here, she's the one who's going to die."

Darcy sighed and looked at Roxy. "Ailish is right. I know you're not like Silver, Roxy. All three of us know it. I'm angry, not just because I don't like Silver, but I'm furious for Key, and I was taking it out on you. I'm sorry."

Roxy sat back in surprise. "You...what just happened?"

"Hell froze over and Darcy apologized," Ailish said with a grin.

"Hell seems to freeze over a lot," Carla said.

"I'm not that bad," Darcy said.

Carla smiled. "Not bad. Passionate and opinionated and we love you for it. Axel does, too."

The witch flashed a huge smile. "He really does." Then she turned to Roxy. "Any more dark family secrets?"

"N...wait. One. I don't think it has anything to do with this, though." Roxy's stomach tightened. It had been drilled into her head to never tell anyone. Shayla was her best friend, also the friend refusing to return her phone calls. "About a cousin. She's a year younger than me and wasn't even born when my mom would have done the spell to summon Dyfyr's soul into Key. I can't see how she'd be involved."

Carla said, "Is she a demon witch?"

"No! She wants her chakras to die off the same as I did. She just wants to be a screenwriter and be left alone. That's all."

"Is that her secret?" Ailish asked.

"No." Roxy really didn't know what to do. Why wasn't Shayla returning her calls or emails now that she had a phone and her laptop? "Her name is Shayla Banfield, and I swear I can't see how her situation would have anything to do with the dragon or the Tear. We had a pact not to awaken our magic, and now she's not even returning my calls."

Carla put her hand on Roxy's arm. "Let's talk about

how you open your third eye in your sixth chakra. If you think of something about Shayla's situation we need to know, then tell us."

Surprised and pleased, she said, "You trust me to make that decision after I kept the identity of my mother from you?"

Carla nodded. "You have more to lose here than any of us."

True. "Okay, so how do I open my third eye?"

"Sex with your soul mirror," Carla began.

She was more than willing to do that. They just had to get Dyfyr to cooperate and then hope he'd be willing to talk to her.

———※———

"How many do you see?" Key said into his Bluetooth as he drove through the town. It was dark; they'd waited until the streets were mostly clear of people to reduce the chances of collateral damage. Then Key had left Phoenix's house, one phone clipped on his hip, the other clutched in his hand. The magic-laced diamond inside the phone pulsed lights strong enough to show through the cracks in the casing. Any rogues with their enhanced vision would see it and believe Key was carrying the Dragon Tear. Key was really counting on drawing Liam out.

Ailish, with the help of Carla, Darcy and Roxy online, had infused the diamond with the magic to make it project colored lights similar to the Tear. Key felt a wave of pride in his witch. Darcy and Carla had spent the day at the condo helping her, teaching her how to circle magic with other witches and then project their power through the computer. She'd done it.

"Got two following you," Phoenix answered him from where he flew overhead. "One in a black SUV, another in a blue Civic. They aren't making any aggressive moves yet."

"How many in the vehicles?" Ram cut in.

Ram, Linc and Eli were stationed at various points on the streets. Axel and Sutton were at the condos as protection for Roxy and ready to fly to the scene if needed.

"I see two in each car, but could be more in back of the SUV," Phoenix answered.

The dragon shifted restlessly on his chest. Ready to fight? Or something else? Once Key thought he knew the dragon, but since he'd forced out claws on Key and gone after Roxy, Key was confused as hell. When he was with Roxy in bed last night, he'd have sworn the dragon loved her. It didn't make sense. But right now, he had to focus on—

His BlackBerry dinged a text message. Looking at the display, he saw it was from Linc. What the hell? Why wasn't he talking through their link on the headset? Softly, he said, "Linc, see anything by you?"

Silence.

"Linc," Axel's voice, was sharp. "Report."

Key opened the text and saw a picture that made his blood run cold. The words under it read, "Bring the Tear to the storage unit."

"Shit, they have Linc." He forwarded the message to the others. It showed Linc chained to a wall, beat to hell, and they were cutting a witch to blood him. Enough witch blood on him would make him insane, and he'd kill the witch. Once he did that, his soul was gone.

"I'm taking the Tear to them now." It was the same storage unit they'd rescued Tyler and his mom from. He turned left and floored it. They thought to use Linc to get the Tear from him. Bastards.

"I'll scout from the air, Key."

"I'm on my way," Axel said. "Sutton stays here. Eli,

go to Phoenix's and stay with Ailish. Ram, check Linc's position."

"Four or five minutes from the house," Eli said.

"On it," Ram answered.

Key shot down the road, heading toward the storage units. At the end of that road was the Rogue Cadre hideout, protected by the mini-Death Daggers. They'd tested how far those daggers could go, and so far, the small knives couldn't leave the actual property of the hideout. The units should be safe from those.

But if Young was anywhere nearby with the original Immortal Death Dagger on his arm, then they were in trouble. "There yet, Phoenix?"

"Yes," the hunter replied. "Activity around the center row of units at the end near the trailer. I don't see Quinn Young."

Key made a decision, parked his truck and got out. "Going invisible, and I'll get in and take a look. Stay in the air and give me vital updates only." He shoved the fake cellphone with the phony Dragon Tear deep in his pocket and took off at a run. Key fleetingly realized he was even faster since bonding with Roxy.

"Linc's car is right where he was supposed to be, glass and blood everywhere," Ram reported. "He put up a hell of a fight. The headset he was wearing is smashed."

Key covered the distance to the storage units in seconds, leaped the fence and dropped onto the asphalt, shielding himself to appear invisible. He turned down the sound on his Bluetooth so that any voice would be a bare whisper. He began moving with ghostly silence.

A tormented female scream split the night.

Hot rage seared through his chest like a silent roar. He slid his knife free of the holster at his back, more than ready to use it.

Another scream began to shrill, then broke into sobs.

His chest rattled as he ran, following the cries. Then a smooth voice said, "Do it, assholes. Witch blood will make me stronger. I'm going to cut off your balls and force them down your throats. By the time I'm done, you'll beg me to kill you."

A chill slide down Key's spine as he raced for the middle row of units.

"Damn it," Sutton snarled. "Heard that through your phone."

Key found them in the end unit. There were no lights; hunters could see in the dark with enough ambient light. Linc was chained against the back wall. His arms were stretched overhead, the chain anchored to a hook in the ceiling. His legs were in irons fastened to the wall. His face was swollen and bruised, cuts and welts all over him. As Key watched, the blood that had been smeared on his chest was vanishing.

Being absorbed.

Key looked into the man's gold eyes, and, swear to Wing Slayer, he saw a feral light taking hold. He quickly assessed the situation. Six rogues and three witches; one was dead, two alive.

Their blood scent pulsed with adrenaline. Key didn't even feel a smidge of bloodlust, but the rogues were starting to lose it.

And Linc was nearly gone, the feral beast inside him taking over. The one that would kill a witch.

"I see rogues hiding behind the trailer. Going to deal with them," Phoenix said.

"I'm on site," Axel said. "Sutton, give me Key's exact location."

Key heard it all, but his gaze caught on a rogue grabbing a witch's arm and dragging her to Linc. Another rogue got in front of her and ripped off her shirt. The witch tried to shield herself and fight.

The man in front of her grabbed and twisted her arm.

The sound of a bone snapping was followed by a piercing scream.

Key ran in, dropped his shield at the last second as he spun the rogue who broke the witch's arm and stabbed him in the heart. He twisted the blade and yanked it out. He turned to see the witch had been thrown to the ground and was out of danger for the moment. The other five rogues swarmed toward him.

Key threw his knife into the first one's throat, taking him down.

The four remaining men rushed him with knives drawn.

No time to grab his backup weapon from his boot. He turned, avoiding a stab to the heart and felt the slice to his arm. The icy-hot shock of pain tripped an internal switch, lining every cell with an inferno-like ferocity. At the same time, a flash of pain shot through the tips of his fingers. Blood spattered as four-inch, razor-sharp claws shot out from his fingers. It flashed in his mind that they seemed to get longer each time they came out.

Key went after the rogues, gouging, slicing and swiftly learning that he could jam a claw into a rogue's heart and, with a twist, snap it off. That seemed to hurt the dying rogue a lot. Yeah, Key liked that, liked hurting the bastards who would break a helpless witch's arm, liked killing them.

He heard a gunshot and a bullet tore into the back of his thigh. Snapping up to his full height he whirled around.

The last rogue stood over a witch, aiming a gun at Key. "Give me the Tear."

Key stared at the bastard. Slowly, he slid two fingers into his pocket and pulled out the fake phone. He cracked it open, hooked the chain over his finger, and let the magic-infused diamond swing, flashing the glittering colors of the rainbow. "Tell Liam to come and get it. Where's the coward hiding?"

The rogue's eyes fastened on the teardrop diamond and he said, "Throw it to me. Now!"

"Nope. If my brother wants it, he'll have to show himself." Was Liam invisible and cowering in a corner? Where the hell was he?

The rogue fired again.

The bullet ripped through his other thigh. He took a step, barely noticing the pain. "You're dead, asshole."

The rogue aimed the gun at Key's heart.

Key spun, and as he completed the circle and snapped his wrist hard, the two remaining claws flew like missiles. One hit the man in his eye, the other in his chest. The rogue dropped the gun, his hands fluttering in a futile effort to dislodge the claws. Then his legs went out, and he collapsed to the ground and died.

Key shoved the necklace into his pocket, then walked over to the witch with the broken arm. She was sitting with the other witch, both of them in pain. He pulled off his shirt and ripped it down the front. "Put your good arm through here," he said gently.

"You're shot. Both legs. And you had claws." She stared at him with huge blue eyes.

"I'm a Wing Slayer Hunter, I won't hurt you." He gently guided her arm into the shirt. It was so big on her, he wrapped it around her broken arm and it easily covered her.

"Them, too?" the second witch asked, pointing to Axel and Phoenix standing in front of a still chained Linc.

Key had heard Axel and Phoenix fighting outside and assumed that more rogues had shown up.

"Don't release me," Linc said, his gold eyes fixed on

the witches. He was straining against the chains, trying to break free even as he warned them not to let him go. The witch blood they had put on him was moving through his veins, working in his brain.

"Tranq him," Axel said.

Phoenix pulled out a humongous needle, uncapped it and buried it in Linc's ass.

Linc looked at Axel. "Rather die than go rogue. Swear it." His eyes were getting heavy.

The hawk put his hand on Linc's shoulder. "I swear to Wing Slayer, if we can't save you, I'll kill you myself."

Linc relaxed and let the drug knock him out.

Phoenix walked over to him. "Claws? Trust you to be a superfreak, comic boy."

"You're wearing blue and purple wings and you think I'm the freak?" Key got up, found his knife in the heart of a dead rogue, pulled it out, and cleaned it. After checking to make sure all his claws were gone, he stowed the knife. He had no intention of losing the knife that Wing Slayer had marked. Then he walked back and carefully lifted the witch with the broken arm.

Axel stepped in front of him. "You have bullet holes in your thighs. We'll take care of the witches, you go have Roxy heal those."

He shook his head. "Can't get near her right now." He didn't trust the dragon, didn't trust himself. Key studied the carnage he'd done in a rage. Yeah, they had all deserved to die, he was down with that. But if Roxy had been nearby, would he have hurt her? He saw Viv's face in his mind again, his knife in her throat, and the last word she ever said, *Why?* echoing in his head. Then the scene switched to Roxy when he'd slid into bed with her early this morning. She'd trusted him to touch her, trusted him in the most intimate, vulnerable way a woman could. He wanted to be the man she seemed to believe he was—a man who could control the beast inside him, but...

Key looked around again. He'd torn the rogues apart with his claws. Christ. Turning back to Axel, he snapped, "My wounds will heal, I've got her."

They had to get the witches to safety and try to save Linc.

≋ 19 ≋

ROXY WALKED INTO AILISH AND Phoenix's house with Darcy and Sutton. Carla had gone over earlier in the day to work with Tyler and his mom. The big man had a handful of chains and padlocks. His face was grim until he spotted Carla. He held out one arm.

The blond witch slipped into his embrace.

Roxy moved past them, giving them a moment of privacy, and wandered into the kitchen. She was surprised to see Tyler sitting at the bar drawing in a sketchbook, and Paige moving around in the kitchen making coffee. "You both look rested." It was amazing. Yesterday, Paige's brown eyes had been haunted, with dark circles, and she couldn't seem to keep the thread of a conversation. Tyler had coped better, but he'd been afraid to leave his mother's side.

"Hi, Roxy." Tyler turned to face her.

Paige turned on the coffeemaker and walked around the counter to stand by her son. "Carla helped us a lot. She used hypnosis."

"And magic," Tyler said.

Roxy was startled.

Carla came into the room. "They deserve the truth," she said gently. "They saw me heal Eli in the

265

warehouse, they've been used and hurt, and they had a right to know why."

Roxy glanced at Paige again. She'd obviously showered, her dark blond hair drying in a sleek sheet to her shoulders in a way her own hair never did. She was built more like Ailish, slim and strong. There were faint lines around her eyes and a world-weariness that suggested a rough life. But she saw relief, too; the woman looked lighter. "Paige, I think they saw me talking to Tyler right before I was kidnapped. I'm so sorry. I would never have endangered your son if I had realized."

"We're safe now. Ailish says we can stay here until we get settled. They've even offered me a job at a nightclub, Axel of Evil."

"Ailish has already shown me some self-defense," Tyler added. "I'm drawing her now. Want to see?"

Roxy smiled at the boy. These people were going to be okay. "Yes, I do." She walked over to look. Tyler had drawn Ailish in some kind of flying kick. Her hair flew out behind her; she wore a short little top and black pants and looked a little bit like the hard-assed women in Key's comics.

Except for the face. He'd captured her strong bones, silvery blue eyes bracketed by scars. There was such strength in the image, then that one heartbreaking spot of vulnerability made the picture come to life. "You have to show Key."

He looked up at her with such hope. "Really?"

She thought of Mural Maze, and all that Kieran did to support artists. "Definitely. Do you know he hung the picture you drew of him and Dyfyr? I saw it."

Tyler's eyes widened. "Awesome."

Ailish walked in. "Tyler, Paige, I'd like you both to go up to the media room and stay there. We're bringing in someone who could be very dangerous. They are going to be here any minute." She turned to face Tyler. "No matter what you hear, stay up there. Understand?"

"Yes." Tyler bit his lower lip. "Will Key be here?"

"Yes. Phoenix is already here, he's downstairs with Sutton. Key and Axel will bring the hunter in."

Paige said, "We'll go now. Tyler, gather up your stuff."

The boy did and headed to the stairs. Paige hung back, and put her hand on Ailish's arm. "If there's something I can do, will you tell me? I mean it, I want to help if I can."

"I'll tell you if there's anything. We don't know if we can save him, so please, keep Tyler upstairs."

"I will." She dropped her hand and walked away.

"That is amazing," Roxy said. "She's like a different person."

Carla shook her head. "She's a strong woman at her core. Her husband died suddenly, and she's been raising Tyler on her own. She had to take in a roommate, and that turned ugly. She couldn't get him to leave...so now she has a chance to start over. She's one of the rare mortals who can accept magic without being freaked."

"Tyler's a great kid," Ailish said. "He was so worried about his mom."

"That's why you showed him self-defense." Roxy had wondered since they'd just been kidnapped, tied up and hurt yesterday. But now she understood. "To help him feel confident."

"The boy wants to be able to protect his mom. We're going to teach him how," Ailish said.

"Wish I could help. I don't know much about self-defense."

"Coming tonight is a big help," Carla said. "We're going to need all the magic we can get to save Linc. We're fighting bloodlust caused by a powerful curse."

"Axel told me that Linc is right on the edge," Darcy

said. "He was sane enough to warn them not to release the chains with the two living witches still in the garage unit. They've tranquilized Linc, which slows down the process."

Roxy listened carefully, trying to follow the logic. She knew about the sex-and-blood curse. She'd spent the first eleven years of her life learning about magic, witches and the like. Additionally, she and Shayla had tried to learn enough to avoid their Awakenings. "We can't cure bloodlust, can we?"

"No," Carla shook her head, her hazel eyes shadowed with regret. "The Ancestors and our knowledge chakras have shown us that. The only cure is a soul mirror. But the hunters can feed the sex part of the curse to push back the bloodlust."

Her stomach tightened with a knot of dread. "And?"

"Roxy, your sex magic is so powerful, we all felt it yesterday and today when we worked with you in the condo. We think you might be able to bring out the sex part of the curse in Linc, overriding the bloodlust enough for him to get control."

A sense of betrayal made her queasy. "You want me to have sex with him?" Exactly how was she supposed to do that? Summon as much magic as she could and make him want her? Then just...it made her shudder. Key had said he'd help her with her needs for her magic. She didn't want to ever get so desperate that she...

"No," Ailish moved up between the two witches and touched Roxy's arm. "Roxy, the three of us have soul mirrors. We know that's just not...no. We wouldn't ask that of you. Any magic that requires actual sex will be with Key."

She nodded, and then remembered Ailish's blindness. "Okay. I guess I jumped to conclusions." This was her issue and she knew it. "What do you want me to do?"

Carla said, "We thought that if you could summon up your sex magic and then touch him, using your communication chakra, it might pull out his sex drive and override the bloodlust. Key will be here; he should be able to help you."

She thought about that. "I'm willing to try."

Carla lifted her hands in frustration. "I don't know if it will work. Depends how far gone he is. Hunters are biologically very advanced. What I'm hoping is that feeding the sex lust will buy enough time for the brain to push back and heal." She dropped her hands. "Sutton was blooded, and much worse than Linc. I was able to save him by calling him as my familiar. Our bond healed the brain damage. We don't know who Linc's soul mirror is, so this is our only shot at saving him."

But no pressure, she thought. "What if it doesn't work? What then?"

"Axel will kill him," Darcy said quietly.

Roxy felt the worry in her words. She didn't want her mate to have to do that. They all cared about this hunter. Linc was their friend.

Carla explained further, "They made the vow that if any of them go rogue, one of the other hunters will kill him before he loses his soul."

A phone rang, and Ailish answered it, then walked toward the front door.

Roxy didn't know Linc, but she did know hunters had pheromones that attracted women. "When I do this, won't Linc need sex?"

"That's why I'm here."

Roxy turned to see the woman with Ailish. "Dee." Ailish's friend who cooked, drove and did a variety of other things. But this?

"Linc and I are friends. I want to do this." She wore cargo pants, a loose shirt and a concerned frown.

Roxy heard the garage door raise and a truck pull in. No more time for pondering. "Let's try it."

※

Key drove through the town to Phoenix's house. Axel sat in the back of the truck with an unconscious Linc. The last thing they wanted was the hunter to wake inside the cab and go apeshit with the bloodlust. The bed of the truck gave Axel more room to control the situation.

Key's thighs were on fire, his gut churned with worry for Linc, and the dragon was shifting restlessly. What did Dyfyr want?

And where the hell was his brother? Had he been there at the storage units? Too much a coward to face Key?

He had to find and kill him.

And he had to help Roxy gain enough power to talk to Dyfyr and find out how to get that Tear out and save her life, so Wing Slayer could give them immortality. His chest tightened at the thought of failing. He couldn't fail.

He couldn't lose Roxy. Damn it, he thought viciously, she'd made him feel too much. He was falling for her, coming to care about her so deeply that she was vital to him.

She believed in him.

He'd never known what that felt like. Not like this. When his claws had come out and he'd nearly scored open her chest, she'd soothed him and healed his hands after he'd smashed off the claws. She refused to believe he'd hurt her. And then she'd let him touch her again. He'd had her in his bed, sliding so deep into her body, it felt like he was touching her heart.

She believed in him.

Key just didn't know if he believed in himself.

He pulled into the circular driveway of Phoenix's house, rolled down his window, and pressed his palm to the security plate that would open the garage. Once the door was up, he drove in.

Right now they had to do what they could to save Linc. Then once he and the dragon were calm, he'd go to Roxy and they'd work on her magic and reaching Dyfyr. He turned off the ignition, got out, and ignored the pain from the gunshots.

Axel was already on his feet with Linc slung over his shoulder. He stepped up on the side and jumped down.

Guess the man didn't need help. Key didn't say a word, seeing the grim set of Axel's square jaw. Without a soul mirror for Linc, hope was slim.

"Knife out," Axel said. "If he wakes and gets near one of the women..."

Key pulled out his blade without needing to hear the rest. He walked ahead.

The garage door to the kitchen opened. Sutton stood there, his eyes steel blue, his knife in his hand. "Down to the gym. Phoenix is there. We've set up restraints."

When Key was even with Sutton, he said, "It's bad."

The big man's chest expanded, then he gave a slow nod. "Witches have a plan."

"We could use a miracle." Key stalked into the kitchen, intending to hit the stairs down to the gym, but the distinct honey-almond scent stopped him.

Whipping his head to the left, he saw the four witches and Dee. They were standing by the refrigerator, probably where Sutton had pushed them back. "Roxy. What are you doing here? Damn it, how did you get here? Liam is—"

Axel came in and strode down to the gym.

Sutton stopped by Key. "I brought her and made sure she was safe." Then he took Carla's hand and they went down to the gym, followed by Ailish, Darcy and Dee.

Key was peripherally aware of them all. When Roxy was near, all his senses went on high-alert protective mode. He would hear a whispered threat against her from the other side of the house. But his gaze was on her, drinking in the sight of her. She was wearing jeans and a high-neck T-shirt that covered the necklace. He was worried about Linc, still buzzed from the adrenaline of the fight, and edgy as hell. He didn't dare touch her. "Are you feeling okay? You were pale this morning." How long did they have to free her from that Tear?

"I'm fine and I want to help. The plan is—" Her gaze suddenly narrowed, going his thighs. "What happened?" She walked to him. "Oh, Kieran!"

Her scent was filling his chest and chasing out the cold detachment he needed to stay in control. "The bullets are out, it'll heal." He'd checked and bandaged the wounds to keep the blood out of his way.

Her witch shimmer began to darken. "Damn right it will. Go sit in a chair." She gestured toward the big kitchen table and then shifted back to him.

"Not right now, I'm still on adrenaline overload and don't want to touch you." Shit, that came out wrong. "I mean that I don't want to risk the dragon claws coming out."

"You don't have to touch me, just go sit down." When he didn't move fast enough to suit her, she added, "If not for me, then for Linc. I'm going to try to save him, and I need your help with my magic. But if you stay like this, all I'm going to feel is your pain."

One glimpse of her diamond-hard will glittering in her green eyes told him he wasn't going to win this argument. He walked over to the table, pulled out the chair and sat down.

Roxy knelt between his thighs and started unwrapping the bloodiest bandage first. As she exposed the bloody hole with the ragged edges, surrounded by red angry skin, she blanched. "Kieran. You walked on this?"

He fisted his hands around the wood seat in case his claws sprang out. "Yeah."

She bent her head without a word and brushed her fingers around the edges with butterfly gentleness. Her magic began swirling around his thigh, then burrowing deeper and deeper until he could feel it all the way to the back of his leg. It also quivered through his insides until it seemed that it was trying to mark his soul. He closed his eyes, fighting not to inhale the dark chocolate scent. His blood heated and, naturally, he got rock hard. Linc was downstairs, fighting for his soul, and Key got a boner. *Shit.* Trying to keep his mind off Roxy and the rising rush of physical need taking hold, he stared at a wine bottle on the counter.

She took her hand from the wound, shifted to his other leg, and began unwrapping that bandage.

He couldn't take any more and looked down at her kneeling there, her hair sliding forward to cover her face. "It's just a cut. Leave—" He noticed the skin of her bare arms—her witch-shimmer was dull and spotted with red pain holes. "Stop!" He shoved the chair back and stood up. Fought to get his breath.

Roxy blinked like he'd struck her, then she stood up. "What now?"

He wanted to use his fingers to smooth that frown from her forehead. "I'm an asshole. I didn't mean to yell at you. I just realized you were taking my pain. I couldn't touch you to draw it back to me."

She lifted a brow. "Not true. You could have touched me. The only shackles on you are your own doubts. And frankly, I have bigger problems to worry about right now. I'm going to try to save your friend if you feel like helping. And after that. I'm just selfish enough to want to save my own life." She turned and walked down the stairs.

Damn, that hurt worse than the gunshots. But could she be right? Could it be that he had enough control to stop anything Dyfyr might do?

≫ 20 ≪

ROXY LOOKED DOWN AT LINC. He was out cold on the mat, lying on his back. Axel stood above his head with a firm hold on the chains binding Linc's wrists. Sutton was at his feet, holding the chains around his ankles. Linc wasn't going anywhere.

Phoenix stood next to her, his arms crossed over his bare chest, the twin tats on his biceps bulging. "You got a mean streak, Elf Witch."

She rolled her eyes. "I should have known you all would hear us talking." Once again, she was on an emotional roller coaster. All the blood on Kieran, and not just from his wounds, made her queasy. Darcy had told her what had happened tonight, but what if he'd had a wound she couldn't heal? What if he'd died? Her heart cringed. She'd never felt this way for anyone.

"Every word," Phoenix said cheerfully.

She looked over at him. "Got something you want to say? Spit it out." Seriously, she was not in the mood. Yes, she got that Kieran had good reasons for not touching her, but she...damn it, it hurt. Dyfyr hadn't hated her last night, he'd held her, stroked her with his wings.

"Nope. I'm good."

She turned to look at the hunter.

He smiled. "Key needs you, Elf Witch. Not just short-term, but long-term. He needs someone who believes in him and doesn't back down just because he's a scary son of a bitch when he loses his temper."

She...what? Phoenix *liked* her? She knew better than to say that to him. Key had told her Phoenix respected strength. "Maybe I'm a scarier son of a bitch when I lose *my* temper."

His face blanked, and then he threw back his head and laughed. Finally, he regained his breath and said, "Doubtful. But I think you can tame the violence in Key and that freak show dragon he's hauling around."

"Dyfyr is not a freak show!" Her blood heated with outrage. "He's a dragon, ancient and smart, but he doesn't think like a man. He thinks like a dragon. When something needs to die, he kills it. Simple. He doesn't get all twisted up in human morality. But he's also fiercely protective, and he doesn't like bullies. A dragon like Dyfyr is truly powerful and..." Roxy blinked, wondering where the hell all that came from. How she knew this stuff. Heat rushed to her face.

After a beat of stillness, Phoenix said, "Damn, Elf Witch, I take it back. You are scary."

She felt strange, and a slight headache formed behind her eyes. "I don't even know where all that came from." Carla put a hand on her shoulder. "Soul memory. You knew him from your past life. The bond between you and him was so strong, the memory is imprinted."

The witch's words grounded her, made her feel a bit more solid. "Okay, that's a better answer than calling me crazy."

Carla smiled. "You're not crazy, Roxy."

Axel cleared his throat and got their attention. "Where the hell is Key? Linc's going to start coming around."

"I'm here." Key strode up to them and shoved Phoenix aside.

Roxy could see he'd washed off all the blood. The dragon watched her with his gleaming eyes, holding the lock of hair. She knew Key had heard everything she'd said, including her defense of Dyfyr—the soul memory, Carla had called it. Before she could think of anything to say, Darcy and Ailish moved behind her and next to Carla. Dee was in the room, too, but they had her back by the stairs out of harm's way.

Carla said, "Once you summon your magic, we'll circle our power and feed you more. Then you touch him and we'll push in as much of the sex magic as we can."

She nodded.

"Key," Carla looked at him. "There's always an exchange. Bringing up his sexual lust is going to push the bloodlust out and into Roxy. She's going to feel the burn and craziness."

"The hell she will. I'll draw it off."

He stepped behind her, so close she could feel the heat of him. But he didn't touch her yet. Would he?

He leaned close to her ear. "I'm going to help you. We'll do this together."

Little sparks danced along her nerves. Her schema woke up and tendrils of desire began branching out. Her response was fast and intense; her chakras popped open quickly from her pelvis to her heart. Her magic began to spin, rushing up and down her spine and pushing at her throat. Her skin tightened, her nipples peaked and she was overwhelmed.

"Damn, Roxy," Key said, his voice strangled.

"Key, help her," Phoenix ground out. "Before we all lose control."

Oh sweet crone, her magic was rushing out and touching them all. Making them feel lust. Humiliation burned through her. She tried to stare down at Linc and focus. He was big like the others, and even in his unconscious state, she could see the cut of his muscles. He had brown hair with gold streaks. His face was elegant with an edge of brutality. He had cuts and bruises all over his chest and arms. She had to get control in order to help him.

Or Axel would have to kill him.

But her magic kept whirling and rushing. Her throat ached. She was failing.

Two hands gripped her waist. "Come here," Key said, tugging her back to his chest. He folded his arms around her.

His warmth surrounded her, the dark spice scent, his strength. She felt the steady, strong beat of his heart. Her magic started to calm until she felt his erection press against her lower back. Oh God.

He leaned closer. "Tell me what's happening."

She forced herself to say, "Too much. My throat..."

"Her communication chakra," Ailish said. "She needs it for the dragon to help her control her magic."

He lifted one hand and drew his fingertips over her throat, then down the center of her chest and back up. "Here?" He kept stroking softly.

Her magic paused; in the internal silence every cell waited for direction. Even her schema stilled. Then the power circled back down and rushed up through her first four chakras right to Key's fingers.

A second later, sweet relief came as her throat chakra opened. A new, vivid awareness scuttled through her and she felt not only one heartbeat against her back, but two. The sound vibrated inside her, and then she felt a gentle sweep of...wings? They swept up her arms, then down, and felt like buttery-soft leather. She tilted her head up. "He's touching me."

"Felt it." He smiled down at her, his dimples flashing. "Your magic is focusing now."

The wings that had been touching her skin were now inside her, resolutely sweeping her magic into a disciplined pattern going up and down her spine, growing and thickening. The brush of the wings was intimate and deeply sensual. She shivered. "He's so powerful."

Key's gray eyes began to burn with a gas-flame blue. "Like your magic."

"That was...intense," Phoenix said. "That's some awesome magic you got there, Elf."

Key kept staring into her eyes. "Phoenix doesn't know when to shut up."

"Either I talk or I drag Ailish out of here," he muttered.

Roxy laughed. "He's *your* friend. I get Ailish."

Key rubbed his thumb over the skin just below her throat. "Unfortunately, they are a package deal."

She felt a touch of sadness. If she didn't find a way to get this Tear off, she'd never have the chance—

"Roxy," Darcy broke in, "we're sending you more power through your communication chakra. You should feel it."

She turned back to focus on Linc. She began to sense the internal touch of the other witches, a bright, warm feeling blending into her magic and strengthening the stream. "Okay, I feel it."

"Good. Are you ready to try?"

"Yes." She pushed Key's arms off her and walked to Linc.

"Focus on your fifth chakra, then funnel the power through it and down your arm."

"Keep your hand away from his teeth," Axel said as he pulled the chains tight. "He's going to be vicious. Phoenix, get your knife out. Key, you be ready to pull Roxy back."

Her nerves stretched spiderweb thin. She crouched down next to the man.

His eyes popped open, so fast that she fell back on her ass. The gold depths burned with a feral light. His muscles went rigid and a vibration rumbled in his chest. His nostrils flared.

Key caught her beneath her arms, lifted her to her feet, and swung her behind him.

Linc began to struggle. "Let go, dickheads!"

Axel wrapped the chains around his forearms and pulled tight. Sutton did the same, stretching Linc to immobility. "He's going to rip out his joints. Now, Roxy."

Roxy responded to the authority in Axel. She moved around Key and refocused, drawing the power up her spine, through her throat chakra and down her arm.

Linc thrashed and bellowed. "Bitch...pricks...kill you...blood...want the blood...not her blood, goddammit." A pause. Then Linc's clarity broke through in his eyes as he glared at Sutton. "Kill me. By all that is holy, kill me!"

The furious desperation in the hunter's words drove her as nothing else had. She dropped to her haunches and laid her hand on his ribs. His skin was hot and dry, as if he burned with a fever.

Linc's body bucked up, almost throwing her hand off.

The chains rattled, the men grunting as they fought for control, but she pushed it all from her mind and focused on Linc. Her magic streamed through her palm and fingers. She concentrated and kept herself open, like a conduit.

Seconds later, she felt a return of something dark and ugly. It began snaking up her fingers, burrowing into her palms, and a sweat broke out on her body. The veins on the back of her hands swelled and distorted. It felt like acid was being injected into her. Ugly red and black welts pulsed. She suddenly felt smothered, like ashes coated in her lungs, making it impossible to get air.

Key crouched next to her, wrapped an arm around her shoulder, and pulled her into his side. "Breathe," he said softly, then put his hand over hers on Linc.

She stared at his bigger, darker hand that was strong enough to kill, yet gentle enough to draw. Followed by the added sensation of dragon wings brushing back and forth, matching the rhythm of the dual heartbeats. Her communication chakra allowed her to feel and hear the dragon so clearly. While Key's arm around her shoulder anchored her in the maelstrom of magic mixing with darkness. *Her Kieran.*

A second later she could pull in a full breath and the pain eased. Her magic flowed, the wings helping her control it. She endured only a fraction of the return before Key siphoned off the pain and smothering blackness. *But now Key is feeling it—is he okay?*

"Keep going, Roxy," Key said. "I'm fine."

She hadn't spoken out loud...had she? With her hand pressed to Linc, she kept the magic flowing, pulling in the extra power from Darcy, Ailish and Carla. She studied Linc's face. Sweat dotted his upper lip, and his color was splotchy. That strange light in his eyes was flickering.

"Head's spinning," he said.

"We're trying to pull out the bloodlust, Linc," Key told him.

"Remember it. The blood on me. Felt so fucking good. More...blood." His body twisted in the throes of some internal cramping.

"His shoulder popped," Axel said. "Keep going, Roxy. Force in more sex magic."

She sucked in a breath and tried. So much power winging through her began to make her skin hurt. Key kept his hand over hers but moved behind her, wrapped his arm around her middle, and settled her on his lap. She just let him, concentrating. She didn't know how to sort her sex magic from her power. It had something to do with the goddess.

He reached his hand down between her thighs.

"Key!" Her magic stuttered with thick embarrassment. What was he doing?

"Just touching your schema. That's all." Through her jeans, he settled his palm over the inside of her upper left thigh. His other hand rested on top of hers pressed against Linc.

His touched ignited a firestorm in her. Rich, thick waves of desire blossomed outward. Filling her body. A roar of need saturated her womb and clenched through her. Her core ached, her breasts ached, her cleft ached, she...needed. *Harness it*. She summoned every little bit of it, and poured it through her magic.

Into Linc.

"Jesus," Phoenix said.

"What the hell kind of magic is that?" Linc asked.

Roxy felt the voice rumble through Linc even as she heard the words. She blinked, and then lifted her head to look at him.

The spottiness was gone. His skin was tanned except for slashes of red over his cheekbones. His gold eyes were clear but the pupils were dilating. He seemed to be panting. She didn't want to look down to his hips.

She already knew he'd be hard.

"Sex magic," she said.

He groaned in a low, throaty voice. The violent twisting of his body slowed into an undulating rhythm. "You have nice hands, love." He rubbed up against her palm. "Little lower..."

Key roared behind her. He jerked her hand away.

Linc ignored him, his eyes on Roxy. "Undo my

pants. Touch me," he arched up, angling toward her.

Another roar behind her, and Key's chest vibrated like a fast-approaching train. It all happened so fast! He stood, lifting her with him, then pushed her behind him toward the witches. Then he whipped around and demanded of Axel, "Let him go!"

Roxy watched in total shock. His back bunched, the muscles popping and twitching. Key was just over six feet and packed 210 pounds of raw strength. All of it rippled now, expanding his back. He held his arms out at his sides, opening and closing his fingers. The threat in him so vivid, it made her mouth go dry and her heart hammer.

"Stand down, Key!" Axel shouted. "Now!"

"Let him go!" Key yelled back.

"Come back, little witch," Linc said. "Give me more of your hot sex magic."

Another current went through Key. He flexed his fingers and claws burst out, spraying blood. His back rippled, the shoulder blades bulged, and a sudden whoosh filled the room.

Then silence. Even Linc shut up, and stopped rattling the chains.

Wings. Magnificent wings that spanned at least six feet on each side, and at the top curve had to reach eight feet, maybe more. They were different from the other men's wings, made from a membrane-like substance and covered with iridescent scales of emerald green and sapphire blue. The bottoms of the wings were scalloped. Stunning.

"Roxy," Axel broke the silence. "Move where Key can see you."

She walked around and realized Phoenix had glued himself to her shoulder. "He's not going to hurt me." Dyfyr hadn't hurt her last time his claws came out in the gym. Roxy really was coming to believe something else was going on.

Phoenix looked down at her. "Probably not, but he's going to kill Linc. The dragon is jealous. It's going to be funny as hell as soon as he calms down."

"Jealous. Of Linc." That meant Dyfyr really did care about her.

Phoenix rolled his eyes. "Elf, unless you want to watch Linc sliced up into bloody strips of jerky, you'd better go tell the dragon to knock that shit off."

Too many feelings crowded her chest. She moved in front of Key.

His gaze was gray like wet cement, and his wings twitched in fury. "Get up," he snarled at Linc.

"Tell them to let go, lizard, and I will."

Lizard? He called her dragon a lizard? "Oh, shut up!" She snapped at the hunter, then turned back to Key. Her breath caught in her lungs. The tattoo on his chest was gone. He had massive muscles in his shoulders, arms and chest, and even down his flat, ripped stomach to handle those wings. The inside of the wings gleamed a light amethyst that changed shades with each movement. Then she looked up to his face.

Lethal.

"Key?"

"Out of the way, Roxy."

She didn't know how to talk to the dragon if he was gone from Key's chest. Instead she reached up a hand and touched the inside of a wing. Soft and warm, and she wanted to burrow herself into the feel of them.

Key shuddered.

She said, "Kieran."

He looked down at her. "Going to kill him."

"No." She put her other hand on his chest. "He's reacting to the sex magic."

He pulled his face tight. "Still want to kill him."

"But you're not going to."

The wing curled around her, stroking her back. "You're mine."

Warmth spread through her. In this moment, Kieran wasn't afraid Dyfyr would hurt her; he was staking his claim. It was stupid, Neanderthal and primitive, yet her magic, and her heart, danced in joy. She stroked her fingers over the inside of his wing. Blue smoke misted his gaze as he added, "He can't have you."

She smiled at him. "No. I only want you and Dyfyr."

He closed his eyes and dragged in a breath. "You're our treasure." He opened his eyes, passion burned in his gaze. "You have to live."

She felt the change as the wing locked around her. Where it had been soft and secure like a blanket, now the wing was hard and unyielding. A second later, Kieran's left hand came toward her, so fast that all she saw were the three-inch claws coming at her.

"No!" Key yelled, his face contorting and he managed to slow the trajectory of his strike.

Roxy couldn't move! Dyfyr's wing held her frozen.

Phoenix dived into Key. The impact loosened the wing's hold on her. Key and Phoenix hit the mat, while she was grabbed and shoved into the group of witches, Darcy clasping her arm so she didn't fall. It all happened in the blink of an eye.

Her heart pounding, fear coating her mouth, she saw Sutton help Phoenix pin Key to the mat. Phoenix's leather vest was shredded, claw marks raked his chest and face. Key's lip was split, and he had fist-sized welts around his ribs. The wings were still out, and twitching. "Dear Ancestors." Roxy slapped her hand over her mouth as the horror began to sink in. Dyfyr had tried to kill her. Everything inside her wanted to reject the idea, to deny it. But she'd seen the claws on Key's hand coming at her, had felt the wing trap her so she couldn't escape.

She turned her gaze to see Axel still holding the chains binding Linc's hands, his face rigid with anger.

Loud breathing echoed in the gym.

Fear gave way to fury. Fiery hot, make-her-head-explode rage. Shaking off Darcy's hand, she walked over toward the men.

"Stay back," Sutton said.

She ignored him and kept going until she stood two feet from Key's ear.

Blood ran down the side of his face from his mouth. "Get away from me!" he snarled.

"I want to talk to Dyfyr. I want to know what the hell I ever did to him. Why one minute he loves me and then the next he's trying to rip out my throat! I have a right to know!" God, she was mad. So mad. And beneath that anger was pain like she'd never felt before. The kind of hurt that eats through any hope and leaves only black despair and loneliness, and the dawning realization that Dyfyr didn't want to save her; he wanted her dead.

Key stared up at her. "I don't know! I was furious at Linc, then there was this overwhelming feeling that you can't leave us. Then I was struggling with Dyfyr. He was going for your heart." He closed his eyes, exhaustion seeming to weigh him down.

She replayed it in her head. "You have to live. That's what you said, you and Dyfyr."

Key opened his eyes. "What?"

Excitement began bubbling deep in her pelvis and moving up through her chakras. "I don't think he was trying to kill me."

"She has a point," Carla said as she came up next to Roxy. "We were all shocked and reacted, but we don't really know what the claws were going to do."

Key shoved the two men off him and rose to his feet. "I know what the claws do, they kill." He stared at her. "You can't keep denying the obvious."

Phoenix and Sutton stood and kept close watch.

Roxy held his gaze. Was she in denial? She shook

her head. "You're our treasure, that's what you said."

Key lifted up his hands with the three-inch claws. "The dragon is insane then. When your mother called his soul into me, something must have broken in him."

She couldn't bear this anymore, the constant tear on her heart. He loves me, he hates me. She had to know, and there was one way to find out. She took a step.

Phoenix and Sutton blocked her path instantly with their huge bodies.

She looked up at them. "Move. We need to see what happens if I touch him."

Sutton looked away from her. "Carly?"

"Let her try."

"No!" Key snarled. "Roxy, don't be stupid."

She glared up at the two men. "Get out of my way, or I'll unleash so much sex magic on you two, you'll forget your own names." She was so drained, it was a bluff, but they couldn't know that.

Phoenix winced. "You're wicked, Elf." He and Sutton both shifted positions to give her room.

Key was six steps away from her. The wings fluttered, the scales twinkling in the lights. Key's muscles tensed. His hands with the claws hung at his side. Her mouth went dry, her heart hammered and her magic hummed. She was afraid, but her magic wasn't. She took a step.

"Roxy..." It came out a growl.

She lifted her gaze, and thought about the way he took care of her after his brother cut her. The picture he drew of her, making love with him...all of it. "I'm not afraid of you, Kieran." She took another two steps.

"You should be."

All eyes in the gym were on her, including Linc's. The hunter was sitting up and Axel was removing the manacles while watching them.

"Dyfyr, I don't want you to claw me. Or cut me."

Ignoring the wary light in Key's eyes, she took another step. Over her breathing, she heard a noise. Several *plops*.

"Look at that," Darcy said. "The claws are falling off."

Key raised his hands. The claws were gone.

She shifted her attention to ten claws on the mat. Dyfyr dropped the claws for her. He'd listened to her. Wild hope soared through her, and she shot her gaze to Key's face.

He stared at her. "Come here."

She went into his arms.

≋ 21 ≋

ROXY WAITED FOR KEY DOWN in the warehouse. Phoenix was showing him how to use his wings, taking off, flying, landing and folding them up. She'd gone back with Darcy and Axel. Axel and Sutton had closed down the club next door. Now they were drinking beer and playing pool with Ram and Eli.

Linc stayed at Ailish and Phoenix's with Dee.

Axel made a shot, then said, "Eli, we're going to do your Induction Ceremony tomorrow night."

Darcy handed Roxy a bottle of water and sat next to her on the couch. "That's the ceremony where Wing Slayer accepts a witch hunter as full Wing Slayer Hunter. Key did the outline of Eli's bird, a griffin, right, Eli?" Darcy asked.

The hunter looked over his shoulder, his light green eyes standing out in his darker face. "Yep."

Darcy returned her gaze to Roxy. "During the ceremony, if Wing Slayer finds him worthy, he'll finish the wings."

She twisted off the cap on her water bottle. "Wing Slayer marked Key's knife." Just thinking of Key made her schema hurt. The need inside her was churning and getting worse. Her magic was *hungry*. And damn, she was tired.

"Axel told me." Darcy looked over. "That was incredible tonight the way the dragon claws just dropped off of Key once you told him not to claw you."

"He's not trying to claw me to hurt me," Roxy said. When it happened, she'd been startled, and seeing wicked-sharp claws coming at her had frightened her. But now looking back... "Dryfr was aiming for the Tear. He's trying to save me." Then all the hunters reacted, stopping the strike. "I have to talk to Dyfyr. Maybe his magic can safely cut the Tear out of me." And to get the strength to do that, she needed to feed her magic.

"Third eye, Roxy," Darcy reminded her. "And after what you did tonight, you should be able to reach your sixth chakra. You and Key can work on it now that you know Dyfyr will listen to you."

Thinking of Key and Dyfyr made her magic try to surge, causing another cramp, and her schema started to burn. Roxy shifted on the couch and watched the pool game. Ram called his shot, bent his long frame over, and made it with military precision.

Sutton laughed. "You lose, Axel. Again. Ram's the only one who can consistently beat you at pool."

Axel glowered.

"I can beat him," Darcy said next to her.

"Yeah, but you cheat." He looked up, his green eyes heating.

Darcy shrugged. "I prefer to think of it as creative winning."

Axel stared at his mate. "Those pictures you put in my head while I'm trying to make a shot are very creative."

The sexual tension was so thick, Roxy felt like a voyeur. But it also gave her a glimpse of the intimacy the soul-mirror bond created. "You can send mental pictures back and forth?"

Darcy nodded. "Yes. It takes time to build the bond, but yes."

"Cool."

"Unless," Ram said, "you're undisciplined like Axel. He loses his concentration when Darcy's around. And he owes me fifty bucks."

Axel glared at the man. "Let's spar and I'll win the fifty bucks back by throwing you on your ass."

"I'll put money on that," Sutton said.

Eli laughed. "I don't know, Ram's a machine. Think I'll put my money on him."

Roxy shook her head as the four men debated who would win. Then she heard the door to the garage open, and Key strode in. She forgot everyone else as his gaze landed on her. He walked around the pool table straight to her. "You're still up."

Her chakras squeezed at the sound of his voice. "I thought I'd wait for you. You said you were coming back." The need in her cramped right down her center. "Did you learn to fly?"

He smiled. "Yep. One crash landing." He held up his left arm. "Then it was easy."

She leaped to her feet and touched the four-inch gash. Her chakras squeezed but she forced the magic up and began healing the cut. As the magic left her, she felt emptier than ever. Her goddess mark sent out long, deep threads of desire, trying to fill the emptiness.

A flush rode up his face; heat poured off him as he covered her hand with his. *You're doing sinful things to me, green eyes.*

His words whispered in her head and she realized he hadn't spoken aloud. Swallowing a gasp of surprise, warmth spread through her. His touch, both physical and mental, helped ease her chakras.

He smiled. *Soul-mirror bond. I started hearing your thoughts tonight when I was helping you with your magic while healing Linc.*

His voice was a gentle internal caress, almost more intimate than when he was inside her body. She tried to project her thoughts to him. *I remember, I was worried how much pain you were feeling.* Lifting her hand from his arm, she said, "It's healed."

Heard you.

She summoned more of her power to answer him, but she groaned at a cramp. It was like squeezing out toothpaste, creating that vacuum that pulls in the sides of the tube.

"Roxy, what's wrong?" Key put his hand on her shoulder.

She opened her eyes. "Nothing." *I think my magic is depleted.* Her head started to pound.

Sex. You need sex. He brushed her mind with the words while drawing her against his side. *You should be able to pull some energy from me now.*

In just seconds, the cramping stopped, and her magic fluttered.

Key stiffened. *Your magic is calling me.*

All four men stopped talking and turned toward them. Darcy looked at them, too. Oh damn, Roxy knew her schema was pounding out the sex magic to call Key.

"That's—shit," Eli sputtered. "I'm leaving. Later."

"Right. I'd better go, too." Ram followed him out the garage door.

I'm sorry. Roxy pushed the thought with her magic, mortified.

Axel put his arm around Darcy. "Roxy."

She lifted her gaze to Axel. "I'll get better control."

"You and your magic saved one of my men tonight. I would have had to kill him if you hadn't done that. Your magic is strong and valuable, and something to be damned proud of. I better not hear of anyone insulting you and your magic. Good night." They turned and walked toward the stairs.

Key pulled her back against his naked chest and growled out, "Count to ten, Roxy."

Oh sweet crone, now even the sound of his voice caused the internal squeezing pain. "Why?"

"Have to wait for them to get far enough ahead. Count." His voice was sharp.

"One, two, three..." *Tell me why.* She didn't know if she had enough strength to connect to him mentally.

"Keep going," his voice was huskier. *Waiting for them to get into the condo before I lose control.*

The silent communication shivered through her. Out loud, she counted, "Four, five..." *I don't understand.*

I feel your need; it's pounding in my blood, in my cock and through my brain. I can scent your caramel heat flowing from between your thighs, and the pain clawing at you.

"Six." She shivered, the sinkhole of need inside of her expanding.

I'm going to get you in the condo, strip you down, and kiss away the pain until there's only rich caramel.

"Seven." She could hardly breathe.

And then, I'm going to hold your sweet ass as I bury my cock in you. Sliding in and out, harder and harder until I fill that need in you and you're boneless with pleasure.

"Eight," she spit out, desperate to get to ten.

Then I'm going to draw you like that, languid and mine. The last word was fierce and hot in her head.

"Nine!" She might have shouted, who could tell with all the blood roaring in her ears.

And then make love to you again. And again. And again.

"Ten!"

He swept her off her feet and into his arms before she finished the word. Roxy buried her face in his chest as he raced at crazy-ass hunter speed up the stairs, shoved into the condo, and closed and locked the door.

$\Longrightarrow$ 22 $\Longleftarrow$

KEY'S HEART WAS POUNDING WITH the raging, out-of-control desire for the witch he held in his arms. Racing up the stairs from the warehouse, he fought the compulsion, the bone-deep need to strip her down and bury his cock inside her right there on the stairs. He desperately wanted to feed her magic and fill her with pleasure.

He made it inside the condo and leaned back against the locked door to draw in a breath to try to temper his lust. He just needed a second so he didn't jump her like some sex-crazed maniac.

The scent of dark chocolate rose while an electric sizzle traveled through his chest. Either he'd just imploded or...

He looked down.

Roxy was naked and so was he. She'd stripped them with magic. Her witch-shimmer glowed, and the Tear buried in the curve of her breast pulsed out soft colored lights. The dragon's rage spiked at the sight, so he shifted his gaze down. Her nipples were dark and pebbled. With her curved in his arms, he looked down her soft belly to the lush curls at her thighs.

Blood roared in his ears. He could smell her desire.

Feel the heat. Nothing mattered but Roxy—giving her what she craved.

He took a step, and swear to Wing Slayer, he nearly stumbled. He could run five miles without pausing, but the walk to the bedroom was beyond him. His cock was hard and getting impossibly harder. He felt her magic streaming from her to dance over his skin at every point of contact: the insides of his arms where he held her and his chest. The soft, sensual touches coiled every muscle with the animal need to possess her, to get inside her and thrust deep enough to touch the very core of Roxy.

"I can't control my magic," she said as she clutched his arm. "I didn't mean to take our clothes."

Her witch-shimmer glowed, and her eyes were losing focus. She was in a grip of pure hunger as her magic fought to get what it needed.

Him.

That snapped the last of his restraint. *She needed him now.* He dropped to his knees and laid her on the thick rug that ran beneath the couch, chair and coffee table. He spread her thighs and looked. The full blue and green color schema on her inner thigh was faded, a sign that she needed sex to feed her power. The outline of the goddess even looked distorted, the middle widening. He shifted his gaze to the rich strawberry-colored curls shielding her sex. He tugged her bottom up on his thighs and used his thumbs to comb through her damp hair and gently separate her.

She was wet, swollen and pink, and he ran his finger along her cleft, feeling her silky heat and the kiss of her magic as he touched her, the sweet need that enticed the hell out of him. No time to taste her now, so he slid two fingers inside her, tunneling deep to make sure she was ready. The feel of her channel surrounding him with slick heat made him break out in a sweat.

Then he used his other hand to feather a finger over the schema, caressing the goddess mark and watching the colors darken from his touch. The magic there was pure sex traveling through him, down his spine and engorging his cock.

She mewled softly, raising her hips higher. "It's not enough!" She squeezed her eyes closed and one tear slid out. "Please," she said.

Her plea rocked him to his soul. "Roxy." He pulled out his fingers and shifted to cover her body with his. He touched that warm tear and his chest fucking hurt. He knew she was being torn apart by the clawing need, yet she was so damned vulnerable. "I'm here for you. I will always be here for you." He leaned down and kissed her. Her magic rushed over his tongue. It hit him then that all her magic was going to him, leaving her empty.

He spread her legs with his hips, reached down and took hold of his cock. He found her entrance, felt the wet heat touch the swollen head, and groaned into her mouth. He pushed in.

She grabbed on to his shoulders and kissed him.

The folds of her walls began to pull and milk, her magic spinning around his cock, sliding into his balls, and driving him wild. He thrust all the way into her. He lifted his head, seeing her kiss-swollen mouth. "Can't stop," he growled the words. He pulled out of her, all the way until just the tip was inside her.

She opened her eyes, and they were brimming with emotion and a burning panic. "I can't get enough."

He snapped. There was a sound, like stepping on a twig in perfect silence, and then he thrust into her, going ball-deep. Her magic went fierce and possessive, tunneling through him with an electric twang. Owning him. Making him hers, until all that mattered was his Roxy. He pumped and stroked, in and out, watching her eyes. She met his movements, but it still wasn't enough for her.

"Bend your legs, hold your knees," he told her.

She lifted her legs, took her hands from his shoulders and pulled her knees up.

She was wide open, trusting, and needing what only he could give her. Pride raced and burned, mixing with the animal lust and dragon protectiveness. "Yes, perfect." He went up on his elbows, held her face with his hands and said, "Now, Roxy." He drove into her, hard. Fast. Over and over. Feeling her body, her magic, almost touching her soul while he held her face. He lost himself and found her. The bliss was unbearable, building and building at the base of his spine, waiting to explode. Waiting to pour out from him and fill her.

But not until she came apart for him.

He pounded in and out, feeling her begin to tighten. Watching her shimmer brighten and blaze with sunset colors. And then she arched her spine, her body bowing, and she cried out, "Kieran!"

He went up on his hands, fighting to draw out her pleasure. Nothing felt so damned good as seeing her face go soft, her witch shimmer take on that last color of sunset, burnt orange. He drove in deep, brushing against her womb and the pleasure burst over him. For a full minute, he kept pumping and filling her body with his seed. Giving her all he had.

When both their tremors stopped, his gaze drifted down to the necklace and something ripped open inside him. "I can't lose you, Roxy." The sheer magnitude of what she meant to him choked him. He pulled out of her body and moved to his side. Sliding his arm beneath her shoulder he pulled her close. They lay together on the rug, the only illumination coming from the soft recessed lighting over the bar behind the couch. This woman had gotten inside him, he'd shared more with her than anyone else and yet...she still believed in him. He told her, "For years I thought I was a creature of hatred and violence, and you showed me I can be something better."

"You are!" She wrapped her arm around him and pressed her warm mouth to him, kissing his neck, shoulders and chest, wherever she could reach. She ran her hand down his spine, and her magic followed, stroking with the same softness.

At the same time, her words brushed in his mind. *I love you.*

His eyes burned and Key was stunned to realize it was with unshed tears at those three words. So small but so powerful. Big, mean-ass rogues hadn't been able to get him to even crack with pain and violence, but this little witch with her huge heart was breaking him with her love. She was so beautiful; his fiery, courageous, strong witch, and she loved him. Trusted him with her body, something she hadn't been able to do with anyone else. She'd tried, although he sure as hell didn't want to think about that, but she hadn't been able to, yet with him—total trust. Him, the man with a dragon soul and very real claws.

He pushed himself up on his elbows. "Roxy, look at me."

She tilted her head back. Her eyes, the color of spring grass were so bottomless with her feelings. Just looking into her face caused a too-full pressure in his chest. This was real, and he wanted it, needed it, knowing that the love of Roxy defined him as worthy. "Tell me again. Out loud."

——✳——

Roxy looked up at Kieran. His harsh face was softened by the vulnerability that added shades of blue to his gray eyes. He'd stayed by her no matter what happened, even when he found out her mother had saddled him with the soul of a dragon.

All Kieran feared was himself. He didn't see the good in him that she did. Just like he was teaching her to trust her magic, she wanted to teach him to trust love. She reached up and cradled his face in her hands. She could feel the tension in him. "I love you, Kieran. You are a good man, strong enough to live with the soul of a dragon, fierce enough to kill bullies, and artistic enough to see the beauty in magic." Her voice thickened. "You make me feel whole. Not half witch and half mortal, but a whole woman."

He stared at her, the intensity shifting the colors in his eyes. "My life has been full of ugliness. So many times I wondered why I survived, how the hell I survived. The only thing that kept me sane was drawing."

She barely breathed and lay still in his arms. Their connection strengthened and grew in those seconds. She could feel their hearts meeting and beginning to beat in sync. All this happened as the truth of Kieran's words sank into her. His lifetime of pain. Fleeting images rushed her mind: cruel moments from his childhood. Bad days while living on the streets. Holding a young woman's body. She was seeing his most painful moments. A multitude of agonies. *Oh, Kieran.* Her mind and magic cried out to him.

Leaning down he kissed her, then raised his head. "Until you. Now I know now why I survived, why I was created in the screwed-up way I was. For you." He stroked her face, then down to the chain on her chest, and finally he touched the Tear flashing the soft light beneath her chest. When he looked up, his eyes burned with emotion. "I love you, Roxy. My entire life taught me how to fight, and I will fight any force of magic and hell to keep you with me. I won't lose you."

Warm shivers raced through her. She'd hoped he

cared for her, maybe loved her, but this? He touched the one true vulnerability of her heart. "I've never had anyone fight for me. No one ever cared enough." She could still remember being eleven and so scared that her mom was sending her to live with her dad. That whole night was one of terror. Her parents had been screaming at each other, then Gwen went into Roxy's room and stared packing her stuff. Roxy cried and begged her mom to let her stay with her. She swore she'd be good. But her mom hadn't wanted her anymore. And then all those years she'd tried so hard to be what her father wanted so he wouldn't stop loving her. But she'd failed again, and he'd fired her from his business and from his life.

I'll never fire you from my life, never stop loving you. His words brushed her mind.

You heard me. She hadn't realized she was projecting to him.

He smiled. "Your parents didn't deserve you, Roxy. I don't think I deserve you, but you're mine, and I will fight for you." His words were fierce, his eyes blazing. "I won't abandon you."

He meant it, she knew he did, yet there was still a thread of fear. "What if I die? Can you handle that?" Could *she*? She didn't want to die alone.

"Roxy, Jesus!" His face tightened, then he lifted her into his arms, rolled over so she was on top of him, and held her to his chest, pressing her face to his heart. "I won't leave you, baby, I swear. No matter what happens, I'll be here with you."

Soft joy chased out the sadness and worry. Knowing she wasn't alone, that he was there with her fueled her courage. She lifted her head and looked at the face of her hunter. "I love you, Kieran, and I'm going to live. For you and for us."

Approval lit up his eyes. "Let's fire up your magic and see if Dyfyr has the answer to getting that Tear out."

Her chest was lighter, yet she felt stronger than ever. Confident. She needed energy from sex to feed her magic, and for the first time, that felt okay. Even good. "You want my magic, you're going to have to work for it, hunter. The other witches tell me the best way to open my third eye is sex."

"Did they?" His voice dropped to a growl. "Demanding little witch, aren't you?" He stroked his hand down her back, to the swell of her butt.

His words would have more effect if his cock wasn't growing against her thigh. "You're already getting hard."

He laughed. "Around you, I get an erection as often as I breathe."

He kept stroking her bottom, creating shivers and getting her schema's full attention. The mark began pulsing out waves of hot desire. "You're supposed to work for it."

Key slid both his hands down to the back of her thighs, spread her open, and tugged her down to his arousal. His eyes gleamed with knowledge and color rose in his face. "I can feel exactly how hot you are for me." He tugged her farther and began filling her, stretching her. Slowly. One inch at a time. His eyes darkened. "Making love to you will never be work."

She settled her hands on his chest, feeling the dual heartbeats of him and the dragon. Her magic started spinning, rushing up her spine, then back to deep between her legs.

"Sweetheart, your magic..." He arched, going deeper, "...can't stop."

Buttery-soft wings caressed her arms, and she sucked in her breath at the sensation of Key filling her. She pushed up and took him all the way until she felt him touch her womb. Her nipples pebbled.

His gaze moved to her breasts, and he cupped them, his thumbs brushing her nipples. The twin sensations of Key and the dragon arrowed straight to her groin. *I feel you both. You and Dyfyr.*

Take it, Roxy. From both of us. Ride me. He thrust up beneath her and she cried out. *We're both going to help you get to your sixth chakra.*

Her folds, clit, and deep inside were so sensitized, every movement rocketed through her. She was freer than she ever had been, safe to immerse herself in sex and magic. *More,* she cried out to him in her mind.

As much as you can take. The words were a whisper, filling her head with such love. She figured out the rhythm, rising then lowering, each slide teasing every nerve ending as Kieran filled her body. He grasped her nipples, tugging lightly as the wings kept brushing. She began moving faster, meeting his thrusts harder. She leaned back, bracing her hands on his solid thighs.

Key's gaze lowered to watch as she took him into her body. He let go of her breasts and circled her clit with his thumb.

Sensations raced through her, and her magic split, half rushing down to pile and push low in her groin, the other half rising to settle in her forehead. Every pulse of pleasure intensified both between her legs and in her head. She couldn't take it...didn't know what was happening.

"I've got you." Key reached up, circled his arm around her shoulders and pulled her to his chest. The feel of Kieran all around and inside her caused her orgasm to burst free. She felt his other hand curl around her hip, and he thrust high, and then he was with her. His body shuddering, his mind tightly merged with hers. They were immersed in a bright prism of colored lights. Every flash of the bright colors rippled through them both as they clung skin to skin.

And then one of those beams of light caught her

and ripped her from Kieran. The sensation was frightening. *No! Kieran! Don't let me go!*

It's okay, I'm still holding you. I won't let go. You're safe, let the magic have you.

His reassurance brushed her mind. She believed him. For the first time ever, Roxy believed someone would hold on to her and not let her go. She closed her eyes, allowing herself to be taken by magic.

Her third eye opened, revealing a dragon sitting on a cliff overlooking the ocean. He was beautiful beyond what her mind could comprehend. Tall as a house, green and blue scales that caught the sunlight, his chest amethyst, and his eyes rubies. He was staring out at the sea. "Dyfyr?" She was maybe a dozen feet away to his right.

He turned, his eyes glowing as he looked at her. "Roxanne, you see me."

"Didn't I always see you?" Worlds were colliding, memories rushing by, like a movie on fast forward.

"Yes. You always did. Until you breathed no more."

"Where am I?" She looked around, and in the process, she saw that she didn't have a shadow. She glanced down and saw no body. It was...unsettling.

"Kieran is holding your corporeal body now and the two of us are funneling your magic. You opened your third eye and came with me here."

"My spirit. And this is where we often came, you and I."

"It's where we first made love, and where I gave you my gift of fertility."

The memory stirred, shaking off the dust of centuries and emerging warm and real. The dragon taking his man form and then taking her. Such a powerful creature, and yet he'd made her feel like the most special woman in the world. "I loved you. I still love you. I could never love anyone else throughout all of time. I reincarnated but could never..." She'd always been alone. Life after life. There had always been a hole in her, leaving her feeling barren. "I was empty without you, but I didn't know why."

"My treasure, you died in my arms, your skin so very fragile by then, your hair gray, but I loved you even more. My magic was powerful, is still powerful, but even I couldn't reach beyond death or I would have followed you as I wanted to."

Dyfyr had always called her his treasure, or his love. Clarity filled her mind with more memories of her life with Dyfyr all those centuries ago. "I loved you too much. I was looking for you, life after life. I had sworn I'd find you again." She remembered that he'd been so distraught, he couldn't hold his man form and held her in his dragon shape. But Roxy had never feared him; even with his razor-sharp claws and ability to breathe fire, he'd never hurt her. He had cherished her, loved her. His grief as she had been dying cut her as nothing else could. And she'd sworn to find a way to return to him.

The dragon nodded. "My body lies here beneath us, a part of this rocky cliff overlooking the ocean. Waiting for you to find me. And you would have," he said fiercely. "Each lifetime, I felt you getting closer to allowing the soul memory of me, of us, to surface."

"Oh Dyfyr, you suffered so long."

His ruby eyes softened with a golden light. "It doesn't matter now, my love. Though it was a twisted path, you woke me, and I have you back. I've gotten to hold you. Taste you. Feel your body against mine. Even as we're talking, I feel you in my arms as Kieran holds you."

This was all so puzzling. "I love Kieran, too." How was this possible? Was she betraying Dyfyr? Or Kieran?

"We are the same. Kieran became my man form when the spell was done." His scales rippled, and his tail twitched. "Foolish women had no idea what mayhem they have wrought; they cared only for their own desires."

His anger trembled within Roxy. "It was my mother, wasn't it?"

"And Kieran's mother, Beth. She could see the Tear Wing Slayer had hidden, in spite of his spell shielding it, because she has dragon blood in her ancestry." He shook his head in disgust.

Roxy had to ask, "Dyfyr, the Tear, it's a god killer. Didn't you know that when you created it?"

The dragon huffed out a breath of flames, searing the gray rock with long black streaks. "You were gone. Gone!" The dragon shuddered and the entire cliff shook. "It was too much to be borne. Even with all my magic, I could not reach you, the one thing I loved beyond reason. I wept with such grief, I created the Tears, infusing them with the magic to allow the other dragons to become mortal."

"Shhh." She felt herself moving, drawn to his pain. She wasn't in her body, but she brushed her spirit, or whatever she was, against his chest.

He sighed a sound of contentment.

She asked him, "Dyfyr, why didn't you use the Tear for yourself?"

He turned his head to look at her as she floated around him. "Because you vowed to return one day."

"You waited for me." All this time, she'd had love and hadn't known it. The memories were racing and flying, taking her all the way back to the first time she'd met Dyfyr. "You were in your dragon form when you first saw me. You swooped down and gathered me into your arms. We flew for days as you showed me your world."

"Oh, my treasure, you saw me. No other human saw me. As you saw the other dragons."

"But none of them were you," she said softly. In

those days with him, her heart had been won. She remembered her early fear; Dyfyr was huge, how would they have physical relations? Then he showed her his man form, and she went into his arms at once.

She wondered, "Why did you show me your dragon form first? You could have approached me in your man form. You were powerful enough to hide your wings." She recalled that some dragons did that, took their man form and seduced humans. That must be how Beth had dragon ancestry.

"You used to ask me that many times over, little treasure. Because I never hid anything from you. I am a dragon, a creature of such power and beauty no mortal could even see me. But you saw me. And you gave me your trust, and your love."

The shimmers of his love washed over her spirit. The warmth was bright and eternal.

"I cannot save you if Kieran doesn't let me. His will is strong, and he believes I am trying to hurt you." The dragon blinked as if perplexed.

She would have laughed at his expression except that too much was at stake. "Is that what you were doing? At the maze and in the gym with your claws?"

"I must get that Tear. The spell that summoned my soul was desperate and flawed." His eyes glowed. "You would never make such a mistake with magic, my treasure. You wielded your power with care. And you trained our daughters and their daughters until time took you from us. Never would they have done such a thing. Forcing a soul from one being into another? It is an abomination!" His voice rumbled and the cliff trembled.

Her spirit bounced from the ripples of his rage, but it didn't bother her. His temper felt familiar and safe, as she knew he never hurt the innocent. She rose until she was near his eyes. "What did they do? What did my mother do?" She had to understand it fully.

"I will show you. Come, Roxanne." He lifted his clawed hand and she settled in the middle. "Look with me, my love."

Roxy fixed her gaze on the sea churning below them. In seconds, the scene re-formed itself. She was looking at a different beach in the moonlight. There were five women wearing flowing dresses in a circle around a lone woman in the center. That woman was naked except for the Dragon Tear hanging from a silver chain between her breasts.

"Kieran's mother."

"Yes, and in her hands she has a dragon carved from stone."

"Symbolic magic," Roxy said. "The carved statue symbolizes your sleeping body." She watched the scene.

"Are you sure this will work?" Beth asked.

Gwen answered, "Yes. We will call the soul of the immortal dragon into your unborn child. It's best to do this with as young a fetus as possible so the dragon doesn't feel a strong threat and kill it even in his sleep. The dragon will become accustomed, then once the child wakes him, he will grant you immortality for helping him wake."

Shock made the scene ripple. Her mother promised immortality to Beth? She turned to look at Dyfyr. "That's not true. You couldn't grant immortality. You're a dragon, not a god."

"You are correct. Or I would have made you immortal. Even our children were not immortal. They lived long, but they eventually died."

"My mother lied. And she knew it. She knew the story of the Dragon's Lover. And logically if you couldn't give your lover immortality, you could not give it to Beth."

"Indeed. But your mother convinced Beth the minor amount of dragon blood running in her veins made it possible. Many humans believe it. They wish to believe it. Instead of embracing the life they have been gifted with, they waste it searching for magic."

"You gave me magic." The rich memory of Dyfyr in his man form spreading her legs and bestowing his magic kiss on her inner thigh enveloped her.

He brushed her spirit with his face. "You gave me your heart."

Warm from the memory, she turned back to the scene Dyfyr showed her.

Gwen pulled a small silver knife from a pocket and sliced Beth's thumb. The woman dropped blood onto the statue. Then her mother and the other witches all did the same. The moonlight gleamed off the drops of blood on the dragon statue cradled in Beth's arms against her breast. The Tear shot beams of colored lights over the scene. Then the five witches stepped back and began to chant:

> *O Sacred Dragon*
> *Who bestowed the magic kiss*
> *Your heart beat for love*
> *And stilled in brutal grief*
>
> *With broken magic*
> *And grieving hearts*
> *We cry for our creator*
> *To rise once more*
> *Return our sex magic!*
> *In our fertile mark!*
>
> *Your body sleeps*
> *In stony slumber*
> *Your goddess swore*
> *To love you eternally*
> *But she cannot find you*
> *Unless you are reborn*

Seek this woman
Wearing your Tear
Burrow deep within her
Your soul to be reborn
Sleep within the child
Until your goddess returns

O Beloved Dragon
Who bestowed the magic kiss
Your heart will beat again
Burying the Tear deep
That you may achieve
Final vengeance on your grief!

The scene vanished, the churning sea below returned. Roxy rested in Dyfyr's claw, stunned and horrified at what her mother had done, at what that spell had done. Her attention caught on trails of smoke rising from Dyfyr's nostrils.

His ruby eyes glittered. "Do you see the flaw in the spell?"

"Final vengeance on your grief." She thought the spell through. "I'm your grief. I'm the reason you cried that Tear. They spelled the Tear to find and kill me. That's why the Tear locked on to me, then following the spell, it *buried deep* and began binding with my life force. How stupid!" She was outraged on multiple levels.

He stared at her. "They wanted me to destroy the Tear. They meant for the Tear to symbolize my grief, and that once you woke me, I would destroy it as final vengeance on my grief."

"Why did my mother do it?"

"She was playing goddess. She spent the next several years trying to call the soul of my lover from Summerland. Eventually she became pregnant with you. She believed that you'd wake me, and I'd return all their power."

"But you can't, can you?"

"No. Again they operated on flawed logic. There were fertility witches present when the demon witches cast their dark spell to bind the captured witch hunters as their familiars. You know the rest: Asmodeus arrived and twisted the spell into a blood and sex curse, and the fertility witches were cursed, too. I cannot undo that. The solution is soul mirrors—finding the other half of your soul as you and Kieran have done. Gwen was desperate when she did the spell. And desperation made her foolish."

"You said you can save me, if Kieran allows you to. By clawing out the Tear?"

He nodded. "Kieran must allow me to fully emerge in him and trust that we will not kill you."

"We?" Roxy tried to grasp it. "You have to work together?"

"We do work together. We have killed rogues and saved witches. Kieran trusts me fully in the heat of battle. It's only with those he loves he fears what we are together." He lifted his clawed hand, caressing her spirit. "Kieran suffered such cruelty by the man who should have loved him. He fears that if he doesn't control both of us, we will kill without conscience." Flames slithered out the sides of Dyfyr's mouth. "Like that bastard who sired him."

Roxy hurt for Kieran. "You shielded him." She knew Dyfyr, he loved children. Being a creature of true power and magic, he detested bullies who picked on the weak to make themselves feel strong.

"I would have woken fully if I could have for that boy and killed his father myself. But alas, I was trapped in my own magic. But Kieran is enough a part of me that I could pull him away from the pain, and I could give him strength." He nuzzled his head against her spirit. "You must get him to trust me and trust himself. Together we will get that Tear out of you."

Roxy's entire spirit shuddered at the memory of Kieran's rage when the claws came out at the maze. He'd bashed his hands against the cement wall in his fury. The idea of hurting someone he loved was unbearable to him. "He won't like it, Dyfyr. I don't know if he can do it. Can you just force him when he's asleep or something?"

"You saw what happened when I tried. His will is strong, as it should be," Dyfyr said with gruff approval. "He loves you, and even asleep, his mind will not allow you to be hurt. You must convince him to trust himself, and to trust my magic. As long as you have your chakras open, I can connect with them and use my magic to separate the Tear from your life force and get it out of you. Our combined magic will heal the wound."

Suspicion and worry for him began to swirl. "And then what happens to the Tear? Wing Slayer couldn't destroy it, how will you?"

Dyfyr tilted his head, reading her as he always did. "I will be fine, little treasure. I am simply going to magically call the Tear back to me, and it will make me mortal, but it won't hurt Key. Just be sure to keep your chakras open until I am finished. No matter what happens, you must keep your chakras open."

"But what of you then?" Panic welled within her. "You won't die, will you? Please, Dyfyr, I have only just found you!"

"No, love, I won't die. I will live as long as Kieran lives. Once my immortality is gone, I will be fully merged into his life force."

"Will I still see you?" She felt such a strong connection with him. "Like I see you now? Will you still have your magic?"

"Sweet treasure, yes. I will not leave you. But you

must think, Roxanne. What would happen now if Kieran died while I am immortal?"

She stared at Dyfyr's ruby eyes. "I guess...your soul would leave?" Would it go back to where his body was beneath them? "But wait, the spell! They needed that Tear, because it's part of you, in order to draw your soul to Kieran. Beth wore the Tear, and Kieran was inside her when they did the spell." The answer hit her so hard, she felt her spirit shake.

Dyfyr caught her in his hands, cradling her gently.

She was furious and sickened. "Liam! He's rogue; he doesn't have a soul. He wants your soul! That's why he's desperate to get the Tear. Then he'd have a soul and the strength of a dragon in him. He'd be a powerful ally for Asmodeus."

"That is also why Beth wore the Tear. If they did kill Kieran, my soul would go to her. She taunted both Kieran's father and Liam that since they didn't have dragon blood in their veins, my soul wouldn't be able to go to them."

Her thoughts spun. "Is that true?"

"Yes. And Asmodeus knew it as well."

"That's why...oh God. That's why Asmodeus and Young infused Liam with fertility witch blood. They are all descended from you...they have dragon blood. He created a vessel for your soul."

Dyfyr's scales glittered with fury, his chest expanded, and a low growl ripped up his throat. "They murdered those witches! Our descendants! They have perverted true sex magic into an abomination, and we will not allow it! You must make Kieran understand. I have to get the Tear from you and end my immortality."

She saw it all so clearly now. "I will try."

"You will succeed. I will not lose you again." Dyfyr calmed down, his ruby eyes glowing. "My love, it's time to go back. You're growing tired and must rest."

"No," she said softly, "I'm not ready to leave you."

"You're not leaving me. You have felt me when you're with Kieran. You know I am with you, love. But I am not the only one."

The warmth of their love began to glow in her spirit. "You mean Kieran?"

Once again his chest puffed up; his scales rippled in incredible beauty. "I mean the child you carry." As he finished saying the words, beams of colored light shot out from his scales, and she was traveling again, but her mind was overflowing with too much wonder to pay attention.

She was pregnant.

≈ 23 ≈

As soon as Key had felt her magic bloom hot and wild in his chest, he'd slipped out of her body and sat up, shifting Roxy onto his lap. Her power rippled through him, heating his blood, making him feel more alive than he'd ever been and firing his need to draw.

Holding her, he rolled to his feet and carefully walked into the bedroom. Roxy was boneless and so damned trusting in his arms, his throat tightened. She knew he'd take care of her body while she did her magic. Never had he been a part of something so intimate and special. Picking up his sketch pad and pencils, he sat on the bed, leaned against the headboard, and settled her against his chest. Her magic continued to strum through him, strong and steady. Naturally, he was hard again. His witch funneled enough sex magic to put Viagra out of business. Not that he needed her magic to get aroused by her. Just her voice, her touch, her scent made him hot. He set the book on the bed next to his thigh, and with his right arm wrapped around Roxy, he flipped it open to a blank page and began to capture the images filling his mind. He had no idea how much time passed before he realized her magic was dialing back in his

JENNIFER LYON

chest. He dropped the pencil, fully aware of what he'd drawn—he could see the witches surrounding his mother, who wore the Tear—but Roxy came first.

Always.

He moved her into the cradle of his arm and she opened her eyes.

"You're back." He stroked her face and felt a slight throb. She must have a headache. He slid his fingers into her hair and gently massaged her scalp, drawing off the ache. "You saw Dyfyr." His voice was husky with pride and the residue of her magic.

Her witch-shimmer was dimming, but it rippled with sudden light. "He's amazing."

He smiled at her, then slipped his fingers from her scalp to trail down to the lights in the Tear flashing where it was buried in the curve of her breast. "Did he tell you how to get the Tear out?"

Her witch-shimmer faded away, and she lifted her gaze to his. "He said he can do it. You have to let him do it." She slid off his thighs and sat facing him, drawing her knees up. Then she saw his sketchbook. "Is this what you were doing while I was in my third eye? What did you draw?" She picked up the book and squinted in the semigloom.

Key leaned over and turned on the bedside lamp for her.

Roxy turned the page. "This is what Dyfyr showed me. The spell to call his soul into you when you were in your mother's womb." She looked up at him. "You saw it?"

He shrugged. "Images bouncing in my head. I don't know if you or Dyfyr were projecting to me, but I got the gist of it. My mother wore the Tear; your mother and other witches performed the spell to summon Dyfyr's soul into her baby."

"Dyfyr is angry, called what they did an abomination."

Key listened as Roxy explained what she'd learned from the dragon. How the spell had gone wrong, causing the Tear to try to kill her. How her mother had done more spells to call the soul of Dyfyr's lover from Summerland. It took all his self-control to keep his growing fury in check at what her bitch of a mother had done to her. He needed to have a clear head, listen to what she'd learned, and save Roxy. That was the important thing. So he asked, "How did she have enough magic to do those things? Witches need high magic to do spell work. This was after the curse when they couldn't access their high magic."

Roxy lowered her chin to her knees. "I didn't ask Dyfyr that, but I think it was the Tear. It had enough of Dyfyr's magic in it, and fertility witches were created by him, so it strengthened their magic enough to call his soul. And maybe enough residual power to call my soul from Summerland, but that took longer. How old are you?"

He didn't even blink at her shift in subjects. "Twenty-eight."

"I'm twenty-four, so it took her at least three years to become pregnant with me."

He couldn't stand not touching her so he wrapped his hand around her calf. After they summoned the dragon into Key, Roxy's mother spent the next three years desperately trying to get pregnant with Dyfyr's lover. He was with her so far. "Your mother believed waking Dyfyr would restore the fertility witches' power?"

Roxy nodded. "But it won't, the curse is demon magic, and Dyfyr can't undo that. Soul mirrors are the only solution. But at the time, no one knew that. Everyone was desperate to find a fix." She lifted her head. "I'm not excusing my mother, what she did was wrong. Even as frightened and desperate as she must have felt after the curse...how did she justify forcing a dragon's soul into a baby?" Her face flushed with anger. "Into you?"

His self-control slipped. "You're the one wearing the death sentence because of her! She spelled that Tear to kill you! And I swear to you if you die, I will kill her." Roxy's spine snapped straight, and hot color flooded her face. "No, you can't! She's not a demon witch—you'll lose your soul." She grabbed his arm. "Swear it, Kieran! Swear you won't kill her!"

He felt her fingers digging into his arm with her pure panic and raw worry. For him. Even facing her own death, she worried about him. He didn't know if he could make that promise, so he said, "Don't die. Just don't leave me, Roxy."

"Kieran..."

Her fingers on his arm softened as her love seeped into him. And with it he also felt how tired she was. Getting himself under control, he said, "Tell me the rest."

She studied his face, then said, "It's about Liam. Why he wants the Tear."

Cold rage tried to dig in again, but Key squelched it. "For Asmodeus."

"Yes, but there's more to it." She took a breath. "Dyfyr is immortal. If you die and Liam has the Tear—"

The truth rang in his head like cymbals clanging. "His soul goes to Liam." His anger broke through. "He wants Dyfyr's strength and violence to kill more witches. They think they can harness the dragon in Liam and make him into a weapon for the demon." Key looked at her. "When I was young, I was exactly what they thought I was, a coward. I didn't know how to fight. It was easier to just let Dyfyr pull me away. To escape. It's wasn't until Phoenix forced me to fight that Dyfyr began to waken and help me fight back. Now I'm a killer that they admire." And one day, he'd lose control and kill another innocent like Vivian and their baby. Key knew it was in him to do it. It had to be—look what he came from. He'd killed his own father. What kind of man does that?

Roxy put her hand on his bunched forearm. "You're not them, Kieran. You are not. Your father deserved to die and you know that or you wouldn't have killed him."

She'd heard his thoughts. Their bond was growing at an astonishing rate. He lifted his eyes to her gaze. "How do you know that?"

"Because I share your soul. And I know how you would lay down your own life, even today, to go back and give Vivian and your child another chance at life. That you regret that mistake every day. That you loved her as much as you were capable at seventeen years old, and that while maybe you didn't quite love the child yet, you loved the *idea* of your own family and you would have loved that baby once you held him in your arms. Your only mistake that day was not realizing Vivian had gotten up. But it was an accident. You did not kill her. Liam killed her by pulling her into the path of your knife."

Key was staggered by her. She was dead-on, so exactly right he almost couldn't draw a breath. He felt such loving respect and acceptance for his memories of Vivian coming from Roxy that he knew he was no longer alone in his guilt and grief, or in anything. He had blamed himself for letting the filth of his past touch Vivian, but he realized that the truth was he hadn't trusted her enough to tell her what he really was, or that he came from killers. They'd been too young to really know what real love was.

But now...he looked up at his witch and knew love was about trust and partnership. It was scary and exhilarating. It made him strive to be worthy of her. Then he looked down at the Tear. He thought he'd known fear before?

Not even close. Losing her would rip his soul apart, taking out all the good and leaving all that was rotten in him. He couldn't lose her. "How do we save you?"

She tensed. "You have to let Dyfyr do it. He's tried twice and both times you shut him down. Your will is so strong, you stopped him. But he's only trying to save me, not hurt me. And remember, he's immortal, so he'll use the Tear on himself, becoming mortal and tied to your life force. Then Wing Slayer can make us both immortal. So the Tear will be gone, no longer a threat—"

"Roxy," he said, interrupting her rapid-fire words. The soft lights from the Tear were pulsing faster, indicating her heart was racing. Her fingers around his hand were white-knuckled.

She blinked, swallowing, then said, "Please, Kieran. You have to."

Dread filled him. "Have to what? Stop dancing around it and tell me. I get the part about Dyfyr being immortal and using the Tear to become mortal. But how does he get the Tear out of you?"

"Dyfyr needs you to let him emerge fully in you and connect with my chakras. Then he'll use his magic to cut the Tear from my lifeline, and draw it into his own life force. He said our combined magic will heal the spot once he removes the Tear."

Removes the Tear. It vibrated in his head. Jerking his hand from hers, he snarled, "You mean where he claws the Tear from your chest right over your heart?" He launched himself from the bed, his heart pounding, blood roaring in his ears. "Do you have any idea what those claws can do? How many rogues I killed with those claws? Not just killed"—he whirled around, so goddamned furious, he felt his veins popping out—"but ripped apart until their intestines were hanging out in bloody strips." The dragon wanted to use those claws on Roxy? And what if the Tear broke inside her? She'd probably die in seconds! "Not a fucking chance!" He paced to the dresser, slapped his hands down on top, and said, "We'll find another way."

"No, we won't. The Tear is Dyfyr's magic, and my mother spelled the Tear to kill me. Either the dragon gets the Tear out or I die." She swiveled around on the bed to face him. "And according to Dyfyr, it's not just me that's going to die."

Key whipped around, his gaze latching on to her. Shit, she was pale, and he could almost feel her fatigue. But this was her life they were talking about! "What the hell does that mean?"

"I'm pregnant."

He froze to the spot under the sheer weight of the words. Pregnant. With his child, their child. And she was going to die. He stared at her sitting on the bed, her arms wrapped around her bent legs. What she was asking? Use the claws to rip open her chest? He looked up to her eyes and felt his gut roll over. Dark circles made her look exhausted and gaunt. It was five A.M., she'd been depleted of magic, had marathon sex, and then used a tremendous amount of magic. She had that Tear in her sucking off her life force.

And now a child. A baby.

He crossed to the bed. "Dyfyr said you're pregnant?" Dare he believe the dragon?

She barely moved, her gaze fixed on his chest. "Yes. And he would know, he's the one that gave witches fertility."

That ripped through his memories until he recalled her mother explaining how she had to wake the dragon. "Your mother said, *It's sex magic. You need your magic, then you call the dragon, he Awakens and fertilizes you.*"

Roxy closed her eyes. "I should have realized...should have known. I just thought fertilize meant you spilling your seed in me."

He stood there, helpless frustration burning through him. Roxy had dreamed of a family, desperately wanted that. Then she'd given up her dream to help him. And then, for reasons that still confounded him, she'd fallen in love with him. Trusted him. Believed him when he'd told her he wouldn't leave her.

But now, he could feel her fatigue, loneliness and fear. He didn't have to read her mind to know that she feared he'd just cut his losses like her father had. He leaned over, scooped her into his arms, and walked toward the bathroom.

"What are you doing?"

"You're exhausted, and I'm taking care of you." He turned on the shower jets, adjusted them, then carried her into the warm spray. Her honey scent flared with a wisp of caramel as he washed her breasts, her belly and deep between her thighs. Even tired and satiated she wanted him.

He dried them both, led her to his bed.

"Wait," she said tiredly, looking around. "Need a shirt."

"Why?" He walked over to the dresser and grabbed her black tank top. Then drew it over her head.

"The Tear, I don't want to wake up and see it."

His guts tightened. She couldn't escape that Tear, not even in sleep. She needed him to get it out, and right now, she didn't believe he would do it. He smoothed the tank over her, picked her up and put her in bed. Climbing in, he pulled her into his arms and settled her against his chest. Then he tilted her head up to see those eyes he loved, and his choice was clear. "Whatever it takes to keep you with me, to have you as my eternal mate, I'll do it. I will fight for you, and if there's a child, I'll fight for him, too. Always."

He kissed her and stroked his hand down her back until she fell into an exhausted sleep.

A child. He and Roxy might have a child. If he could save her by digging into her chest with dragon claws. His heart iced and hot sweat burned his skin. Christ. Would he be able to take her pain or would they have to hold her down while she screamed?

And if Key failed, if he killed Roxy, the other hunters had better kill him. Or he was going to unleash his fury on the world.

⚜

Roxy woke to see Kieran sitting in a chair next to the bed. He had on a pair of jeans, one ankle crossed over his knee, and his sketchbook propped on his thigh. His arm and shoulders bunched and undulated as he drew with fast, sharp movements. The dragon sat on his chest, looking at her with his ruby eyes.

Her schema flared to life. She shifted and realized she was barely covered.

"Morning, green eyes."

She looked up, and her heart caught. His eyes were alive with blue. Just the feel of his gaze burned through her. She sat up, and the sheet slid down, reminding her that she had the tank top on. She could still see the soft lights of the Tear pulsing, but the shirt muted it a little. She returned her gaze to Key. "What are you drawing?"

He grinned. "Want to see?"

Forgetting the Tear, another shiver raced down her center, and her magic woke up. "Yes."

He sat forward and handed her the pad. Roxy looked down. He'd drawn a pencil sketch of the two of them. Key had his wings out, he was holding Roxy as they flew.

Naked.

And given the way her legs were wrapped around his waist, her head tilted back and the expression on her face...she looked up at him. "I think you can get arrested for this."

His grin widened, but his eyes darkened to a sensual heat. "For drawing it or doing it?"

Her nipples ached, her core throbbed and she wanted him. "You're in a good mood."

"Look closer. See the way you're leaning back, showing me your breasts while I stroke my cock deep inside you?"

She clenched with need at his raw voice. Could feel his desire crashing through her. She tried to do what he said and looked at her breasts. He'd drawn them full with large areolas, tightly budded nipples.

What's missing, love?

His words in her head made her magic sing. She stared and saw the soft colors of lights flashing on the page, that came from the Tear—*The Tear!* It wasn't there in the picture. She looked up and saw the glint of determination in his gaze. "You're willing to let Dyfyr get the Tear out?"

Key stared back. "I'm willing to do anything it takes to save you. And our child." He grinned and added, "I'm going to make love to you for hours to fill your sex magic. I want you strong and ready to get that Tear out—we'll do it tonight after Eli's Induction Ceremony. And then," he dropped his gaze to the book. "We're going to work on the flying sex I promised you at the maze."

Hope soared through her, and she didn't even think, just tossed off the sheet and scooted to the edge of the bed.

Key took the book from her fingers and tossed it aside. His gaze burned into hers, and he settled his warm hands on her thighs. "I noticed last night that your schema is changing."

"The color? That's—"

He shook his head. "No. I know your schema." The

teasing in his face firmed to seriousness. "I feel your magic stream through me. I've touched it, tasted it; your goddess mark and I are connected. Maybe because Dyfyr is in me, maybe because we're soul mirrors and I'm your familiar. I just know exactly what she should look like. And last night, I realized the shape of your schema was different. I was so wrapped up in feeding your magic, into the *feel* of you, that I didn't think about what it meant."

She put her hands on Kieran's. "I saw it yesterday in the shower. You think she's telling us I'm pregnant? Like Dyfyr said?" Roxy believed Dyfyr, but Kieran needed more.

He lifted their hands from her thighs and threaded their fingers together. "She is you, Roxy. She'll change with you." He stood and gently pushed her back to the bed. Color darkened his cheekbones and his voice roughened. "I'm going to kiss you and work my way down to spreading your legs and seeing the schema. She'll tell us if you're pregnant, just like she tells me when you need me."

Roxy realized he'd been sitting here planning this. She could part her thighs and look, but Kieran wanted to do this, he wanted to discover the answer his way. With her fingers laced in his, she reclined on the bed, drinking in the feel of him looming over her. He pressed her hands to the mattress, leaned down, and kissed her. Slow and soft, he eased his way inside her mouth with sensual strokes of his tongue.

She tilted her head, giving him more. Meeting the wet strokes of his tongue with hers, inhaling his taste, just letting the sensation of him wash over and fill her. Drive out all her days, weeks and years of loneliness, of never knowing where she belonged.

She belonged to Kieran and his dragon.

Key lifted his head, his eyes nearly blue. "You're our treasure. You will always belong to us. And together, we are going to get that Tear out of you so that nothing can ever separate us again."

Her heart swelled, and a wild sense of freedom swirled in her—freedom to be herself, a witch gifted with sex magic.

He ran his gaze down her body to her legs. "I caught the scent of your desire just after you woke up. It's making me insane with the need to touch you, taste you. You want that, don't you?"

She couldn't deny him. "Yes."

"Pull the shirt up."

She gathered the stretchy material in her fingers and tugged it up to her stomach.

"Higher." His voice rumbled as he watched her. "I want to see all of you."

She drew it up until she'd revealed her breasts. Her nipples tightened beneath his hot gaze. He lowered himself, the muscles of his arms bulging as he supported his weight, and closed his mouth around a nipple. The lights from the Tear flashed green, blue and red over his face, but then he swirled his tongue and her thoughts were filled with only Kieran. He pulled deeper on her nipple until she arched beneath the sensation.

He kissed the valley between her breasts, then kissed and suckled the other nipple until her magic was spinning and her nerves were so sensitive that just the scrape of his teeth had her raising her hips in silent begging.

Kieran lifted his head, his eyes fierce, powerful arms holding him over her. "You never have to beg me for your pleasure. Ever." He pushed off the bed, onto his knees, and spread her legs wide.

She could feel the heat of his gaze.

"So damned lovely. Creamy pink folds, your clit exposed and swollen, all surrounded by your curls." He turned his gaze to the left. "And there, your schema. The faded color showing me how hungry you are for me." He moved his thumb to stroke the mark.

Roxy lifted her head to see him. His stare was fixed on her inner thigh. Then he turned his gaze to her. Her heart turned over at the vulnerable joy there. "And telling us that you're growing our child. I can see the softening in the middle of the mark."

She didn't try to see the mark. What was important was the connection between her and Kieran. "Sex magic," she said softly, realizing that creating a child was true magic.

"Our magic." He kept stroking her schema, sending deep shivers through her.

Her need was there, but she realized something profound—there was no fear attached to it anymore. Kieran would always feed her magic.

An intimate smile curved his mouth. "Oh yeah." He leaned in and kissed the mark.

His mouth released a flood of hormones, swamping her with tides of sensuality until she writhed in it. "Kieran," she cried his name from the depths of her heart.

"I know, baby." He slid his hands beneath her, lifted her, and blew gently.

She sucked in a breath, her stomach contracting.

Then he leaned in with a soft brush of his lips, followed by his tongue sliding through her folds and caressing her clit. Lightning bolts raced through her. Her thighs tightened over his shoulders.

He groaned, lifting her higher to press his mouth to her entrance, and lapped with maddening slowness, as if to savor her. Holding her up with one hand, he used his thumb to tease her clit.

Then it changed, his kiss grew hotter, more demanding. Faster strokes. Deeper. Her magic raced and bubbled. Pleasure built and climbed. He kept finding her spots, giving her more. Making her feel more. Circling her clit, thrusting and licking with his tongue. Even a gentle rasp of teeth. Too much!

She cried out, and Kieran filled her mind, the man and the dragon. *You are so beautiful I can't get enough.*

She splintered, and the intense pressure released in swirling lights of pleasure. She gave herself up to it, feeling bliss and Kieran as she soared. Shudders rippled through her, and every tremor was pure joy.

Finally Key stood and began unbuttoning his jeans. She took in his wide chest, his hard stomach. As she watched, he undid two buttons, the material sliding low on his hips, revealing a dusting of his crisp pubic hair and his huge erection straining the remaining buttons. His fingers were at the third button. She sat up, pulled her shirt down and said, "Stop."

He jerked his head up, his fingers stilling. "What's wrong?"

He looked hot enough to burn her fingers if she touched him. As she rose to her feet, a wave of dizziness made her catch her breath. Before she could recover, Key caught her in his arms and sat on the chair with her on his lap. "Are you sick?"

≥ *24* ≥

WORRY MADE HIM IGNORE THE bite of the buttons from his jeans pressing into his erection. "Roxy?"

She lifted her head. "No, it was just a little dizziness." Her scent was rich with caramel desire and no sickness. Was it from being pregnant or that Tear?

Frowning, he said, "Why did you stop me?" She was seated on his thighs, her shoulder pressed against his chest. Her scent climbed up his nose and burrowed into his skin.

She leaned close, pressing her mouth to his neck. *I want to make love to you.*

Her mind merged with his, and he felt her *want*...the want to touch him, taste him, learn him. The touch of her thoughts to his shuddered straight through to his soul. His cock engorged even more, but this was more than sex. She was showing him her true self; the desires and needs that she'd fought all her life that she'd now freed. The sheer intimacy and willingness to reveal herself to him. Hot male pride lit him up, while his heart felt the pure glow of her love.

She rose up on her knees and kissed him. *Let me make love to you.* She feathered hot kisses over his jaw, down his neck, and licked his shoulder.

Let? He'd have laughed if she hadn't rendered him speechless. Fire raced through him, sizzling along his nerves until all he knew was Roxy. His witch, the slide of her breasts barely covered in the tank, her thighs straddling his jean-covered hips, her hands skimming and touching, creating a path of magical heat...

She slid down to lick his nipple.

Key bowed up from the chair, his hand pressing against her lower back to hold her. Words failed him. Thought failed him. He was consumed with just her, his witch.

Her silky hair slid over his chest and arms as she eased her way down between his thighs. She pressed her hot, damp mouth to his stomach and he groaned. Growled.

She stopped.

He looked down. He was so hard, so engorged the head of his dick jutted up from his partially buttoned jeans. His shaft was trapped inside.

She stroked his straining head with the pad of her finger.

Icy stars of sensation shot through him, rushing and shivering. Key couldn't move and locked his hands around the arms of the chair.

She drew her finger down over the head, to the first closed button. Magic teased, and the button popped open.

Then the second one, and he sprang free.

Roxy curled her warm fingers around his shaft, and he was gloved in skin and magic. Blood pounded in his ears. He couldn't look away as she lowered her head.

Toward his cock.

He squeezed the chair arms harder.

She licked him. A slow swipe of her tongue, and his brain melted. Then he saw her face. The softening of her mouth, the sensual sweep of her lashes as she closed her eyes and savored the taste. Her scent bloomed hot and rich with caramel desire; she liked the taste of him. Sliding her hand down lower on his shaft, she took him in her mouth.

He lost his mind in the heat of her. Her mouth sliding over him, magic swirling, and his pants vanished and her hand cupped his balls.

"Roxy," he growled out, cradling her head as she suckled him. Too much! The hot pleasure swirled and raged, gathered, then shot down his spine. He tried to pull her away. *Going to explode!* He couldn't stop it; he was pumping into her mouth.

Mine. She whispered back to him, the word heavy with love.

His entire body lit on fire as his pleasure burst out. The flames licked his skin and burned through him. Even before he'd finished coming, he reached down, lifted her to his chest, and held her tight against his heart and Dyfyr's.

⟶✤⟵

"I talked to the Ancestors," Carla said.

Roxy tried to concentrate. Carla, Darcy and Ailish were in the warehouse because there was more room. Key, Phoenix and Sutton were out trying to draw Liam from the rogue hideout protected by the mini-Death Daggers. She was worried Key would venture too close and get stabbed.

"Roxy?" Carla said softly.

"Sorry." She snapped out of it. "What did the Ancestors say?"

"They said Dyfyr can absolutely work through your chakras. He created your gift of magic, so that will work. But you should have your third eye open. That's where you connected with him, and it will give him the most access. You must try to keep it open. Even if Key can't take all your pain." She paused.

Darcy sat forward. "I think we should be there, Roxy. We can help you."

She flushed. "I can't." She'd never be able to release her sex magic to get to her third eye with them there, watching. And if they had to have sex... Before she'd Awakened, the idea had horrified her on a purely moral level. But now, it was a special intimacy she shared with Key, she couldn't...

"I know," Darcy put her hand on her arm. "I wouldn't like it either. But this is your life, and your baby's."

"I have a better idea," Ailish said. "Roxy, you and Key use our backyard. For one thing, it has power there, it's where Phoenix and I both reached Wing Slayer when we needed him. Second, Phoenix and I will stay in the house. But if you need help, I'll come out." She grinned then. "I can't see, so I won't care if you're both naked, oiled and covered in purple glitter."

That image caused her to choke.

"But more important, I'm a siren witch. I can sing and enhance your magic, and possibly the dragon's magic working through you. I know that I can help you hold your chakras open and take your pain. Basically, you'll have privacy unless you're in trouble."

"That's an excellent idea," Carla said.

"Brilliant," Darcy said. "And we can always lend our power through Ailish if you need it."

She looked at the three witches and was humbled. Carla was smart and compassionate, Darcy was passionate and loyal, Ailish was brash and strong with a huge heart. And they accepted her. "Thank you. I—" The door opened, and the three hunters strode in. Roxy leaped to her feet and met Key by the pool table. He wasn't wearing a shirt, and Dyfyr sat on his chest, little tendrils of smoke rising from his nostrils. "What's he mad about?" Roxy asked, reaching out to stroke the dragon. The smoke vanished.

Key put his hand over hers and looked down, his eyes full of gray menace. "Can't get to Liam. We fought those mini-Death Daggers, but we can't destroy them. Dyfyr senses Liam, I think."

Roxy agreed. "He's furious at Liam, and at the demon for killing his fertility witches to regrow Liam's heart."

"We won't let him get the Tear." Key ground his jaw; his gaze dropped to where it pulsed under her shirt.

Phoenix handed out bottles of cold beer. "You come from a long line of geniuses, comic boy. Your mother trying to get the soul of an enraged dragon into you. Yeah..."

Roxy shuddered at the memory of Liam when she'd been at his mercy. "He doesn't care," she said softly. "His eyes...blue and empty. Except when I screamed, he liked that."

Key set the beer on the pool table and hauled her to his chest, his arms wrapping around her. "You're safe. We're not going to let him get you again, Roxy." He spread his hand over her lower back.

Comfort eased through her muscles. She lifted her head to look at him. "I know that. I'm trying to explain what I saw, what he is. Said he was blood-born, but he's still empty and soulless and..." She turned out of his embrace, leaning her hands on the pool table. "He survived by the blood of fertility witches. It's made him stronger, faster. He thinks he can control Dyfyr. In his crazed mind, the witch blood brought him back from the dead, so it'll also allow him to control Dyfyr. Then he'll have a soul. He will be completely reborn. Blood-born."

"Bat-shit crazy is more like it," Phoenix snarled.

Key put his hands on her shoulders. "He'll never get the chance to find out," he said fiercely. "We're getting that Tear out of you tonight." His fingers tightened. "Maybe we should do it now. Liam is planning something—both Dyfyr and I feel it."

Ailish said, "Key, we have a plan for you and Roxy to get the Tear out after Eli's ceremony. Phoenix and I will stay in the house, but if Roxy needs me, I can use my voice."

Axel strode in from the back of the warehouse. "And if you wait until after the ceremony, Wing Slayer's god powers will be strengthened. Every hunter who commits to him increases his power."

"Roxy?"

She met his gaze and her heart squeezed. She wanted to live. Desperately. "Tonight. At Ailish and Phoenix's house."

⚜

Key joined all the hunters out in Phoenix's backyard. The witches stayed inside. This was a ceremony between Wing Slayer and his chosen. Key took off his shirt, laid it on the patio table, and walked down the stairs to the sloping grass. The night air was damp with the faintest whiff of the sea.

The recruits who hadn't yet achieved Wing Slayer Hunter status all stood about ten feet back on the left, watching. Eli stood with them. Phoenix's house was on the top of a hill overlooking a tract of homes. Axel took the point, looking down over the development. The moonlight showed his powerful back as his brown and gold hawk wings sprang out.

Sutton's wings flashed out, and he moved to Axel's left, and Ram stepped up next, his thunderbird tattoo showing on his chest. Key moved to Axel's right, and his wings popped out. Phoenix stood next to him, his phoenix wings whooshing out. Linc fell in behind them, his falcon tattoo visible on his back. They were in wing formation.

The silence settled with a quiet reverence. The wind blew the grass, and the trees bent and moved so that long shadows of the branches swayed over them.

Axel nodded, and Eli broke from the other recruits and walked to stand before the hawk. The outline of his griffin tat was clearly visible on his back; the head of an eagle looking to the side, dramatic wings rising from the lion's body, with each feather distinct. Eli handed the hawk his silver knife.

Axel said, "Your test?"

Eli answered, "Follow the law of protection by taking a knife strike meant to kill a mortal woman and her son."

"Did you know them?"

"No. It makes no difference. They were innocents."

Key felt Eli's passion and anger. His own sister had been threatened and used to try to force him to kill a witch and go rogue. Phoenix had shown up in time to save his sister. Eli had been in a hellish situation. He understood helplessness, and he would fight to his death to defend those in that position.

"Accepted," Axel said. "Your vow."

Eli's head lifted, his shoulders spread, and he said in a clear voice, "I vow my allegiance to Wing Slayer, god of the witch hunters. I take the ancient oath of protection for the innocent and justice for the damned. And I swear to fight the curse to my death."

"And your sacrifice." He handed the knife to Eli.

The hunter took it and said, "My life's blood for protection and justice in the name of Wing Slayer." He sliced his arm, letting the blood drip onto the grass at his feet.

Silence spread out, and even the breeze stilled.

This was the moment that Wing Slayer would accept or reject Eli. A change in the air vibrate in Key's wings. A fierce wind whipped across the grounds, blowing grass and leaves; the shadows of the tree branches bent and swelled. Time slowed with expectation—

Then was shattered by piercing alarms from all their cellphones.

Key jerked his phone out. The alarms at the club and his loft were going off.

"The witches are getting alarms, too." Sutton scrolled through the screens.

"Hold formation!" Axel said, his voice thundering.

Each man stilled. A sharp, tangy scent surrounded them as a large, winged outline fell over Eli.

The edge of the heavy darkness touched Key, creating an electrical rush, a power so intense, he couldn't breathe.

Wing Slayer.

Then the shadow vanished, gone as quickly as it came. The wind faded back to a breeze, the trees grew calm, the scent left.

Axel said, "Eli Stone, in our wing formation. You are marked a Wing Slayer Hunter."

Eli moved to stand next to Ram, the griffin tat on his back completed. The wings were bronze and gold, filling the shape Key had outlined. The eagle head and lion body were all there, the creature looking as fiercely intelligent as the mythology claimed.

It was a moment to celebrate, but the alarms were still blaring. Axel broke formation, striding toward the house, his wings disappearing instantly. "Sutton, status!"

"Three reports of witches taken," Sutton said. "If they have their cells we can track them. Alarm at the club going off, cameras show a broken window, nothing else. Key's loft—"

"On fire." Key stared at the flames on his phone before the camera at his loft died. All he could think was, thank Wing Slayer Roxy was safe here at Phoenix's house.

Axel led them inside. "It's an organized attack. Ram, you coordinate and mobilize."

Key's wings folded up and vanished as he walked through the door. Then Roxy slammed into him. He got his arm around her to steady her.

"My parents! He has my parents!" Her face was so white, the scattering of freckles looked like blood. Grabbing her phone from her, he looked at the picture text, recognizing Gwen; she was cut in multiple places and tied up. Next to her was a man in his fifties sporting fresh bruises beneath thick white hair and also tied up. The text read, "I'll kill your mother first, then your father. Ten minutes until the real fun starts here at Grace Chapel." He felt Roxy's terror, her guilt at what Liam had been doing.

"That's the little church close to the cemetery," Phoenix said, looking over Key's shoulder.

Key nodded. "I'll get them, Roxy. You stay here. Don't step outside." Urgency rode his spine.

"Going with you," Phoenix said. "It's a setup, but I don't see how they think they'll get Roxy."

"Fire department is at your loft, Key," Ram said. "Linc went to handle the club. Recruits are fanning out. Sutton and Axel, you two go after the missing witches. I'll stay here with the women and coordinate. If you have headsets or Bluetooths, get them on and go."

Key kissed Roxy and hauled ass out the back door. His wings sprang out; he leaped into the air and climbed. Phoenix flew his left flank. Both of them put on their Bluetooths so they could communicate with each other and Ram.

As he flew, hot anger stabbed him. He should have gotten the Tear from Roxy today. Not waited. They weren't immortal, and if Key died tonight, she had no chance of getting that Tear out.

His chest burned with his own and Dyfyr's rage.

Liam wanted to meet Dyfyr? Key was going to introduce them.

They both circled the church with the A-line roof. Key spotted four rogues outside, and more had to be invisible. The church itself was about thirteen hundred square feet. The main chapel had four long, stained glass windows on either side.

"Ram, we need some recruits to take down the guards outside."

"I have them in the area," Ram responded. "ETA one to two minutes."

While they waited, Key said, "See the stained glass windows. Ever flown through one?"

"Only you, comic boy. Birds die from hitting windows."

"We aren't birds. Besides, I have an idea. Keep watching." Holding his invisible shield, Key called out his claws. Then he flew to the second window on one side, pulled the shield around himself and muted the sound waves, then he scored the glass in a rectangle. Carefully he eased back, then flew to the other side and did the same.

He returned closer to Phoenix. "Hit the second window, the one with the angel on it. I'll go in the other side."

Key saw four witch hunters materialize on the grounds and attack the rogues. The battle grew hot and bloody in seconds, the sounds echoing. Flying to his side of the church, Key said, "Now!" He flew straight for the window and hit it with his shoulder, and the glass popped out. His wings tangled. Key pulled them to his back, dropped to the floor in a roll, and came up holding his knife.

Phoenix, his wings tight to his sides, exploded through the glass and sailed up to the ceiling, catching hold of the rafters and hanging there.

"Last time I listen to you, dragon boy," he bellowed.

Key ignored him and took in the Scene. There weren't any rogues, just the bodies of Roxy's parents. Her mother was drained, her father had his throat cut. Key strode up to them. "He killed them and left. Murdered her parents." He stared down at the witch who had summoned Dyfyr's soul into Key. He didn't feel anything now but sadness.

"I have to tell Roxy." He glanced at her father. The man who'd fired her for releasing her magic. Such a waste. His Roxy was a special woman, and Key couldn't fathom how her father had just thrown her away.

"Key, there's more trouble," Phoenix said. "Hell's breaking loose all over."

He turned and ran out.

Ailish's living room was turning into a witch triage. They'd helped four witches the hunters had rescued and healed any injuries the men had suffered, then sent them back out. It was a hellish night.

What about her parents? She hadn't heard anything yet.

More witches were taken. The alarms kept going off. The Circle Witches were all trying to help by checking to make sure other witches weren't missing that they didn't know about. Ram stayed in the kitchen, keeping everything and everyone coordinated.

Roxy felt a strange sadness coming from Key. She knew in her heart her parents were dead. He was just waiting to tell her in person. Ram knew it, too. Roxy was pretty sure Phoenix had told him; she could see it in his blue eyes.

Her baby wouldn't have any grandparents now. Her chest hurt. Ram pressed a bottle of green tea into her hand. "Go sit down." She took the tea and walked back into the living room, sinking onto the couch. Her father had probably blamed her as he died.

Her phone rang, and she took it out and was surprised at the name on the screen. She answered, "Shayla, where are you?"

"In a motel." Her voice was thin and strained. "They left me here."

Roxy sat up, slapping the tea on the coffee table. "What?" She clutched the phone tighter. "They?"

"Rogues. Two rogues. They've had me since...what day is it?"

When her cousin hadn't returned her calls, she'd thought... "Shayla, are they there now? Are you hurt? I'll send help!"

"I'm alone. I need you, Roxy. You have to help me." Her voice broke. "They cut off my schema."

Cut off—her mind rebelled. She jumped to her feet. "You'll die! Tell me where you are!" Her head spun with the horror. Their schema was a representation of their true self. If it died off naturally, then they became mortal, but to cut it off before that would kill them.

"Glassy Waves Motel. C-8. Hurry—"

"I'll send hunters and—"

"You can't. I'm Awakening, or I was."

She was struck dumb. "Awakening?" That meant that she'd begun to spread infertility. Shit, she couldn't just stand here. "Okay, I'll come." She hung up. Looked around. Keys. Where were Kieran's keys? Wait, she had magic. She held out her hand and called the keys to his truck. They materialized in her palm.

She got up and headed to the front door. When she opened it, sirens blared.

"Roxy, what are you doing?" Darcy chased her, followed by Ram.

"My cousin, she's at the Glassy Waves Motel.

Rogues cut off her schema. She'd dying. I'm going—"

Ram grabbed her arm. "No. I'll send Axel."

"You can't." She looked at Darcy. "That secret? It's that Shayla is an infertility witch. She said she was beginning to Awaken. I have to go."

Darcy's face went tight. "Doesn't matter, we can't let you go alone."

"She's dying! She's all I have left. I know my parents are dead—"

"I'll take her."

Roxy jumped at the smooth voice behind her. Jerking around, she looked at Linc. Tall, handsome, and gold eyes. "You could end up sterile."

"You saved my life. I owe you. Let's go." He took her arm and said to Ram, "I'll protect her, and you get Key to fly his lizard ass over there." He tugged her to his car, a low-slung Viper, settled her into the passenger seat, got in, fired up the car and they roared out.

"Thank you." She didn't really know this hunter.

He down-shifted around a corner and said, "I wasn't myself when we met. I am really sorry for the things I said. Your magic saved my soul. That's not a debt I'll forget, Roxy."

"I hope it can save my cousin."

"Sugar, if you can pull my soul back from the claws of Asmodeus, you can save her. I'm a betting man, little witch, and I'd bet my soul on you any day."

She took a breath. "You're much nicer when you're not chained down." Wincing she said, "That came out wrong."

He let out a bark of laughter.

Her phone rang. After looking at the screen, she answered quickly. "Key?"

"Tell me, baby."

She thought he'd yell at her, lecture her, be mad. But no, he understood that she had to do this. It all spilled out. "Shayla, she's an infertility witch, said rogues had her, cut her schema off...and then—" Her mind shifted gears midthought. "They're dead, aren't they?" Her parents were gone, she knew it.

"Yes. I'm sorry. But right now we're going to get your cousin. I'm flying as fast as I can, I'll meet you there. Until you see me, do what Linc tells you. Swear to me, Roxy."

"I swear," she said as Linc circled the motel and then pulled in.

"See you in a few." He hung up.

Linc swung the car around and backed into a space in front of the door. Roxy fought her urge to jump out, but she waited for Linc to come and stand by the door to C-8, knife in one hand. "I'm going into the room first."

She nodded and hurried to the door. Linc's long, lean body was taut and ready to spring. He strode in, barely looking at Shayla, instead checking the bathroom and closet.

Roxy stopped inside the room. The only sound was Shayla's harsh, shallow breathing. The room was standard, small table and two chairs below the window. Dresser on the left with a TV, bed on the right.

Shayla lay on the bed, wearing a green T-shirt, panties and too many cuts. Her right thigh was wrapped in a bloodstained towel. Her face was waxy pale, her dark blond hair sweaty. Her eyes were closed, her chest barely moving.

Roxy wasted no more time. She went around the other side, climbed on the bed, and knelt by Shayla's right thigh.

Linc came to the other side of the bed. His face cracked into lines; his eyes tightened.

Roxy pulled off the towels. "Oh sweet crone." The cut was rough and brutal, around two to three inches in diameter. Her inner thigh looked like a chunk of raw meat, there was so much blood. Roxy began opening chakras, desperate to save her.

"We'll put her in the car," Linc said. "You can—"

Roxy shook her head. "No time. We have to stop the bleeding." Her power moved a steady pace up and down her spine. She worked to gather more and more and began to push it higher and faster. Finally her fifth released, and she focused it into a stream down her arm. She put a hand on the bloody wound.

Wicked hot pain burned into her fingers. Sharp. As if her hand were being held over an inferno, each layer of skin torn away. Her stomach twisted. The pain traveled up her arm, through her skin, searing every nerve, then down her side and hit her schema.

Her fifth chakra closed. Her magic weakened; She squeezed her eyes shut, thinking of the dragon, reaching...

The chakra quivered but the pain was too intense, she couldn't keep her concentration. She could feel Shayla's life force dimming. "No!" She fought harder, trying to push through the pain.

"I need Kieran!"

≈ 25 ≈

KEY HEARD HER CRY IN his head. She was so desperate, she reached out to him mentally. Landing in the parking lot, he was close enough now to clearly feel her distress and projected back to her, *I'm here, Roxy.* He could smell a faint residue of rogues, but nothing fresh. What the hell were Liam and the rogues up to? He was going to help Roxy stabilize her cousin and get them out of here. He folded his wings, ran across the lot and shoved open the door. He automatically noted Linc standing at the side of the unconscious witch on the bed, but the sight of Roxy made his chest hurt. Her face was pale and tear-stained; he could feel her pain. The room smelled of blood and sweaty desperation with an edge of heavy grief.

Her magic was sparse. He hurried to her, got on the bed, and put his thighs around hers. She was wearing a simple little cotton dress, and the back was damp with sweat, her scent acrid. She was so tense, he couldn't get much of her pain.

She'd been trying to do this alone!

"I'm going to do a perimeter check," Linc said and left the room.

Key covered Roxy's hand with his. He curled his

arm around her and pulled her against him. "Let go of the pain, sweetheart. You're clenching, holding on too tight. Relax against me and Dyfyr." He spread his hand on her stomach, trying to encourage her chakras.

Her frozen magic thawed and began rushing, and Key started drawing off the pain. It was hot and vicious; he had no idea how she had endured it. He was used to pain, built to withstand it, but she wasn't. The dragon wings began working, helping her with her magic until a steady flow of healing energy streamed out. Key held her, siphoning off the pain and funneling her magic while listening for any sounds of trouble.

"Not enough. Need more." She was panting with the effort.

Key tried to think, then he remembered Carla healing Eli. "Blood, Roxy. Use our blood. I've seen the other witches do it." Key reached back and got his knife out. He took her free hand and sliced the palm. Then he cut his, and laid it on hers. "Feel it?"

Hope brightened her witch-shimmer. "Yes, it's like lightning whipping through me." She switched hands, laying the one with their combined blood on Shayla's inner thigh.

The woman arched and moaned. Key put his hand over Roxy's, taking the pain from both of them.

Anxiety tightened his spine. "Is she strong enough yet? We need to get out of here."

"Let me just heal the other cuts and then—"

"Who is that?" the woman on the bed said.

Key eyed the woman and smelled the sudden suspicion. She looked different from his Roxy; longer, leaner, with a hot anger just beneath her skin.

"It's Kieran." Roxy moved her hands to the cuts on Shayla's arm, then one on her thigh.

Her gaze clouded. "You've Awakened."

Key got off the bed and went to the door. "Linc. Let's roll."

The other hunter was scanning the lot. "Viper's going to be a tight fit for the four of us."

The other man's increasing tension tightened Key's neck muscles. He could feel the threat weighing down the air but he couldn't see it. "You take Shayla, Roxy will fly with me."

Linc strode into the room, straight to the bed, and said, "Hey there, Shayla. I'm Linc, and we're going to go for a ride."

Key followed, seeing Roxy healing a cut on the woman's side. Pain holes were forming in Roxy's shimmer. Hurrying back, he put his hand over hers.

Shayla shoved them all away and sat up. "I'm not going anywhere with a witch hunter." She turned to her cousin. "They broke into my house and dragged me out." Fury poured off her.

Roxy put her hand on her cousin's arm. "Shayla, we have to get you to safety."

"I don't trust them. I can't trust anyone now." She turned to Linc. "I'm not going with you."

Linc sighed and looked at Key.

He nodded, leaned over and lifted Roxy out of the way.

Linc moved in a flash, shifting Shayla onto the comforter, wrapping her in it to trap her arms and legs, then scooping her up.

"You bastard! Scum-sucking troll! Donkey-screwing asshole!" Her voice faded as Linc got her into his car.

Key turned Roxy to face him, seeing her tear-stained face and pain-filled eyes. Her parents had been murdered, and she was terrified of losing the only family she had left. "Linc won't hurt her, but we have to get out of here."

She nodded.

He grabbed her waist and lifted her. "Put your legs around me," he said as he heard Linc's Viper roar off.

Then, another car squealed into the parking lot.

No time! Key turned and ran, blowing through the opened door and snapping out his wings. He took in a large, dark SUV and two motel room doors opening at the same time.

Guns! Two men ran out of the rooms with guns. Fuck! He concentrated to go invisible when he felt a prick in his thigh. Then his neck. *Run! Fly!* His wings weren't pumping right. Too slow...clumsy. Pain didn't stop him so why wasn't he flying yet? His strides were uncoordinated. Felt like Roxy was slipping from his hold—

"Kieran! You have a dart in your neck!"

Dart? He became aware of the icy-hot pain slithering through his veins. "Poison..." His mouth felt thick. *Don't drop Roxy!* He fought the drug, struggled to run, to get her to safety. Sweat slicked down his back. It was like running under water, he couldn't get any speed.

He saw Roxy put her hand on his neck where the dart must be. Tried to scream, *No! Don't touch it!* Couldn't get the words out. Needed to warn her not to get the drug on her. Had to get her to safety! He was halfway across the parking lot. Get to the street, get someone to help Roxy. *Run. Walk. Move!*

It took all his will to force his left leg up. He had to fight to keep his grip on her. Then a man slammed into him, throwing both of them to the ground. Key landed on his side, felt the impact jar him, felt the pain, but his muscles wouldn't move. Not his legs, not his arms, not his fingers. Drawing in a breath was a strain.

Roxy screamed.

Couldn't turn his head, but he felt her pain. Hot slices of agony as they cut her. *Roxy!* He couldn't move! Couldn't get to her. It was like being trapped in a nightmare.

Two rogues picked him up, dragged him into the motel room, and threw him down. His head bounced off the floor and he stayed where he landed. Where was Roxy?

I'm here.

He clung to her presence in his mind. He'd find a way to get her help. Then black boots and pants entered his vision. The toe of a boot caught his shoulder and kicked him over onto his back. His wings were gone, at some point they'd folded up and disappeared into the tattoo. His head and eyes wouldn't move, and he was forced to stare straight up.

Liam stood there.

Old hatred spewed up inside him. Key was helpless once more, as helpless as he'd been all those years ago. Impotent fury burned and seethed, and there wasn't a goddamned thing he could do about it. He heard Roxy breathing, felt her fear and pain. His entire being fought the drug to get to her. He struggled to move, but the most he could do was blink once, and that effort made spots dance in front of his eyes. Key stilled his futile attempts to fight the drug and, while he stared at Liam, took stock of who was in the room. He heard only one other male moving around. The others must be outside.

The other Wing Slayer Hunters knew where he was, they would come. Just hold on, keep Roxy alive.

His brother's cold blue eyes gleamed with triumph. "Did you get a chance to meet my mortal sharpshooters? Those darts are coated in enough Tubocurarine to bring down an elephant. Or a dragon." He laughed at his own joke. "If you were a regular man, you'd die. Soon. But witch hunters have advanced biology, so you should keep breathing even though the rest of your system is paralyzed. Until I kill you anyway. But first..." He turned away, "Bring her over here."

Roxy was shoved, landing on Key's chest, her hand on the dragon tat. The scent of her pain ripped through his veins, fueling his internal rage, but he still couldn't move.

"Kieran, what did they do to you?" He felt her magic rise, flowing through her hand on his chest. The dragon twitched.

Then Liam caught a handful of her hair and jerked her off him. He locked an arm around her waist, grabbed the front of her dress, ripping down and exposing the swell of her breasts in her black bra. The Tear pulsed frantically with her heart.

The sound and sight tore through Key's mind. He strained against his frozen muscles, felt the dragon struggling, too. He realized he could move his fingers, shift his eyes. Was the drug wearing off?

Roxy fought, trying to break free. Kicking, using her elbows, struggling to get to him.

No! Stop it, Roxy! He screamed at her in his mind, terror for her bleeding through his brain. *Stall him!*

She shook her head, fighting harder.

Liam stabbed his knife into her thigh, and her entire body bucked so hard, she kicked Key in the ribs. Then her blood poured down her leg and onto his stomach. She was panting, wheezing with the agony. It filled his head, the searing burn that was hurting his witch, his sweet Roxy. Her blood pooled on his stomach, rolled down his side. *I'm so sorry,* he cried to her.

Blood, trying to keep chakras open.

He felt her magic then, felt it seeping into him...holy shit! She was bleeding on him intentionally. She'd thrown herself on him intentionally. Hoping that the soul-mirror blood was the antidote to the drug, like it was for the Immortal Death Dagger. Key felt his muscles begin to burn as her magic chased out the drug. He could move his hands, arms and legs more and more, but he wasn't fully online yet. It took every ounce of will he had to remain still. He could do nothing until he had full control of his muscles.

Then Liam lifted his knife, pressing the tip to the swell of her breast. "This will only hurt enough to kill you." He shoved the knife in.

Roxy cried out hoarsely. *No more. Can't. Hurts!* She sobbed in Key's mind, and his vision grayed out until all he saw was Roxy and blood. The dragon roared in his head. Logic and reason shattered. Key exploded up from the ground; his claws burst out.

The scent of Roxy's blood and agony were fuel on the flames. He grabbed Liam's wrist and snapped it. Raked his claws over the bastard's face and gouged his eyes.

Instinctively, the other man let go of Roxy. Key shoved her behind him, heard her fall to the ground.

Liam came at him, his face bloody, one eye gone, and he bellowed in rage. He had a knife, but Key went low, shoved his shoulder into his stomach, and landed on top of his brother. Before Liam could move, Key slashed his chest, ripped apart his ribs, and clawed out his heart.

Liam's mouth opened, but only a gurgle came out. Key looked into his remaining eye. "You're an abomination. Enjoy eternity as a shade, fucker." He jumped to his feet and threw the organ as the other rogue fired a gun at him.

The bullet missed, and Key ripped out the gunman's throat. The door blew open, and he snatched out his knife and threw it into the heart of the man. He eviscerated the next rogue who ran in.

They stopped coming into the room, but the fight outside continued. The other Wing Slayer Hunters had arrived. Key retrieved his knife and raced to Roxy. She was crumpled between the bed and dresser. So much blood! Carefully he turned her over and his heart squeezed. Gently, he wiped away some blood and saw the edge of the Tear. Cold fear hit his gut. Liam had gotten the knife under the Tear and pried it partway out. She was bleeding badly, but that Tear was killing her. The brilliant pulsing and the vivid colors were stealing her from him.

Roxy was dying.

"No!" Something in him broke, shattered. Time fractured. Black memories tortured him—holding his beloved treasure in his arms as she took her last breaths, her body old and frail as she swore she'd find a way to return to him. It was too much to bear, the wrenching pain. He knew the dragon's memories were invading his own, their combined love for her merging past all barriers of time and magic. Other memories: The first time Key had seen her so beautiful and real. Their first kiss. The first time he slid into her body and she gave him her heart. The way she'd wielded her powerful magic to save Linc, how she'd fought to save her cousin. His Roxy...she willingly put herself at risk and suffered pain to save another.

His love for her erupted in ferocious determination. He'd sworn to her he'd fight for her. With the battle raging outside, he slid his right arm beneath her, holding her still and vulnerable, while he swelled with the ancient strength of the dragon as they fused their will.

Roxy gasped, her breath stuttering. "Kieran..." Her eyes opened, pain and fear dulling her gaze. She lifted her hand, touching his chest, him and Dyfyr. "Love you. Don't want to...leave..."

"Roxy." His throat tightened, and his heart surged in his chest, trying to reach her, to grab on to her and hold her to him. Her hand on his chest felt like a stain on his soul. "I'll get the Tear out! You'll live!"

"Not your fault." Her fingers spasmed. "Hurts. Not brave like you."

He was a damned coward! He should have ripped that fucking Tear out the first time when Dyfyr tried. But he'd been afraid. He could feel her pain, feel the squeezing pressure on her chest. Key lifted her to his face. Pressed his mouth to her dry lips. Tried to fill her with his life. "I have to—" Hurt her more. Rip farther into her chest.

"I know. Let Dyfyr get the Tear. Become mortal..." Her body shook as she dragged in a breath. "Maybe find you both again." Tears rolled down her face.

"No!" The fingers on his left hand burned, fresh claws burst out. He wouldn't let her leave them. He focused on the soft swell of her breast where the Tear pulsed, obscenely beautiful as it killed her.

Don't lose her! Rip out that Tear! As she lay dying and defenseless, he felt her magic somehow rise. She opened at least one chakra, maybe two as she struggled to breathe. Now! He had to do it now. Key struck, his claws ruthlessly shoving into her wound and latching on to the Tear. He yanked, pulled the Tear out of her, and freed the silver chain from her skin.

She screamed brokenly, her muscles locking with the hot agony. A loud crack echoed and the Tear he held in his claw burst open. Then the room filled with violent, piercing lights, red, green, blue and yellow exploded in streaks of wild color. Then a second later they shot to the spot where Roxy's hand lay against the tattoo of Dyfyr.

Then the colors vanished and the Tear disappeared, leaving just the chain hanging loose around her neck. The dragon shuddered violently on his chest, then stilled. The last thread of Roxy's magic shut off. Her hand fell away. *Love you. Find you again...*echoed in his head as her spirit began to drift away.

He'd failed. She was leaving him. A keening cry of mad grief tore up his throat and filled the room.

≋ 26 ≋

THE DESPERATE GRIEF ROLLED THROUGH him in pounding waves, and he held her tight to his chest, refusing to let her go. Hands grabbed him, jerked him to his feet as he clutched Roxy.

Axel glared at him with hot urgency vibrating through him. "Get to the witches with her! Now!"

The order of his leader cut through his pain. A flicker of hope sparked. He spun and raced out the door, his wings springing out as he took to the skies. He flew with the speed of a dragon, spotting Phoenix's house and landing in the yard.

"Key!" Ailish Darcy, and Carla raced across the yard toward him. They all dropped to their knees, Key cradling Roxy on his thighs, the witches on the other side of her. They laid their hands on her and their magic rose, filling the air, their witch-shimmers lighting the night.

"She's not gone yet," Carla said. "She's still nearby!"

"Cut your hand, Key. Give her more blood to call her spirit back," Darcy said.

He lifted his hand and dug his claws in, ripping open his flesh. Then he covered the ragged wound over her heart with his palm. He poured everything he had into Roxy. "Live, baby. You have to live. I can't go on without you!"

Phoenix landed behind Ailish, blood spattered on his chest, his eyes dark and troubled. "Look through me," he told Ailish as he put his hands on her shoulders.

Sutton and Axel dropped down behind Carla and Darcy, feeding their strength through their witches. Key looked up and saw them all coming together to save Roxy. He'd been created in perverted magic, grown up in violence and hate, and thought he was tainted by it. Now he was surrounded by strength and love.

"I think...yes..." Ailish said. Then she tilted back her head and began to sing; her voice soared and trilled with her siren magic.

Holding his bleeding hand over her heart, Key pleaded, "Roxy, feel how much you are loved!"

Wind rose through the trees, bending the grass and scenting the air with metal and the faintest whiff of flowers. Then the hairs on Key's arms stood straight up, and he felt the heavy, furious, electric presence of another being.

Wing Slayer appeared on his right. He towered over them, his shoulder-length, golden hair blowing back from an unforgiving face. His eyes were deep-set, gleaming gold with a tinge of red. His wings were a dark bloody bronze. Key's bones shivered in reaction. The being radiated hellish anger.

"Dyfyr holds their spirits. Call them!" He thundered over Ailish's powerful singing.

His voice was like surround sound inside Key's chest. It boomed with a command that his body scrambled to obey, and he looked at Roxy's too-still face. *Please, Roxy, come back to me! Bring our child!* He reached out with everything he had, looking for her. Needing her. Determined to find her and bring her back. He could almost feel her, catching the slightest scent of honey-almond, a faint ripple of her magic. The witches were pouring in their magic, forcing her body to heal, as Ailish kept singing. His heart pounded, his head throbbed, and he felt his soul cry out for her.

Then his very skin rippled. Stunned, he looked down to see a larger, bronzed hand settled over Roxy's stomach, where their child should be. *Wing Slayer?*

Warmth began to bloom beneath his hand. The scent of her magic drifted up, teasing him for an instant, then it took hold and grew. A low hum rose in his chest and stomach.

<hr />

Roxy saw the vivid colors of the dragon scales and his ruby eyes as he stared down into his cupped hands. "Dyfyr?"

"Come look, my love."

His voice rumbled with purr-like sound. Curious, she drifted toward him, closer and closer, straining to see. But there was nothing there...then she saw it. A tiny flickering light, floating in the cage of his lethal claws. Warmth traveled through her, touching the very core of her. "It's...breathtaking. And alive." She recognized that light but couldn't quite grasp it. She tore her gaze away to look at the dragon she loved beyond time. "Dyfyr, what is it?"

His scales rippled and glowed impossibly brighter. "Meet your daughter. She is as exquisite as her mother."

"That's her spirit?" Roxy must be dead then. What was happening? She'd tried to hold on, to stay with Kieran, but—

Dyfyr reached out, sweeping Roxy into the cradle of

his hands. She felt her spirit touch the baby's, and the heat of maternal love, along with Dyfyr's, surrounded them in a safe bubble. "You were ripped away from me once, and I couldn't stop it. This time, before you and the child's spirits left, I pulled them into the tattoo. The baby came first, and you followed her. I'm holding you, to give Kieran and the others time to find a way to save you both. Kieran and I won't let you go."

The bubble of Dyfyr's love, safe and familiar, wrapped her and her daughter's spirit tight against her dragon's beating heart. "I love you, Dyfyr."

He rumbled his deep pleasure noise in his chest. "I know, my treasure. My heart has always beaten for you."

"Did you get the Tear? Are you mortal?"

He nodded. "You found the strength to open your magic to me, even while suffering. To see you so..." he shuddered, and smoke streamed from his nose and mouth. "Losing you can break even a dragon."

"Dyfyr..." How could love hurt so much?

"Roxy."

The voice stunned her. Turning, she stared. "Mom?" She couldn't believe it. Where the spirit of her child floated, her mother appeared as Roxy had always known her. "How can I see you? Are you...dead?"

"I'm at rest in Summerland, but Our Sacred Dragon granted me this one gift. To see you and your baby."

Tears burned her eyes even though Roxy had no body on this plane of existence. "You wanted to see me? I'm sorry, Mom. Kieran tried to get there in time to save you and Dad." Her voice broke. She had never been enough for her parents, always disappointed them. "I'm sorry..."

Her mother floated to her, wrapped her arms around Roxy. "Roxy, no. I love you, always loved you. But I did a terrible thing by forcing the dragon's soul into Kieran. We were all so frightened when we lost our high magic, and the hunters who always protected us were going rogue and killing us. That's no excuse." She sighed. "Roxy, being your mother taught me the lesson of my lifetime. Magic is a gift we must use with love, not fear." She leaned back and looked into Roxy's eyes. "You taught me that. I will always love you, and I'm proud of you."

The angst of grief eased within her. "You came back to tell me that?"

"I did. And that your father died trying to protect me and begged me to ask you to forgive him. His last words were, 'Tell Roxy I love her.'"

"Oh Mom. Thank you."

Gwen's gaze drifted to the tiny light hovering next to Roxy. "May I?"

"Yes." Roxy watched as her mother pulled the tiny light to her chest, holding gently. "She's perfect." Then her mother lifted her head, looking around. "I must go."

Roxy reached out. "Mom..." She tried to touch her one last time.

But Gwen's image broke apart in hundreds of tiny lights and vanished.

"I love you," she sobbed as emotions swamped her.

Dyfyr gathered her and the baby to his heart once more. "She knows, sweet treasure. She is at rest now."

Please, Roxy, come back to me! Bring our child!

"That's Kieran." She began to feel actual sensation as if she were in her body again. Ailish's powerful siren witch voice trembled around them.

She could feel the distance between her and Kieran closing. Could almost reach him...

"Roxy, my love, open your eyes."

His voice! She felt his arm around her shoulders, and others were touching her, too. Power swelled and rippled, calling out her magic. Slowly, she lifted her eyelids.

Kieran filled her vision. His gray eyes flamed with blue fire. She reached up, touched his face, and found it wet. *Tears?* Her heart wrenched, and she sat up, pitching herself into his arms.

He held her tight against him. *For you, yes. I couldn't bear losing you.* His love poured over her mind, her body, and her magic.

I didn't want to leave! I fought, and then Dyfyr caught my spirit and... She leaned her head back, looking into his face. "I saw our daughter's spirit. She is perfect." Then she felt a wave of panic. "Did she come back? Where—"

"Peace, witch, she is within you now, safe and secure."

The voice rolled through her, shivered her chakras, and commanded her attention. Roxy turned and saw the golden brilliance of a god. "Wing Slayer." She scrambled off Key's lap, digging her knees into the grass. "I felt you, felt the electric touch of your god power bring us back to my body." She bowed her head, humbled that Kieran's god had done that. "Thank you."

Key shifted to kneel by her side. "My thanks, too." *When he first arrived, his wings were dark bronze and his eyes flickered with red. Now he's glowing gold.*

Roxy reached out and clutched Kieran's hand. *Angry at us?*

"I can hear you," the god thundered.

Roxy fought to keep her balance as the ground shook. "Sorry."

"I was not angry at you. You two fought with true hearts. Asmodeus is the one who brings out my anger. He tried to get that Tear to kill me and gain control of Earth."

Roxy cringed as his fury crashed over them.

"Roxy."

Her name from the god surprised her into looking up.

"You nearly lost your life to safeguard that Tear. I am not just Kieran's god, but I am yours." He was suddenly in front of her. "At the last moment, as you were dying, you forced open your chakras just enough for Dyfyr to use his dragon magic and take back the Tear. Only the chain remains." He reached out and touched the silver chain. "Wear the wings of your dragon over your heart."

A warm twang slid around her neck and pooled at the curve of her left breast. She looked down. The dress was no longer torn—either the witches or the god had repaired it. In the gap of the material, where the Tear once marked her, there was a pair of silver dragon wings embedded into her skin.

You wear my wings, marking you as our treasure, Kieran whispered in her mind.

How do you thank a god for something so precious? "I am honored."

Wing Slayer said, "Kieran DeMicca, you have the heart and soul of a dragon. You have stood against evil all of your life. But it was your love for Roxy and your child that allowed Dyfyr and me to save them."

"I am grateful."

"Hunter, your knife."

Key handed the blade to the god.

"Lift your joined hands." Wing Slayer then looked at Roxy. "Roxanne, your Ancestors are here."

She raised her head, her green eyes softening. "I see them. I wondered...the other witches have seen them, but I never did. They look like radiant stars gleaming in the night." Like her mother had when she left Roxy.

She was able to project their beauty to him as Key raised their joined hands.

Wing Slayer smiled. "They were always there, Roxanne. But you gravitated to Dyfyr. And the dragon will tell you that he is so beautiful, you could see nothing but him. Dragons are singularly vain creatures, but when they love, they love for eternity."

Then he turned to Key. "You and Dyfyr will never be without your witch again."

Key saw the blur of his silver knife and looked down to see the twin rings appear around the base of their thumbs. "Immortality."

Wing Slayer wrapped his large hand around theirs. "As true soul mirrors, may the two of you reflect the faith, courage, honor, strength and cunning to fight the curse and protect the innocent. We give you the gift of time to aid you."

With their minds joined, the touch of the god seared through them right down to their cells. Roxy felt them being redrawn, reshaped, a stronger life force emerging. Her long hair blew back behind her from the force, but Kieran's thoughts stayed firmly linked with hers as the internal shifting crested, and then it was done.

Key said reverently, "Thank you." He bowed his head. "For giving me back Roxy, my treasure, and safeguarding her with immortality."

Wing Slayer began to fade from their view. "Guard her well, hunter." And then he was gone.

Key swept her up in his arms. "For all eternity."

Her mind was spinning, her body humming with magic and love. Kieran had fought for her, right to the death as he'd sworn. His love was a swirling silver light in her mind.

His face softened. "I love you, Roxy. I promised you I'd fight for you. You're mine. I will fight for you and with you, but I will never walk away from you."

Joy crowded her heart, and tears filled her eyes. "I've been looking for you so many lifetimes, to finally have found you...I've come home."

≫ 27 ≪

A Week Later

ROXY SAT ON THE GRASS in the moonlight with her cousin, gazing at the graves of her parents. Key had drawn the image of her mother holding the tiny, brilliant light that was their daughter's spirit on her mother's headstone. And for her father, Key had drawn his hand reaching down from the heavens to touch his daughter, as he had touched Roxy when her mom gave her the message from him.

Her heart was at peace for her parents. It was Shayla she worried about. "Where will you go?"

Her cousin looked thinner, anxious. Roxy could feel only weak flickers of her magic.

Shayla shook her head. "I never wanted this, never wanted to Awaken. And now...I can't be around people. At least not anyone who wants children." Twisting her mouth, she said, "I could hire out to frat parties."

Roxy squeezed Shayla's hand, her heart breaking for her. "I have my high magic, maybe I can figure out what happened to cause infertility witches and find the answer."

Shayla looked at her mounting frustration. "You can try, but before the curse, no one ever could find the cause or reason that an infertility witch is born once each generation. In the meantime, I can't stay here, I can't be near him. I'm...it's building. The need, the restlessness and I have to go. Get away."

"Shayla, he could be your soul mirror. Maybe that would break this infertility thing, and free you."

"This existed before the curse. You know that. And what man would want a woman who not only is infertile but would make him, and everyone around them, infertile?" She sucked in a breath, the old anger rising.

Roxy winced, knowing she had a point. "Still, the other soul-mirror witches and I might be able to find an answer."

Shayla pulled her hand from Roxy's. "No. You trust them, I get that. I don't. I can't."

She sighed. Shayla had her reasons, but this was tearing Roxy apart. She tried bribery. "I'm taking over my father's production company, and I'm going to buy the rights to the Eternal Assassins. I want you to write the script."

"Good try. I can write the script anywhere. I just need to leave." She stood up.

It was inevitable. She hated letting her go, but Roxy had learned a truth; they each had their own journey. She rose and hugged her.

Shayla hugged her back and said, "How long do I have until you tell Ram?"

"I don't know. What would I tell him? *That wasn't a supersized weapon you got zapped with in my apartment, that was my cousin. You're her Awakening, and the jolt was just chemistry.* Unless he was her soul mirror. But then there's the whole infertility witch problem. And who knew how Ram, who ate, slept and breathed discipline, would react.

Shayla's eyes clouded. "He won't come after me anyway. Tell him, I don't care." She turned to walk to her car in the parking lot. She hesitated and turned back. "You'll be all right here?"

They'd come together in the same car. "Yes, Key's on his way now."

"I'll call you."

"Shayla, I love you, and I'll always be here for you." Her cousin nodded, turned and left.

Her heart ached. A few seconds later she felt the breeze behind her, and then Kieran's wings wrapped around her. "We have to tell him, Roxy."

Of course Kieran knew. She didn't lie or hold secrets from him. "I know." She turned and looked up at him. "How's Tyler? Was he excited?"

His eyes caught the moonlight. "Oh yeah. The kid couldn't believe it when I told him he was getting his own wall at Mural Maze. We spent an hour sketching out ideas. That boy has some big-ass talent going on." Tyler and his mom were moving into their own place next week and doing well. She lifted her face to Key. "You're going to be a great dad."

He traced his finger over her clavicle to the silver dragon wings woven into her skin. He loved that design, and Roxy cherished it as Wing Slayer's gift. "You give me the strength to overcome my childhood to give our daughter the love and support she needs."

Tremors of warm pleasure filled her heart while her magic streamed out to follow his touch. She studied him in the moonlight pouring over his face, shoulders, and his chest powerful enough to handle his incredible scaled wings spread out behind him. Kieran had fully merged the dragon and the man into this magnificent hunter she loved. He was fierce, lethal and just. *And hers.*

He smiled at her, lifting his hand to her face. "You are my treasure, Roxy."

Her schema warmed and fired her magic with desire.

Key groaned. "Damn, witch, you're going to bring me to my knees."

She felt him harden against her belly and loved it. "I don't want you on your knees."

His eyes took on blue heat. "Liar, you love me on my knees." His voice dropped. "Your goddess adores my kiss."

Her chakras shivered with pleasure. But she had something else in mind. "You drew me a picture, remember?"

His eyes gleamed and his mouth curved. "So I did." He reached down and lifted her. "Put your legs around me."

She linked her ankles behind him. Key turned and launched into a run, his wings pumping in powerful strokes. Soon they lifted off, rising higher and higher into the skies of Glassbreakers. She lay against his chest, listening to the dual heartbeats. The wind blew away her lingering worries about Shayla, leaving her filled with love and joy.

In the picture, we were naked, no? Key's voice caressed her mind.

Roxy easily controlled her magic and made their clothes vanish. Then she looked up into his eyes.

He lifted her, until she felt the pressure of his erection pressing against her. Her body tightened with anticipation, her magic pooled in heavy need, and her nipples ached. Just when it became unbearable, Key slid home, driving into her until they were one. Then he moved a hand to the center of her back. *Show me.*

She leaned back against his hand supporting her.

He looked down at her breasts, and she knew he once more looked at the dragon wings spread out in fine, delicate silver. She saw the heat color his face as he began to thrust, somehow holding her at a slight incline, flying while plying her with deep, intimate strokes that made her body sing. Her power rushed up and down her spine, fifth chakra opened, sixth... *Kieran...*

His voice was a deep purr in her head. *Now, baby, let me watch. Let me see the magic take you.* She was completely at his mercy as he flew them through the skies, thrusting into her body, her magic pulsing and spinning, while filling her head with love. The pleasure of such trust and love shattered through her, spinning her into a bliss of sensation while Kieran's strong arms held her.

—※—

Her magic was winging through him, so freaking hot, he'd had to land before he lost control. He chose the maze by the waterfall. Her power pulsed and squeezed his cock buried inside her. With care, he laid her on the ground and followed her, never breaking their joining.

Roxy opened her eyes, and their green depths captivated him. He leaned down and kissed her, then said, "I believe that's called a power surge."

She lifted her hands to his face. "Entirely your fault," she said softly and moved her hips. "Just the feel of you fires my magic and pleasure." She lifted higher, taking him deeper.

Key's control shattered. He took her mouth and filled her body, surrounding himself in Roxy. Losing himself in her. His heart pounded and his blood roared as hot, silky pleasure consumed them. Her scent, her taste, the feel of her skin, her body open and taking him, while her magic caressed him. Roxy had fearlessly chased out the darkness inside him and replaced it with love.

Key broke from her mouth, rising up on his hands,

pumping into her, feeding her, giving her everything he had. He looked down into the eyes of his sweet, sinfully perfect witch and felt her body tightening around his.

She wrapped her arms around him. *Together. We'll fly together this time.*

Her husky whisper in his mind sent him over the edge with her. They merged in soul-deep pleasure and eternal love.

The End

Dear Readers,

Thank you for reading Sinful Magic! I have always loved witches and dragons, and having the chance to weave them together into a story of timeless love was an amazing experience. I know Sinful Magic is fiction...but for a little while there, Dyfyr felt very real to me, along with Key and Roxy. I hope you enjoyed their story!

Next up is the beginning of Ram and Ginny's epic love story in the novella Forbidden Magic. Have you ever craved the forbidden? Can you resist? Ram thought he could...

Wishing you all a little magic in your lives!

~Jen

Other Books By Jennifer Lyon

The Wing Slayer Hunter Series

Blood Magic (Book #1)
Soul Magic (Book #2)
Night Magic (Book #3)
Sinful Magic (Book #4)
Forbidden Magic (Book #4.5 a novella)
Caged Magic (Book #5)

The Plus One Chronicles Trilogy

The Proposition (Book #1)
Possession (Book #2)
Obsession (Book #3)
The Plus One Chronicles Boxed Set

Anthology

The Beast Within Anthology
with Erin McCarthy and Bianca D'Arc

WRITING AS JENNIFER APODACA

ONCE A MARINE SERIES

The Baby Bargain (Book #1)
Her Temporary Hero (Book #2)
Exposing The Heiress (Book #3)

THE SAMANTHA SHAW MYSTERY SERIES

Dating Can Be Murder (Book #1)
Dying To Meet You (Book #2)
Ninja Soccer Moms (Book #3)
Batteries Required (Book #4)
Thrilled To Death (Book #5)

SINGLE TITLE NOVELS

The Sex On The Beach Book Club
Extremely Hot

ANTHOLOGIES

Wicked Women Whodunit Anthology
with Mary Janice Davidson, Amy Garvey & Nancy J. Cohen
Sun, Sand, Sex Anthology
with Linda Lael Miller and Shelly Laurenstron

ABOUT THE AUTHOR

Bestselling author Jennifer Lyon lives in Southern California where she continually plots ways to convince her husband that they should get a dog. So far, she has failed in her doggy endeavor. She consoles herself by pouring her passion into writing books. To date, Jen has published more than fifteen books, including a fun and sexy mystery series and a variety of contemporary romances under the name Jennifer Apodaca, and a dark, sizzling paranormal series as Jennifer Lyon. She's won awards and had her books translated into multiple languages, but she still hasn't come up with a way to persuade her husband that they need a dog.

Jen loves connecting with fans. Visit her website at www.jenniferlyonbooks.com or follow her at https://www.facebook.com/jenniferlyonbooks.